Amanda M. D

A Little Girl in Old Boston

Amanda M. Douglas

A Little Girl in Old Boston

1st Edition | ISBN: 978-3-75231-757-2

Place of Publication: Frankfurt am Main, Germany

Year of Publication: 2020

Outlook Verlag GmbH, Germany.

Reproduction of the original.

A LITTLE GIRL IN OLD BOSTON

By AMANDA M. DOUGLAS

CHAPTER I

DORIS

"I do suppose she is a Papist! The French generally are," said Aunt Priscilla, drawing her brows in a delicate sort of frown, and sipping her tea with a spoon that had the London crown mark, and had been buried early in revolutionary times.

"Why, there were all the Huguenots who emigrated from France for the sake of worshiping God in their own way rather than that of the Pope. We Puritans did not take all the free-will," declared Betty spiritedly.

"You are too flippant, Betty," returned Aunt Priscilla severely. "And I doubt if her father's people had much experimental religion. Then, she has been living in a very hot-bed of superstition!"

"The cold, dreary Lincolnshire coast! I think it would take a good deal of zeal to warm me, even if it was superstition."

"And she was in a convent after her mother died! Yes, she is pretty sure to be a Papist. It seems rather queer that second-cousin Charles should have remembered her in his will."

"But Charles was his namesake and nephew, the child of his favorite sister," interposed Mrs. Leverett, glancing deprecatingly at Betty, pleading with the most beseeching eyes that she should not ruffle Aunt Priscilla up the wrong way.

"But what is that old ma'shland good for, anyway?" asked Aunt Priscilla.

"Why they are filling in and building docks," said Betty the irrepressible. "Father thinks by the time she is grown it will be a handsome fortune."

Aunt Priscilla gave a queer sound that was not a sniff, but had a downward tendency, as if it was formed of inharmonious consonants. It expressed both doubt and disapproval.

"But think of the expense and the taxes! You can't put a bit of improvement on anything but the taxes eat it up. I want my hall door painted, and the cornishes,"—Aunt Priscilla always would pronounce it that way,—"but I mean to wait until the assessor has been round. It's the best time to paint in cool weather, too. I can't afford to pay a man for painting and then pay the city for the privilege."

No one controverted Mrs. Perkins. She broke off her bread in bits and sipped

2

her tea.

"Why didn't they give her some kind of a Christian name?" she began suddenly. "Don't you suppose it is French for the plain, old-fashioned, sensible name of Dorothy?"

Betty laughed. "Oh, Aunt Priscilla, it's pure Greek. Doris and Phyllis and Chloe——"

"Phyllis and Chloe are regular nigger names," with the utmost disdain.

"But Greek, all the same. Ask Uncle Winthrop."

"Well, I shall call her Dorothy. I'm neither Greek nor Latin nor a college professor. There's no law against my being sensible, fursisee"—which really meant "far as I see." "And the idea of appointing Winthrop Adams her guardian! I did think second-cousin Charles had more sense. Winthrop thinks of nothing but books and going back to the Creation of the World, just as if the Lord couldn't have made things straight in the beginning without his help. I dare say he will find out what language they talked before the dispersion of Babel. People are growing so wise nowadays, turning the Bible inside out!" and she gave her characteristic sniff. "I'll have another cup of tea, Elizabeth. Now that we're through with the war, and settled solid-like with a President at the helm, we can look forward to something permanent, and comfort ourselves that it was worth trying for. Still, I've often thought of that awful waste of tea in Boston harbor. Seems as though they might have done something else with it. Tea will keep a good long while. And all that wretched stuff we used to drink and call it Liberty tea!"

"I don't know as we regret many of the sacrifices, though it came harder on the older people. We have a good deal to be proud of," said Mrs. Leverett.

"And a grandfather who was at Bunker Hill," appended Betty.

Aunt Priscilla never quite knew where she belonged. She had come over with the Puritans, at least her ancestors had, but then there had been a title in the English branch; and though she scoffed a little, she had great respect for royalty, and secretly regretted they had not called the head of the government by a more dignified appellation than President. Her mother had been a Church of England member, but rather austere Mr. Adams believed that wives were to submit themselves to their husbands in matters of belief as well as aught else. Then Priscilla Adams, at the age of nineteen, had wedded the man of her father's choice, Hatfield Perkins, who was a stanch upholder of the Puritan faith. Priscilla would have enjoyed a little foolish love-making, and she had a

3

carnal hankering for fine gowns; and, oh, how she did long to dance in her youth, when she was slim and light-footed!

In spite of all, she had been a true Puritan outwardly, and had a little misgiving that the prayers of the Church were vain repetitions, the organ wickedly frivolous, and the ringing of bells suggestive of popery. There had been no children, and a bad fall had lamed her husband so that volunteering for a soldier was out of the question, but he had assisted with his means; and some twelve years before this left his widow in comfortable circumstances for the times.

She kept to her plain dress, although it was rich; and her housemaid was an elderly black woman who had been a slave in her childhood. She devoted a good deal of thought as to who should inherit her property when she was done with it. For those she held in the highest esteem were elderly like herself, and the young people were flighty and extravagant and despised the good old ways of prudence and thrift.

They were having early tea at Mrs. Leverett's. Aunt Priscilla's mother had been half-sister to Mrs. Leverett's mother. In the old days of large families nearly everyone came to be related. It was always very cozy in Sudbury Street, and Foster Leverett was in the ship chandlery trade. Aunt Priscilla *did* love a good cup of tea. Whether the quality was finer, or there was some peculiar art in brewing it, she could never quite decide; or whether the social cream of gentle Elizabeth Leverett, and the spice of Betty, added to the taste and heightened the flavor beyond her solitary cup.

Early October had already brought chilling airs when evening set in. A century or so ago autumn had the sharpness of coming winter in the early morning and after sundown. There was a cheerful wood fire on the hearth, and its blaze lighted the room sufficiently, as the red light of the sunset poured through a large double window.

The house had a wide hall through the center that was really the keeping-room. The chimney stood about halfway down, a great stone affair built out in the room, tiled about with Scriptural scenes, with two tiers of shelves above, whereon were ranged the family heirlooms—so high, indeed, that a stool had to be used to stand on when they were dusted. Just below this began a winding staircase with carved spindles and a mahogany rail and newel, considered quite an extravagance in that day.

This lower end was the living part. In one of the corners was built the buffet, while a door opposite led into the wide kitchen. Across the back was a porch where shutters were hung in the winter to keep out the cold.

The great dining table was pushed up against the wall. The round tea table was set out and the three ladies were having their tea, quite a common custom when there was a visitor, as the men folk were late coming in and a little uncertain.

On one side the hall opened in two large, well-appointed rooms. On the other were the kitchen and "mother's room," where, when the children were little, there had been a cradle and a trundle bed. But one son and two daughters were married; one son was in his father's warehouse, and was now about twenty; the next baby boy had died; and Betty, the youngest, was sixteen, pretty, and a little spoiled, of course. Yet Aunt Priscilla had a curious fondness for her, which she insisted to herself was very reprehensible, since Betty was such a feather-brained girl.

"It is to be hoped the ship did get in to-day," Aunt Priscilla began presently. "If there's anything I hate, it's being on tenterhooks."

"She was spoken this morning. There's always more or less delay with pilots and tides and what not," replied Mrs. Leverett.

"The idea of sending a child like that alone! The weather has been fine, but we don't know how it was on the ocean."

"Captain Grier is a friend of Uncle Win's, you know," appended Betty.

"Betty, do try and call your relatives by their proper names. An elderly man, too! It does sound so disrespectful! Young folks of to-day seem to have no regard for what is due other people. Oh——"

There was a kind of stamping and shuffling on the porch, and the door was flung open, letting in a gust of autumnal air full of spicy odors from the trees and vines outside. Betty sprang up, while her mother followed more slowly. There were her father and her brother Warren, and the latter had by the hand the little girl who had crossed the ocean to come to the famous city of the New World, Boston. Almost two hundred years before an ancestor had crossed from old Boston, in the ship *Arabella*, and settled here, taking his share of pilgrim hardships. Doris' father, when a boy, had been sent back to England to be adopted as the heir of a long line. But the old relative married and had two sons of his own, though he did well by the boy, who went to France and married a pretty French girl. After seven years of unbroken happiness the sweet young wife had died. Then little Doris, six years of age, had spent two years in a convent. From there her father had taken her to Lincolnshire and placed her with two elderly relatives, while he was planning and arranging his affairs to come back to America with his little daughter. But one night, being out with a sailing party, a sudden storm had caught them and swept them out of life in an instant.

Second-cousin Charles Adams had been in correspondence with him, and advised him to return. Being in feeble health, he had included him and his

5

heirs in his will, appointing his nephew Winthrop Adams executor, and died before the news of the death of his distant relative had reached him. The Lincolnshire ladies were too old to have the care and rearing of a child, so Mr. Winthrop Adams had sent by Captain Grier to bring over the little girl. Her father's estate, not very large, was in money and easily managed. And now little Doris was nearing ten.

"Oh!" cried Betty, hugging the slim figure in the red camlet cloak, and peering into the queer big hat tied down over her ears with broad ribbons that, what with the big bow and the wide rim, almost hid her face; but she saw two soft lovely eyes and cherry-red lips that she kissed at once, though kissing had not come in fashion to any great extent, and was still considered by many people rather dubious if not positively sinful.

"Oh, little Doris, welcome to Boston and the United Colonies and the whole of America! Let me see how you look," and she untied the wide strings.

The head that emerged was covered with fair curling hair; the complexion was clear, but a little wind-burned from her long trip; the eyes were very dark, but of the deepest, softest blue, that suggested twilight. There was a dimple in the dainty chin, and the mouth had a half-frightened, half-wistful smile.

"Captain Grier will send up her boxes to-morrow. They got aground and were delayed. I began to think they would have to stay out all night. The captain will bring up a lot of papers for Winthrop, and everything," explained Mr. Leverett. "Are you cold, little one?"

Doris gave a great shiver as her cloak was taken off, but it was more nervousness than cold, and the glances of the strange faces. Then she walked straight to the fireplace.

"Oh, what a beautiful fire!" she exclaimed. "No, I am not cold"—and the wistful expression wandered from one to the other.

"This is my daughter Betty, and this is—why, you may as well begin by saying Aunt Elizabeth at once. How are you, Aunt Priscilla? This is our little French-English girl, but I hope she will turn into a stanch Boston girl. Now, mother, let's have a good supper. I'm hungry as a wolf."

Doris caught Betty's hand again and pressed it to her cheek. The smiling face won her at once.

"Did you have a pleasant voyage?" asked Mrs. Leverett, as she was piling up the cups and saucers, and paused to smile at the little stranger.

"There were some storms, and I was afraid then. It made me think of papa. But there was a good deal of sunshine. And I was quite ill at first, but the captain was very nice, and Mrs. Jewett had two little girls, so after a while we played together. And then I think we forgot all about being at sea—it was so like a house, except there were no gardens or fields and trees."

Mrs. Leverett went out to the kitchen, and soon there was the savory smell of frying sausage. Betty placed Doris in a chair by the chimney corner and began to rearrange the table. Warren went out to the kitchen and, as by the farthest window there was a sort of high bench with a tin basin, a pail of water, and a long roller towel, he began to wash his face and hands, telling his mother meanwhile the occurrences of the last two or three hours.

Aunt Priscilla drew up her chair and surveyed the little traveler with some curiosity. She was rather shocked that the child was not dressed in mourning, and now she discovered, that her little gown was of brocaded silk and much furbelowed, at which she frowned severely.

True, her father had been dead more than a year; but her being an orphan made it seem as if she should still be in the depths of woe. And she had earrings and a brooch in the lace tucker. She gave her sniff—it was very wintry and contemptuous.

"I suppose that's the latest French fashion," she said sharply. "If I lived in England I should just despise French clothes."

"Oh," said Doris, "do you mean my gown? Miss Arabella made it for me. When she was a young lady she went up to London to see the king crowned, and they had a grand ball, and this was one of the gowns she had—not the ball dress, for that was white satin with roses sprinkled over it. She's very old now, and she gave that to her cousin for a wedding dress. And she made this over for me. I got some tar on my blue stuff gown yesterday, and the others were so thin Mrs. Jewett thought I had better put on this, but it is my very best gown."

The artless sincerity and the soft sweet voice quite nonplused Aunt Priscilla. Then Warren returned and dropped on a three-cornered stool standing there, and almost tilted over.

"Now, if I had gone into the fire, like any other green log, how I should have sizzled!" he said laughingly.

"Oh, I am so glad you didn't!" exclaimed Doris in affright. Then she smiled softly.

"Does it seem queer to be on land again?"

"Yes. I want to rock to and fro." She made a pretty movement with her slender body, and nodded her head.

7

"Are you very tired?"

"Oh, no."

"You were out five weeks."

"Is that a long while? I was homesick at first. I wanted to see Miss Arabella and Barby. Miss Henrietta is—is—not right in her mind, if you can understand. And she is very old. She just sits in her chair all day and mumbles. She was named for a queen—Henrietta Maria."

Aunt Priscilla gave a disapproving sniff.

"Supper's ready," said Mr. Leverett. "Come."

Warren took the small stranger by the hand, and she made a little courtesy, quite as if she were a grown lady.

"What an airy little piece of vanity!" thought Aunt Priscilla. "And whatever will Winthrop Adams do with her, and no woman about the house to train her!"

Betty came and poured tea for her father and Warren. Mr. Leverett piled up her plate, but, although the viands had an appetizing fragrance, Doris was not hungry. Everything was so new and strange, and she could not get the motion of the ship out of her head. But the pumpkin pie was delicious. She had never tasted anything like it.

"You'll soon be a genuine Yankee girl," declared Warren. "Pumpkin pie is the test."

Mr. Leverett and his son did full justice to the supper. Then he had to go out to a meeting. There were some clouds drifting over the skies of the new country, and many discussions as to future policy.

"So, Aunt Priscilla, I'll beau you home," said he; "unless you have a mind to stay all night, or want a young fellow like Warren."

"You're plenty old enough to be sensible, Foster Leverett," she returned sharply. She would have enjoyed a longer stay and was curious about the newcomer, but when Betty brought her hat and shawl she said a stiff good-night to everybody and went out with her escort.

Betty cleared away the tea things, wiped the dishes for her mother and then took a place beside Warren, who was very much interested in hearing the little girl talk. There was a good deal of going back and forth to England although the journey seemed so long, but it was startling to have a child sitting by the fireside, here in his father's house, who had lived in both France and England. She had an odd little accent, too, but it gave her an added daintiness. She

8

remembered her convent life very well, and her stay in Paris with her father. It seemed strange to him that she could talk so tranquilly about her parents, but there had been so many changes in her short life, and her father had been away from her so much!

"It always seemed to me as if he must come back again," she said with a serious little sigh, "as if he was over in France or down in London. It is so strange to have anyone go away forever that I think you can't take it in somehow. And Miss Arabella was always so good. She said if she had been younger she should never have agreed to my coming. And all papa's relatives were here, and someone who wrote to her and settled about the journey."

She glanced up inquiringly.

"Yes. That's Uncle Winthrop Adams. He isn't an own uncle, but it seems somehow more respectful to call him uncle. Mr. Adams would sound queer. And he will be your guardian."

"A—guardian?"

"Well, he has the care of the property left to your father. There is a house that is rented, and a great plot of ground. Cousin Charles owned so much land, and he never was married, so it had to go round to the cousins. He was very fond of your father as a little boy. And Uncle Winthrop seems the proper person to take charge of you."

Doris sighed. She seemed always being handed from one to another.

She was sitting on the stool now, and when Betty slipped into the vacant chair she put her arm over the child's shoulder in a caressing manner.

"Do you mean—that I would have to go and live with him?" she asked slowly.

Warren laughed. "I declare I don't know what Uncle Win would do with a little girl! Miss Recompense Gardiner keeps the house, and she's as prim as the crimped edge of an apple pie. And there is only Cary."

"Cary is at Harvard—at college," explained Betty. "And, then, he is going to Europe for a tour. Uncle Win teaches some classes, and is a great Greek and Latin scholar, and translates from the poets, and reads and studies—is a regular bookworm. His wife has been dead ever since Cary was a baby."

"I wish I could stay here," said Doris, and, reaching up, she clasped her arms around Betty's neck. "I like your father, and your mother has such a sweet voice, and you—and him," nodding her head over to Warren. "And since that —the other lady—doesn't live here——"

"Aunt Priscilla," laughed Betty. "I think she improves on acquaintance. Her

9

bark is worse than her bite. When I was a little girl I thought her just awful, and never wanted to go there. Now I quite like it. I spend whole days with her. But I shouldn't spend a night in praying that Providence would send her to live with us. I'd fifty times rather have you, you dear little midget. And, when everything is settled, I am of the opinion you will live with us, for a while at least."

"I shall be so glad," in a joyous, relieved tone.

"Then if Uncle Win should ask you, don't be afraid of anybody, but just say you want to stay here. That will settle it unless he thinks you ought to go to school. But there are nice enough schools in Boston. And I am glad you want to stay. I've wished a great many times that I had a little sister. I have two, married. One lives over at Salem and one ever so far away at Hartford. And I am Aunt Betty. I have five nephews and four nieces. And you never can have any, you solitary little girl!"

"I think I don't mind if I can have you."

"This is love at first sight. I've never been in love before, though I have some girl friends. And being in love means living with someone and wanting them all the time, and a lot of sweet, foolish stuff. What a silly girl I am! Well— you are to be my little sister."

Oh, how sweet it was to find home and affection and welcome! Doris had not thought much about it, but now she was suddenly, unreasonably glad. She laid her head down on Betty's knee and looked at the dancing flames, the purples and misty grays, the scarlets and blues and greens, all mingling, then sending long arrowy darts that ran back and hid behind the logs before you could think.

Mrs. Leverett kneaded her bread and stirred up her griddle cakes for morning. It was early in the season to start with them, but with the first cold whiff Mr. Leverett began to beg for them. Then she fixed her fire, turned down her sleeves, took off the big apron that covered all her skirt, and rejoined the three by the fireside.

"That child has gone fast asleep," she exclaimed, looking at her. "Poor thing, I dare say she is all tired out! And, man-like, your father never thought of her nightgown or anything to put on in the morning, and that silk is nothing for a child to wear. I saw that it shocked Aunt Priscilla."

"And she told the story of it so prettily. It is a lovely thing—and to think it has been to London to see the king!"

"You must take her in your bed, Betty."

"Oh, of course. Mother, don't you suppose Uncle Win will consent to her staying here? I want her."

"It would be a good thing for you to have someone to look after, Betty. It would help steady you and give you some sense of responsibility. The youngest child always gets spoiled. Your father was speaking of it. I can't imagine a child in Uncle Winthrop's household."

Betty laughed. "Nor in Aunt Priscilla's," she appended.

"Poor little thing! How pretty she is. And what a long journey to take—and to come among strangers! Yes, she must go to bed at once."

"I'll carry her upstairs," said Warren.

"Nonsense!" protested his mother.

But he did for all that, and when he laid her on Betty's cold bed she roused and smiled, and suffered herself to be made ready for slumber. Then she slipped down on her knees, and said "Our Father in Heaven" in soft, sleepy French. Her mother had taught her that. And in English she repeated:

"Now I lay me down to sleep," in remembrance of her father, and kissed Betty. But she had hardly touched the pillow when she was asleep again in her new home, Boston.

CHAPTER II

IN A NEW HOME

The sun was shining when Doris opened her eyes, and she rubbed them to make sure she was not dreaming. There was no motion, and her bed was so soft and wide. She sat up straight, half-startled, and she seemed in a well of fluffy feathers. There were two white curtained windows and a straight splint chair at each one, with a queer little knob on the top of the post that suggested a sprite from some of the old legends she had been used to hearing.

What enchantment had transported her thither? Oh, yes—she had been brought to Cousin Leverett's, she remembered now; and, oh, how sleepy she had been last night as she sat by the warm, crackling fire!

"Well, little Doris!" exclaimed a fresh, wholesome voice, with a laughing sound back of it.

"Oh, you are Betty! It is like a dream. I could not think where I was at first. And this bed is so high. It's like Miss Arabella's with the curtains around it. And at home I had a little pallet—just a low, straight bed almost like a bench, with no curtains. You slept here with me?"

"Yes. It is my bed and my room. And it was delightful to have you last night. I think you never stirred. My niece Elizabeth was here in the summer from Salem, and after two nights I turned her out—she kicked unmercifully, and I couldn't endure it. Now, do you want to get up?"

"Oh, yes. Must I jump out or just slip."

"Here is a stool."

But Doris had slipped and come down on a rug of woven rags almost as soft as Persian pile. Her nightdress fell about her in a train; it was Betty's, and she looked like a slim white wraith.

"Now I will help you dress. Here is a gown of mine that I outgrew when I was a little girl, and it was so nice mother said it should be saved for Elizabeth. We call her that because my other sister Electa has a daughter she calls Bessy. They are both named after mother. And so am I, but I have always been called Betty. So many of one name are confusing. But yours is so pretty and odd. I never knew a girl called Doris."

"I am glad you like it," said Doris simply. "It was papa's choice. My mother's name was Jacqueline."

"That is very French."

"And that is my name, too. But Doris is easier to say."

Betty had been helping her dress. The blue woolen gown was not any too long, but, oh, it was worlds too wide! They both laughed.

"*I* wasn't such a slim little thing. See here, I will pin a plait over in front, and that will help it. Now that does nicely. And you must be choice of that beautiful brocade. What a pity that you will outgrow it! It would make such a splendid gown when you go to parties. I've never had a silk gown," and Betty sighed.

They went downstairs. It would seem queer enough now to attend to one's toilet in the corner of the kitchen, but it was quite customary then. In Mrs. Leverett's room there were a washing stand with a white cloth, and a china bowl and ewer in dark blue flowers on a white ground, picked out with gilt edges. The bowl had scallops around the edge, and the ewer was tall and slim. There were a soap dish and a small pitcher, and they looked beautiful on the thick white cloth, that was fringed all around. It had been brought over from England by Mrs. Leverett's grandmother, and was esteemed very highly, and had been promised to Betty for her name. But Mrs. Leverett would have considered it sacrilege to use it.

It is true, many houses now began to have wash rooms, which were very nice in summer, but of small account in winter, when the water froze so easily, unless you could have a fire.

When people sigh for the good old times they forget the hardships and the inconveniences.

Doris brushed out her hair and curled it in a twinkling; then she had some breakfast. Mrs. Leverett was baking bread and making pies and a large cake full of raisins that Betty had seeded, which went by the name of election cake.

The kitchen was a great cheery place with some sunny windows and a big oven built at one side, a capacious working table, a dresser, some wooden chairs, and a yellow-painted floor. The kitchen opened into mother's room as well as the hall.

Doris sat and watched both busy women. At Miss Arabella's they had an old serving maid and the kitchen was not a place of tidiness and beauty. It had a hard dirt floor, and Barby sat out of doors in the sunshine to do whatever work she could take out there, and often washed and dried her dishes when the weather was pleasant.

But here the houses were close enough to smile at each other. After the great spaces these yards seemed small, but there were trees and vines, and Mrs. Leverett had quite a garden spot, where she raised all manner of sweet herbs and some vegetables. Mr. Leverett had a shop over on Ann Street, and attended steadily to his business, early and late, as men did at that time.

The dining table was set out at noon, and soon after twelve o'clock the two men made their appearance.

"Let me look at you," said Mr. Leverett, taking both of Doris' small hands. "I hardly saw you yesterday. You were buried in that big hat, and it was getting so dark. You have not much Adams about you, neither do you look French."

"Miss Arabella always said I looked like papa. There is a picture of him in my box. He had dark-blue eyes."

"Well, yours would pass for black. Do they snap when you get out of temper?"

Doris colored and cast them down.

"Don't tease her," interposed Mrs. Leverett. "She is not going to get angry. It is a bad thing for little girls."

"I don't remember much of anything about your father. Both of your aunts are dead. You have one cousin somewhere—Margaret's husband married and went South—to Virginia, didn't he? Well, there is no end of Adams connection even if some of them have different names. Captain Grier dropped into the warehouse with a tin box of papers, and your things are to be sent this afternoon. He is coming up this evening, and I've sent for Uncle Win to come over to supper. Then I suppose the child's fate will be settled, and she'll be a regular Boston girl."

"I do wonder if Uncle Win will let her stay here? Mother and I have decided that it is the best place."

"Do *you* think it a good place?"

He turned so suddenly to Doris that her face was scarlet with embarrassment.

"It's splendid," she said when she caught her breath. "I should like to stay. And Aunt Elizabeth will teach me to make pies."

"Well, pies are pretty good things, according to my way of thinking. There's lots for little girls to learn, though I dare say Uncle Win will think it can all come out of a book."

"Some of it might come out of a cookbook," said Betty demurely.

"Your mother's the best cookbook I know about—good enough for anyone."

"But we can't send mother all round the world."

"We just don't want to," said Warren.

Mrs. Leverett smiled. She was proud of her ability in the culinary line.

Mr. Leverett looked at Doris presently. "Come, come," he began good-naturedly, "this will never do! You are not eating enough to keep a bird alive. No wonder you are so thin!"

"But I ate a great deal of breakfast," explained Doris with naïve honesty.

"And you are not homesick?"

Doris thought a moment. "I don't want to go away, if that is what you mean."

"Yes, that's about it," nodding humorously.

Warren thought her the quaintest, prettiest child he had ever seen, but he hardly knew what to say to her.

When the men had eaten and gone, the dishes were soon washed up, and then mother and daughter brought their sewing. Mrs. Leverett was mending Warren's coat. Betty darned a small pile of stockings, and then she took out some needlework. She had begun her next summer's white gown, and she meant to do it by odd spells, especially when Aunt Priscilla, who would lecture her on so much vanity, was not around.

Mrs. Leverett gently questioned Doris—she was not an aggressive woman, nor unduly curious. No, Doris had not sewed much. Barby always darned the stockings, and Miss Easter had come to make whatever clothes she needed. She used to go to Father Langhorne and recite, and Mrs. Leverett wondered whether she and the father both were Roman Catholics. What did she study? Oh, French and a little Latin, and she was reading history and "Paradise Lost," but she didn't like sums, and she could make pillow lace. Miss Arabella made beautiful pillow lace, and sometimes the grand ladies came in carriages and paid her ever so much money for it.

And presently dusk began to mingle with the golden touches of sunset, and Mrs. Leverett went to make biscuit and fry some chicken, and Uncle Winthrop came at the same moment that a man on a dray brought an old-fashioned chest and carried it upstairs to Betty's room. But Betty had already attired Doris in her silk gown.

Doris liked Uncle Winthrop at once, although he was so different from Uncle Leverett, who wore all around his face a brownish-red beard that seemed to grow out of his neck, and had tumbled hair and a somewhat weather-beaten face. Mr. Winthrop Adams was two good inches taller and stood up very straight in spite of his being a bookworm. His complexion was fair and rather pale, his features were of the long, slender type, which his beard, worn in the Vandyke style, intensified. His hair was light and his eyes were a grayish blue, and he had a refined and gentle expression.

"So this is our little traveler," he said. "Your father was somewhat older, perhaps, when we bade him good-by, but I have often thought of him. We corresponded a little off and on. And I am glad to be able to do all that I can for his child."

Doris glanced up, feeling rather shy, and wondering what she ought to say, but in the next breath Betty had said it all, even to declaring laughingly that as Doris had come to them they meant to keep her.

"Doris," he said softly. "Doris. You have a poetical name. And you are poetical-looking."

She wondered what the comparison meant. "Paradise Lost" was so grand it tired her. Oh, there was the old volume of Percy's "Reliques." Did he mean like some of the sweet little things in that? Miss Arabella had said it wasn't quite the thing for a child to read, and had taken it away until she grew older.

Uncle Winthrop took her hand again—a small, slim hand; and his was slender as well. No real physical work had hardened it. He dropped into the high-backed chair beside the fireplace, and, putting his arm about her, drew her near to his side. Uncle Leverett would have taken her on his knee if he had been moved by an impulse like that, but he was used to children and grandchildren, and the bookish man was not.

"It is a great change to you," he said in his low tone, which had a fascination for her. "Was Miss Arabella—were there any young people in the old Lincolnshire house?"

"Oh, no. Miss Henrietta was very, very old, but then she had lost her mind and forgotten everybody. And Miss Arabella had snowy white hair and a sweet wrinkled face."

"Did you go to school?"

"There wasn't any school except a dame's school for very little children. I used to go twice a week to Father Langhorne and read and write and do sums."

"Then we will have to educate you. Do you think you would like to go to school?"

"I don't know." She hung her head a little, and it gave her a still more winsome expression. There was an indescribable charm about her.

"What did you read with this father?"

"We read 'Paradise Lost' and some French. And I had begun Latin."

Winthrop Adams gave a soft, surprised whistle. By the firelight he looked her over critically. Prodigies were not to his taste, and a girl prodigy would be an abhorrence. But her face had a sweet unconcern that reassured him.

"And did you like it—'Paradise Lost'?"

"I think I did—not," returned Doris with hesitating frankness. "I liked the verses in Percy's 'Reliques' better. I like verses that rhyme, that you can sing to yourself."

"Ah! And how about the sums?"

"I didn't like them at all. But Miss Arabella said the right things were often hard, and the easy things——"

"Well, what is the fault of the easy things that we all like, and ought not to like?"

"They were not so good for anyone—though I don't see why. They are often very pleasant."

He laughed then, but some intuition told her he liked pleasant things as well.

"What do you do in such a case?"

"I did the sums. It was the right thing to do. And I studied Latin, though Miss Arabella said it was of no use to a girl."

"And the French?"

"Oh, I learned French when I was very little and had mamma, and when I was in the convent, too. But papa talked English, so I had them both. Isn't it strange that afterward you have to learn so much about them, and how to make right sentences, and why they are right. It seems as if there were a great many things in the world to learn. Betty doesn't know half of them, and she's as sweet as——Oh, I think the wisest person in the world couldn't be any sweeter."

Winthrop Adams smiled at the eager reasoning. Betty was a bright, gay girl. What occult quality was sweetness? And Doris had been in a convent. That startled him the first moment. The old strict bitterness and narrowness of Puritanism had been softened and refined away. The people who had banished Quakers had for a long while tolerated Roman Catholics. He had known Father Matignon, and enjoyed the scholarly and well-trained John Cheverus, who had lately been consecrated bishop. The Protestants had even been generous to their brethren of another faith when they were building their church. As for himself he was a rather stiff Church of England man, if he

17

could be called stiff about anything.

"And—did you like the convent?" he asked, after a pause, in which he generously made up his mind he would not interfere with her religious belief.

"It's so long ago"—with a half-sigh. "I was very sad at first, and missed mamma. Papa had to go away somewhere and couldn't take me. Yes, I liked sister Thérèse very much. Mamma was a Huguenot, you know."

"You see, I really do not know anything about her, and have known very little about your father since he was a small boy."

"A small boy! How queer that seems," and she gave a tender, rippling laugh. "Then you can tell me about him. He used to come to the convent once in a while, and when he was ready to go to England he took me. Yes, I was sorry to leave Sister Thérèse and Sister Clare. There were some little girls, too. And then we went to Lincolnshire. Miss Arabella was very nice, and Barby was so queer and funny—at first I could hardly understand her. And then we went to a pretty little church where they didn't count beads nor pray to the Virgin nor Saints. But it was a good deal like. It was the Church of England. I suppose it had to be different from the Church of France."

"Yes." He drew her a little closer. That was a bond of sympathy between them. And just then Uncle Leverett and Warren came in, and there was a shaking of hands, and Uncle Leverett said:

"Well, I declare! The sight of you, Win, is good for sore eyes—well ones, too."

"I am rather remiss in a social way, I must confess. I'll try to do better. The years fly around so, I have always felt sorry that I saw so little of Cousin Charles until that last sad year."

"It takes womenkind to keep up sociability. Charles and you might as well have been a couple of old bachelors."

Uncle Win gave his soft half-smile, which was really more of an indication than a smile.

"Come to supper now," said Mrs. Leverett.

Doris kept hold of Uncle Win's hand until she reached her place. He went around to the other side of the table. She decided she liked him very much. She liked almost everybody: the captain had been so friendly, and Mrs. Jewett and some of the ladies on board the vessel so kind. But Betty and Uncle Win went to the very first place with her.

The elders had all the conversation, and it seemed about some coming trouble to the country that she did not understand. She knew there had been war in

France and various other European countries. Little girls were not very well up in geography in those days, but they did learn a good deal listening to their elders.

They were hardly through supper when Captain Grier came with the very japanned box papa had brought over from France and placed in Miss Arabella's care. His name was on it—"Charles Winthrop Adams." Oh, and that was Uncle Win's name, too! Surely, they *were* relations! Doris experienced a sense of gladness.

Betty brought out a table standing against the wainscot. You touched a spring underneath, and the circular side came up and made a flat top. The captain took a small key out of a curious long leathern purse, and Uncle Win unlocked the box and spread out the papers. There was the marriage certificate of Jacqueline Marie de la Maur and Charles Winthrop Adams, and the birth and baptismal record of Doris Jacqueline de la Maur Adams, and ever so many other records and letters.

Mr. Winthrop Adams gave the captain a receipt for them, and thanked him cordially for all his care and attention to his little niece.

"She was a pretty fair sailor after the first week," said the captain with a twinkle in his eye. He was very much wrinkled and weather-beaten, but jolly and good-humored. "And now, sissy, I'm glad you're safe with your folks, and I hope you'll grow up into a nice clever woman. 'Taint no use wishin' you good looks, for you're purty as a pink now—one of them rather palish kind. But you'll soon have red cheeks."

Doris had very red cheeks for a moment. Betty leaned over to her brother, and whispered:

"What a splendid opportunity lost! Aunt Priscilla ought to be here to say, 'Handsome is as handsome does.'"

Then Captain Grier shook hands all round and took his departure.

Afterward the two men discussed business about the little girl. There must be another trustee, and papers must be taken out for guardianship. They would go to the court-house, say at eleven to-morrow, and put everything in train.

Betty took out some knitting. It was a stocking of fine linen thread, and along the instep it had a pretty openwork pattern that was like lace work.

"That is to wear with slippers," she explained to Doris. "But it's a sight of work. 'Lecty had six pairs when she was married. That's my second sister, Mrs. King. She lives in Hartford. I want to go and make her a visit this winter."

Mrs. Leverett's stocking was of the more useful kind, blue-gray yarn, thick and warm, for her husband's winter wear. She did not have to count stitches and make throws, and take up two here and three there.

"Warren," said his mother, when he had poked the fire until she was on 'pins and needles,'—they didn't call it nervous then,—"Warren, I am 'most out of corn. I wish you'd go shell some."

"The hens do eat an awful lot, seems to me. Why, I shelled only a few nights ago."

"I touched bottom when I gave them the last feed this afternoon. By spring we won't have so many," nodding in a half-humorous fashion.

"Don't you want to come out and see me? You don't have any Indian corn growing in England, I've heard."

"Did it belong to the Indians?" asked Doris.

"I rather guess it did, in the first instance. But now we plant it for ourselves. We don't, because father sold the two-acre lot, and they're bringing a street through. So now we have only the meadow."

Doris looked at the uncles, but she couldn't understand a word they were saying.

"Come!" Warren held out his hand.

"Put the big kitchen apron round her, Warren," said Betty, thinking of her silk gown.

He tied the apron round her neck and brought back the strings round her waist, so she was all covered. Then he found her a low chair, and poked the kitchen fire, putting on a pine log to make a nice blaze. He brought out from the shed a tub and a basket of ears of corn. Across the tub he laid the blade of an old saw and then sat on the end to keep it firm.

"Now you'll see business. Maybe you've never seen any corn before?"

She looked over in the basket, and then took up an ear with a mysterious expression.

"It won't bite you," he said laughingly.

"But how queer and hard, with all these little points," pinching them with her dainty fingers.

"Grains," he explained. "And a husk grows on the outside to keep it warm. When the winter is going to be very cold the husk is very thick."

"Will this winter be cold?"

"Land alive! yes. Winters always *are* cold."

Warren settled himself and drew the ear across the blade. A shower of corn rattled down on the bottom of the tub.

"Oh! is that the way you peel it off?"

He threw his head back and laughed.

"Oh, you Englisher! We *shell* it off."

"Well, it peels too. You peel a potato and an apple with a knife blade. Oh, what a pretty white core!"

"Cob. We Americans are adding new words to the language. A core has seeds in it. There, see how soft it is."

Doris took it in her hand and then laid her cheek against it. "Oh, how soft and fuzzy it is!" she cried. "And what do you do with it?"

"We don't plant that part of it. That core has no seeds. You have to plant a grain like this. The little clear point we call a heart, and that sprouts and grows. This is a good use for the cob."

He had finished another, which he tossed into the fire. A bright blaze seemed to run over it all at once and die down. Then the small end flamed out and the fire crept along in a doubtful manner until it was all covered again.

"They're splendid to kindle the fire with. And pine cones. America has lots of useful things."

"But they burn cones in France. I like the spicy smell. It's queer though," wrinkling her forehead. "Did the Indians know about corn the first?"

"That is the general impression unless America was settled before the Indians. Uncle Win has his head full of these things and is writing a book. And there is tobacco that Sir Walter Raleigh carried home from Virginia."

"Oh, I know about Sir Walter and Queen Elizabeth."

"He was a splendid hero. I think people are growing tame now; there are no wars except Indian skirmishes."

"Why, Napoleon is fighting all the time."

"Oh, that doesn't count," declared the young man with a lofty air. "We had some magnificent heroes in the Revolution. There are lots of places for you to see. Bunker Hill and Lexington and Concord and the headquarters of Washington and Lafayette. The French were real good to us, though we have had some scrimmages with them. And now that you are to be a Boston girl ____"

"But I was in Old Boston before," and she laughed. "Very old Boston, that is so far back no one can remember, and it was called Ikanhoe, which means Boston. There is the old church and the abbey that St. Botolph founded. They came over somewhere in six hundred, and were missionaries from France— St. Botolph and his brother."

"Whew!" ejaculated Warren with a long whistle, looking up at the little girl as if she were hundreds of years old.

Betty opened the door. "Uncle Win is going," she announced. "Come and say good-by to him."

He was standing up with the box of papers in his hand, and saying:

"I must have you all over to tea some night, and Doris must come and see my old house. And I have a big boy like Warren. Yes, we must be a little more friendly, for life is short at the best. And you are to stay here a while with good Cousin Elizabeth, and I hope you will be content and happy."

She pressed the hand Uncle Win held out in both of hers. In all the changes she had learned to be content, and she had a certain adaptiveness that kept her from being unhappy. She was very glad she was going to stay with Betty, and glanced up with a bright smile.

They all said good-night to Cousin Adams. Mr. Leverett turned the great key in the hall door, and it gave a shriek.

"I must oil that lock to-morrow. It groans enough to raise the dead," said Mrs. Leverett.

CHAPTER III

AUNT PRISCILLA

There was quite a discussion about a school.

Uncle Win had an idea Doris ought to begin high up in the scale. For really she was very well born on both sides. Her father had left considerable money, and in a few years second-cousin Charles' bequest might be quite valuable, if Aunt Priscilla did sniff over it. There was Mrs. Rawson's.

"But that is mostly for young ladies, a kind of finishing school. And in some things Doris is quite behind, while in others far advanced. There will be time enough for accomplishments. And Mrs. Webb's is near by, which will be an object this cold winter."

"I shouldn't like her to forget her French. And perhaps it would be as well to go on with Latin," Cousin Adams said.

Mrs. Leverett was a very sensible woman, but she really did not see the need of Latin for a girl. There was a kind of sentiment about French; it had been her mother's native tongue, and one did now and then go to France.

There had been a good deal of objection to even the medium education of women among certain classes. The three "R's" had been considered all that was necessary. And when the system of public education had been first inaugurated it was thought quite sufficient for girls to go from April to October. Good wives and good mothers was the ideal held up to girls. But people were beginning to understand that ignorance was not always goodness. Mrs. Rawson had done a great deal toward the enlightenment of this subject. The pioneer days were past, unless one was seized with a mania for the new countries.

Mrs. Leverett was secretly proud of her two married daughters. Mrs. King's husband had gone to the State legislature, and was considered quite a rising politician. Mrs. Manning was a farmer's wife and held in high esteem for the management of her family. Betty was being inducted now into all household accomplishments with the hope that she would marry quite as well as her sisters. She was a good reader and speller; she had a really fine manuscript arithmetic, in which she had written the rules and copied the sums herself. She had a book of "elegant extracts"; she also wrote down the text of the Sunday morning sermon and what she could remember of it. She knew the difference between the Puritans and the Pilgrims; she also knew how the thirteen States were settled and by whom; she could answer almost any question about the French, the Indian, and the Revolutionary wars. She could do fine needlework and the fancy stitches of the day. She was extremely "handy" with her needle. Mrs. Leverett called her a very well-educated girl, and the Leveretts considered themselves some of the best old stock in Boston, if they were not much given to show.

It might be different with Doris. But a good husband was the best thing a girl could have, in Mrs. Leverett's estimation, and knowing how to make a good home her greatest accomplishment.

They looked over Doris' chest and found some simple gowns, mostly summer ones, pairs of fine stockings that had been cut down and made over by Miss Arabella's dainty fingers, and underclothes of a delicate quality. There were the miniatures of her parents—that of her mother very girlish indeed—and a few trinkets and books.

"She must have two good woolen frocks for winter, and a coat," said Mrs. Leverett. "Cousin Winthrop said I should buy whatever was suitable."

"And a little Puritan cap trimmed about with fur. I am sure I can make that. And a strip of fur on her coat. She would blow away in that big hat if a high wind took her," declared Betty.

"And all the little girls wear them in winter. Still, I suppose Old Boston must have been cold and bleak in winter."

"It was not so nearly an island."

There was a good deal of work to do on Friday, so shopping was put off to the first of the week. Doris proved eagerly helpful and dusted very well. In the afternoon Aunt Priscilla came over for her cup of tea.

"Dear me," she began with a great sigh, "I wish I had some nice young girl that I could train, and who would take an interest in things. Polly *is* too old. And I don't like to send her away, for she was good enough when she had any sense. There's no place for her but the poorhouse, and I can't find it in my conscience to send her there. But I'm monstrous tired of her, and I do think I'd feel better with a cheerful young person around. You're just fortunate, 'Lizabeth, that you and Betty can do for yourselves."

"It answers, now that the family is small. But last year I found it quite trying. And Betty must have her two or three years' training at housekeeping."

"Oh, of course. I'm glad you're so sensible, 'Lizabeth. Girls are very flighty, nowadays, and are in the street half the time, and dancing and frolicking round at night. I really don't know what the young generation will be good for!"

Mrs. Leverett smiled. She remembered she had heard some such comments when she was young, though the lines were more strictly drawn then.

"Has Winthrop been over to see his charge? How does he feel about it? Now, if she had been a boy——"

"He was up to tea last night, and he and Foster have been arranging the business this morning. Foster is to be joint trustee, but Winthrop will be her guardian."

"What will he do with a girl! Why, she'll set Recompense crazy."

"She is not going to live there. For the present she will stay here. She will go to Mrs. Webb's school this winter. He has an idea of sending her to boarding school later on."

"Is she that rich?" asked Aunt Priscilla with a little sarcasm.

"She will have a small income from what her father left. Then there is the rent of the house in School Street, and some stock. Winthrop thinks she ought to be well educated. And if she should ever have to depend on herself, teaching seems quite a good thing. Even Mrs. Webb makes a very comfortable living."

"But we're going to educate the community for nothing, and tax the people who have no children to pay for it."

"Well," said Mrs. Leverett with a smile, "that evens up matters. But the others, at least property owners, have to pay their share. I tell Foster that we ought not grudge our part, though we have no children to send."

"How did people get along before?"

"I went to school until I was fifteen."

"And when I was twelve I was doing my day's work spinning. There's talk that we shall have to come back to it. Jonas Field is in a terrible taking. According to him war's bound to come. And this embargo is just ruining everything. It is to be hoped we will have a new President before everything goes."

"Yes, it is making times hard. But we are learning to do a great deal more for ourselves."

"It behooves us not to waste our money. But Winthrop Adams hasn't much real calculation. So long as he has money to buy books, I suppose he thinks the world will go on all right. It's to be hoped Foster will look out for the girl's interest a little. But you'll be foolish to take the brunt of the thing. Now it would be just like you 'Lizabeth Leverett, to take care of this child, without

25

a penny, just as if she was some charity object thrown on your hands."

Mrs. Leverett did give her soft laugh then.

"You have just hit it, Aunt Priscilla," she said. "Winthrop wanted to pay her board, but Foster just wouldn't hear to it, this year at least. We have all taken a great liking to her, and she is to be our visitor from now until summer, when some other plans are to be made."

"Well—if you have money to throw away——" gasped Aunt Priscilla.

"She won't eat more than a chicken, and she'll sleep in Betty's bed. It will help steady Betty and be an interest to all of us. I really couldn't think of charging. It's like having one of the grandchildren here. And she needs a mother's care. Think of the poor little girl with not a near relative! Aunt Priscilla, there's a good many things money can't buy."

Aunt Priscilla sniffed.

"Take off your bonnet and have a cup of tea," Mrs. Leverett had asked her when she first came in. "It's such a long walk back to King Street on an empty stomach. The children are making cookies, but Betty shall brew a cup of tea at once, unless you'll wait till the men folks come in."

Aunt Priscilla sat severe and undecided for a moment. The laughing voices in the other room piqued and vexed and interested her all in a breath. She had come over to hear about Doris. There was so little interest in her methodical old life. Mrs. Leverett sincerely pitied women who had no children and no grandchildren.

"They're quite as queer as old maids without the real excuse," she said to her husband. "They've missed the best things out of their lives without really knowing they were the best."

And perhaps at this era more respect was paid to age. There were certain trials and duties to life that men and women accepted and did not try to evade. A modern happy woman would have been bored at the call of a dissatisfied old woman every few days. But since the death of Mehitable Doule, Priscilla's own cousin, who had been married from her house, she had clung more to the Leveretts. Foster was too easy-going, otherwise she had not much fault to find with him. He had prospered and was forehanded, and his married son and daughters had been fairly successful.

"Well, I don't care if I do," said Aunt Priscilla, with a half-reluctance. "Though I hadn't decided to when I came away, and Polly'll make a great hole in that cold roast pork, for I never said a word as to what she should have for supper. She's come to have no more sense than a child, and some things are bad to eat at night. But if she makes herself sick she'll have to suffer."

"I'll have some tea made——"

"No, 'Lizabeth, don't fuss. I shan't be in any hurry, if I do stay, and the men will be in before long. So Winthrop wasn't real put out when he saw the girl?"

"I think he liked her. He's not much hand to make a fuss, you know. He feels she must be well brought up. Her mother, it seems, was quite quality."

"Queer the mother's folks didn't look after her."

"Her mother was an only child. Winthrop has the records back several generations. And when *she* died the father was alive, you know."

"Winthrop is a great stickler for such things. It's good to have folks you're not ashamed of, to be sure, but family isn't everything. Behaving counts."

Aunt Priscilla took off her bonnet and shawl, and hung them in the "best" closet, where the Sunday coats and cloaks were kept.

"You might just hand me that knitting, 'Lizabeth. I guess I knit a little tighter'n you do, on account of my hand being out. I've more than enough stockings to last my time out and some coarse ones for Polly. They spin yarn so much finer now. Footing many stockings this fall?"

"No. I knit Foster new ones late in the spring. He's easy, too. Warren's the one to gnaw out heels, though young people are so much on the go."

Aunt Priscilla took up the stocking and pinned the sheath on her side. How gay the voices sounded in the kitchen! Then the door opened.

"Just look, Aunt Elizabeth! Aren't they lovely! Betty let me cut them out and put them in the pans. Oh——"

Doris stood quite abashed, with a dish of tempting brown cookies in one hand. Her cheeks were like roses now, and Betty's kitchen apron made another frock over hers of gay chintz, that had been exhumed from the chest.

"Good-afternoon," recovering herself.

"The cookies look delightful. I must taste one," Mrs. Leverett said smilingly.

She handed the plate to Aunt Priscilla.

"It'll just spoil my supper if I eat one. But you may do up some in a paper, and I'll take them home. I'm glad to see you at something useful. Did you help about the house over there in England?"

"Oh, no. We had Barby," answered the child simply.

"Well, there's a deal for you to learn. I made bread just after I had turned ten years old. Girls in old times learned to work. It wasn't all cooky-making, by a long shot!"

Doris made a little courtesy and disappeared.

"I'd do something to that tousled hair, 'Lizabeth. Have her put it up or cut it off. It's good to cut a girl's hair; makes it thick and strong. And curls do look so flighty and frivolous."

"The new fashion is a wig with all the front in little curls. It's so much less trouble if it is made of natural curly hair."

"Are you going to set up for fashion in these hard times?" asked the visitor disdainfully.

"Not quite. But Betty Pickering is to be married in great state next month, and we have been invited already. I suppose I ought to consider her in some sort a namesake."

"I'm glad I haven't any fine relatives to be married," and the sniff was made to do duty.

Mrs. Leverett put down her sewing. She had drawn the threads and basted the wristbands and gussets for Betty to stitch, as they had come to shirt-making. The new ones of thick cotton cloth would be good for winter wear. One had always to think ahead in this world if one wanted things to come out even.

Then she went out to the kitchen, and there was a gay chattering, as if a colony of chimney swallows had met on a May morning. Aunt Priscilla pushed up nearer the window. She had good eyesight still, and only wore glasses when she read or was doing some extra-fine work.

Betty came in and rolled out the table as she greeted her relative. Aunt Priscilla had a curiously lost feeling, as if somehow she had gone astray. No one ever would know about it, to be sure. There were times when it seemed as if there must be a third power, between God and the Evil One. There were things neither good nor bad. If they were good the Lord brought them to pass, —or ought to,—and if they were bad your conscience was troubled. Aunt Priscilla had been elated over her idea all day yesterday. It looked really generous to her. Of course Cousin Winthrop couldn't be bothered with this little foreign girl, and the Leveretts had a lot of grandchildren. She might take this Dorothy Adams, and bring her up in a virtuous, useful fashion. She would go to school, of course, but there would be nights and mornings and Saturdays. In two years, at the latest, she would be able to take a good deal of charge of the house. All this time her own little fortune could be augmenting, interest on interest. And if she turned out fair, she would do the handsome thing by her—leave her at least half of what she, Mrs. Perkins, possessed.

And yet it was not achieved without a sort of mental wrestle. She was not quite sure it was spiritual enough to pray over; in fact, nothing just like this had come into her life before. She was not the kind of stuff out of which missionaries were made, and this wasn't just charitable work. She would expect the girl to do something for her board, but Polly would be good for a year or two more. Time did hang heavy on her hands, and this would be interest and employment, and a good turn. When matters were settled a little she would broach the subject to Elizabeth.

If Winthrop Adams meant to make a great lady out of her—why, that was all there was to it! Times were hard and there might be war. Winthrop had a son of his own, and perhaps not so much money as people thought. And it did seem folly to waste the child's means. If she had so much—enough to go to boarding school—she oughtn't be living on the Leveretts. Foster was having pretty tight squeezing to get along.

They all wondered what made Aunt Priscilla so unaggressive at supper time. She watched Doris furtively. All the household had a smile for her. Foster Leverett patted her soft hair, and Warren pinched her cheek in play. Betty gave her half a dozen hugs between times, and Mrs. Leverett smiled when Doris glanced her way.

The quarter-moon was coming up when Priscilla Perkins opened the closet door for her things.

"I'll walk over with Aunt Priscilla," said Warren. "It's my night for practice."

"Oh, yes." His father nodded. Warren had lately joined the band, but his mother thought she couldn't stand the cornet round the house.

"I aint a mite afraid in the moonlight. I come so often I ought not put anyone out."

"Now that the evenings are cool it seems lonesomer," said Mr. Leverett, settling in his armchair by the fire, really glad his son could be attentive without any special sacrifice.

Doris brought the queer little stool and sat down beside him. She looked as if she had always lived there.

"You'll all spoil that child," Aunt Priscilla said to Warren when they had stepped off the stoop.

"I don't believe there's any spoil to her," said Warren heartily. "She's the sweetest little thing I ever saw; so wise in some ways and so honestly ignorant in others. I never saw Uncle Win so taken—he never seems to quite know what to do with children. And he's asked us all over to tea some night next week. I was clear struck."

Mrs. Perkins made no reply. About once a year he invited her over to tea with some of the old cousins, and he called on her New Year's Day, which was not specially kept in any fashionable way.

Mrs. Perkins always said King Street, though in a burst of patriotism the name had been changed after the Revolution. It had dropped down very much and was being given over to business. There was a narrow hall floor set in a little distance, with a few steps, and the shop front with the plain sign of "Jonas Field, Flour, Grain, and Feed." The stairway led to an upper hall and a very comfortable suite of rooms, where Mrs. Perkins had come as a young wife, and where she meant to end her days. It was plenty good enough inside, and she "didn't live in the street."

The best room occupied the whole front and had three windows. Priscilla had been barely nineteen when she was married, and Hatfield Perkins quite a bachelor. And, as no children had come to disturb their orderly habits, they had settled more securely in them year after year.

Next to the parlor was the sleeping chamber. Now, it was the spare room, though no one came to stay all night who was fine enough to put in it. The smaller one adjoining she had used since her husband's death. There was a little tea room, and a big kitchen at the back. Downstairs the store part had been built out, and on the roof of this the clothes were dried. Polly always sat out here in pleasant weather, to prepare vegetables and do various chores. The lot was deep, and at the back were some fruit trees, and the patch of herbs every woman thought she must have, and a square of grass for bleaching.

A lighted lamp stood at the head of the stairs. Polly was dozing in the kitchen. Mrs. Perkins sent her to bed in short order. There were two rooms and a storage closet upstairs in the gables. One was Polly's. The other was the guest chamber that was good enough "for the common run of folks."

The moon was shining in the back windows. Priscilla snuffed out the candle; there was no use wasting candle light. She sat down in a low rocker, the only one she owned; and several list seats had been worn out in it besides the original one of rushes. She had never been really lonely in the sixty-five years of her life for she had kept busy, and was replete with old-fashioned methods that made work. She was very particular. Everything was scrubbed and scoured and swept and dusted and aired. The dishes were polished until they were lustrous. The knives and forks and spoons were speckless. There were napery and bedding that had been laid by for her marriage outfit, and not all worn out yet, though in the early years she had kept replenishing for possible children. There was plenty for twenty years to come, and though her people had been strong and healthy, they never went much over seventy. She was the youngest, and all the rest were gone. Her few real nieces and nephews were scattered about; she had made up her mind long ago she shouldn't ever have anyone hanging on her.

No one wanted to. No one even leaned on her. Yet somehow the life had never seemed real solitary until now. She had comforted her years with the thought that children were a great deal of trouble and did not always turn out well. She could see the picture the little foreign girl made as she folded her arms on Foster Leverett's knee. She wouldn't have that mop of frowzly hair flying about, and she would like to fat her up a little—she was rather peaked. She had imagined her going about in this old place, sewing, learning to work properly, reading and studying, and going to church every Sabbath. She had really meant to do something for a human being day after day, not in a spasmodic fashion. And this was the end of it.

She sprang up suddenly, lighted the candle again, went out to the kitchen to

31

see that everything was right and there was no danger of fire. She opened the outside door and glanced around. There was an autumnal chill in the air, but there were no mysterious shadows creeping about in the yard below that might presage burglars. Then she bolted the door with a snap, and stood a moment in the middle of the floor.

"You are an old fool, Priscilla Perkins! The idea of all Boston being turned upside down for the sake of one little girl! People have come over from England before, big and little, and there's been a war and there may be another, and no end of things to happen. To be sure, I'd done my duty by her if I'd had her; and if the others spoil her—I aint to blame, the Lord knows!"

CHAPTER IV

OUT TO TEA

"There! Does it look like Old Boston?"

They were winding around Copp's Hill. Warren had been given part of a day off, and the use of the chaise and Jack, to show the little cousin something of Boston before they went to Uncle Winthrop's to tea.

Doris had her new coat, which was a sort of fawn color, and the close Puritan cap to keep her neck and ears warm. For earache was quite a common complaint among children, and people were careful through the long cold winter. A strip of beaver fur edged the front, and went around the little cape at the back. Its soft grayish-brown framed in her fair face like a picture, and her eyes were almost the tint of the deep, unclouded blue sky.

They had a fine view of Old Boston, but they could hardly dream of the Boston that was to be. There were still the three elevations of Beacon Hill, lowered somewhat, to be sure, but not taken away entirely. And there was Fort Hill in the distance.

"Why, it looks like a chain of islands, and instead of a great sea the water runs round and round. At home the Witham comes down to the winding cove called The Wash. Boston is sort of set between two rivers, but it is fast of the mainland, and doesn't look so much like floating off. You can go over to the Norfolk shore, and you look out on the great North Sea. But it isn't as big as the Atlantic Ocean."

"Well, I should say not!" with disdain. "Why, you can look over to Holland!"

"You can't see Holland, but it's there, and Denmark."

"And we shall have to be something like the Dutch, if ever we mean to have a grand city. We shall have to dike and fill in and bridge. I have a great regard for those sturdy old Dutchmen and the way they fought the Spanish as well as the sea."

Doris didn't know much about Holland, even if she could make pillow lace and read French verses with a charming accent.

"That's the Mill Pond. And all that is the back part of the bay. And over there a grand battle was fought—but you were not born before the Revolutionary War."

"I guess you were not born yourself, Warren Leverett," said Betty, with

33

unnecessary vigor.

"Well, I am rather glad I wasn't; I shall have the longer to live. But grandfather and ever so many relatives were, and father knows all about it. I am proud, too, of having been named for General Warren."

"And down there near the bay is Fort Hill. Boston wasn't built on seven hills like Rome, and though there are acres and acres of low ground, we are not likely to be overflowed, unless the Atlantic Ocean should rise and sweep us out of existence. And there is the old burying ground, full of queer names and curious epitaphs."

The long peninsula stretched out in a sort of irregular pear-shape, and then was connected to another portion by a narrow neck. The little villages about had a rural aspect, and some of them were joined to the mainland by bridges. And cows were still pastured on the commons and in several tracts of meadow land in the city. Many people had their own milk and made butter. There were large gardens at the sides of the houses, many of them standing with the gable end to the street, and built mostly of wood. But nearly all the leaves had fallen now, and though the sun shone with a mellow softness, it was quite evident the reign of summer was ended.

They drove slowly about, Warren rehearsing stories of this and that place, and wishing there was more time so they might go over to Charlestown.

"But Doris is to stay, and there will be time enough next summer. It is confusing to see so many places at once. And mother said we must be at Uncle Win's about four," declared Betty.

It *was* rather confusing to Doris, who had heard so little of American history in her quiet home. War seemed a dreadful thing to her, and she could not take Warren's pride in battle and conquest.

So they turned and went down through the winding streets.

"Do you know why they are so crooked?" Warren asked.

"No; why?" asked Doris innocently.

"Well, William Blackstone's cows made the paths. He came here first of all and had an allotment. Then when people began to come over from Charlestown he sold out for thirty pounds English money. Grandfather used to go over to the old orchard for apples. But think of Boston being bought for thirty pounds!"

"It wasn't *this* Boston with the houses and churches and everything. Come, do get along, or else let me drive," said Betty.

There was quite a descent as they came down. Streets seemed to stop suddenly, and you had to make a curve to get into the next one. From Main they turned into Fish Street, and here the wind from the harbor swept across to the Mill Pond.

"That's Long Wharf, and it has lots of famous stories connected with it. And just down there is father's. And now we could cut across and go over home."

"As if we meant to do any such foolish thing?" ejaculated Betty.

"I said we *could*. There are a great many things possible that are not advisable," returned the oracular young man. "And I have heard the longest way round was the surest way home. We shall reach there about nine o'clock to-night."

"Like the old woman and her pig. I should laugh if we found mother already at Uncle Win's."

"She's going to wait for father, and something always happens to him."

They crossed Market Square, and passed Faneuil Hall, that was to grow more famous as the years went on; then they took Cornhill and went over to Marlborough Street.

"That's Fort Hill. It's lovely in summer, when the wind doesn't blow you to shreds. Now we will take Marlborough, and to-night you will be surprised to see how straight it is to Sudbury Street."

They drove rapidly down, and made one turn. It was like a beautiful country road, over to Common Street, and there was the great tract of ground that would grow more beautiful with every decade. Tall, overarching trees; ways that were grassy a month ago, but now turning brown.

"Here we are," and they turned up a driveway at the side of the long porch upheld with round columns. Betty sprang out on the stepping block and half-lifted Doris, while Warren drove up to the barn.

Uncle Winthrop came out to welcome them, and smiled down into the little girl's face.

"But where is your mother?" he asked.

"Oh, she had some shopping to do and then she was to meet father. We have been driving up around Copp's Hill and giving Doris a peep at the country."

"The wind begins to blow up sharply, though it was very pleasant. I am glad to see you, little Doris, and I hope you have not grown homesick sighing for Old Boston. For if you should reach the threescore-and-ten, things will have changed so much that this will be old Boston; and, Betty, you will be telling your grandchildren what it was like."

Betty laughed gayly.

There was the same wide hall as at home, but it wasn't the keeping-room here. It had a great fireplace, and at one side a big square sofa. The floor was inlaid with different-colored woods, following geometric designs, much like those of to-day. Before the fire was a rug of generous dimensions, and a high-backed chair stood on each of the nearest corners. There was a bookcase with some busts ranged on the top; there were some portraits of ancestors in military attire, and women with enormous head-dresses; there was one in a Puritan cap, wide collar, and a long-sleeved gown, that quite spoiled the effect of her pretty hands. Over the mantel was a pair of very large deer's antlers. Down at one corner there were two swords crossed and some other firearms. Just under them was a cabinet with glass doors that contained many curiosities.

A tall, thin woman entered from a door at the lower end of the hall and greeted Betty with a quiet dignity that would have seemed cold, if it had not been the usual manner of Recompense Gardiner, who could never have been effusive, and who took it for granted that anyone Mr. Winthrop Adams invited to the house was welcome. Her forehead was high and rather narrow, her brown hair was combed straight back and twisted in a little knot high on her head, in which in the afternoon, or on company occasions, she wore a large shell comb. Her features were rather long and spare, and she wore plain little gold hoops in her ears because her eyes had been weak in youth and it was believed this strengthened them. Anyhow, she could see well enough at five-and-forty to detect a bit of dust or dirt, or lint left on a plate from the towel, or a chair that was a trifle out of its rightful place. She was an excellent housekeeper, and suited her master exactly.

"This is the little English girl I was telling you about, Recompense—Cousin Charles' grandniece, and my ward," announced Mr. Adams.

"How do you do, child! Let me take off your hood and cloak. Why, she isn't very stout or rosy. She might have been born here in the east wind. And she is an Adams through and through."

"Do you think so?" with an expression of pleasure, as Recompense held her off and looked her over.

"Are her eyes black?" rather disapprovingly.

"No, the very darkest blue you can imagine," said Mr. Adams.

"Betty, run upstairs with these things. Your feet are younger than mine, and haven't done so much trotting round. Lay them on my bed. Why, where's your mother?" in a tone of surprise.

Betty made the proper explanation and skipped lightly upstairs.

Mr. Adams took one of the large chairs, drawing it closer to the fire. Recompense brought out a stool for the little girl. It was covered with thick crimson brocade, a good deal faded, but it had a warm, inviting aspect. Children were not expected to sit in chairs then, or to run about and ask what everything was for.

There had been children, little girls of different relatives, sitting at the fireside before. His own small boy had dozed in the fascinating warmth of the fire and hated to go to bed, and he had weakly indulged him, as there had been no mother to exercise authority. But Doris was different. She was alone in the world, and had been sent to him by a mysterious providence. He knew the responsibility of a girl must be greater. He couldn't send her to the Latin school and then to Harvard, and he really wondered how much education a girl ought to have to fit her for the position Doris would be able to take.

She was like a quaint picture sitting there. Betty had tied a cluster of curls high on her head with a blue ribbon, and just a few were left to cling about her neck over the lace tucker. Her slim hands lay in her lap. He glanced at his own—yes, they were Adams hands, and looked little like hard work. He was rather proud that Recompense should discern a family likeness.

Betty came flying down the oaken staircase, and Warren entered from the back door. For a few moments there was quite a confusion of tongues, and Recompense wondered how mothers stood it all the time.

"How queer not to have anyone know about Boston," began Warren with a teasing glance over at Doris. "We have been looking at it from Copp's Hill, and going through the odd places."

"And I wondered if people came to be fed in White Bread Alley," exclaimed Doris quickly.

"And I dare say Warren didn't know."

"Why, yes—a woman baked bread there."

"Women have baked bread in a great many places," returned Uncle Win, with a quizzical smile.

"Oh, I didn't mean just that."

"It was John Tudor's mother," appended Betty.

"Mrs. Tudor made the first penny rolls offered for sale in Boston, and little John, as he was then, took them around for sale."

"And Mr. Benjamin Franklin didn't make them famous either," laughed

37

Warren.

"And Salutation Alley with its queer sign—its two old men with cocked hats and small clothes, bowing to each other," said Betty. "It always suggests a couplet I found in an old book:

"'O mortal man who lives by bread,
What is it makes your nose so red?
O mortal man with cheeks so pale,
'Tis drinking Levi Puncheon's ale!'"

"It is said the resolutions for the destruction of the tea were drawn up in the old tavern. It was famous for being the rendezvous of the patriots."

"It would be nice to drive all around Boston shore."

"Let it be summer time, then," rejoined Betty. "Or, like the Hollanders, we might do it on skates. Of course you do not know how to skate, Doris?"

Doris admitted with winsome frankness that she did not. But she could ride a pony, and she could row a little.

"There are some delightful summer parties when we do go out rowing. At least, the boys row mostly, because

"'Satan finds some mischief still
For idle hands to do!'"

and Betty laughed.

"And the girls always take their knitting," appended Warren. "There's never any mischief for them to get into."

"I suppose it doesn't look much like Old Boston," inquired Miss Recompense. "And what do the little girls do there, my dear?"

Warren opened his eyes wide. The idea of Miss Recompense saying "my dear" to a child.

It had slipped out in a curiously unpremeditated fashion. There was something about the little girl—perhaps it was the fact of her having come so far, and being an orphan—that moved Recompense Gardiner.

"I didn't know any real little girls," answered Doris modestly, "except the farmer's children. They worked out of doors in the summer in the fields."

"And I was the youngest of five sisters," said Miss Recompense. "There were three boys."

"It would be so nice to have a sister of one's very own. There were Sallie and Helen Jewett on the vessel."

"I think I like the sisters to be older," said Betty archly. "There are the weddings and the nieces and nephews. And they are always begging you to visit them."

"And I had no sisters," said Uncle Win, as if he would fain console Doris for her loneliness.

She glanced up with sympathetic sweetness. He was a little puzzled at the intuitive process.

"Fix up the fire, Warren. Your mother and father will be cold when they get in."

Warren gave the burned log a poke, and it fell in two ends, neither dropping over the andirons. Then he pushed them a little nearer and a shower of sparks flew about.

"Oh, how beautiful!" and Doris leaned over intently.

Warren placed a large log back of them, then he piled on some smaller split pieces. They began to blaze shortly. He picked up the turkey's wing and brushed around the stone hearth.

"That was very well done," remarked Miss Recompense approvingly.

"Warren knows how to make a fire," said his uncle, "and it is quite an art."

"That is a sign he will make a good husband," commented Betty. "And I shall get a bad one, for my fires go out half the time."

"You are too heedless," said Miss Recompense.

"Now, we ought to tell some ghost stories," suggested Warren. "Or we could wait until it gets a little darker. The sun is going down, and the fire is coming up, and just see how they are fighting at the Spanish Armada. Uncle Win, when you break up housekeeping you can leave me that picture."

They all turned to look at the picture in the cross light, with one of the wonderful fleet ablaze from the broadside of her enemy. It was a vigorous if somewhat crude painting by a Dutch artist.

"Oh, Uncle Win," cried Betty; "do you really think there will be war when we have a new President?"

"I sincerely hope not."

"We ought to have an Armada. Well, I don't know either," continued Warren dubiously. "If it should go to pieces like that one," nodding his head over to the scene, growing more vivid by the reflection of the red light in the west. "Doris, do you know what happened to the Spanish Armada?"

"Indeed I do," returned Doris spiritedly. "I may not know so much about America, except that you fought England, and were called rebels and—and ____"

"That we were the upper dog in the fight, and now we are citizens of a great and free Republic and rebels no longer."

"But the Spanish did not conquer England. Some of the ships were destroyed by English men-of-war, and then a terrific storm wrecked them, and there were only a few to return to Spain."

"Pretty good," said Uncle Win smilingly. "And now, Warren, maybe you can tell about the French Armada that was going to destroy Boston."

"Why, the French—came and helped us. Oh, there was the French and English war, but did they have a real Armada?"

"Why, after Louisburg was taken by the colonists—we were only Colonies in 1745. The French resolved to destroy all the towns the colonists had planted on the coast. You surely can't have forgotten?"

"The Revolution seems so much greater to this generation," said Miss Recompense. "That is almost seventy years ago. My father was called out for the defense of Boston. Governor Shirley knew it would be the first town attacked."

"And a real Armada!" said Warren, big-eyed.

"They didn't call it that exactly. Perhaps they thought the name unlucky. But there were twenty transports and thirty-four frigates and eleven ships of the line. Quite a formidable array, you must admit. The Duc d'Anville left Brest with five battalions of veterans."

"And then what happened? Warren, we do not know the history of our own city, after all. But surely they did not take it?"

"No, it is safely anchored to a bit of mainland yet," said Uncle Win dryly. "Off Cape Sable they encountered a violent storm. The Duc succeeded in reaching the rendezvous, but in such a damaged condition that he felt a victory would be impossible. Conflans with several partly disabled ships returned to France, and some steered for friendly ports in the West Indies. The Duc died in less than a week, of poison it was said, unwilling to endure the misfortune. The Governor General of Canada ordered the Vice Admiral to proceed and strike one blow at least. But he saw so many difficulties in the way, that he worried himself ill with a fever and put himself to death with his own sword. Boston was so well prepared for them by this time, the fleet decided to attack Annapolis, but encountering another furious storm they returned to France with the remnant. So Armadas do not seem to meet with brilliant success."

"Why, that is quite a romance, Uncle Win, and I must hunt it up. Curious that both should have shared so nearly the same fate."

"That was a special interposition of Providence," said Miss Recompense.

People believed quite strongly in such things then, and it certainly looked like it, since the storm was of no human agency.

Miss Recompense began to light the candles, and the steps of the tardy ones were heard on the porch. Betty sprang up and opened the door.

"I began to think I never should get here," exclaimed Mrs. Leverett. "I waited and waited for your father, and I thought something had surely happened."

"And so it had. Captain Conklin is going to start for China in a few days, and there was so much to talk about I couldn't get away."

"If I had been real sure he would have come on I would have started. It has blown off cold. Didn't you have a breezy ride? Were you warm enough, Doris?"

"It was splendid," replied Doris, her eyes shining. "And I have seen so many things."

"Now get good and warm and come out to supper."

"If you call this cold I don't know what you will do at midwinter."

"Well, it is chilly, and we are not used to it. But we must have our Indian summer yet."

Betty had been carrying away her mother's hat and shawl, and now Uncle Win led the way to the dining room. The table was bountifully spread; it was a sort of high tea, and in those days people ate with a hearty relish and had not yet discovered the thousand dangers lurking in food. If it was good and well cooked no one asked any farther questions. At least, men did not. Women took recipes of this and that, and invented new ways of preparing some dish with as much elation as some of the greater discoveries have given.

The men talked politics and the possibilities of war. There was an uneasy feeling all along the border, where Indian troubles were being fomented. There were some unsettled questions between us and England. Abroad, Napoleon was making such strides that it seemed as if he might conquer all Europe.

Mrs. Leverett and Miss Recompense compared their successes in pickling and preserving, and discussed the high prices of dry goods and the newer scant skirts that would take so much less cloth and the improvement in home-made goods. Carpets of the higher grades were beginning to be manufactured in Philadelphia.

Warren, with the appetite of a healthy young fellow, thought everything tasted uncommonly good, and really had nothing to say. Doris watched one and another, with soft dark eyes, and wondered if it would be right to like Uncle Win any better than she did Uncle Leverett, and why she had any desire to do so, which troubled her a little. Uncle Win *was* the handsomest. She liked the something about him that she came to know afterward was culture and refinement. But she was a very loyal little girl, and Uncle Leverett had welcomed her so warmly, even on board the vessel.

After supper they went into Uncle Winthrop's study a while. There were more bookcases, and such a quantity of books and pamphlets and papers. There were busts of some of the old Roman orators and emperors, and more paintings. There was a beautiful young woman with a head full of soft curls and two bands passed through them in Greek fashion. A scarf was loosely wound around her shoulders, showing her white, shapely throat, and her short sleeves displayed almost perfect arms that looked like sculpture. Later Doris came to know this was Uncle Winthrop's sweet young wife, who died when her little boy was scarcely a year old.

There were many curiosities. The walls were wainscoted in panels, with moldings about them that looked like another frame for the pictures. The chimney piece was of wood, and exquisitely carved. There was an old escritoire that was both carved and gilded, and in the center of the room a large round table strewn with books and writing materials. At the windows were heavy red damask curtains, lined with yellow brocade. They were always put up the first of October and taken down punctually the first day of April. Uncle Win had a luxurious side to his nature, and there was a soft imported rug in the room as well.

Carpets were not in general use. Many floors were polished, some in the finer houses inlaid. Rag carpets were used for warmth in winter, and some were beautifully made. Weaving them was quite a business, and numbers of women were experts at it. Sometimes it was in a hit-or-miss style, the rags sewed just as one happened to pick them up. Then they were made of the ribbon pattern, a broad stripe of black or dark, with narrower and wider colors alternating. The rags were often colored to get pretty effects.

It was a long walk home, but in those days, when there were neither cars nor cabs, people were used to walking, and the two men would not mind it. Betty could drive Jack by night or day, as he was a sure-footed, steady-going animal, and for a distance the road was straight up Beacon Street.

"Some day I will come up and take you out to see a little more of your new home," said Uncle Winthrop to Doris. "When does she go to school, Elizabeth?"

"Why, I thought it would be as well for her to begin next week. From eight to twelve. And she is so young there is no real need of her beginning other things. Betty can teach her to sew and do embroidery."

"There is her French. It would be a pity to drop that."

"She might teach me French for the sake of the exercise," returned Betty laughingly when Uncle Win looked so perplexed.

"To be sure. We will get it all settled presently." He felt rather helpless where a girl was concerned, yet when he glanced down into her soft, wistful eyes he wished somehow that she was living here. But it would be lonely for a child.

Warren brought Jack around and helped in the womenkind when they had said all their good-nights, and Uncle Wrin added that he would be over some evening next week to supper.

It was a clear night, but there was no moon. Jack tossed up his head and trotted along, with the common on one side of him.

Boston had been improving very much in the last decade, and stretching herself out a little. But it was quite country-like where Uncle Win lived. He liked the quiet and the old house, the great trees and his garden that gave him all kinds of vegetables and some choice fruit, though he never did anything more arduous than to superintend it and enjoy the fruits of Jonas Starr's labor.

CHAPTER V

A MORNING AT SCHOOL

Our ancestors for some occult reason held early rising in high esteem. Why burning fire and candle light in the morning, when everything was cold and dreary, should look so much more virtuous and heroic than sitting up awhile at night when the house was warm and everything pleasant, is one of the mysteries to be solved only by the firm belief that the easy, comfortable moments were the seasons especially susceptible to temptation, and that sacrifice and austerity were the guide-posts on the narrow way to right living.

Mr. and Mrs. Leverett had been reared in that manner. They had softened in many ways, and Betty was often told, "I had no such indulgences when I was a girl." But, mother-like, Mrs. Leverett "eased up" many things for Betty. Electa King half envied them, and yet she confessed in her secret heart that she had enjoyed her girlhood and her lover very much. She and Matthias King had been neighbors and played as children, went to church and to singing school together, and on visitors' night at the debating society she was sure to be the visitor. Girls did not have just that kind of boy friends now, she thought.

The softening of religious prejudices was softening character as well. Yet the intensity of Puritanism had kindled a force of living that had done a needed work. People really discussed religious problems nowadays, while even twenty years before it was simply belief or disbelief, and the latter "was not to be suffered among you."

Mrs. Leverett kept to her habit of early rising. True, dark and stormy mornings Mr. Leverett allowed himself a little latitude, for very few people came to buy his wares early in the morning. But breakfast was a little after six, except on Sunday morning, when it dropped down to seven.

And Mrs. Webb's school began at eight from the first day of February to the first day of November. The intervening three months it was half-past eight and continued to half-past twelve.

Doris came home quite sober. "Well," began Uncle Leverett, "how did school go?"

"I didn't like it very much," she answered slowly.

"What did you do?"

"I read first. Four little girls and two boys read. We all stood in a row."

"What then?"

"We spelled. But I did not know where the lesson was, and I think Mrs. Webb gave me easy words."

"And you did not enjoy that?" Uncle Leverett gave a short laugh.

"I was glad not to miss," she replied gravely.

"Mrs. Webb uses Dilworth's speller," said Mrs. Leverett, "and so I gave her Betty's. But she has a different reader. She thought Doris read uncommon well."

"And what came next?"

"They said tables all together. Why do they call them tables?"

"Because a system of calculation would be too long a name," he answered dryly.

Doris looked perplexed. "Then there was geography. What a large place America is!" and she sighed.

"Yes, the world is a good-sized planet, when you come to consider. And America is only one side of it."

"I don't see how it keeps going round."

"That must be viewed with the eye of faith," commented Betty.

"All that does very well. I am sorry you did not like it."

"I did like all that," returned Doris slowly. "But the sums troubled me."

"She's very backward in figures," said Mrs. Leverett. "Betty, you must take her in hand."

"I must study all the afternoon," said Doris.

"Oh, you'll soon get into the traces," said Uncle Leverett consolingly.

It was Monday and wash-day in every well-ordered family. Mrs. Leverett and Betty had the washing out early, but it was not a brisk drying day, so no ironing could be done in the afternoon. Betty changed her gown and brought out her sewing, and Doris studied her lessons with great earnestness.

"I wish I was sure I knew the spelling," she said wistfully.

"Well, let me hear you." Betty laid the book on the wide window sill and gave out the words between the stitches, and Doris spelled every one rightly but "perceive."

"Those i's and e's used to bother me," said Betty. "I made a list of them once and used to go over them until I could spell them in the dark."

"Is it harder to spell in the dark?"

"Oh, you innocent!" laughed Betty. "That means you could spell them anywhere."

Spelling had been rather a mysterious art, but Mr. Dilworth, and now Mr. Noah Webster, had been regulating it according to a system.

"Now you might go over some tables. You can add and multiply so much faster when you know them. Suppose we try them together."

That was very entertaining and, Doris began to think, not as difficult as she had imagined in the morning.

"Betty," said her mother, when there was a little lull, "what do you suppose has become of Aunt Priscilla? I do hope she did not come over the day we were at Cousin Winthrop's. But she never was here once last week."

"There were two rainy days."

"And she may be ill. I think you had better go down and see."

"Yes. Don't you want to go, Doris? The walk will be quite fun."

Doris could not resist the coaxing eyes, though she felt she ought to stay and study. But Betty promised to go over lessons with her when they came back. So in a few moments they were ready for the change. Mrs. Leverett sent a piece of cake and some fresh eggs, quite a rarity now.

The houses and shops seemed so close together, Doris thought. And they met so many people. Doris had not lived directly in Old Boston town, but quite in the outskirts. And King Street was getting to be quite full of business.

Black Polly came to the door. "Yes, missus was in but she had an awful cold, and been all stopped up so that she could hardly get the breath of life."

Aunt Priscilla had a strip of red flannel pinned around her forehead, holding in place a piece of brown paper, moistened with vinegar, her unfailing remedy for headache. Another band was around her throat, and she had a well-worn old shawl about her shoulders, while her feet rested on a box on which was placed a warm brick.

"Is it possible you have come? Why, one might be dead and buried and no one the wiser. I crawled out to church on Sunday, and took more cold, though I have heard people say you wouldn't catch cold going to church. Religion ought to keep one warm, I s'pose."

"I'm sorry. Mother was afraid you were ill."

"And I have all the visiting to do. It does seem as if once in an age some of you might come over. You went to Cousin Winthrop's!" in an aggrieved tone.

"But mother had not been there since last summer, when 'Lecty was on making her visit. And we took all the family along, just as you can," in a merry tone. "But if you like to have mother come and spend the day, I'll keep house. You see, there's always meals to get for father and Warren."

"Yes, I kept house before you were born, Betty Leverett, and had a man who needed three stout meals a day. But he want a mite of trouble. I never see a man easier to suit than Hatfield Perkins. And I didn't neglect him because he could be put off and find no fault. There are men in the world that it would take the grace of a saint to cook for, only in heaven among the saints if there aint any marryin' you can quite make up your mind there isn't any cooking either. Well—can't you get a chair? There's that little low one for Dorothy."

"If you please," began Doris, with quiet dignity, "my name is not Dorothy."

"Well, you ought to hear yourself called by a Christian name once in a while."

"Still it isn't a Scriptural name," interposed Betty. "I looked over the list to see. And here are some nice fresh eggs. Mother has had several splendid layers this fall."

"I'm obliged, I'm sure. I do wish I could keep a few hens. But Jonas Field wants so much room, and there's my garden herbs. I've just been dosing on sage tea and honey, and it has about broke up my cough. I generally do take one cold in autumn, and then I go to March before I get another. Well, I s'pose Recompense Gardiner stays at your uncle's? There was some talk I heard about some old fellow hanging round. After I'd lived so long single, I'd stay as I was."

"I can't imagine Miss Recompense getting her wedding gown ready. What would it be, I wonder?"

Betty laughed heartily.

"She could buy the best in the market if she chose," said Aunt Priscilla sharply. "She must have a good bit of money laid by. Cousin Winthrop would be lost without her. Not but what there are as good housekeepers in the world as Recompense Gardiner."

Then Aunt Priscilla had to stop and cough. Polly came in with some posset.

"I'll have one of those eggs beaten up in some mulled cider, Polly," she said.

Doris glanced curiously at the old colored woman. She was tall and still very

47

straight, and, though kept in strict subjection all her life, had an air and bearing of dignity, as if she might have come from some royal race. Her hair was snowy white, and the little braided tails hung below her turban, which was of gay Madras, and the small shoulder shawl she wore was of red and black.

"You're too old a woman to be fussed up in such gay things," Aunt Priscilla would exclaim severely every time she brought them home, for she purchased Polly's attire. "But you've always worn them, and I really don't know as you'd look natural in suitable colors."

"I like cheerful goin' things, that make you feel as if the Lord had just let out a summer day stead'er November. An', missus, you don't like a gray fire burned half to ashes, nuther."

Truth to tell, Aunt Priscilla did hanker after a bit of gayety, though she frowned on it to preserve a just balance with conscience. And no one knew the parcels done up in an old oaken chest in the storeroom, that had been indulged in at reprehensible moments.

Just then there was a curious diversion to Doris. A beautiful sleek tiger cat entered the room, and, walking up to the fire, turned and looked at the child, waving his long tail majestically back and forth. He came nearer with his sleepy, translucent eyes studying her.

"May I—touch him?" she asked hesitatingly.

"Land, yes! That's Polly's Solomon. She talks to him till she's made him most a witch, and she thinks he knows everything."

Solomon settled the question by putting two snowy white paws on Doris' knee, and stretching up indefinitely with a dainty sniffing movement of the whiskers, as if he wanted to understand whether advances would be favorably received.

There was a cat at the Leveretts', but it haunted the cellar, the shed, and the stable, and was hustled out of the kitchen with no ceremony. Aunt Elizabeth was not fond of cats, and cat hairs were her abomination. Doris had uttered an ejaculation of delight when she saw it one morning, a big black fellow with white feet and a white choker.

"Don't touch him—he'll scratch you like as not!" exclaimed Mrs. Leverett in a quick tone. "Get out, Tom! We don't allow him in the house. He's a good mouser, but it spoils cats to nurse them. And I never could abide a cat around under my feet."

Doris had made one other attempt to win Tom's favor as she was walking

48

about the garden. But Tom eyed her askance and discreetly declined her overture. There had always been cats at Miss Arabella's, and two great dogs as well as her pony, and birds so tame they would fly down for crumbs.

"Oh, kitty!" She touched him with her dainty fingers. "Solomon. What a funny name! Oh, you beautiful great big cat!"

Solomon rubbed his head on her arm and began to purr. He was sure of a welcome.

"You can't get in her lap, for it isn't big enough," said Aunt Priscilla. "Polly's got him spoiled out of all reason, though I s'pose a cat's company when there's no one else."

"If you would let me—sit on the rug," ventured Doris timidly. She had been rather precise of late in her new home.

"Well, I declare! Sit on the floor if you want to. The floor was plenty good enough to sit on when I was a child. Me and my sisters had a corner of our own, and we'd sit there and sew."

Betty had been about to interpose, but at Aunt Priscilla's concession Doris had slidden down and taken Solomon in her arms, and rubbed her soft cheek against his head. Polly came in with the egg and cider.

"Why, little missy, you just done charm him! He's mighty afeared of the boys around, and there aint no little gals. Do just see him, Mis' Perkins. He acts as if he was rollin' in a bed of sweet catnip."

"One is about as wise as the other," declared Aunt Priscilla, nodding her head. She was rather glad there was something in her house to be a rival to Cousin Winthrop and the Leveretts, since Doris Adams was to be held up on a high plane and spoiled with indulgence. She had not yet made up her mind whether she would like the child or not.

"Yes, she had started at Mrs. Webb's school. Uncle Win was going to make some arrangement about her French and her writing when he came over. They'd had a letter from 'Lecty, and as the legislature was to meet in Hartford there would be quite gay times, and she did so hope she could go. Mary wasn't very well, and wanted mother to come on for a week or two presently," and Betty made big eyes at Aunt Priscilla, while that lady nodded as well as her bundled up head would admit, to signify that she understood.

"I'm sure you ought to know enough to keep house for your father and Warren," was the comment.

Then Betty said they must go, and Aunt Priscilla tartly rejoined that they might look in and see whether she was dead or alive.

49

"Can I come and see Solomon again?" asked Doris.

"Of course, since Solomon is head of the house."

"Thank you," returned Doris simply, not understanding the sarcasm.

"Wonderful how Solomon liked little missy," said Polly, straightening the chairs and restoring order.

"My head aches with all the talking," said Aunt Priscilla. "I want to be alone."

But she felt a little conscience-smitten as Polly stepped about in the kitchen getting supper and sang in a thick, soft, but rather quivering voice, her favorite hymn:

"'Hark, from the tombs a doleful sound,
Mine ears, attend the cry.'"

Yes, Polly was a faithful old creature, only she had grown forgetful, and she was losing her strength, and black people gave out suddenly. But there, what was the use of borrowing trouble, and the idea of having a child around to train and stew over, and no doubt she would be getting married just the time when she, Mrs. Perkins, would need her the most. The Lord hadn't seen fit to give her any children to comfort her old age; after all, would she want a delicate little thing like this child with a heathenish name!

It was quite chilly now, and Doris, holding Betty's hand tight, skipped along merrily, her heart strangely warm and gay.

"She's very queer, and her voice sounds as if she couldn't get the scold out of it, doesn't it? And I felt afraid of the black woman first. I never saw any until we were on the ship. But the beautiful cat!" with a lingering emphasis on the adjective.

"Well—cats are cats," replied Betty sagely. "I don't care much about them myself, though we should be overrun with rats and mice if it wasn't for them. I like a fine, big dog."

"Oh, Betty!" and a girl caught her by the shoulder, turning her round and laughing heartily at her surprise.

"Why, Jane! How you startled me."

"And is this your little foreign girl—French or something?"

"English, if you please, and her father was born here in Boston. And isn't it queer that she should have lived in another Boston? And her name is Doris Adams."

"I'm sure the Adams are sown thickly enough about, but Doris sounds like verses. And, oh, Betty, I've been crazy to see you for two days. I am to have a real party next week. I shall be seventeen, and there will be just that number invited. The girls are to come in the afternoon and bring their sewing. There will be nine. And eight young men," laughing—"boys that we know and have gone sledding with. They are to come to tea at seven sharp. Cousin Morris is to bring his black fiddler Joe, and we are going to dance, and play forfeits, and have just a grand time."

"But I don't know how to dance—much."

Betty's highest accomplishments were in the three R's. Her manuscript arithmetic was the pride of the family, but of grammar she candidly confessed she couldn't make beginning nor end.

"I'm going to coax hard to go to dancing school this winter. Sam is going, and he says all the girls are learning to dance. Mother's coming round to-morrow. We want to be sure about the nine girls. Good-by, it's getting late."

"Now, let's hurry home," exclaimed Betty.

The table was laid, and Mrs. Leverett said:

"Why didn't you stay all night?"

"Aunt Priscilla has her autumn cold. She was quite cross at first. She was sick last week, and went to church yesterday, and is worse to-day. But she was glad about the eggs."

"There comes your father. Be spry now."

After supper Warren went out to look after Jack. Mr. Leverett took his chair in the corner of the wide chimney and pushed out the stool for the little girl. She smiled as she sat down and laid her hands on his knee.

"So you didn't like the school," he began, after a long silence.

"Yes—I liked—most of it," rather reluctantly.

"What was it you didn't like—sitting still?" "No—

not that."

"The lessons? Were they too hard?"

"She said I needn't mind this morning."

"But the figuring bothered you."

"Of course I didn't know," she said candidly.

"You will get into it pretty soon. Betty'll train you. She's a master hand at figures, smarter than Warren."

Doris made no comment, but there was an unconfessed puzzle in her large eyes.

"Well, what is it?" The interest he took in her surprised himself.

"She whipped a boy on his hands with a ruler very hard because he couldn't remember his lesson."

"That's a good aid to memory. I've seen it tried when I was a boy."

"But if I had tried and tried and studied I should have thought it very cruel."

"I guess he didn't try or study. What did Miss Arabella do to you when you were careless and forgot things? Or were you never bad?"

Doris hung her head, while a faint color mounted to her brow.

"When I was naughty I couldn't go out on the pony nor take him a lump of sugar. And he loved sugar so. And sometimes I had to study a psalm."

"And weren't children ever whipped in your country?"

"The common people beat their children and their wives and their horses and dogs. But Miss Arabella was a lady. She couldn't have beaten a cat."

There was a switch on the top of the closet in the kitchen that beat Tom out of doors when he ventured in. Doris' tender heart rather resented this.

Foster Leverett smiled at this distinction.

"I do suppose people might get along, but boys are often very trying."

"Don't grown-up people ever do anything wrong? And when they scold dreadfully aren't they out of temper? Miss Arabella thought it very unladylike to get out of temper. And what is done to grown people?"

Uncle Leverett laughed and squeezed the soft little hands on his knee. Yes, men and women flew into a rage every day. Their strict training had not given them control of their tempers. It had not made them all honest and truthful. Yet it might have been the best training for the times, for the heroic duties laid upon them.

"She was very cross once, and her forehead all wrinkled up, and her eyes were so—so hard; and when she is pleasant she has beautiful brown eyes. I like beautiful people."

"We can't all be beautiful or good-tempered."

"But Miss Arabella said we could, and that beauty meant sweetness and grace and truth and kindliness, and that"—she lowered her voice mysteriously —"where one really tried to be good God gave them grace to help. I don't quite know about the grace, I'm so little. But I want to be good."

Was there a beautiful side to goodness? Foster Leverett had been for some time weakening in the old faith.

"Now I'm ready," exclaimed Betty briskly. "We can say tables without any book."

Uncle Leverett laughed and squeezed the soft little stranger at his hearth. But affection was not demonstrative in those days, and it looked rather weak in a man.

They had grand fun saying addition and multiplication tables. They went up to the fives, and Doris found that here was a wonderful bridge.

"You could add clear up to a hundred without any trouble," the child declared gleefully. "But you couldn't multiply."

"Why, yes," said Betty. "I had not exactly thought of it before. Five times thirteen would be sixty-five, and so on. Five times twenty would be a hundred. Why, we do it in a great many things, but I suppose they—whoever invented tables thought that was far enough to go."

"Who did invent them?"

"I really don't know. Doris, we will ask Uncle Win when he comes over. He knows about everything."

"It would take a great many years to learn everything," said the child with a sigh.

"But the knowledge goes round," said Betty with arch gayety. "One has a little and the other a little and they exchange, and then women don't have to know as much as men."

"I'd like to see the man that knew enough to keep house," declared Mrs. Leverett. "And didn't Mrs. Abigail Adams farm and bring up her children and pay off debts while her husband was at congress and war and abroad? It isn't so much book learning as good common sense. Just think what the old Revolutionary women did! And now it is high time Doris went to bed. Come, child, you're so sleepy in the morning."

Doris had her dress unbuttoned and untied her shoes to make sure there were no knots to pick out. Knots in shoe-strings were very perplexing at this period when no one had dreamed of button boots. I doubt, indeed, if anyone would have worn them. The shoes were made straight and changed every morning, so as to wear evenly and not get walked over at the side. And people had pretty feet then, with arched insteps, and walked with an air of dignity. Some of the gouty old men had to be measured for a tender place here or a protuberance there, or allowance made for bad corn.

Doris said good-night and went upstairs. Miss Arabella had always kissed her. Betty did sometimes, and said "What a sweet little thing you are!" or "What a queer little thing you are!" She said her prayers, hung her clothes over a chair, put her little shoes just right for morning, and stepping on the chair round vaulted over to her side of the bed.

What a long, long day it had been! The most beautiful thing in it was the big cat Solomon, and if she could nurse him she shouldn't be very much afraid of Aunt Priscilla. Oh, how soft his fur was, and how he purred, just as if he was glad she had come! Perhaps he sometimes tired of Aunt Priscilla and black Polly, and longed for a little girl who didn't mind sitting on the floor, and who knew how to play.

Then there was the spelling, and she tried to think over the hard words, and the tables, and her small brain kept up such a riot that she was not a bit sleepy.

Betty brought out her work after lighting another candle. Mr. Leverett sat and dozed and thought. When Warren had finished up the chores he went around to the other side of Betty's table, and was soon lost in a history of the French War. When the tall old clock struck nine it was time to prepare for bed.

Betty was putting up some wisps of hair in tea leads, when Doris sat up.

"Oh, you midget! Are you not asleep yet?" she exclaimed.

"No. I've been thinking of everything. And, Betty, can you go to the party? I went to the May party when I was home, but that was out of doors, and we danced round the May pole."

"The party——"

"Yes, did you ask Aunt Elizabeth?" eagerly.

"Oh, no. I wasn't going to be caught that way. She would have had time to think up ever so many excellent reasons why I shouldn't go. And now Mrs. Morse will take her by surprise, and she will not have any good excuse ready and so she will give in."

"But wouldn't she want you to go?" Doris was rather confused by the reasoning.

"I suppose she thinks I am young to begin with parties. But it isn't a regular grown-up affair. And I am just crazy to go. I'm so glad you did not blurt it out, Doris. I'll give you a dozen kisses for being so sensible. Now lie down and go to sleep this minute."

The child gave a soft little laugh, and a moment later Betty was "cuddling" her in her arms.

The result of Foster Leverett's cogitation over the fire led him to say the next morning to his son:

"Warren, you run on. I have a little errand to do."

He turned in another direction and went down two squares. There was Mrs. Webb sweeping off her front porch and plank path.

"Good-morning," stopping and leaning on her broom as he halted.

"I'm glad to see you, Mrs. Webb. I suppose the little girl wasn't much trouble yesterday. She's never been to school before."

"Trouble! Bless you, no. If they were all as good as that I should feel frightened, I really should, thinking they wouldn't live long. She's a bit timid——"

"She's backward in some things—figures, for instance. And a little strange, I suppose. So if you would be kind of easy-going with her until she gets settled to the work——"

"Oh, you needn't be a mite afraid, Mr. Leverett. She's smart in some things, but, you see, she's been run on different lines, and we'll get straight presently. She's a nice obedient little thing, and I do like to see children mind at the first bidding."

"Your school is so near we thought we would try it this winter. Yes, I think all will go right. Good-morning," and his heart lightened at the thought of smoothing the way for Doris.

CHAPTER VI

A BIRTHDAY PARTY

Doris sat in the corner studying. Betty had gone over to Mme. Sheafe's to make sure she had her lace stitch just right. They had been ironing and baking all the morning, and now Mrs. Leverett had attacked her pile of shirts, when Mrs. Morse came in. She had her work as well. Everybody took work, for neighborly calls were an hour or two long.

Doris had been presented first, a kind of attention paid to her because she was from across the ocean. Everybody's health had been inquired about.

"I came over on a real errand," began Mrs. Morse presently. "And you mustn't make excuses. My Jane is going to have a little company week from Thursday night. She will be seventeen, and we are going to have seventeen young people. The girls will come in the afternoon, and the young men at seven to tea. Then they will have a little merrymaking. And we want Warren and Betty. We are going to ask those we want the most first, and if so happen anything serious stands in the way, we'll take the next row."

"You're very kind, I'm sure. Warren does go out among young people, but I don't know about Betty. She's so young."

"Well, she will have to start sometime. My mother was married at sixteen, but that is too young to begin life, though she never regretted it, and she had a baker's dozen of children."

"I'm not in any hurry about Betty. She is the last girl home. And the others were past nineteen when they were married."

"We feel there is no hurry about Jane. But I've had a happy life, and all six of us girls were married. Not an old maid among us."

"Old maids do come in handy oftentimes," subjoined Mrs. Leverett.

Yet in those days every mother secretly, often openly, counted on her girls being married. The single woman had no such meed of respect paid her as the "bachelor maids" of to-day. She often went out as housekeeper in a widower's family, and took him and his children for the sake of having a home of her own. Still, there were some fine unmarried women.

"Yes, they're handy in sickness and times when work presses, but they do get queer and opinionated from having their own way, I suppose."

Alas! what would the single woman, snubbed on every side, have said to that!

57

Then they branched into a chatty discussion about some neighbors, and as neither was an ill-natured woman, it was simply gossip and not scandal. Mrs. Morse had a new recipe for making soap that rendered it clearer and lighter than the old one and made better soap, she thought. And to-morrow she was going at her best candles, so as to be sure they would be hard and nice for the company.

"But you haven't said about Betty?"

"I'll have to think it over," was the rather cautious reply.

"Elizabeth Leverett! I feel real hurt that you should hesitate, when our children have grown up together!" exclaimed Mrs. Morse rather aggrieved.

"It's only about putting Betty forward so much. Why, you know I don't mind her running in and out. She's at your house twice as often as Jane is here. And when girls begin to go to parties there's no telling just where to draw the line. It's very good of you to ask her. Yes, I do suppose she ought to go. The girls have been such friends."

"Jane would feel dreadfully disappointed. She said: 'Now, mother, you run over to the Leveretts' first of all, because I want to be sure of Betty.'"

"Well—I'll have to say yes. Next Thursday. There's nothing to prevent that I know of. I suppose it isn't to be a grand dress affair, for I hadn't counted on making Betty any real party gown this winter? I don't believe she's done growing. Who else did you have in your mind, if it isn't a secret?"

"I'd trust it to you, anyhow. The two Stephens girls and Letty Rowe, Sally Prentiss and Agnes Green. That makes six, with Betty. We haven't quite decided on the others. I dare say some of the girls will be mad as hornets at being left out, but there can be only nine. Of course we do not count Jane."

These were all very nice girls of well-to-do families. Mrs. Leverett did feel a little proud that Betty should head the list.

"They are all to bring their sewing. I had half a mind to put on a quilt, but I knew there'd be a talk right away about Jane marrying, and she has no steady company. I tell her she can't have until she is eighteen."

"That's plenty young enough. I don't suppose there will be any dancing?"

"They've decided on proverbs and forfeits. Cousin Morris is coming round to help the boys plan it out. Are you real set against dancing, Elizabeth?"

"Well—I'm afraid we are going on rather fast, and will get to be too trifling. I can't seem to make up my mind just what is right. Foster thinks we have been too strait-laced."

"I danced when I was young, and I don't see as it hurt me any. And some of the best young people here-about are going to a dancing class this winter. Joseph has promised to join it, and his father said he was old enough to decide for himself."

Mrs. Morse had finished her sewing and folded it, quilting her needle back and forth, putting her thimble and spool of cotton inside and slipping it in her work bag. Then she rose and wrapped her shawl about her and tied on her hood.

"Then we may count on Warren and Betty? Give them my love and Jane's, and say we shall be happy to see them a week from Thursday, Betty at three and Warren at seven. Come over soon, do."

When she had closed the door on her friend Mrs. Leverett glanced over to the corner where Doris sat with her book. She had half a mind to ask her not to mention the call to Betty, then she shrank from anything so small.

Doris studied and she sewed. Then Betty came in flushed and pretty.

"I didn't have the stitch quite right," she said to her mother. "And I have been telling her about Doris. She wants me to bring her over some afternoon. She is a little curious to see what kind of lace Doris makes. She has a pillow—I should call it a cushion."

"Doris ought to learn plain sewing——"

"Poor little mite! How your cares will increase. Can I take her over to Mme. Sheafe's some day?"

"If there is ever any time," with a sigh.

"Do you know your spelling?" She flew over to Doris and asked a question with her eyes, and Doris answered in the same fashion, though she had a fancy that she ought not. Betty took her book and found that Doris knew all but two words.

"If I could only do sums as easily," she said, with a plaintive sound in her voice.

"Oh, you will learn. You can't do everything in a moment, or your education would soon be finished."

"What is Mme. Sheafe like?" she asked with some curiosity, thinking of Aunt Priscilla.

"She is a very splendid, tall old lady. She ought to be a queen. And she was quite rich at one time, but she isn't now, and she lives in a little one-story cottage that is just like—well, full of curious and costly things. And now she gives lessons in embroidery and lace work, and hemstitching and fine sewing, and she wears the most beautiful gowns and laces and rings."

"Your tongue runs like a mill race, Betty."

"I think everybody in Boston is tall," said Doris with quaint consideration that made both mother and daughter laugh.

"You see, there is plenty of room in the country to grow," explained Betty.

"Can I do some sums?"

"Oh, yes."

Plainly, figures were a delusion and a snare to little Doris Adams. They went astray so easily, they would not add up in the right amounts. Mrs. Webb did not like the children to count their fingers, though some of them were very expert about it. When the child got in among the sevens, eights, and nines she was wild with helplessness.

Supper time came. This was Warren's evening for the debating society, which even then was a great entertainment for the young men. There would be plenty of time to give them the invitation. Mrs. Leverett was sorry she had consented to Betty's going, but it would have made ill friends.

The next day Mrs. Hollis Leverett, the eldest son's wife, came up to spend the day, with her two younger children. Doris was not much used to babies, but she liked the little girl. The husband came up after supper and took them home in a carryall. Doris was tired and sleepy, and couldn't stop to do any sums.

Betty was folding up her work, and Warren yawning over his book, when Mrs. Leverett began in a rather jerky manner:

"Mrs. Morse was in and invited you both to Jane's birthday party next Thursday night."

"Yes, I saw Joe in the street to-day, and he told me," replied Warren.

"I said I'd see about you, Betty. You are quite too young to begin party-going."

"Why, I suppose it's just a girl's frolic," said her father, wincing suddenly. "They can't help having birthdays. Betty will be begging for a party next."

"She won't get it this year," subjoined her mother dryly. "And, by the looks of things, we have no money to throw away."

Betty looked a little startled. She had wanted so to really question Doris, but it did not seem quite the thing to do. And perhaps she was not to go, after all.

She would coax her father and Warren, she would do almost anything.

Warren settled it as they were going up to bed. His mother was in the kitchen, mixing pancakes for breakfast, and he caught Betty's hand.

"Of course you are to go," he said. "Mother doesn't believe in dealing out all her good things at once. I wish you had something pretty to wear. It's going to be quite fine."

"Oh, dear," sighed Betty. "Jane has such pretty gowns. But of course I have only been a little school-girl until this year, and somehow it is very hard for the mothers to think their girls are grown-up in any respect except that of work."

Warren sighed as well, and secretly wished he had a regular salary, and could do what he liked with a little money. His father was training him to take charge of his own business later on. He gave him his board and clothing and half a dollar a week for spending money. When he was twenty-one there would be a new basis, of course. There was not much call for money unless one was rich enough to be self-indulgent. One couldn't spend five cents for a trolley ride, even if there was a downpour of rain. And as Mr. Leverett had never smoked, he had routed the first indications of any such indulgence on the part of his son.

The amusements were still rather simple, neighborly affairs. The boys and girls "spent an evening" with each other and had hickory nuts, cider, and crullers that had found their way from Holland to Boston as well as New York. And when winter set in fairly there was sledding and skating and no end of jest and laughter. Many a decorous love affair sprang into shy existence, taking a year or two for the young man to be brave enough to "keep company," if there were no objections on either side. And this often happened to be a walk home from church and an hour's sitting by the family fireside taking part in the general conversation.

To be sure, there was the theater. Since 1798, when the Federal Street Theater had burned down and been rebuilt and opened with a rather celebrated actress of that period, Mrs. Jones, theater-going was quite the stylish amusement of the quality. Mr. Leverett and his wife had gone to the old establishment, as it was beginning to be called, to see the tragedy of "Gustavus Vasa," that had set Boston in a furore. They were never quite settled on the point of the sinfulness of the pleasure. Indeed, Mr. Leverett evinced symptoms of straying away from the old landmarks of faith. He had even gone to the preaching of that reprehensible young man, Mr. Hosea Ballou, who had opened new worlds of thought for his consideration.

"It's a beautiful belief," Mrs. Leverett admitted, "but whether you can quite square it with Bible truth——"

"I'm not so sure you can square the Westminster Catechism either."

"If you must doubt, Foster, do be careful before the children. I'm not sure but the old-fashioned religion is best. It made good men and women."

"Maybe if you had been brought up a Quaker you wouldn't have seen the real goodness of it. Isn't belief largely a matter of habit and education? Mind, I don't say religion. That is really the man's life, his daily endeavor."

"Well, we won't argue." She felt that she could not, and was ashamed that she was not more strongly fortified. "And do be careful before the children."

Her husband was a good, honest, upright man—a steady churchgoer and zealous worker in many ways. The intangible change to liberalness puzzled her. If you gave up one point, would there not be a good reason for giving up another?

Neither could she quite explain why she should feel more anxious about Betty than she had felt about the girlhood of the two elder daughters.

Of course Warren accepted the invitations for himself and his sister. If her new white frock was only done! She had outgrown her last summer's gowns. There was a pretty embroidered India muslin that her sister Electa had given her. If she might put a ruffle around the bottom of the skirt.

Aunt Priscilla came over and had her cup of tea so she could get back before dark. She was still afraid of the damp night air. Aunt Priscilla had a trunk full of pretty things she had worn in her early married life. If she, Betty, could be allowed to "rummage" through it!

Saturday was magnificent with a summer softness in the air, and the doors could be left open. There were sweeping and scrubbing and scouring and baking. Doris was very anxious to help, and was allowed to seed some raisins. It wasn't hard, but "putterin'" work, and took a good deal of time.

But after dinner Uncle Winthrop came in his chaise with his pretty spirited black mare Juno. It was such a nice day, and he had to go up to the North End on some business. There wouldn't be many such days, and Doris might like a ride.

There was a flash of delight in the child's eyes. Betty went to help her get ready.

"You had better put on her coat, for it's cooler riding," said Mrs. Leverett. "And by night it may turn off cold. A fall day like this is hardly to be trusted."

"But it is good while it lasts," said Uncle Win, with his soft half-smile.

"Elizabeth, don't pattern after Aunt Priscilla, who can't enjoy to-day because there may be a storm to-morrow."

"I don't know but we are too ready to cross bridges before we come to them," she admitted.

"A beautiful day goes to my inmost heart. I want to enjoy every moment of it."

Doris came in with her eager eyes aglow, and Betty followed her to the chaise, and said:

"Don't run away with her, Uncle Win; I can't spare her."

That made Doris look up and laugh, she was so happy.

They drove around into Hanover Street and then through Wing's Lane. There were some very nice lanes and alleys then that felt quite as dignified as the streets, and were oftentimes prettier. He was going to Dock Square to get a little business errand off his mind.

"You won't be afraid to sit here alone? I will fasten Juno securely."

"Oh, no," she replied, and she amused herself glancing about. People were mostly through with their business Saturday afternoon. It had a strange aspect to her, however—it was so different from the town across the seas. Some of the streets were so narrow she wondered how the horses and wagons made their way, and was amazed that they did not run over the pedestrians, who seemed to choose the middle of the street as well. Many of the houses had a second story overhanging the first, which made the streets look still narrower.

"Now we will go around and see the queer old things," exclaimed Uncle Win, as he jumped into the chaise. "For we have some interesting points of view. A hundred years seems a good while to us new people. And already streets are changing, houses are being torn down. There are some curious things you will like to remember. Did Warren tell you about Paul Revere?"

"Oh, yes. How he hung the lantern out of the church steeple."

"And this was where he started from. More than thirty years ago that was, and I was a young fellow just arrived at man's estate. Still it was a splendid time to live through. We will have some talks about it in the years to come."

"Did you fight, Uncle Win?"

"I am not much of a war hero, though we were used for the defense of Boston. You are too young to understand all the struggle."

Doris studied the old house. It was three stories, the upper windows seeming just under the roof. On the ground floor there was a store, with two large windows, where Paul Revere had carried on his trade of silver-smith and engraver on copper. There was a broken wire netting before one window, and quite an elaborate hallway for the private entrance, as many people lived over their shops.

Long afterward Doris Adams was to be interested in a poet who told the story of Paul Revere's ride in such vivid, thrilling words that he was placed in the list of heroes that the world can never forget. But it had not seemed such a great deed then.

Old North Square had many curious memories. It had been a very desirable place of residence, though it was dropping down even now. There were quaint warehouses and oddly constructed shops, taverns with queer names almost washed out of the signs by the storms of many winters. There were the "Red Lion" and the "King's Arms" and other names that smacked of London and had not been overturned in the Revolution. Here had stood the old Second Church that General Howe had caused to be pulled down for firewood during the siege of Boston, the spot rendered sacred by the sermon of many a celebrated Mather. And here had resided Governor Thomas Hutchinson, who would have been sacrificed to the fury of the mob for his Tory proclivities during the Stamp Act riot but for his brother-in-law, the Rev. Samuel Mather, who faced the mob and told them "he should protect the Governor with his life, even if their sentiments were totally dissimilar." And when he came to open court the next morning he had neither gown nor wig, very important articles in that day. For the wigs had long curling hair, and those who wore them had their hair cropped close, like malefactors.

And here was the still stately Frankland House, whose romance was to interest Doris deeply a few years hence and to be a theme for poet and novelist. But now she was a good deal amused when her uncle told her of a Captain Kemble in the days of Puritan rule who, after a long sea voyage, was hurrying up the Square, when his wife, who had heard the vessel was sighted, started to go to the landing. As they met the captain took her in his arms and kissed her, and was punished for breaking the Sabbath day by being put in the stocks.

"But did they think it so very wrong?" Her face grew suddenly grave.

"I suppose they did. They had some queer ideas in those days. They thought all exhibitions of affection out of place."

Doris looked thoughtfully out to the harbor. Perhaps that was the reason no one but Betty kissed her.

Then they drove around to the Green Dragon. This had been a famous inn, where, in the early days, the patriots came to plan and confer and lay their far-reaching schemes. It was said they went from here to the famous Tea Party. Uncle Winthrop repeated an amusing rhyme:

"'Rally, Mohocks, bring out your axes,
And tell King George we'll pay no taxes
      On his foreign tea.
His threats are vain, he need not think
To force our wives and girls to drink,
      His vile Bohea.'"

"I shouldn't like to be forced to drink it," said Doris, with a touch of repugnance in her small face.

"It does better when people get old and queer," said Uncle Winthrop. "Then they want some comfort. They smoke—at least, the men do—and drink tea. Now you can see the veritable Green Dragon."

The house was low, with small, old-time dormer windows. The dragon hung out over the doorway. He was made of copper painted green, his two hind feet resting on a bar that swung out of the house, his wings spread out as well as his front feet, and he looked as if he really could fly. Out of his mouth darted a red tongue.

"He is dreadful!" exclaimed Doris.

"Oh, he doesn't look as fierce now as I have seen him. A coat of paint inspires him with new courage."

"Then I am glad they have not painted him up lately. Uncle Win, is there any such thing as a real dragon? Of course I've read about St. George and the dragon," and she raised her eyes with a perplexed light in them.

"I think we shall have to relegate dragons to the mythical period, or the early ages. I have never seen one any nearer than that old fellow, or with any more life in him. There are many queer signs about, and queer corners, but I think now we will go over to Salem Street and look at some of the pretty old houses, and then along the Mill Pond. Warren took you up Copp's Hill?"

"Oh, yes."

"You see, you must know all about Boston. It will take a long while. Next summer we will have drives around here and there."

"Oh, that will be delightful!" and she smiled with such a sweet grace that he began to count on it himself.

The sun was going over westward in a soft haze that wrapped every leafless tree and seemed to caress the swaying vines into new life. The honeysuckles had not dropped all their leaves, and the evergreens were taking on their winter tint. On some of the wide lawns groups of children were playing, and their voices rang out full of mirth and merriment. Doris half wished she were with them. If Betty was only twelve instead of sixteen!

The Mill Pond seemed like a great bay. The placid water (there was no wind to ruffle it) threw up marvelous reflections and glints of colors from the sky above, and the sun beyond that was now a globe of softened flame, raying out lance-like shapes of greater distinctness and then melting away to assume some new form or color.

Doris glanced up at Uncle Winthrop. It was as if she felt it all too deeply for any words. He liked the silence and the wordless enjoyment in her face.

"We won't go home just yet," he said. They were crossing Cold Lane and could have gone down Sudbury Street. "It is early and we will go along Green Lane and then down to Cambridge Street. You are not tired?"

"Oh, no. I think I never should be tired with you, Uncle Winthrop," she returned with grave sweetness, quite unconscious of the delicate compliment implied.

What was there about this little girl that went so to his heart?

"Uncle Winthrop," she began presently, while a soft pink flush crept up to the edge of her hair, "I heard you and Uncle Leverett talking about some money the first night you were over—wasn't it *my* money?"

"Yes, I think so," with a little dryness in his tone. What made her think about money just now, and with that almost ethereal face!

"Is it any that I could have—just a little of it?" hesitatingly.

"Why? Haven't you all the things you want?"

"I? Oh, yes. I shouldn't know what to wish for unless it was someone to talk French with," and there was a sweet sort of wistfulness in her tone.

"I think I can supply that want. Why we might have been talking French half the afternoon. Do you want some French books? Is that it?"

"No, sir." There was a lingering inflection in her tone that missed satisfaction.

"Are you not happy at Cousin Leverett's?"

"Happy? Oh, yes." She glanced up in a little surprise. "But the money would be to make someone else happy."

"Ah!" He noddedencouragingly.

"Betty is going to a party."

"And she has been teasing her mother for some finery?"

"She hasn't any pretty gown. I thought this all up myself, Uncle Win. Miss Arabella has such quantities of pretty clothes, and they are being saved up for me. If she was here I should ask her, but I couldn't get it, you know, by Thursday."

She gave a soft laugh at the impossibility, as if it was quite ridiculous.

"And you want it for her?"

"She's so good to me, Uncle Win. For although I know some things quite well, there are others in which I am very stupid. A little girl in school said yesterday that I was 'dreadful dumb, dumber than a goose.' Aunt Elizabeth said a goose was so dumb that if it came in the garden through a hole in the fence it never could find it again to get out."

"That is about the truth," laughed Uncle Win.

"I couldn't get along in arithmetic if it wasn't for Betty. She's so kind and tells me over and over again. And I can't do anything for Aunt Elizabeth, because I don't know how, and it takes most of my time to study. But if I could give Betty a gown—Miss Arabella went to so many parties when she was young. If I was there I know she would consent to give Betty *one* gown."

Uncle Winthrop thought of a trunk full of pretty gowns that had been lying away many a long year. He couldn't offer any of those to Betty. And that wouldn't be a gift from Doris.

"I wonder what would be nice? An old fellow like me would not know about a party gown."

"Warren would. He and Betty talked a little about it last night. And that made me think—but it didn't come into my mind until a few moments ago that maybe there would be enough of my own money to buy one."

Doris glanced at him with such wistful entreaty that he felt he could not have denied her a much greater thing. He remembered, too, that Elizabeth Leverett had refused to take any compensation for Doris, this winter at least, and he had been thinking how to make some return.

"Yes, I will see Warren. And we will surprise Betty. But perhaps her mother would be a better judge."

"I think Aunt Elizabeth doesn't quite want Betty to go, although she told Mrs. Morse she should."

"Oh, it's at the Morses'? Well, they are very nice people. And young folks do go to parties. Yes, we will see about the gown."

67

"Uncle Winthrop, you are like the uncles in fairy stories. I had such a beautiful fairy book at home, but it must have been mislaid."

She put her white-mittened hand over his driving glove, but he felt the soft pressure with a curious thrill.

They went through Cambridge Street and Hilier's Lane and there they were at home.

"It has been lovely," she said with a happy sigh as he lifted her out. Then she reached up from the stepping-stone and kissed him.

"It isn't Sunday," she said naïvely, "and it is because you are so good to me. And this isn't North Square."

He laughed and gave her a squeeze. Cousin Elizabeth came out and wished him a pleasant good-night as he drove away.

What a charming little child she was, so quaintly sensible, and with a simplicity and innocence that went to one's heart. How would Recompense Gardiner regard a little girl like that? He would have her over sometime for a day and they would chatter in French. Perhaps he had better brush up his French a little. Then he smiled, remembering she had called herself stupid, and he was indignant that anyone should pronounce her dumb.

CHAPTER VII

ABOUT A GOWN

Saturday evening was already quiet at the Leveretts'. Elizabeth had been brought up to regard it as the beginning of the Sabbath instead of the end of the week. People were rather shocked then when you said Sunday, and quite forgot the beautiful significance of the Lord's Day. Aunt Priscilla still believed in the words of the Creation: that the evening and the morning were the first day. In Elizabeth's early married life she had kept it rigorously. All secular employments had been put by, and the children had studied and recited the catechism. But as they changed into men and women other things came between. Then Mr. Leverett grew "lax" and strayed off—after other gods, she thought at first.

He softened noticeably. He had a pitiful side for the poor and all those in trouble. Elizabeth declared he used no judgment or discrimination.

He opened the old Bible and put his finger on a verse: "While we have time let us do good unto all men; and especially unto them that are of the household of faith."

"You see," he said gravely, "the household of faith isn't put first, it is 'all men.'"

She was reading the Bible, not as a duty but a delight, skipping about for the sweetness of it. And she found many things that her duty reading had overlooked.

The children did not repeat the catechism any more. She had been considering whether it was best to set Doris at it; but Doris knew her own catechism, and Cousin Winthrop was a Churchman, so perhaps it wasn't wise to meddle. She took Doris to church with her.

Now, on Saturday evening work was put away. Warren was trying to read "Paradise Lost." He had parsed out of it at school. Now and then he dropped into the very heart of things, but he had not a poetical temperament. His father enjoyed it very much, and was quite a reader of Milton's prose works. Betty had strayed off into history. Doris sat beside Uncle Leverett with her arms on his knee, and looked into the fire. What were they doing back in Old Boston? Aunt Elizabeth had already condemned the fairy stories as untrue, and therefore falsehoods, so Doris never mentioned them. The child, with her many changes and gentle nature, had developed a certain tact or adaptiveness, and loved pleasantness. She was just a little afraid of Aunt Elizabeth's sharpness. It was like a biting wind. She always made comparisons in her mind, and saw things in pictured significance.

It ran over many things now. The old house that had been patched and patched, and had one corner propped up from outside. The barn that was propped up all around and had a thatched roof that suggested an immense haystack. Old Barby crooning songs by the kitchen fire, sweet old Miss Arabella with her great high cap and her snowy little curls. Why did Aunt Priscilla think curls wrong? She had a feeling Aunt Elizabeth did not quite approve of hers, but Betty said the Lord curled them in the beginning. How sweet Miss Arabella must have been in her youth—yes, she must surely have been young—when she wore the pretty frocks and went to the king's palace! She always thought of her when she came to the verses in the Psalms about the king's daughters and their beautiful attire. If Betty could have had one of those!

Her heart beat with unwonted joy as she remembered how readily Uncle Winthrop had consented to her wish. Oh, if the frock would be pretty! And if Betty would like it! She stole a glance or two at her. How queer to have a secret from Betty that concerned her so much. Of course people did not talk about clothes on Sunday, so there would be no temptation to tell, even if she had a desire, which she should not have. Monday morning everything would be in a hurry, for it was wash-day, and she would have to go over her lessons. Uncle Win said the gown would be at the house Monday noon.

"What are you thinking of, little one?"

Uncle Leverett put his hand over the small one and looked down at the face, which grew scarlet—or was it the warmth of the fire?

She laughed with a sudden embarrassment.

"I've been to Old Boston," she said, "and to new Boston. And I have seen such sights of things."

"You had better go to bed. And you have almost burned up your face sitting so close by the fire. It is bad for the eyes, too," said Aunt Elizabeth.

She rose with ready obedience.

"I think I'll go too," said Betty with a yawn. The history of the Reformation was dull and prosy.

When Doris had said her prayers, and was climbing into bed, Betty kissed her good-night.

"I'm awfully afraid Uncle Win will want you some day," she said. "And I just couldn't let you go. I wish you were my little sister."

There was a service in the morning and the afternoon on Sunday. Uncle Leverett accompanied them in the morning. He generally went out in the evening, and often some neighbor came in. It was quite a social time.

When Doris came home from school Monday noon Aunt Elizabeth handed her a package addressed to "Miss Doris Adams, from Mr. Winthrop Adams."

"It is a new frock, I know," cried Betty laughingly. "And it is very choice. I can tell by the way it is wrapped. Open it quick! I'm on pins and needles."

"It is a nice cord; don't cut it," interposed Aunt Elizabeth.

Betty picked out the knot. There was another wrapper inside, and this had on it "Miss Betty Leverett. From her little cousin, Doris Adams."

Mr. Leverett came at Betty's exclamation and looked over her shoulder.

"Are you sure it is for me? Here is a note from Uncle Win that is for you. Oh! oh! Doris, was this what you did Saturday?"

A soft shimmering China silk slipped out of its folds and trailed on the floor. It was a lovely rather dullish blue, such as you see in old china, and sprays of flowers were outlined in white. Betty stood transfixed, and just glanced from one to the other.

"Oh, do you like it?" cried Warren, impatient for the verdict. "Uncle Win asked me to go out and do an errand with him. I was clear amazed. But it's Doris' gift, and bought out of her own money. We looked over ever so many things. He said you wanted something young, not a grandmother gown. And we both settled upon this."

Betty let it fall and clasped Doris in her arms.

"Down on the dirty floor as if it was nothing worth while!" began Mrs. Leverett, while her husband picked up the slippery stuff and let it fall again until she took it out of his hands. "And do come to dinner! There's a potpie made of the cold meat, and it will all be cold together, for I took it up ever so long ago. And, Betty, you haven't put on any pickles. And get that quince sauce."

"I don't know what to say." There were tears in Betty's eyes as she glanced at Doris.

"Well, you can have all winter to say it in," rejoined her mother tartly. "And your father won't want to spend all winter waiting for his dinner."

They had finished their washing early. By a little after ten everything was on the line, and now the mornings had grown shorter, although you could piece them out with candlelight. Betty had suggested the cold meat should be made into a potpie, and now Mrs. Leverett half wished she had kept to the usual wash-day dinner—cold meat and warmed-over vegetables. She felt undeniably cross. She had not cordially acquiesced in Betty's going to the party. The best gown she had to wear was her gray cloth, new in the spring. It had been let down in the skirt and trimmed with some wine-colored bands Aunt Priscilla had brought her. It would be a good discipline for Betty to wear it. When she saw the other young girls in gayer attire, she would be mortified if she had any pride. Just where proper pride began and improper pride ended she was not quite clear. Anyhow, it would check Betty's party-going this winter. And now all the nice-laid plans had come to grief.

Doris stood still, feeling there was something not quite harmonious in the atmosphere.

"You were just royal to think of it," said Warren, clasping both arms around Doris. "Uncle Win told me about it. And I hope you like our choice. Betty had a blue and white cambric, I think they called it, last summer, and she looked so nice in it, but it didn't wash well. Silk doesn't have to be washed. Oh, you haven't read your letter."

Uncle Leverett had been folding and rolling the silk and laid it on a chair. The dinner came in just as Doris had read two or three lines of her note.

"Aunt Elizabeth,"—when there was a little lull,—"Uncle Winthrop says he will come up to supper to-night."

"He seems very devoted, suddenly."

"Well, why shouldn't he be devoted to the little stranger in his charge, if she isn't exactly within his gates? She is in ours."

A flush crept up in Elizabeth Leverett's face. She did not look at Doris, but she felt the child's eyes were upon her—wondering eyes, asking the meaning of this unusual mood. It was unreasonable as well. Elizabeth had a kindly heart, and she knew she was doing not only herself but Doris an injustice. She checked her rising displeasure.

"I should have enjoyed seeing you and Uncle Win shopping," she said rather jocosely to Warren.

Betty glanced up at that. The sky was clearing and the storm blowing over. But, oh, she had her pretty gown, come what might!

"I don't believe but what I would have been a better judge than either of them," said Uncle Leverett.

"Uncle Win wasn't really any judge at all," rejoined Warren laughingly. "He would have chosen the very best there was, fine enough for a wedding gown. But I knew Betty liked blue, and that girls wanted something soft and delicate."

"You couldn't have suited me any better," acknowledged Betty, giving the chair that held her treasure an admiring glance. "I shall have to study all the afternoon to know what to say to Uncle Win. As for Doris——"

Doris was smiling now. If they were all pleased, that was enough.

"I hope Uncle Win won't let you spend your money this way very often," said Uncle Leverett, "or you will have nothing left to buy silk gowns for yourself when you are a young woman."

"Maybe no one will ever ask me to a party," said Doris simply.

"I will give one in your honor," declared Warren. "Let me see—in seven years you will be sixteen. I will save up a little money every year after I get my freedom suit."

"Your freedom suit?" in a perplexed manner. "Yes—

when I am twenty-one. That will be next July."

"You will have to buy her a silk gown as well," said his father with a twinkle of humor in his eye.

"Then I shall strike for higher wages."

"We shall have a new President and we will see what that brings about. The present method is simply ruinous."

The dinner was uncommonly good, if it had been made of cooked-over meat. And the pie was delicious. Any woman who could make a pie like that, and have the custard a perfect cream, ought to be the happiest woman alive.

Mr. Leverett followed his wife out in the kitchen, and gave the door a push with his foot. But the three young people were so enthusiastic about the new gown, now that the restraint was removed, that they could not have listened.

"Mother," he began, "don't spoil the little girl's good time and her pleasure in the gift."

"Betty did not need a silk gown. The other girls didn't have one until they were married. If I had considered it proper, I should have bought it myself."

"But Winthrop hadn't the heart to refuse Doris."

"If he means to indulge every whim and fancy she'll spend everything she has before she is fairly grown. She's too young to understand and she has been brought up so far in an irresponsible fashion. Generosity is sometimes foolishness."

"You wouldn't catch Hollis' little boy spending his money on anyone," and Sam's grandfather laughed. Sam was bright and shrewd, smart at his books and good at a barter. He had a little money out at interest already. Mr. Leverett had put it in the business, and every six months Sam collected his interest on the mark.

"Winthrop isn't as slack as you sometimes think. He could calculate compound interest to a fraction."

"I'm glad someone has a little forethought," was the rather tart reply.

"Winthrop isn't as slack as you sometimes think. He doesn't like business, but he has a good head for it. And he will look out for Doris. He is mightily interested in her too. But if you must scold anyone, save it for him to-night, and let Doris be happy in her gift."

"Am I such a scold?"

"You are my dear helpmeet." He put his arm over her shoulder and kissed her. People were not very demonstrative in those days, and their affection spoke oftener in deeds than words. In fact, they thought the words betrayed a strand of weakness. "There, I must be off," he added. "Come, Warren," opening the door. "Meade will think we have had a turkey dinner and stayed to polish the bones."

Betty had been trying the effect of trailing silk and enjoying her brother's admiration. Now she folded it again decorously, and began to pile up the cups and plates, half afraid to venture into the kitchen lest her dream of delight should be overshadowed by a cloud.

Mrs. Leverett was doing a sober bit of thinking. How much happiness ought one to allow one's self in this vale of tears? Something she had read last night recurred to her—"Inasmuch as ye have done it unto the least of these——" Done what? Fed bodies and warmed and clothed them. And what of the hungry longing soul? All her life she had had a good tender husband. And now, when he had strayed from the faith a little, he seemed dearer and nearer than ever before. God had given her a great deal to be thankful for. Five fine children who had never strayed out of the paths of rectitude. Of course, she had always given the credit to their "bringing up." And here was a little girl reared quite differently, sweet, wholesome, generous, painstaking, and grateful for every little favor.

Astute Betty sent Doris in as an advance guard.

"You may take the dish of spoons, and I'll follow with the cups and saucers."

74

Aunt Elizabeth looked up and half smiled.

"You and Uncle Win have been very foolish," she began, but her tone was soft, as if she did not wholly believe what she was saying. "I shall save my scolding for him, and I think Betty will have to train you in figures all winter long to half repay for such a beautiful gift."

"Oh, Aunt Elizabeth, I *thought* of it, you know," she cried in sweet eagerness, "and if there is anything wrong——"

"There isn't anything wrong, dear." Mrs. Leverett stooped and kissed her. "I don't know as Betty needed a silk gown, for many a girl doesn't have one until she is married. I shall have to keep a sharp eye on you and Uncle Win hereafter."

Betty went back and forth. The dishes were washed and the kitchen set to rights, while the bits of talk flowed pleasantly.

"I think I will iron this afternoon," announced Betty. "I see some of the clothes are dry. Didn't you mean to go and see about the carpet, mother?"

"I had thought of it. I want to have my warp dyed blue and orange, and some of the rags colored. Mrs. Jett does it so well, and she's so needy I thought I would give her all the work. Your father said I had better. And she might dip over that brown frock of yours. The piece of new can go with it so it will all be alike."

Betty wanted to lift up her heart in thanksgiving. The dyeing tub was her utter abomination—it took so long for the stain to wear out of your hands.

"Well—if you like." This referred to the ironing. "I don't know how you'll get your gown done."

"I might run over and get some patterns from Jane, if I get through in time," suggested Betty. For a horrible fear had entered her mind that her mother's acceptance of the fact foreboded some delay in the making.

"Don't go until I get back."

"Oh, no."

Betty took down the clothes and folded them. They were just right to iron. She arranged her table, and Doris brought her books and sat at one end.

"It would be so much nicer to talk about the party," she said gravely, "but the lessons are so hard. Oh, Betty, do you think I shall ever be smart like other girls? I feel ashamed sometimes. My figures are just dreadful. Robert Lane said this morning they looked like hen tracks. His are beautiful. And he is only seven years old. Oh, dear!"

"Robbie has been at school three years. Wait until you have been a year!"

"And writing. Oh, Betty, when will I be able to write a letter to Miss Arabella? Now, if you could talk across the ocean!"

"The idea! One would have to scream pretty loud, and then it wouldn't go a mile." Betty threw her head back and laughed.

But Doris was to live long enough to talk across the ocean, though no one really dreamed of it then; indeed, at first it was quite ridiculed.

"It is a nice thing to know a good deal, but it is awful hard to learn," said the little girl presently.

"Now, it seems to me I never could learn French. And when you rattle it off in the way you do, I am dumb-founded."

"What is that, Betty?"

Betty flushed and laughed. "Surprised or anything like that," she returned.

"But, you see, I learned to talk and read just as you do English. And then papa being English, why I had both languages. It was very easy."

"Patience and perseverance will make this easy."

"And I can't knit a stocking nor make a shirt. And I haven't pieced a bedspread nor worked a sampler. Mary Green has a beautiful one, with a border of strawberries around the edge and forget-me-nots in the corner. Her father is going to have it framed."

"Oh, you must not chatter so much. Begin and say some tables."

"I know 'three times' skipping all about. But when you get good and used one way you have to fly around some other way. I can say 'four times' straight, but I have to think a little."

"Now begin," said Betty.

They seemed to run races, until Doris' cheeks were like roses and she was all out of breath. At last she accomplished the baleful four, skipping about.

"Mrs. Webb said I must learn four and five this week. And five is easy enough. Now, will you hear me do some sums in addition?"

She added aloud, and did quite well, Betty thought.

"When I can make nice figures and do sums that are worth while, I am to have a book to put them in, Mrs. Webb says. What is worth while, Betty?"

"Why it's—it's—a thing that is really worth doing well. I don't know everything," with a half-laughing sigh.

Betty had all her pieces ironed before the lessons were learned. Doris thought ironing was easier. It finished up of itself, and there was nothing to come after.

"Well—there is mending," suggested Betty.

"I know how to darn. I shall not have to learn that."

"And you darn beautifully."

While Mrs. Leverett was out she thought she would run down to Aunt Priscilla's a few moments, so it was rather late when she returned. But Betty had a pan of biscuits rising in the warmth of the fire. Then she was allowed to go over to the Morses' and tell Jane the wonderful news. Uncle Winthrop walked up, so there would be no trouble about the horse; then, he had been writing all day, and needed some exercise.

"And how did the silk suit?" he asked as he took both of the child's hands in his.

"It was just beautiful. Betty was delighted, and so surprised! Uncle Winthrop, isn't it a joyful thing to make people happy!"

"Why—I suppose it is," with a curious hesitation in his voice, as he glanced down into the shining eyes. He had not thought much of making anyone happy latterly. Indeed, he believed he had laid all the real joys of life in his wife's grave. He was proud of his son, of course, and he did everything for his advancement. But a simple thing like this!

"We have been studying all the afternoon, Betty and I. She is so good to me. And to think, Uncle Win, she had read the Bible all through when she was eight years old, and made a shirt. All the little girls make one for their father. And he gave her a silver half-dollar with a hole in it, and she put a blue ribbon through it and means to keep it always. But I haven't any father. And I began to read the Bible on Sunday. It will take me two years," with a long sigh. "I used to read the Psalms to Miss Arabella, and there was a portion for every day. They are just a month long, when the month has thirty days."

Her chatter was so pleasant. Several times through the day her soft voice had haunted him.

Aunt Elizabeth came in with her big kitchen apron tied over her best afternoon gown. She didn't scold very hard, but she thought Uncle Win might better be careful of the small fortune coming to Doris, since she had neither father nor brother to augment it. And they would make Betty as vain as a peacock in all her finery.

Betty returned laden with patterns and her eyes as bright as stars. Jane Morse had promised to come over in the morning and help her cut her gown. Jane was a very "handy" girl, and prided herself on knowing enough about "mantua making" to get her living if she had need. At that period nearly every family did the sewing of all kinds except the outside wear for men. And fashions were as eagerly sought for and discussed among the younger people as in more modern times. The old Puritan attire was still in vogue. Not so many years before the Revolution the Royalists' fashions, both English and French, had been adopted. But the cocked hats and scarlet coats, the flowing wigs and embroidered waistcoats, had been swept away by the Continental style. For women, high heels and high caps had run riot, and hoops and flowing trains of brocades and velvets and glistening silks. And now the wife of the First Consul of France was the Empress Josephine, and the Empire style had swept away the pompadour and everything else. It had the advantage of being more simple, though quite as costly.

Uncle Win and Uncle Leverett talked politics after supper, one sitting one side of the chimney and one the other. Doris had gone over to Uncle Winthrop's side, and she wished she could be two little girls just for the evening. She was trying very hard to understand what they meant by the Embargo and the Non-Intercourse Act, and she learned they were going to have a new President in March. She did not think politics very interesting—she liked better to hear about the war that had begun more than thirty years ago. Uncle Leverett was quite sure there would be another war before they were done with it; that all the old questions had not been fought out, and there could be no lasting peace until they were. Did men like war so much, she wondered?

Betty stole around to Uncle Win's side before he went away and thanked him again for the interest he had taken in Doris' desire. Yes, she was a pretty girl; and how much cheer there seemed around the Leverett fireside! Warren was a fine young fellow, too, older by two years than his own son. He missed a certain cordial living that would have cheered his own life. When his boy came home he would have it different. And by that time he would have decided about Doris.

Betty and Jane had plenty of discussions the next morning. Waists were short and full, and with a square neck and a flat band, over which there was a fall of lace, and short, puffed sleeves for evening wear.

"But she isn't likely to go to another party this winter, and she will want it for a best dress all next summer," said Mrs. Leverett.

"Oh, I should have long sleeves, as well, and just baste them in. And there's so much silk I should make a fichu to tie round in the back with two long ends. You can make that any time. And a scant ruffle not more than an inch wide when it is finished. A ruffle round the skirt about two inches when that is done. Letty Rowe has three ruffles around her changeable taffeta. 'Twas made for her cousin's wedding, and it is just elegant."

"It is a shame to waste stuff that way," declared Mrs. Leverett.

"But the frills are scant, and skirts are never more than two and a half yards round. Why, last summer mother said I might have that fine sprigged muslin of hers to make over, and I'm sure I have enough for another gown. Mrs. Leverett, it doesn't take half as much to make a gown for us as it did for our mothers," said Jane with arch humor.

"She had better save the piece for a new waist and sleeves," declared the careful mother.

"Well, maybe fichus and capes will go out before another summer. I would save the piece now, at any rate," agreed Jane.

Jane was extremely clever. The girls had many amusing asides, for Mrs. Leverett was ironing in the kitchen. There was nothing harmful about them, but they were full of gay promise. Jane cut and basted and fitted. There were the bodice and the sleeves. "You can easily slip out the long ones," she whispered, "and there was the skirt with the lining all basted, and the ruffles cut and sewed together."

"You'll have a nice job hemming them. I should do it over a cord. It makes them set out so much better. And if you get in the drag I'll come over to-morrow. I'm to help mother with the nut cake this afternoon. It cuts better to be a day or two old. We made the fruit cake a fortnight ago."

"How good you are! I don't know what I should have done without you!"

"And I don't know how Betty will ever repay you," said Mrs. Leverett.

"I know," returned Jane laughingly. "I have planned to get every stitch out of her. I am going to quilt my 'Young Man's Ramble' this winter, and mother's said I might ask in two or three of the best quilters I know—Betty quilts so beautifully!"

The "Young Man's Ramble" was patchwork of a most intricate design, in which it seemed that one might ramble about fruitlessly.

"I am glad there is some way of your getting even," said the mother with a little pride.

Jane took dinner with them and then ran off home. Warren went a short distance with her, as their way lay together.

"I hope you didn't say anything about the dancing," he remarked. "Mother is rather set against it. But Sister Electa gives dancing parties, and Betty's going to Hartford this winter. She ought to know how to dance."

"Trust me for not letting the cat out of the bag!"

Betty sewed and sewed. She could hardly attend to Doris' lessons and sums. She hemmed the ruffle in the evening, and hurried with her work the next morning. Everything went smoothly, and Mrs. Leverett was more interested than she would have believed. And she was quite ready to take up the cudgel for her daughter's silken gown when Aunt Priscilla made her appearance. Of course she would find fault.

But it is the unexpected that happens. Aunt Priscilla was in an extraordinary mood. Some money had been paid to her that morning that she had considered lost beyond a peradventure. And she said, "It was a great piece of foolishness, and Winthrop Adams at his time of life ought to have had more sense, but what could you expect of a man always browsing over books! And if she had thought Betty was dying for a silk frock, she had two laid away that would come in handy some time. She hadn't ever quite decided who should fall heir to them, but so many of the girls had grown up and had husbands to buy fine things for them, she supposed it would be Betty."

"What is going round the neck and sleeves?" she asked presently.

"Mother has promised to lend me some lace," answered Betty. "The other girls had a borrowed wear out of it."

"I'll look round a bit. I never had much real finery, but husband always wanted me to dress well when we were first married. We went out a good deal for a while, before he was hurt. I'll see what I have."

And the next morning old Polly brought over a box with "Missus' best compliments." There was some beautiful English thread lace about four inches wide, just as it had lain away for years, wrapped in soft white paper, with a cake of white wax to keep it from turning unduly yellow.

"Betty, you are in wonderful luck," said her mother. "Something has stirred up Aunt Priscilla."

Just at noon that eventful Thursday Mr. Manning came in from Salem for his mother-in-law. Mrs. Manning's little daughter had been born at eight that morning, and Mary wanted her mother at once. She had promised to go, but hardly expected the call so soon.

There were so many charges to give Betty, who was to keep house for the next week. Nothing was quite ready. Mother fashion, she had counted on doing this and that before she went; and if Betty couldn't get along she must ask Aunt Priscilla to come, just as if Betty had not kept house a whole week last summer. There was advice to father and to Warren, and he was to try to bring Betty home by nine o'clock that evening. What Doris would do in the afternoon, she couldn't see.

"Go off with an easy heart, mother," said Mr. Leverett; "I will come home early this afternoon."

CHAPTER VIII

SINFUL OR NOT?

"You should have seen me when Jane tied a white sash about my waist. Then I was just complete."

"But you looked beautiful before—like a—well, a queen couldn't have looked prettier. Or the Empress Josephine."

Betty laughed and kissed the little girl whose eyes were still full of admiration. She had not come home until ten, and found her father waiting at the fireside, but Doris was snuggled up in bed and soundly asleep. She had risen at her father's call, made the breakfast, and sent the men off in time; then heard the lesson Doris wasn't quite sure of, and sent her to school; and now the dinner was cleared away and they were sitting by the fire.

The Empress Josephine was in her glory then, one of the notables of Europe.

"And Mrs. Morse said such lace as that would be ten dollars a yard now. Think of that! Thirty dollars! But didn't you get lonesome waiting for father?"

"He came just half an hour afterward. And, oh, we had such a grand, funny time getting supper. It was as good as a party. I poured the tea. And he called me Miss Adams, like a grown lady. And, then, what do you think? We played fox and geese! And do you know I thought the geese were dumb to let the fox get them all. And then he took the geese and soon penned my fox in a corner. Then he told me about the fox and the goose and the measure of corn and the man crossing the stream. It was just delightful. I wanted to stay up until you came home, but I did get so sleepy. And was the party splendid? I don't think anyone could have been prettier than you!"

"Sally Prentiss had a pink silk frock, and the ruffles were fringed out, which made them fluffy. It was beautiful! Oh, I should have felt just awful in my gray cloth or my blue winter frock. And I owe most of the delight to you, little Doris. I've been thinking—sometime I will work you a beautiful white frock, fine India muslin."

"And what did they do?"

"We didn't sew much," Betty laughed. "We talked and talked. I knew all but one girl, and we were soon acquainted. Jane didn't have a thing to do, of course. Then the gentlemen came and we went out to supper. The table was like a picture. There was cold turkey and cold ham and cold baked pork. They were all delicious. And bread and biscuits and puffy little cakes quite new. Mrs. Morse's cousin brought the recipe, and she has promised it to mother. And there were jams and jellies and ever so many things, and then all the plates and meats were sent away, and the birthday cake with seventeen tiny candles was lighted up. And cake of every kind, and whipped cream and nuts and candies. Then we went back to the parlor and played "proverbs" and "What is my thought like?" and then black Joe came with his fiddle. First they danced the minuet. It was beautiful. And then they had what is called cotillions. I believe that is the new fashionable dance. It takes eight people, but you can have two or three at the same time. They dance in figures. And, oh, it is just delightful! I *do* wonder if it is wrong?"

"What would make it wrong?" asked Doris gravely.

"That's what puzzles me. A great many people think it right and send their children to dancing-school. On all great occasions there seems to be dancing. It is stepping and floating around gracefully. You think of swallows flying and flowers swinging and grass waving in the summer sun."

"But if there is so much of it in the world, and if God made the world gay and glad and rejoicing and full of butterflies and birds and ever so many things that don't do any real work but just have a lovely time——"

Doris' wide-open eyes questioned her companion.

"They haven't any souls. I don't know." Betty shook her head. "Let's ask father about it to-night. When you are little you play tag and puss-in-the-corner and other things, and run about full of fun. Dancing is more orderly and refined. And there's the delicious music! All the young men were so nice and polite,—so kind of elegant,—and it makes you feel of greater consequence. I don't mean vain, only as if it was worth while to behave prettily. It's like the parlor and the kitchen. You don't take your washing and scrubbing and scouring in the parlor, though that work is all necessary. So there are two sides to life. And my side just now is getting supper, while your side is studying tables. Oh, I do wonder if you will ever get to know them!"

Doris sighed. She would so much rather talk about the party.

"And your frock was—pretty?" she ventured timidly.

"All the girls thought it lovely. And I told them it was a gift from my little cousin, who came from old Boston—and they were so interested in you. They thought Doris a beautiful name, but Sally said the family name ought to be grander to go with it. But Adams is a fine old name, too—the first name that was ever given. There was only one man then, and when there came to be such hosts of them they tacked the 's' on to make it a noun of multitude."

"Did they really? Some of the children are learning about nouns. Oh, dear, how much there is to learn!" said the little girl with a sigh.

Betty went at her supper. People ate three good stout meals in those days. It made a deal of cooking. It made a stout race of people as well, and one heard very little about nerves and indigestion. Betty was getting to be quite a practiced cook.

Mr. Leverett took a good deal of interest hearing about the party. Warren had enjoyed it mightily. And then they besieged him for an opinion on the question of dancing. Warren presented his petition that he might be allowed to join a class of young men that was being formed. There were only a few vacancies.

"I do not think I have a very decided opinion about it," he returned slowly. "Times have changed a good deal since I was young, and amusements have changed with them. A hundred or so years ago life was very strenuous, and prejudices of people very strong. Yet the young people skated and had out-of-door games, and indoor plays that we consider very rough now. And you remember that our ancestors were opposed to nearly everything their oppressors did. Their own lives were too serious to indulge in much pleasuring. The pioneers of a nation rarely do. But we have come to an era of more leisure as to social life. Whether it will make us as strong as a nation remains to be seen."

"That doesn't answer my question," said Warren respectfully.

"I am going to ask you to wait until you are of age, mostly for your mother's sake. I think she dreads leaving the old ways. And then Betty will have no excuse," with a shrewd little smile.

Warren looked disappointed.

"But I danced last night," said Betty. "And we used to dance last winter at school. Two or three of the girls were good enough to show us the new steps. And one of the amusing things was a draw cotillion. The girls drew out a slip of paper that had a young man's name on it, and then she had to pass it over to him, and he danced with her. And who do you think I had?" triumphantly.

"I do not know the young men who were there," said her father.

"I hope it was the very nicest and best," exclaimed Doris.

"It just was! Jane's cousin, Morris Winslow. And he was quite the leader in everything, almost as if it was his party. And he is one of the real quality, you know. I was almost afraid to dance with him, but he was so nice and told me what to do every time, so I did not make any serious blunders. But it is a pleasure to feel that you know just how."

"There will be years for you to learn," said her father. "Meanwhile the ghost of old Miles Standish may come back."

"What would he do?" asked Doris, big-eyed.

Warren laughed. "What he did in the flesh was this: The Royalists—you see, they were not all Puritans that came over—were going to keep an old-time festival at a place called Merry Mount. They erected a May pole and were going to dance around it."

"That is what they do at home. And they have a merry time. Miss Arabella took me. And didn't Miles Standish like it?"

"I guess not. He sent a force of men to tear it down, and marched Morton and his party into Plymouth, where they were severely reprimanded—fined as well, some people say."

"We do not rule our neighbors quite as strictly now. But one must admire those stanch old fellows, after all."

"I am glad the world has grown wider," said Warren. But he wished its wideness had taken in his mother, who had a great fear of the evils lying in wait for unwary youth. Still he would not go against her wishes while he was yet under age. Young people were considered children in their subjection to their parents until this period. And girls who stayed at home were often in subjection all their lives. There were men who ruled their families with a sort of iron sway, but Mr. Leverett had always been considered rather easy.

Doris begged to come out and dry the dishes, but they said tables instead of talking of the seductive party. Mr. Leverett had to go out for an hour. Betty sat down and took up her knitting. She felt rather tired and sleepy, for she had gone on with the party the night before, after she was in bed. A modern girl would be just getting ready to go to her party at ten. But then she would not have to get up at half-past five the next morning, make a fire, and cook breakfast. Suddenly Betty found herself nodding.

"Put up your book, Doris. I'll mix the cakes and we will go to bed. You can dream on the lessons."

The party had demoralized Doris as well.

Among the real quality young men came to inquire after the welfare of the ladies the next morning, or evening at the latest. But people in the middle classes were occupied with their employments, which were the main things of their lives.

And though the lines were strongly drawn and the "quality" were aristocratic, there were pleasant gradations, marked by a fine breeding on the one side and a sense of fitness on the other, that met when there was occasion, and mingled and fused agreeably, then returned each to his proper sphere. The Morses were well connected and had some quite high-up relatives. For that matter, so were the Leveretts, but Foster Leverett was not ambitions for wealth or social distinction, and Mrs. Leverett clung to the safety of the good old ways.

Jane ran over in the morning with a basket of some of the choicer kinds of cake, and some nuts, raisins, and mottoes for the little girl. There were so many nice things she was dying to tell Betty,—compliments,—and some from Cousin Morris. And didn't she think everything went off nicely?

"It was splendid, all through," cried Betty enthusiastically. "I would like to go to a party—well, I suppose every week would be too often, but at least twice a month."

"The Chauncey Winslows are going to have a party Thanksgiving night. They are Morris' cousins and not mine, but I've been there; and Morris said last night I should have an invitation. It will be just splendid, I know."

"But you are seventeen. And mother thinks I am only a little girl," returned Betty.

"Oh, yes; I didn't go scarcely anywhere last winter. Being grown up is ever so much nicer. But it will come for you."

"Electa wants me to visit her this winter. The assembly is to meet, you know, and she has plenty of good times, although she has three children. I *do* hope I can go! And I have that lovely frock."

"That would be delightful. I wish I had a sister married and living away somewhere—New York, for instance. They have such fine times. Oh, dear! how do you get along alone?"

"It keeps me pretty busy."

Jane had come out in the kitchen, so Betty could go on with her dinner preparations.

"Mother thinks of keeping Cousin Nabby all winter. She likes Boston so, and it's lonely up in New Hampshire on the farm. That will ease me up wonderfully."

"If I go away mother will have to get someone."

"Although they do not think we young people are of much account," laughed Jane. "Give your little girl a good big chunk of party cake and run over when you can."

"But I can't now."

"Then I will have to do the visiting."

Dinner was ready on the mark, and Mr. Leverett praised it. Doris came home in high feather. She had not missed a word, and she had done all her sums.

"I think I am growing smarter," she announced with a kind of grave exultation. "Don't you think Aunt Elizabeth will teach me how to knit when she comes back?"

Not to have knit a pair of stockings was considered rather disgraceful for a little girl.

Aunt Priscilla came over early Saturday afternoon. She found the house in very good order, and she glanced sharply about, too. They had not heard from Mary yet, but the elder lady said no news was good news. Then she insisted on looking over the clothes for the Monday's wash and mending up the rents. Tuesday she would come in and darn the stockings. When she was nine years old it was her business to do all the family darning, looking askance at Doris.

"Now, if you had been an only child, Aunt Priscilla, and had no parents, what a small amount of darning would have fallen to your share!" said Betty.

"Well, I suppose I would have been put out somewhere and trained to make myself useful. And if I'd had any money that would have been on interest, so that I could have some security against want in my old age. Anyway, it isn't likely I should have been allowed to fritter away my time."

Betty wondered how Aunt Priscilla could content herself with doing such a very little now! Not but what she had earned a rest. And Foster Leverett, who managed some of her business, said *sub rosa* that she was not spending all her income.

"You can't come up to your mother making tea," she said at the supper table. "Your mother makes the best cup of tea I ever tasted."

Taking it altogether they did get on passably well without Mrs. Leverett during the ten days. She brought little James, six years of age, who couldn't go the long distance to school in cold weather with the two older children, and so was treated to a visit at grandmother's.

Mary was doing well and had a sweet little girl, as good as a kitten. Mr. Manning's Aunt Comfort had come to stay a spell through the winter. And now there was getting ready for Thanksgiving. There was no time to make mince pies, but then Mrs. Leverett didn't care so much for them early in the season. Hollis' family would come up, they would ask Aunt Priscilla, and maybe Cousin Winthrop would join them. So they were busy as possible.

Little James took a great liking to his shy cousin Doris, and helped her say tables and spell. He had been at school all summer and was very bright and quick.

"But, Uncle Foster," she declared, "the children in America are much smarter than English children. They understand everything so easily."

Then came the first big snowstorm of the season. There had been two or three little dashes and squalls. It began at noon and snowed all night. The sky was so white in the early morning you could hardly tell where the snow line ended and where it began; but by and by there came a bluish, silvery streak that parted it like a band, and presently a pale sun ventured forth, hanging on the edge of yellowish clouds and growing stronger, until about noon it flooded everything with gold, and the heavens were one broad sheet of blue magnificence.

Doris did not go to school in the morning. There were no broken paths, and boys and men were busy shoveling out or tracking down.

"It is a heavy snow for so early in the season," declared Uncle Leverett. "We are not likely to see bare ground in a long while."

Doris thought it wonderful. And when Uncle Winthrop came the next day and took them out in a big sleigh with a span of horses, her heart beat with unwonted enjoyment. But the familiarity little James evinced with it quite startled her.

Thanksgiving Day was a great festival even then, and had been for a long while. Christmas was held of little account. New Year's Day had a greater social aspect. Commencement, election, and training days were in high favor, and every good housewife baked election cake, and every voter felt entitled to a half-holiday at least. Then there was an annual fast day, with church-going and solemnity quite different from its modern successor.

The Hollis Leveretts, two grown people and four children, came up early. Sam, or little Sam as he was often called to distinguish him from his two uncles, was a nice well-grown and well-looking boy of about ten. Mrs. Hollis had lost her next child, a boy also, and Bessy was just beyond six. Charles and the baby completed the group.

Uncle Leverett made a fire in the best room early in the morning. Doris was a little curious to see it with the shutters open. It was a large room, with a "boughten" ingrain carpet, stiff chairs, two great square ottomans, a big sofa, and some curious old paintings, besides a number of framed silhouettes of different members of the family.

The most splendid thing of all was the great roaring fire in the wide chimney.

The high shelf was adorned with two pitchers in curious glittering bronze, with odd designs in blue and white raised from the surface. The children brought their stools and sat around the fire.

Adjoining this was the spare room, the guest chamber *par excellence*. Sometimes the old house had been full, when there were young people coming and going, and relatives from distant places visiting. Electa and Mary had both married young, though in the early years of her married life Electa had made long visits home. But her husband had prospered in business and gone into public life, and she entertained a good deal, and the journey home was long and tedious. Mary was much nearer, but she had a little family and many cares.

Sam took the leadership of the children. He had seen Doris for a few minutes on several occasions and had not a very exalted opinion of a girl who could only cipher in addition, while he was over in interest and tare and tret. To be sure he could neither read nor talk French. This year he had gone to the Latin school. He hadn't a very high opinion of Latin, and he did not want to go to college. He was going to be a shipping merchant, and own vessels to go all over the world and bring cargoes back to Boston. He meant to be a rich man and own a fine big house like the Hancock House.

Doris thought it would be very wonderful for a little boy to get rich.

"And you might be lord mayor of Boston," she said, thinking of the renowned Whittington.

"We don't have *lord* mayors nor lord anything now, except occasionally a French or English nobleman. And we don't care much for them," said the uncompromising young republican. "I should like to be Governor or perhaps President, but I shouldn't want to waste my time on anything else."

Grandfather Leverett smiled over these boyish ambitions, but he wished Sam's heart was not quite so set on making money.

There were so few grown people that by bringing in one of the kitchen tables and placing it alongside they could make room for all. Betty was to be at the end, flanked on both sides by the children; Mrs. Hollis at the other end. There was a savory fragrance of turkey, sauces, and vegetables, and the table seemed literally piled up with good things.

Just as they were about to sit down Uncle Winthrop came in for a moment to express his regrets again at not being able to make one of the family circle. Doris thought he looked very handsome in his best clothes, his elegant brocaded waistcoat, and fine double-ruffled shirt-front. He wore his hair brushed back and tied in a queue and slightly powdered.

He was to go to a grand dinner with some of the city officials, a gathering that was not exactly to his taste, but one he could not well decline. And when Doris glanced up with such eager admiration and approval, his heart warmed tenderly toward her, as it recalled other appreciative eyes that had long ago closed for the last time.

What a dinner it was! Sam studied hard and played hard in the brief while he could devote to play, and he ate accordingly. Doris was filled with amazement. No wonder he was round and rosy.

"Doesn't that child ever eat any more?" asked Mrs. Hollis. "No wonder she is so slim and peaked. I'd give her some gentian, mother, or anything that would start her up a little."

Doris turned scarlet.

"She's always well," answered Mrs. Leverett. "She hasn't had a sick day since she came here. I think she hasn't much color naturally, and her skin is very fair."

"I do hope she will stay well. I've had such excellent luck with my children, who certainly do give their keeping credit. I think she's been housed too much. I'm afraid she won't stand the cold winter very well."

"You can't always go by looks," commented Aunt Priscilla.

After the dinner was cleared away and the dishes washed (all the grown people helped and made short work of it), the kitchen was straightened, the chairs being put over in the corner, and the children who were large enough allowed a game of blindman's buff, Uncle Leverett watching to see that no untoward accidents happened, and presently allowing himself to be caught. And, oh, what a scattering and laughing there was then! His arms were so large that it seemed as if he must sweep everybody into them, but, strange to relate, no one was caught so easily. They dodged and tiptoed about and gave little half-giggles and thrilled with success. He did catch Sam presently, and the boy did not enjoy it a bit. Not that he minded being blindfolded, but he should have liked to boast that grandfather could not catch him.

Sam could see under the blinder just the least bit. Doris had on red morocco boots, and they were barely up to her slim ankles. They were getting small, so Aunt Elizabeth thought she might take a little good out of them, as they were by far too light for school wear. Sam was sure he could tell by them, and he resolved to capture her. But every time he came near grandfather rushed before her, and he didn't want to catch back right away, neither did he want Bessy, whose half-shriek betrayed her whereabouts.

Mrs. Leverett opened the door.

"I think you have made noise enough," she said. People believed in the old adage then that children should "be seen and not heard," and that indoors was no place for a racket. "Aunt Priscilla thinks she must go, but she wants you to sing a little."

This was for Mr. Leverett, but Sam had a very nice boy's voice and felt proud enough when he lifted it up in church.

"I'll come, grandmother," he said with some elation, as if he alone had been asked. And as he tore off the blinder he put his head down close to Doris, and whispered:

"It was mean of you to hide behind grandfather every time, and he didn't play fair a bit."

But having a peep at the red shoes as they went dancing round was fair enough!

Hollis Leverett sang in the choir. They had come to this innovation, though they drew the line at instrumental music. He had a really fine tenor voice. Mr. Leverett sang in a sort of natural, untrained tone, very sweet. Mrs. Hollis couldn't sing at all, but she was very proud to have the children take after their father. There were times when Aunt Priscilla sang for herself, but her voice had grown rather quivering and uncertain. So Betty and her mother had to do their best to keep from being drowned out. But the old hymns were touching, with here and there a line of rare sweetness.

Hollis Leverett was going to take Aunt Priscilla home and then return for the others. Sam insisted upon going with them, so grandfather roasted some corn for Bessy and Doris. They had not the high art of popping it then and turning it inside out, although now and then a grain achieved such a success all by itself. Bessy thought Doris rather queer and not very smart.

The two little ones were bundled up and made ready, and the sleigh came back with a jingle for warning. Mrs. Hollis took her baby in her arms, grandfather carried out little Foster, and they were all packed in snugly and covered up almost head and ears with the great fur robes, while little Sam shouted out the last good-night.

Mrs. Leverett straightened things in the best room until all the company air had gone out of it. Doris felt the difference and was glad to come out to her own chimney corner. Then Betty spread the table and they had a light supper, for, what with dinner being a little late and very hearty, no one was hungry. But they sipped their tea and talked over the children and how finely Sam was getting along in his studies, and Mrs. Leverett brought up the Manning children, for much as she loved Hollis, her daughter Mary's children came in for a share of grandmotherly affection. And in her heart she felt that little James was quite as good as anybody.

Warren had promised to spend the evening with some young friends. Betty wished she were a year older and could have the privilege of inviting in schoolmates and their brothers, and that she might have fire in the parlor on special occasions. But, to compensate, some of the neighbors dropped in. Doris and James played fox and geese until they were sleepy. James had a little cot in the corner of grandmother's room.

CHAPTER IX

WHAT WINTER BROUGHT

Oh, what a lovely white world it was! The low, sedgy places were frozen over and covered with snow; the edges of the bay, Charles River, and Mystic River were assuming their winter garments as well. And when, just a week after, another snowstorm came, there seemed a multitude of white peaks out in the harbor, and the hills were transformed into veritable snow-capped mountains. Winter had set in with a rigor unknown to-day. But people did not seem to mind it. Even the children had a good time sledding and snowballing and building snow forts and fighting battles. There were mighty struggles between the North Enders and the South Enders. Louisburg was retaken, 1775 was re-enacted, and Paul Revere again swung his lantern and roused his party to arms, and snowballs whitened instead of darkening the air with the smoke of firearms. Deeds of mighty prowess were done on both sides.

But the boys had the best of it surely. The girls had too much to do. They were soon too large for romping and playing. There were stockings to knit and to darn. There were long overseams in sheets; there was no end of shirt-making for the men. They put the hems in their own frocks and aprons, they stitched gussets and bands and seams. People were still spinning and weaving, though the mills that were to lead the revolution in industries had come in. The Embargo was taxing the ingenuity of brains as well as hands, and as more of everything was needed for the increase of population, new methods were invented to shorten processes that were to make New England the manufacturing center of the new world.

When the children had nothing else to do there was always a bag of carpet rags handy. There were braided rugs that were quite marvels of taste, and even the hit-or-miss ones were not bad.

Still they were allowed out after supper on moonlight nights for an hour or so, and then they had grand good times. The father or elder brothers went along to see that no harm happened. Fort Hill was one of the favorite coasting places, and parties of a larger growth thronged here. But Beacon Hill had not been shorn of all its glory.

Uncle Winthrop came over one day and took the children and Betty to see the battle at Fort Hill. The British had intrenched themselves with forts and breastworks and had their colors flying. It really had been hard work to enlist men or boys in this army. No one likes to go into a fight with the foregone conclusion that he is to be beaten. But they were to do their best, and they did it. The elders went out to see the fun. The rebels directed all their energies to the capture of one fort instead of opening fire all along the line, and by dusk they had succeeded in demolishing that, when the troops on both sides were summoned home to supper and to comfortable beds, an innovation not laid down in the rules of warfare.

Little James had been fired with military ardor. Cousin Sam was the leader of one detachment of the rebel forces. Catch him anywhere but on the winning side!

Doris had been much interested as well, and that evening Uncle Leverett told them stories about Boston thirty years before. He was a young man of three-and-twenty when Paul Revere swung his lantern to give the alarm. He could only touch lightly upon what had been such solemn earnest to the men of that time, the women as well.

"I'm going to be a soldier," declared James, with all the fervor of his youthful years. "But you can't ever be, Doris."

"No," answered Doris softly, squeezing Uncle Leverett's hand in both of hers. "But there isn't any war."

"Yes there is—over in France and England, and ever so many places. My father was reading about it. And if there wasn't any war here, couldn't we go and fight for some other country?"

"I hope there will never be war in your time, Jimmie, boy," said his grandmother. "And it is bedtime for little people."

"Why does it come bedtime so soon?" in a deeply aggrieved tone. "When I am a big man I am going to sit up clear till morning. And I'll tell my grandchildren all night long how I fought in the wars."

"That is looking a long way ahead," returned grandfather.

Besides the lessons, Doris was writing a letter to Miss Arabella. That lady would have warmly welcomed any little scrawl in Doris' own hand. Uncle Winthrop had acknowledged her safe arrival in good health, and enlarged somewhat on the pleasant home she had found with her relatives. Betty had overlooked the little girl's letter and made numerous corrections, and she had copied and thought of some new things and copied it over again. She had added a little French verse also.

"Dear me!" exclaimed Aunt Elizabeth, "when will the child ever learn anything useful! There doesn't seem any time. The idea of a girl of ten years old never having knit a stocking! And she will be full that and more!"

"But everybody doesn't knit," said Betty.

"Oh, yes, you can buy those flimsy French things that do not give you any wear. And presently we may not be able to buy either French or English. She is not going to be so rich either. It's nonsense to think of that marshy land ever being valuable. Whatever possessed anyone to buy it, I can't see! And if Doris was to be a queen I think she ought to know something useful."

"I do not suppose I shall ever need to spin," Betty said rather archly.

Mrs. Leverett had insisted that all her girls should learn to spin both wool and flax. Betty had rebelled a little two years ago, but she had learned nevertheless.

"And there was a time when a premium was paid to the most skillful spinner. Your grandmother, Betty, was among those who spun on the Common. The women used to go out there with their wheels. And there were spinning schools. The better class had to pay, but a certain number of poor women were taught on condition that they would teach their children at home. And it is not a hundred years ago either. There was no cloth to be had, and Manufactory House was established."

Betty had heard the story of spinning on the Commons, for her own grandmother had told it. But she had an idea that the world would go on rather than retrograde. For now they were turning out cotton cloth and printing calico and making canvas and duck, and it was the boast of the famous *Constitution* that everything besides her armament was made in Massachusetts.

Uncle Winthrop thought Doris' letter was quite a masterpiece for a little girl. At least, that was what he said. I think he was a good deal more interested in that than in the sampler she had begun. And he agreed privately with Betty that "useless" sometimes was misspelled into "useful."

Another letter created quite a consternation. This was from Hartford. Mrs. King wrote that a friend, a Mr. Eastman, was going from Springfield to Boston on some business, and on his return he would bring Betty home with him. His wife was going on to Hartford a few days later and would be very pleased to have Betty's company. She did not know when another chance would offer, for not many people were journeying about in the winter.

Betty was to bring her nicest gowns, and she needed a good thick pelisse and heavy woolen frock for outside wear. The new hats were very large, and young girls were wearing white or cream beaver. Some very handsome ones had come from New York recently. There was a big bow on the top, and two feathers if you could afford it, and ribbon of the same width tied under the chin. She was to bring her slippers and clocked stockings, her newest white frock, and if she had to buy a new one of any kind it need not be made until she came to Hartford.

"I never heard of such a thing!" declared Mrs. Leverett, aghast. "She must think your father is made of money. And when 'Lecty and Matthias were married they went to housekeeping in three rooms in old Mrs. Morton's house, and 'Lecty was happy as a queen, and had to save at every turn. She wasn't talking then about white hats and wide ribbons and feathers and gewgaws. The idea!"

"Of course I can't have the hat," returned Betty resignedly. "But my brown one will do. And, oh, isn't it lucky my silk is made and trimmed with that beautiful lace! If I only had my white skirt worked! And that India muslin might do with a little fixing up. If I had a lace ruffle to put around the bottom!"

"I don't know how I can spare you, Betty. I can't put Doris to doing anything. When any of my girls were ten years old they could do quite a bit of housekeeping. If she wasn't so behind in her studies!"

Betty had twenty plans in a moment, but she knew her mother would object to every one. She would be very discreet until she could talk the matter over with her father.

"Everything about the journey is so nicely arranged," she began; "and, you see, Electa says it will not cost anything to Springfield. There may not be a chance again this whole winter."

"The summer will be a good deal pleasanter."

"But the Capital won't be nearly so"—"gay," she was about to say, but changed it to "interesting."

"Betty, I do wish you were more serious-minded. To think you're sixteen, almost a woman, and in some things you're just a companion for Doris!"

Betty thought it was rather hard to be between everything. She was not old enough for society, she was not a young lady, but she was too old to indulge in the frolics of girlhood. She couldn't be wise and sedate—at least, she did not want to be. And were the fun and the good times really wicked?

She was on the lookout for her father that evening. Warren was going to the house of a friend to supper, as the debating society met there, and it saved him a long walk.

"Father, Electa's letter has come," in a hurried whisper. "She's planned out my visit, but mother thinks—oh, do try and persuade her, and make it possible! I want to go so much."

But Betty began to think the subject never would be mentioned. Supper was cleared away, Doris and James studied, and she sat and worked diligently on her white gown. Then she knew her mother did not mean to say a word before her and presently she went to bed.

Mrs. Leverett handed the letter over to her husband. "From 'Lecty," she said briefly.

He read it and re-read it, while she knit on her stocking.

"Yes"—slowly. "Well—Betty might as well go. She has been promised the visit so long."

"I can't spare her. Even if I sent James home, there's Doris. And I am not as spry as I was ten years ago. The work is heavy."

"Oh, you must have someone. John Grant was in from Roxbury to-day. He has two girls quite anxious to go out this winter. I think the oldest means to marry next spring or summer, and wants to earn a little money."

"We can't take in everyone who wants to earn a little money."

"No," humorously. "It would bankrupt us these hard times. The keep would be the same as for Betty, and a few dollars wages wouldn't signify."

"But Betty'll want no end of things. It does seem as if 'Lecty had turned into a fine lady. Whether it would be a good influence on Betty! She's never been serious yet."

"And Electa joined the church at fourteen. I think you can trust Betty with her. To be sure, Mat's prospered beyond everything."

Prosperity and every good gift came from the Lord, Mrs. Leverett fully believed. And yet David had seen the "ungodly in great prosperity." She had a mother's pride in Mr. and Mrs. King, but they were rather gay with dinner parties and everything.

"She will have to take Betty just as she is. Her clothes are good enough."

Mr. Leverett re-read the letter. He wasn't much judge of white hats and wide ribbons, and, since the time was short, perhaps Electa could help her to spend the money to better advantage, and there would be no worry. He would just slip a bill or two in Betty's hand toward the last.

"Betty's a nice-looking girl," said her father.

"I should be sorry to have her niceness all come out in looks," said Betty's mother.

There was no reply to this.

"I really do not think she ought to go. There will be other winters."

"Well—we will sleep on the matter. We can't tell about next winter."

Warren thought she ought to go. Aunt Priscilla came over a day or two after in Jonas Field's sleigh. He was out collecting, and would call for her at half-past five, though she still insisted she was pretty sure-footed in walking.

Mr. Perkins in a moment of annoyance had once said to his wife: "Priscilla, you have one virtue, at least. One can always tell just where to find you. You are sure to be on the opposition side."

She had a faculty of always seeing how the other side looked. She had a curious sympathy with it as well. And though she was not an irresolute woman, she did sometimes have a longing to go over to the enemy when it was very attractive.

She listened now—and nodded at Mrs. Leverett's reasoning, adding the pungency of her sniff. Betty's heart dropped like lead. True, she had not really counted on Aunt Priscilla's influence.

"I just do suppose if 'Lecty was ill and alone, and wanted Betty, there'd be no difficulty. It's the question between work and play. There wan't much time to play when I was young, and now I wish I had some of the work, since I'm too old to play. I do believe the thing ought to be evened up."

This was rather non-committal, but the girl's heart rose a little.

"Oh, if 'Lecty was ill—but you know, Aunt Priscilla, they keep a man beside the girl, and it seems to me she is always having a nurse when the children are ailing, or a woman in to sew, or some extra help. She doesn't *need* Betty, and it seems as if I did."

"Now, if that little young one was good for anything!"

"She's at her lessons all the time, and she must learn to sew. I should have been ashamed of my girls if they had not known how to make one single garment by the time they were ten year old."

"But Doris isn't ten," interposed Betty. "And here is Electa's letter, Aunt Priscilla."

"No, I don't see how I can spare Betty," said Mrs. Leverett decisively.

Aunt Priscilla took out her glasses and polished them and then adjusted them to her rather high nose.

"Well, 'Lecty's got to be quite quality, hasn't she? And Matthias, too. I suppose it's proper to give folks their whole name when they're getting up in the world and going to legislatures. But land! I remember Mat King when he was a patched-up, barefooted little boy. He was always hanging after 'Lecty, and your uncle thought she might have done better. 'Lecty was real good-looking. And now they're top of the heap with menservants and maidservants, and goodness knows what all."

"Yes, they have prospered remarkably."

"The Kings were a nice family. My, how Mis' King did keep them children, five of them, when their father died, and not a black sheep among them! Theron's a big sea captain, and Zenas in Washington building up the Capitol, and I dare say Mat is thinking of being sent to Congress. Joe is in the Army, and the young one keeps his mother a lady in New York, I've heard say. Mis' King deserves some reward."

Betty glanced up in surprise. It was seldom Aunt Priscilla praised in this wholesale fashion.

"And this about the hat is just queer, Betty. You should have seen old Madam Clarissa Bowdoin, who came to call yesterday, with a fine sleigh and driver and footman. She just holds on to this world's good things, I tell you, and she's past seventy. My, how she was trigged out in a black satin pelisse lined with fur! And she had a black beaver bonnet or hat, whatever you call it, with a big bow on top, and two black feathers flying. I should hate to have my feathers whip all out in such a windy day."

"Oh, yes, that is the first style," said Betty. "Hartford can't keep it all."

"Hartford can't hold a candle to Boston, even if Mat King is there. Stands to reason we can get fashions just as soon here, if theirs do come from New York. Madam was mighty fine. You see, I do have some grand friends, Betty. Your uncle was a man well thought of."

"Madam Bowdoin holds her age wonderfully," said Mrs. Leverett.

"Yes. But she's never done a day's work in her life, and I don't remember when I didn't work. Let me see—I've most forgot the thread of my discourse. Oh, you never would believe, Betty, that twenty year ago there was just such a fashion. I had a white beaver—what possessed me to get it I don't know. Everything was awful high. I had an idea that white would be rather plain, but when it had that great bow on top, and strings a full finger wide—well, I didn't even dare show it to your uncle! So I packed it away with white wax and in a linen towel, and when she'd gone yesterday I went and looked at it. 'Taint white now, but it's just the color of rich cream when it's stood twenty-four hours or so. Fursisee, they were just as much alike as two peas except as to color and the feathers. I declare I *was* beat! Now, if you were going to be married, Betty, it might do for a wedding hat."

"But I'm not going to be married," with a sigh.

"I should hope not," said her mother—"at sixteen."

"My sister Patty was married when she was sixteen, and Submit when she was seventeen. The oldest girls went off in a hurry, so the others had to fill their places. Well—it just amazes me reading about this bonnet. And whatever I'll do with mine except to give it away, I don't know. I did think once of having it dyed. But the bow on top was so handsome, and I've kept paper wadded up inside, and it hasn't flatted down a mite. Now, Elizabeth, she has that silk we all thought so foolish, and her brown frock and pelisse will be just the thing to travel in. And maybe I could find something else. The things will be scattered when I am dead and gone, and I might as well have the good of giving them away. Most of the girls are married off and have husbands to provide for them. I used to think I'd take some orphan body to train and sort of fill Polly's place, for she grows more unreliable every day. Yet I do suppose it's Christian charity to keep her. And young folks are so trifling."

"Go make a cup of tea, Betty," said Mrs. Leverett.

"Now, Elizabeth," when Betty had shut the door, "I don't see why you mightn't as well let Betty go as not. 'Tisn't as if it was among strangers. And there's really no telling what may happen next year. We haven't any promise of that."

Mrs. Leverett looked up in surprise.

"'Tisn't every day such a chance comes to hand. She couldn't go alone on a journey like that. And 'Lecty seems quite lotting on it."

"But Betty's just started in at housekeeping, and she would forget so much."

"Betty started in full six months ago. And the world swings round so fast I dare say what she learns will be as old-fashioned as the hills in a few years. I didn't do the way my mother taught me—husband used to laugh me out of it. She'll have time enough to learn."

The tea, a biscuit, and a piece of pie came in in tempting array. Aunt Priscilla was at her second cup when Jonas Field arrived, good ten minutes before the time.

"You come over to-morrow, Betty," said Aunt Priscilla. "You and Dorothy just take a run; it'll do you good. That child will turn into a book next. She's got some of the Adams streaks in her. And girls don't need so much book learning. Solomon's wise, and he don't even know his letters."

That made Doris laugh. She was getting quite used to Aunt Priscilla. She rose and made a pretty courtesy, and said she would like to come.

Polly had forgotten to light the lamp. She had been nursing Solomon, and the fire had burned low. Aunt Priscilla scolded, to be sure. Polly was getting rather deaf as well.

"It's warm out in the kitchen," said Polly.

"I want it warm here. I aint going to begin to save on firing at my time of life! I have enough to last me out, and I don't suppose anybody will thank me for the rest. Bring in some logs."

Aunt Priscilla sat with a shawl around her until the cheerful warmth began to diffuse itself and the blaze lightened up the room. Polly out in the kitchen was rehearsing her woes to Solomon.

"It's my 'pinion if missus lives much longer she'll be queerer'n Dick's hatband. That just wouldn't lay anyhow, I've heerd tell, though I don't know who Dick was and what he'd been doing, but he was mighty queer. 'Pears to me he must a-lived before the war when General Washington licked the English. And there's no suitin' missus. First it's too hot and you're 'stravagant, then it's too cold and she wants to burn up all the wood in creation!"

Aunt Priscilla watched the flame of the dancing scarlet, blue, and leaping white-capped arrows that shot up, and out of the side of one eye she saw a picture on the end of the braided rug—a little girl with a cloud of light curls sitting there with a great gray cat in her lap. The room was so much less lonely then. Perhaps she was getting old, real old, with a weakness for human kind. Was that a sign? She did enjoy the runs over to the Leveretts'. What would happen if she should not be able to go out!

She gave a little shudder over that. Of all the large family of sisters and brothers there was no one living very near or dear to her. She was next to the youngest. They had all married, some had died, one brother had gone to the Carolinas and found the climate so agreeable he had settled there. One sister had gone back to England. There were some nieces and nephews, but in the early part of her married life Mr. Perkins *had* objected to any of them making a home at his house. "We have no children of our own," he said, "and I take it as a sign that if the Lord had meant us to care for any, he would have sent them direct to us, and not had us taking them in at second-hand."

They had both grown selfish and only considered their own wants and comforts. But the years of solitude looked less and less inviting to the woman, who had been born with a large social side that had met with a pinch here, been lopped off there, and crowded in another person's measure. If the person had not been upright, scrupulously just in his dealings, and a good provider, that would have altered her respect for him. And wives were to obey their husbands, just as children were trained to obey their parents.

But children were having ideas of their own now. Well, when she was sixteen she went to Marblehead and spent a summer with her sister Esther, who was having hard times then with her flock of little children, and who a few years after had given up the struggle. Mr. Green had married again and gone out to the lake countries and started a sawmill, where there were forests to his hand.

But this long-ago summer had been an epoch in her life. She had baked and brewed, swept and scrubbed, cooked and put in her spare time spinning, while poor Esther sewed and took care of a very cross pair of twins and crawled about a little. There had been some merrymaking that would hardly have been allowed at home, and a young man who had sat on the doorstep and talked, who had taken her driving, and with whom she had wickedly and frivolously danced one afternoon when a party of young people had a merrymaking after the hay was in. It was the only time in her life she had ever danced, and it was a glimpse of fairy delight to her. But she was frightened half to death when she came home, and began to have two sides to her life, and she had never gotten rid of the other side.

She had a vague idea that next summer she would go again. Meanwhile Mr. Perkins began to come. There was an older sister, and no one surmised it was Priscilla, until in March, when he spoke to Priscilla's father.

"I declare I was clear beat," said the worthy parent. "Seems to me Martha would be more suitable, but his heart's set on Priscilla. He's a good, steady man, forehanded and all that, and will make her a good husband, and she'll keep growing older. There is nothing to say against it."

The idea that Priscilla would say anything was not entertained for a moment. Mr. Perkins began to walk home from church with her and come to tea on Sunday evening, and it was soon noised about that they were keeping steady company. Martha went to Marblehead that summer and one of the twins died. In the fall Priscilla was married and went to housekeeping in King Street, over her husband's place of business. She was engrossed with her life, but she dreamed sometimes of the other side and the young man who had remarked upon the gowns she wore and put roses in her hair, and she had ideas of lace and ribbons and the vanities of the world in that early married period. Her attire was rich but severely plain; she was not stinted in anything. She was even allowed to "lay by" on her own account, which meant saving up a little money. She made a good, careful wife. And some months before he died, touched by her attentive care, her husband said:

"Silla, I don't see but you might as well have all I'm worth, as to divide it round in the family. They will be disappointed, I suppose, but they haven't earned nor saved. You have been a good wife, and you just take your comfort on it when I'm gone. Then if you should feel minded to give back some of it —why, that's your affair."

The Perkins family had *not* liked it very well. They knew Aunt Priscilla would marry again, and all that money go to a second husband. But she had not married, though there had been opportunities. Later on she almost wished she had. She had entertained plans of taking a girl to bring up, and had considered this little orphaned Adams girl,—who she had imagined in a vague way would be glad of a good home with a prospect of some money,—if she behaved herself rightly. She had pictured a stout, red-cheeked girl who needed training, and not a fine little lady like Doris Adams.

But she was glad Doris had sat there on the rug with the cat in her lap. And she was glad there had been the summer at Marblehead, and the young man who had said more with his eyes than with his lips. He had never married, and had been among the earliest to lay down his life for his country. She always felt that in a way he belonged to her. And if in youth she had had one good time, why shouldn't Betty? Perhaps Betty might marry in some sensible way that would be for the best, and this visit at Hartford would illume all her life.

There were things about it she had never confessed. When her conscience upbraided her mightily she called them sins and prayed over them. There were other matters—the white bonnet had been one. She had purchased it of a friend who was going in mourning, who had made her try it on, and said:

"Just look at yourself in the glass, Priscilla Perkins. You never had anything half so becoming. You look five years younger!"

She did look in the glass. She could have pirouetted around the room in delight. She was in love with her pretty youthful face.

So she bought the hat—at a bargain, of course. She put it away when it came home, and visited it surreptitiously, but somehow never had the courage to confess, or to propose wearing it, though other women of her age indulged in as much and more gayety. In the spring she bought a new silk gown, a gray with a kind of lilac tint, and cut off the breadths to make sure of it.

Mr. Perkins viewed it critically.

"I'm not quite certain, Priscilla, that it is appropriate. And a brown would give you so much more good wear. It looks too—too youthful."

He never remembered there were fifteen years between himself and Priscilla.

"I—I think I would change it."

"Oh," with the best accent of regret she could assume, "I have cut off the breadths and begun to sew them up. It's the spring color. And summer is coming."

"Uu—um——" with a reluctant nod.

She wore it to a christening and a wedding, but the real delight in it had to be smothered. And when her husband proposed she should have it dyed she laid it away.

There were other foolish indulgences. Bows and artificial flowers that she had put on bonnets and worn in her own room with locked doors, then pulled them off and laid them away. She was so fond of pretty things, gay things, the pleasures of life—and she was always relegated to the prose! Other people wore finery with a serene calmness, and went about their daily duties, to church, on missions of mercy, and were well thought of. Where was the sin? Her clothes cost quite as much. Mr. Perkins was a close manager but not stingy with his wife.

She used to think she would confess to her mother about the dancing, but she never had. She ought to bring out these "sins of the eye" and lay them before her husband, but she never found the right moment and the courage. She had meant to deal them out to the Leverett girls, especially Electa—but Electa seemed to prosper so amazingly! She *must* do something with them, and clear up her life, sweep, and garnish before the summons came. She was getting to be old now, and if she went off suddenly someone would come in and take possession and scatter her treasures. Likely as not it would be the Perkinses, for she hadn't made any will.

Why shouldn't Betty have some of them and go off on her good time. It wouldn't be housekeeping and spinning and looking after fractious children. But those evenings out on the stoop, and the timid invitations to take a walk, the pressure of the hand, the smile out of the eyes—oh, why——

All her life she had been asking "Why?"—taking the hard and distasteful because she thought there was a virtue in it, not because she had been trained to believe goodness must have a severe side and that really pleasant things were wicked. The "Whys" had never been answered, much as she had prayed about them.

She would never take the girl to bring up now. As for Doris Adams—Cousin Winthrop would be thinking presently that the ground wasn't good enough for her to walk on. So there was only Betty, unless she took up some of the

Perkins girls. Abby was rather nice. But, after all, her father was only a half-brother to Aunt Priscilla's husband. And she must make that will.

"Missus, aint you goin' to come to supper? I told you 'twas ready full five minutes ago," said an aggrieved voice.

Aunt Priscilla sprang up and gave herself a kind of mental shaking. She stepped around to avoid the little girl on the rug with the cat in her lap. Polly went on grumbling. The toast was cold, the tea had drawn too long, and for once the mistress never said a word in dispraise.

"She's goin' off," thought Polly. "That's a bad sign, though she does sit over the fire a good deal, and you can't tell by that. Land alive! I hope she'll live my time out, or I'll sure have to go to the poorhouse!"

Aunt Priscilla went back to her fire and the vision of the little girl who had made a curious impression on her by a kind of sweetness quite new in her experience. It had disturbed her greatly. Nothing about the child had been as she supposed.

Everybody went down to her, which meant that she had some subtle, indescribable charm, but Aunt Priscilla would have said she had no dictionary words to explain it, though there had been a speller and definer in her day.

The little girl had come to "seven times" in the tables. She had studied an hour, when Betty said they had better go and get back by dark. Jamie boy gave a little "snicker" as she shut her book. The disdain of her young compeer was quite hard to bear, but she meekly accepted the fact that she "wasn't smart." If she had known how he longed to go with them, she would have felt quite even, but he kept that to himself.

All Boston was still hooded in snow, for every few days there came a new fall. Oh, how beautiful it was! Everybody walked in the middle of the street, —it was so hard and smooth,—though you had to keep turning out for vehicles, but one didn't meet them very often.

Boots were not made high for girls and women then, but everybody had a pair of thick woolen stockings, some of them with a leather sole on the outside, which was more durable. The children pulled them well up over their knees and kept good and warm. Some people had leather leggings, but rubber boots had not been invented.

Boys were out snowballing—girls, too, for that matter. Someone sent a ball that flew all over Doris, but she only laughed. She snowballed with little James now and then.

So they were bright and merry when they reached the sign of "Jonas Field," and Doris gave her pretty, rather formal greeting. She was never quite sure of Aunt Priscilla.

"I suppose *you* came to see Solomon!" exclaimed that lady.

"Not altogether," replied Doris.

"Well, he is out in the kitchen. And, Betty, what is the prospect to-day?"

"Oh, Aunt Priscilla, I almost think I'll get off. Father is on my side, and mother did really promise 'Lecty last summer. Mother couldn't get along alone, you know, and Jimmie boy is doing so well at school that she would like to keep him all winter. Father knows of a girl who would be very glad to come in and work for three dollars a month, though he says everybody gives four or more. But Mr. Eastman will be here so soon. Father said I might get some things in Hartford."

"We'll see what Boston has first," returned Aunt Priscilla with a little snort. "I've been hunting over *my* things."

People in those days thought it a great favor to have clothes left to them, as you will see by old wills. And occasionally the grandmothers brought out garments beforehand, and did not wait until they were dead and gone.

"I have a silk gown that I never wore above half a dozen times. I could have it dyed, I suppose, but they're so apt to get stringy afterward. Maybe you wouldn't like it because it's a kind of gray. You're free to leave it alone. I shan't be a mite put out."

The old spirit of holding on reasserted itself. Of course, if Betty didn't like it, *her* duty would be done.

"Oh, Aunt Priscilla! It looks like moonlight over the harbor. It's beautiful."

The elder woman had shaken it out and made ripples with it, and Betty stood in admiring wonderment. It looked to her like a wedding gown, but she knew Aunt Priscilla's had been Canton crape, dyed brown first and then black and then worn out. There was an old adage to the effect that one never could get rich until one's wedding clothes were worn out.

"It's spotted some, I find—just a faint kind of yellow, but that may cut out. I never had any good of it," and she sighed. "It isn't what you might call gay; but, land alive! I might as well have bought bright red! There's plenty of it to make over. They weren't wearing such skimping skirts then, and I had an extra breadth put in so that it would all fade alike. Well——" And she gave a half-reluctant sigh.

"Why, I feel as if it ought to be saved for a wedding gown," declared Betty, her eyes alight with pleasure. "It's the most beautiful thing. Oh, Aunt

Priscilla!"

A modern girl would have thrown her arms around Aunt Priscilla's neck and kissed her, if one could imagine a modern girl being grateful for a gown a quarter of a century old, except for masquerading purposes. People who could remember the great Jonathan Edwards awakening still classed all outward demonstrations of regard as carnal affections to be subdued. The poor old life hungered now for a little human love without understanding what its want really was, just as it had hungered for more than half a century.

"Well, child, maybe 'Lecty can plan to make something out of it. You better just take it to her. And here's a box of ribbons, things I've had no use for this many a year. You see I had a way of saving up—I didn't have much call for wearing such."

Aunt Priscilla felt that she was renouncing idols. How many times she had fingered these things with exquisite love and longing and a desire to wear them! Madam Bowdoin, almost ten years older, wore her fine ribbons and laces and her own snowy white hair in little rings about her forehead. No one accused her of aping youth. Aunt Priscilla had worn a false front under her cap for many a year that was now a rusty, faded brown. Her own white hair was cut off close.

"Oh, Aunt Priscilla, I think my ship has come in from the Indies. I never can thank you enough. I'm so glad you saved them. You see, times *are* hard, and if father had to pay a girl for taking my place at home, he wouldn't feel that he could afford me much finery. And the journey, too. But I have only to pay from Springfield to Boston, for Mr. Eastman has his own conveyance—a nice big covered sleigh. And now all these beautiful things! I feel as rich as a queen."

Doris had been standing there big-eyed and never once asked for Solomon.

Aunt Priscilla began to fold the gown. It still had a crackle and rustle delightful to hear. And there was a roll of new pieces.

"Why, next summer I could have a lovely drawn bonnet—only it *does* cost so much to have one made. I wish I knew how," said Betty.

"I suppose—you don't want to see my old thing?" rather contemptuously.

"The hat, do you mean? Oh, I just should! I've thought so much about it, and how queer it is that old-fashioned articles should come round."

"Every seven years, people say; but I don't believe it's quite as often as that."

From the careful way it was pinned up, one would never imagine it had been out that very morning. The bows were filled with paper to keep them up, and bits of paper crumpled up around, so they could not be crushed. Its days of whiteness were over, but it was the loveliest, softest cream tint, and looked as if it had just come over from France. The beaver was almost like plush, and the puffed satin lining inside was as fresh as if its reverse plaits had just been laid in place.

"Oh, do put it on!" cried Doris eagerly.

Betty held the strings together under her fair round chin.

"You look like a queen!" said the child admiringly.

"Why it *is* just as they are wearing them now, the tip-top style. 'Lecty couldn't have described this hat any better if she had seen it. And if I can have it, Aunt Priscilla, I shall not care a bit about feathers. It's beautiful enough without."

"Yes, yes, take them all and have a good time with them. Now you see if you can pack it up—you'll have to learn."

Aunt Priscilla dropped into her chair. She had cast out her life's temptations, and it had been a great struggle.

"Not that way—make the bow stand up. The bandbox is large enough. And give the strings a loose fold, so. Now put that white paper over. It's like making a gambrel roof. Then bring up the ends of the towel and pin them. Polly shall go along and carry it home for you."

"I'm a thousand times obliged. I wish I knew what to do in return."

"Have a good time, but don't forget that a good time is not all to life. Child—why do you look at me so?" for Doris had come close to Aunt Priscilla and seemed studying her.

"Were you ever a little girl, and what was your good time like?"

Doris' wondering eyes were soft and seemed more pitying than curious.

"No, I never was a little girl. There were no little girls in my time." She jerked the words out in a spasmodic way, and put her hand to her heart as if there was a pain or pressure. "When I was three year old I had to take care of my little brother. I stood up on a bench to wash dishes when I was four, and scoured milk-pans and the pewter plates we used then. And at six I was spinning on the little wheel and knitting stockings. I went to school part of every year, and at thirteen I was doing a woman's work. No, I never was a little girl."

Doris put her soft hand over the one that had been strained and made coarse and large in the joints, and roughened as to skin while yet it was in its tender youth. And all the pay there had been from her father's estate had been three hundred dollars to each girl, the remainder being divided evenly among the boys. She felt suddenly grateful to Hatfield Perkins for the easier times of her married life.

"Now, both of you go out in the kitchen and get a piece of Polly's fresh gingerbread. She hasn't lost her art in that yet. Then you must run off home, for it will soon be dark, and Betty will be needed about the supper."

The gingerbread was splendid. Doris broke off little crumbs and fed them to Solomon, and told him sometime she would come and spend the afternoon with him. She should be so lonesome when Betty went away.

Polly carried the bandbox and bundle for them, and Betty took the box of ribbons. Aunt Priscilla brought out the light-stand and set her candle on it and turned over the leaves of her old Bible to read about the daughters of Zion with their tinkling feet and their cauls and their round tires like the moon, the chains and the bracelets and the bonnets, the earrings, the mantles, the wimples and the crisping pins, the fine linen and the hoods and the veils—and all these were to be done away with! To be sure she did not really know what they all were, but her few had been snares and a source of secret idolatry for years and years. She had nothing to do now but to consider the end of all things and prepare for it. But there was the dreaded will yet to make. If only there was someone who really cared about her!

CHAPTER X

CONCERNING MANY THINGS

When Providence overruled, in the early part of the century, people generally gave in. The stronger tide was called Providence. Perhaps there was a small degree of fatalism in it. So Mrs. Leverett acquiesced, and recalled the fact that she had promised Electa that Betty should come.

Aunt Priscilla's generosity was astonishing. The silken gown would not be made over until Betty reached Hartford. She worked industriously on her white one, but her mother found so many things for her to do. Then Martha Grant came—a stout, hearty, pink-cheeked country girl who knew how to "take hold," and was glad of an opportunity to earn something toward a wedding gown. Doris was so interested that she hardly remembered how much she should miss Betty, though Warren promised to help her with her lessons.

So the trunk was packed. Luckily the bandbox could go in it, for it was quite small. Most of the bandboxes were immense affairs in which you could stow a good many things besides the bonnet. Then they had a calico cover with a stout cord run through the hem.

Mr. Eastman looked rather askance at the trunk—he had so many budgets of his own, and for his wife. However, they strapped it on the back securely, and the good-bys were uttered for a whole month.

Doris had said hers in the morning. She could not divest herself of a vague presentiment that something would happen to keep Betty until to-morrow. But Martha was to sit in her place at the table.

Now that the reign of slavery was over, the farmers' girls from the country often came in for a while. They were generally taken in as one of the family —indeed, few of them would have come to be put down to the level of a common servant. Many had their old slaves still living with them, and numbers of the quality preferred colored servants.

Jamie boy went out to snowball after dinner. Doris worked a line across her sampler. She was going to begin the alphabet next. There were three kinds of letters. Ordinary capitals like printing, small letters, and writing capitals. These were very difficult, little girls thought.

She put up her work presently, studied her spelling, and went over "nine times." She could say the ten and eleven perfectly, but that very day she had missed on "nine times," and Mrs. Webb told her she had better study it a little more.

"I do wonder if you will ever get through with the multiplication tables!" said Aunt Elizabeth.

Doris sighed. It was hard to be so slow at learning.

"'Nine times' floored me pretty well, I remember," confessed Martha Grant. "There's great difference in children. Some have heads for figures and some don't. My sister Catharine could go all round me. But she's that dumb about sewing—I don't believe you ever saw the beat! She just hates it. She'd like to teach school!"

Doris was very glad to hear that someone else had been slow.

Betty had been out to tea occasionally, and Doris tried to make believe it was so now. They would have missed her more but Martha was a great talker. There were seven children at the Grants', and one son married. They had a big farm and a good deal of stock. Martha's lover had bought a farm also, with a small old house of two rooms. *He* had to build a new barn, so they would wait for their house. She had a nice cow she had raised, a flock of twelve geese, and her father had promised her the old mare and another cow. She wanted to be married by planting time. She had a nice feather bed and two pairs of pillows and five quilts, beside two wool blankets.

Mrs. Leverett was a good deal interested in all this. It took her back to her own early life. City girls *did* come to have different ideas. There was something refreshing in this very homeliness.

Martha knit and sewed as fast as she talked. Mrs. Leverett said "she didn't let the grass grow under her feet," and Doris wondered if she would tread it out in the summer. Of course, it couldn't grow in the winter.

"Aunt Elizabeth," she said presently, in a sad little voice, "am I to sleep all alone?"

"Oh dear, no. You would freeze to an icicle. Martha will take Betty's place."

They wrapped up a piece of brick heated pretty well when Doris went to bed. For it was desperately cold. But the soft feathers came up all around one, and in a little while she was as warm as toast. She did not even wake when Martha came to bed. Sometimes Betty cuddled the dear little human ball, and only half awake Doris would return the hug and find a place to kiss, whether it was cheek or chin.

"Aunt Elizabeth," when she came in from school one day, "do you know that Christmas will be here soon—next Tuesday?"

"Well, yes," deliberately, "it is supposed to be Christmas."

"But it really is," with child-like eagerness. "The day on which Christ was born."

"The day that is kept in commemoration of the birth of Christ. But some people try to remember every day that Christ cams to redeem the world. So that one day is not any better than another."

Doris looked puzzled. "At home we always kept it," she said slowly. "Miss Arabella made a Christmas cake and ever so many little ones. The boys came around to sing Noël, and they were given a cake and a penny, and we went to church."

"Yes; it is quite an English fashion. When you are a larger girl and more used to our ways you will understand why we do not keep it."

"Don't you really keep it?" in surprise.

"No, my dear."

The tone was kind, but not encouraging to further enlightenment. Doris experienced a great sense of disappointment. For a little while she was very homesick for Betty. To have her away a whole month! And a curious thing was that no one seemed really to miss her and wish her back. Mrs. Leverett scanned the weather and the almanac and hoped they would get safely to Springfield without a storm. Mr. Leverett counted up the time. It had not stormed yet.

No Christmas and no Betty. Not even a wise old cat like Solomon, or a playful, amusing little kitten. The school children stared when she talked about Christmas.

Two big tears fell on her book. She was frightened, for she had not meant to cry. And now a sense of desolation rushed over her. Oh, what could she do without Betty!

Then a sleigh stopped at the door. She ran to the window, and when she saw that it was Uncle Winthrop she was out of the door like a flash.

"Well, little one?" he said in pleasant inquiry, which seemed to comprehend a great deal. "How do you get along without Betty? Come in out of the cold. I've just been wondering if you would like to come over and keep Christmas with me. I believe they do not have any Christmas here."

"No, they do not. Oh, Uncle Win, I should be so glad to come, if I wouldn't trouble you!"

The eyes were full of entreating light.

"I have been thinking about it a day or two. And Recompense is quite willing. The trouble really would be hers, you know."

"I would try and not make any trouble."

"Oh, it was where we should put you to sleep this cold weather. You would be lost in the great guest chamber. But Recompense arranged it all. She has put up a little cot in the corner of her room. I insisted last winter that she should keep a fire; she is a little troubled with rheumatism. And now she enjoys the warmth very much."

"Oh, how good you are!"

She was smiling now and dancing around on one foot. He smiled too.

"Where's Aunt Elizabeth?" said Uncle Winthrop.

Doris ran to the kitchen and, not seeing her, made the same inquiry.

"She's gone up to the storeroom to find a lot of woolen patches for me, and I'm going to start another quilt. She said she'd never use them in the days of creation, and they wan't but six. She'll be down in a minute," said Martha.

"Uncle Winthrop," going back to him beside the fire, and wrinkling up her brow a little, "is not Christmas truly Christmas? Has anyone made a mistake about it?"

"My child, everybody does not keep it in the same manner. Sometime you will learn about the brave heroes who came over and settled in a strange land, fought Indians and wild beasts, and then fought again for liberty, and why they differed from their brethren. But I always keep it; and I thought now that Betty was gone you might like to come and go to church with me."

"Oh, I shall be glad to!" with a joyful smile.

Aunt Elizabeth entered. Cousin Winthrop presented his petition that he should take Doris over this afternoon and bring her back on Wednesday, unless there was to be no school all the week.

"I'm afraid she will bother Recompense. You're so little used to children. I keep my hand in with grandchildren," smilingly.

"No word from Betty yet? About Doris now—oh, you need not be afraid; I think Recompense is quite in the notion."

"Well, if you think best. Doris isn't a mite of trouble, I will say that. No, we can't hear from Betty before to-morrow. Mr. Eastman thought likely he'd find someone coming right back from Springfield, and I charged Betty to send if she could. I'm glad there has been no snow so far."

"Very fair winter weather. How is Foster and business?"

"Desperately dull, both of them," and Mrs. Leverett gave a piquant nod that would have done Betty credit.

"Go get your other clothes, Doris, and Martha will see to you. And two white aprons. Recompense keeps her house as clean as a pink, and you couldn't get soiled if you rolled round the floor. But dirt doesn't stick to Doris. There, run along, child."

Martha scrubbed her rigorously, and then helped her dress. She came back bright as a new pin, with her two high-necked aprons in her hand, and her nightgown, which Aunt Elizabeth put in her big black camlet bag.

"I wish you'd see that she studies a little, Winthrop. She is so behind in some things."

He nodded. Then Doris put on her hood and cloak and said good-by to Martha, while she kissed Aunt Elizabeth and left a message for the rest.

"It's early, so we will take a little ride around," he said, wrapping her up snug and warm.

The plan had been in his mind for several days. The evening before he had broached it to Recompense. Not but what he was master in his own house, but he hardly knew how to plan for a child.

"If Doris was a boy I could put him on the big sofa in my room. Still, Cato can look after a fire in the guest chamber. It would be too cruel to put a child alone in that great cold barn."

There was a very obstinate impression that it was healthy to sleep in cold rooms, so people shut themselves up pretty close, and sometimes drew the bedclothes over their heads. But Winthrop Adams had a rather luxurious side to his nature; he called it a premonition of old age. He kept a fire in his dressing room, where he often sat and read a while at night. His sleeping room adjoined it.

"Why, we might bring a cot in my room," she said. "I remember how the child delights in a fire. She's such a delicate-looking little thing."

"She is standing our winter very well and goes to school every day. I'm afraid she might disturb you?"

"Not if she has a bed by herself. And there is the corner jog; the cot will just fit into it."

When they put it there in the morning it looked as if it must have taken root long ago. Then Recompense arranged a nice dressing table with a white cover and a pretty bowl and ewer, and a low chair beside it covered with chintz cushions. Her own high-post bedstead had curtains all around it of English damask, and the curiously carved high-back chairs had cushions tied in of the same material. There was no carpet on the painted floor, but a rug beside the bed and one at the stand, and a great braided square before the fire. It was a well-furnished room for the times, though that of Mr. Adams was rather more luxurious.

He was very glad that Recompense had assented so readily, for he was beginning to feel that he ought to take a deeper interest in his little ward.

There were numberless sleighs out on some of the favorite thoroughfares. For even now, in spite of the complaints of hard times, there was a good deal of real wealth in Boston, fine equipages with colored coachmen and footmen. There were handsome houses with lawns and gardens, some of them having orchards besides. There were rich furnishings as well, from France and England and from the East. There were china and plate and glass proud of their age, having come through several generations.

And though there were shades and degrees of social position, there was a fine breeding among the richer people and a kind of pride among the poorer ones. There were occasions when they mingled with an agreeable courtesy, yet each side kept its proper and distinctive relations; real worth was respected and dignified living held in esteem. From a printer's boy, Benjamin Franklin had stood before kings and added luster to his country. From a farm at Braintree had come one of the famous Adamses and his not less notable wife, who had admirably filled the position of the first lady of the land.

Yet the odd, narrow, crooked streets of a hundred years before were running everywhere, occasionally broadened and straightened. There were still wide spaces and pasture fields, declivities where the barberry bush and locust and May flower grew undisturbed. There were quaint nooks with legends, made famous since by eloquent pens; there were curious old shops designated by queer sign and symbols.

But even the pleasures were taken in a leisurely, dignified way. There was no wild rush to stand at the head or to outdo a neighbor, or astonish those who might be looking on and could not participate.

Doris enjoyed it wonderfully. She had a sudden accession of subtle pride when some fine old gentleman bowed to Uncle Win, or a sleigh full of elegantly attired ladies smiled and nodded. There were large hats framing in pretty faces, and bows and nodding plumes on the top such as Mrs. King had written about. Oh, how lovely Betty would look in hers! What was Hartford like; and New Haven, with its college; then, farther on, New York; and

Washington, where the Presidents lived while they held office? She was learning so many things about this new home.

Over here on the Common the boys were drawn up in two lines and snowballing as if it was all in dead earnest. And this was the rambling old house with its big porch and stepping block, and its delightful welcome.

"Are you not most frozen?" asked Miss Recompense. "Here is the fire you like so much. Take off your cloak and hood. We are very glad to have you come and make us a visit."

"Oh, are you?" Doris' face was a gleam of delight. "And I am glad to come. I was beginning to feel dreadfully lonesome without Betty. I ought not when there were so many left," and a bright color suffused her face. "Then there is little James."

"And we have no small people."

"I never had any over home, you know. And so many people here have such numbers of brothers and sisters. It must be delightful."

"But they are not all little at once."

"No," laughed Doris. "I should like to be somewhere in the middle. Babies are so cunning, when they don't cry."

Miss Recompense smiled at that.

There was a comfortable low chair for Doris, and Uncle Win found her seated there, the ruddy firelight throwing up her face like a painting. Miss Recompense went out to see about the supper. There was a good-natured black woman in the kitchen to do the cooking, and Cato, who did the outside work and waited on Dinah and Miss Recompense—a tall, sedate, rather pompous colored man.

Some indefinable charm about the house appealed to Doris. The table was arranged in such an attractive manner. Nothing could be more delightful than Aunt Elizabeth's cooking, but she stopped short at an invisible something. The china was saved for company, though there was one pretty cup they always gave to Aunt Priscilla. The everyday dishes were earthen, such as ordinary people used, and being of rather poor glaze they soon checked. Doris knew these pretty plates and the tall cream jug and sugar dish had not been brought out especially for her, though she had supposed they were when they all came over to a company tea.

She started so when Uncle Winthrop addressed her in French, and glanced at him in amaze; then turned to a pink glow and laughed as she collected her scattered wits to answer.

What a soft, exquisite accent the child had! Miss Recompense paused in her pouring tea to listen.

Uncle Win smiled and continued. They were around the pretty tea table in a sort of triangle. Uncle Win passed the thin, dainty slices of bread. Miss Recompense, when she was done with the tea, passed the cold chicken. Then there were cheese and two kinds of preserves, plain cake and fruit cake.

Children rarely drank tea, so Doris had some milk in a glass which was cut with just a sparkle here and there that the light caught and made brilliant.

"How you _can_ understand any such talk as that beats me," said Miss Recompense in a sort of helpless fashion as she glanced from one to the other.

"And if we were abroad talking English the forsigners would say the same thing," replied Mr. Adams.

"But there is some sense in English."

He laughed a little. "And if we lived in China we would think there was a good deal of sense in Chinese, which is said to be one of the queerest languages in the world."

We did not know very much about China in those days, and our knowledge was chiefly gleaned from rather rude maps and some old histories, and the wonderful tales of sea captains.

"It would be a pity for you to fall back when you are such a good scholar," Uncle Win said, looking over to Doris. "One forgets quite easily. I find I am a little lame. But you like your school, and it is near by this cold weather. Perhaps you and I can keep up enough interest to exercise our memories. You have some French books?"

"Two or three. I tried to read 'Paul and Virginia' to Betty, but it took so long to tell the story over that she didn't get interested. There were so many lessons, too."

She did not say that Aunt Elizabeth had discountenanced it. People were horrified by French novels in those days. Rousseau and Voltaire had been held in some degree responsible for the terrible French Revolution. And people shuddered at the name of Tom Paine.

At first the Colonies, as they were still largely called, had been very much interested in the new French Republic. Lafayette had been so impressed with the idea of a government of the people when he had lent his assistance to America, that he had joined heartily in a plan for the regeneration of France. But after the king was executed, Sunday abolished, and the government passed into the hands of tyrants who shouted "liberty" and yet brought about the slavery of terror, he and many others had stood aside—indeed, left their beloved city to the mob. Then had come the first strong and promising theories of Napoleon. He had been first Consul, then Consul for life, then Emperor, and was now the scourge of Europe.

To Mrs. Leverett all French books were as actors and plays, to be shunned. That any little girl should have read a French story or be able to repeat French verses was quite horrifying. She had a feeling that it really belittled the Bible to appear in the French language.

"Yes," returned Uncle Winthrop assentingly. He could understand the situation, for he knew Mrs. Leverett's prejudices were very strong, and continuous. That she was a thoroughly good and upright woman he readily admitted.

The supper being finished they went to the cozy hall fire again. You had to sit near it to keep comfortable, for the rooms were large in those days and the outer edges chilly. Some people were putting up great stoves in their halls and the high pipes warmed the stairs and all around.

Miss Recompense brought out some knitting. She was making a spread in small squares,—red, white, and blue,—and it would be very fine when it was done. Doris was very much interested when she laid down the squares to display the pattern.

"I suppose you knit?" remarked Miss Recompense.

"No. I don't know how. Betty showed me a little. And Aunt Elizabeth is going to teach me to make a stocking. It seems very easy when you see other people do it," and Doris sighed. "But I am afraid I am not very smart about a good many things besides tables."

That honest admission rather annoyed Uncle Win. Elizabeth had said it as well. For his part he did not see that reading the Bible through by the time you were eight years old and knitting a pile of stockings was proof of extraordinary ability.

"What kind of fancy work can you do?" asked Miss Recompense.

"I've begun a sampler. That isn't hard. And Miss Arabella taught me to hem and to darn and to make lace."

"Make lace! What kind of lace?"

"Like the beautiful lace Madam Sheafe makes. Only I never did any so wide. But Miss Arabella used to. Betty took me there one afternoon. Madam Sheafe has such a lovely little house. And, oh, Uncle Win, she can talk French a little."

He smiled and nodded.

"You see," began Doris with sweet seriousness, "there was no one to make shirts for, and I suppose Miss Arabella thought it wasn't worth while. But I hemmed some on Uncle Leverett's, and Aunt Elizabeth said it was very nicely done."

"I dare say." She looked as if anything she undertook would be nicely done, Miss Recompense thought.

"Betty was learning housekeeping when she went to Hartford. I think that is very nice. To make pies and bread and cake, and roast chickens and turkeys and everything. But little girls have to go to school first. Six years is a long time, isn't it?"

A half-smile crossed the grave face of Miss Recompense.

"It seems a long time to a little girl, no doubt, but when you are older it passes very rapidly. There are years that prove all too short for the work crowded in them, and then they begin to lengthen again, though I suppose that is because we no longer hurry to get a certain amount of work done."

"I wish the afternoons could be longer."

"They will be in May. I like the long afternoons too, though the winter evenings by a cheerful fire are very enjoyable."

"The world is so beautiful," said Doris, "that you can hardly tell which you do like best. Only the summer, with its flowers and the sweet, green out-of-doors, fills one with a kind of thanksgiving. Why did they not have Thanksgiving in the summer?"

"Because we give thanks for a bountiful harvest."

"Oh," Doris responded.

Uncle Winthrop watched her as she chattered on, her voice like a soft, purling rill. Presently Dinah called Miss Recompense out in the kitchen to consult her about the breakfast, for she went to bed as soon as she had the kitchen set to rights. Then Doris glanced over to him in a shy, asking fashion, and brought her chair to his side. He inquired about Father Langhorne, and found he had been educated in Paris, and was really a Roman priest.

Perhaps it was the province of childhood to see good in everybody. Or was it due to the simple life, the absence of that introspection, which had already done so much to make the New England conscience supersensitive and strenuous.

When Miss Recompense returned she found them deep in French again. Doris laughed softly when Uncle Winthrop blundered a little, and perhaps he did it now and then purposely.

The big old clock that said "Forever, never!" long before Longfellow's time, measured off nine hours.

"It's funny," said Doris, "but I'm not a bit sleepy, and at Uncle Leverett's I almost nod, sometimes. Maybe it's the French."

"I should not wonder," and Uncle Win smiled.

"We will both go—it is about my time," remarked Miss Recompense. "Your uncle sits up all hours of the night."

"And would like to sleep all hours of the morning," he returned humorously, "but Miss Recompense won't let me. If she raises her little finger the whole house moves."

"Then she doesn't raise it very often," said that lady. "But it does seem a sin to sleep away good wholesome daylight."

There were some candlesticks on a kind of secretary with a shelf-like top, and she lighted one, stepping out in the kitchen to see that all was safe and to bid Cato lock up. When she returned the candle was sending out its cheerful beam, so she nodded to Doris, who said good-night to Uncle Winthrop and followed her.

Doris had an odd, company-like feeling. Her little bed was pretty, and the room had a fragrance of summer time, of roses and lavender. Miss Recompense stirred the fire and put on a big log. Then she sat down by the stand and read her nightly chapter, turning a little to give Doris a kind of privacy.

"I hope you will sleep well. Your uncle thought you would be lonesome in the guest chamber."

"I would ever so much rather be here. And the bed is so small and cunning, just the bed for a little girl. Thank you ever so many times."

She said her prayers and breathed a soft good-night to the fire. And though she did not feel strange nor sleepy, and wondered about Betty and a dozen other things, one of the last remembrances was the glimmer of the candle on the wall, and the soft rustling of the blaze, that said "Snow, snow, snow."

CHAPTER XI

A LITTLE CHRISTMAS

Sure enough, it snowed the next morning—one of the soft, clinging storms that loaded every branch with a furry aspect, made mounds of the shrubs, and wrapped the south sides of the houses with a mantle of dazzling whiteness. Now and then a patch fell off, and a long pendant would swing from the trees, and finally drop. It was a delight to see them.

The breakfast was laid on the same small table in use last night, but Cato brought in everything hot, and "waited" as Barby used at home. Uncle Winthrop said she looked bright as a rose, and her cheeks had a delicate pink.

Afterward he invited her in his study and told her she might look about and perhaps find a book to entertain herself with while he wrote some letters.

"Thank you. I hope I shall not disturb you."

"Oh, no." He felt somehow he could answer for her. She was so gentle in her movements, and he really wanted to see how he liked having a little girl about. There was a vague idea in his mind that he might decide to have her here some day, since Miss Recompense had taken a sort of fancy to her.

Oh, what a luxury it was to wander softly about and read titles and look at bindings and speculate on what she would like! They had very few books at Uncle Leverett's. Some volume of sermons, a few biographies that she had found rather dreary, a history of the French-Canadian War, and some of Poor Richard's Almanacs, which she thought the most amusing of all.

There was a circulating library that Warren patronized occasionally. There was also the nucleus of a free library, but so far people had been too busy to think much about reading, except the scholarly minds. Books were expensive, too, and very few persons accumulated any stock of them. Of Mr. Adams' collection some had come to him from his father, and Cousin Charles, who had been called a "queer stick," had some English, Latin, and Italian poets that he had bequeathed to the book lover.

Winthrop Adams was a collector of several things beside books. Now and then at an auction sale on someone's death he picked up odd articles that were of value. And so his study was a kind of conglomerate. He had a cabinet of coins from different parts of the world and curios from India and Egypt. Napoleon's campaign in Egypt had awakened a good deal of interest in the country of the Pharaohs.

Doris was so still he glanced around presently. She was curled up in the corner of the chimney, a book on her knees and her head bent over until the curls fell about her in a cloud. When Elizabeth had spoken of the benefit it might be to a growing child to have them cut he had protested at once. They were rarely beautiful, he decided now, gleaming gold in the firelight.

She had a feeling presently that someone was looking at her, so she raised her head, shook away the curls, and smiled.

"Did you find something?"

"'The Vicar of Wakefield,' Uncle Winthrop. Oh, it is delightful! You said I might read anything!" with a touch of hesitation.

"That was quite a wide permission," and he smiled. He couldn't see how that would hurt anyone, but he was not sure of a girl's reading.

"I opened it at a picture—'Preparing Moses for the Fair.' It made me think of Betty going to Hartford. It was so interesting to wonder what you would do, and then to have things happen just right. Aunt Priscilla was so nice. I thought I couldn't like her at first, but I do now. You can't find out all about anyone in a minute, can you?"

"I think not," rather humorously.

"So then I turned to the first of the book. And the Vicar's wife must have known a good deal to read without much spelling. There are some awful hard words in the back of Betty's spelling book. Do you suppose she learned tables and all that?"

"I don't believe she did."

"And she could keep house."

"They were a notable couple."

He took up his pen again and she turned to her book.

Suddenly a flood of golden sunshine poured across the floor, fairly dimming the fire.

"Oh, Uncle Winthrop!" With her book pressed tightly against her body, she flew over to the window like a bird, disturbing nothing, and making only a soft flutter.

"Isn't it glorious!"

The edges of the snow everywhere were illumined with the prismatic rays in proper order. The tree branches caught them, the corners of the houses, the window hoods, the straggling bushes, the fences. Everywhere the sublime beauty was repeated until everything quivered with the excess.

"It is like the New Jerusalem," she said.

The air had softened a great deal. The sun on the window panes spoke of latent warmth. A slight breeze stirred the air, and down came the clinging snow in showers, leaving the trees bare and brown, except the few evergreens.

"It is warmer," Mr. Adams said. "Though it is nearing noon, the warmest part of the day. And so far you have stood the cold weather very well, little Doris," smiling down in the eager face.

"I've snowballed too, and it is real fun. I can slide ever so far, and I've ridden on Jimmie boy's sled. Betty thinks I would soon learn to skate. I would like to very much."

"Then you must have some skates."

"But I am afraid Betty may not come home in time to teach me."

"Someone else might."

"Do you skate?" in soft inquiry.

"Not now; I used to. But I am not a young man, and not very energetic. I like warm firesides and a nice book. I am afraid I shall make an ease-loving old man."

"But isn't it right to be"—what word would express it?—"happy, comfortable? For why should you try to make anyone happy if it was wrong?"

"It is not wrong."

The sky was very blue now, and the snow began to have an ethereal look. Cato came out to shovel and clear away some paths. He struck the young hemlocks and firs with a stick and beat the snow out of them.

"The snow settles in the branches and sometimes freezes and that kills a little place," said Uncle Winthrop in answer to the questioning eyes.

They walked back to the table, with his arm over her shoulder.

"I am done my writing for to-day," he began. "I wonder if you would mind answering a few questions?"

"Oh, no—if I knew the answers," smilingly.

"Then tell me first of all how far you went in Latin. This is a grammar."

She turned some leaves. "I didn't know it very well," skimming over the pages. "It was not like this book, and"—hanging her head a little—"I did not like it—that and the sums."

"Who put you to studying it?"

"Oh, the father did. He said Latin was the key to all other languages. I wonder how many I shall have to learn? Miss Arabella said it was foolishness, except the French."

"Let me hear you read a little. This is not difficult."

He was not sure there was any call for a girl to know Latin. French seemed quite necessary.

She began in a hesitating manner and blundered somewhat at first, but as she went on gained courage, her voice growing firmer and clearer.

"Why, that is very well. You ought to be at a higher school than Mrs. Webb's. And now let us consider these dreadful sums. The paper and a pencil will do."

He put down quite a sum in addition. There were several nines and sevens in it.

She drew a long breath.

"It is a big sum. I haven't done any as large as that."

"Well, begin. Add as I call them off."

Alas! After three figures, in puzzling over an eight, the amount went out of her mind and she had to begin again. Uncle Winthrop made a mark at one figure and put down the amount beside it. After a while she reached the top of the column. Clearly heaven had not meant her for a mathematician. There was no rapport between her figures.

Her eyes were limpid, almost as if there were tears in them.

"Maybe that was pretty difficult for a little girl. I know most about big boys and young men."

"Betty just guesses, this way—eight and nine, and it comes quite as easy as if I had said two and three are five."

Uncle Win gave his gentle smile and it comforted her greatly.

"This quickness comes by practice. When you have had six years' study you may know as much as Betty in arithmetic, and you will know more in some other branches."

"If I can just know as much," she said wistfully.

Cato gave a gentle rap on the open door.

"Juno's ready," he announced. "Will master take little missy out, or shall I go for Master Cary?"

"I had not thought. Would you like to go, Doris?"

Her eyes answered him before she could speak.

"You may put in the other seat, Cato, and drive."

Cato bowed in a dignified manner.

"Now run and bundle up well," said Uncle Win.

Miss Recompense seemed to know a good deal about little girls, if she had none of her own. She tied a soft silk kerchief over Doris' ears before she put on her hood. Then she told Dinah to slip the soapstone in the foot-stove, and drew the long stockings up over her knees.

"Now you could go up to Vermont and not get cold," she said pleasantly.

But after all it was not so very cold. The sun shone in golden magnificence and almost dazzled your eyes out. Uncle Win had on his smoked glasses, and he looked very queer, but she saw other people with this protection. Some of the glasses were green.

The streets were really merry. Children were out with sleds, and snowballing parties were in the field. They went over to State Street for the mail. Cato sprang out and returned with quite a budget. There was one English letter with a big black seal, but Mr. Adams covered it quickly with the papers and drew the package under the buffalo robe.

There was a quaint old bookstore in Cornhill with the sign of Heart and Crown, that was quite a meeting place for students and bookish people, and they drove thither. A young lad came running out, making a bow and greeting his father politely. To have said "Hillo!" in those days would have been horrifying. And to have called one's father the "governor" or the "old gentleman" would have been little short of a crime.

"This is the little English cousin, Doris Adams," said Uncle Win, "and this is my son Cary."

Cary made a bow to her and said he was glad to meet her, then inquired after his father's health and stepped into the sleigh, picking up the reins and motioning Cato to the other side.

Oh, how they spun along! Cary said one or two things, but the words were carried away by the wind. There were sleighs full of ladies and children, great family affairs with three seats; there were cutters with some portly man and a black driver; there were well-known people and unknown people who were to come to the fore in a few years and be famous.

For Boston was throbbing even then with the mighty changes transforming her into a great city. Although she had suffered severely at the first of the war and held many priceless memories of it, the early evacuation of the town had left her free for domestic matters, which had prospered despite poverty and hard times and the great loss of population. Many of the old Tory families had returned to England, and the remnants of the provincial aristocracy were being lessened by death and absorbed by marriage. The squires and gentry of the small towns, most of them intense patriots, had filled their places and given tone to social life, that was still formal, if some of the old stateliness had slipped away.

The French Revolution had brought about some other changes. The State possessed fine advantages for maritime commerce, and all the seaports were veritable hives of industry in the early part of the century. This laid a foundation of respect for fortunes acquired by energy rather than inheritance. The United States, being the only neutral nation in the fierce conflicts raging round the world, had been reaping a rich harvest for several years. Sea captains and merchants had been thriving splendidly until the last year or two, when seizures began to be made by the British Government that roused a ferment of warlike spirit again.

But while men talked politics the women and those who thought it wiser to take neither side, still amused themselves with card parties, tea parties and dances, with now and then an evening at the theater, and driving. There were so many fine long roads not yet cut up into blocks that were great favorites on a day like this. Doris felt the exhilaration and her eyes shone like stars.

Presently Cary turned, and here they were at Common Street.

"That has been fine!" he began as he drew up to the door. "It sets your blood all a-sparkle. Have I taken your breath away, little cousin?"

He came around and offered his hand to his father. Then he lifted Doris as if she had been a feather, and stood her on the broad porch. That recalled Warren Leverett to her mind.

"It was splendid," answered Doris.

They all walked in together, and Cary shook hands cordially with Miss Recompense.

He was almost as tall as his father, with a fair, boyish face and thick light hair that did not curl, but tumbled about and was always falling over his forehead.

Warren was stouter and had more color, and there was a kind of laughing expression to his face. Cary's had a certain resolution and that loftiness we are given to calling aristocratic.

When Doris had carried the foot-stove to Dinah, and her own wraps upstairs, she stood for a moment uncertain. Cary and his father were talking eagerly in the study, so she sat down by the hall fire and began to think about the Vicar and Mrs. Primrose, and wanted to know what Moses did at the Fair. She had been at one town fair, but she could not recall much besides the rather quaintly and gayly dressed crowd. Then there was a summons to supper.

"Oh," cried Cary, "sit still a moment. You look like a page of Mother Goose. You can't be Miss Muffet, for you have no curds and whey, and you are not Jack Horner——"

She sprang up then and caught Uncle Winthrop's hand. "Nor Mother Goose," she rejoined laughingly.

The plates were moved just a little. Cary sat between her and his father.

"I have heard quite a good deal about you," he began. "Are you French or English?"

She caught a tiny gleam in Uncle Win's eye, and gravely answered in French.

"How do you get along there in Sudbury Street? Who does the talking?" he asked in surprise.

"We all talk," she answered.

He flushed a little and then gave an amused nod.

"Upon my word, you are not slow, if the weather is cold. And you *parlez-vous* like a native. Now, if you and father want to say anything bad about me, you may hope to keep it a secret, but I warn you that I can understand French to some extent."

"I shall not say anything bad," she returned naïvely. Adding, "Why, I don't know anything bad."

"Oh, Miss Recompense, isn't it nice to be perfect in someone's eyes?" he laughed.

"Wait until she has known you several years."

"But you have known me several years," appealingly.

"It is best to begin with an unbiased opinion."

"I shall get Betty to speak a good word for me. You have confidence in Betty?"

"I love Betty," Doris said simply.

"And Boston. That begins with a B too. You must love Boston, and the State

127

of Massachusetts, and the whole United States. And if there comes another war you must be true to the flag and the country. No skipping off to England, mind."

"I couldn't skip across the whole Atlantic."

"Then you would have to stay. Which is the nicest, Sudbury Street or this?"

"Cary, you have teased enough," said his father.

"I think the out-of-doors of this will be the prettiest in the summer," replied Doris gravely, "and when I came off the ship I thought the indoors in Sudbury Street just delightful. There was such a splendid fire, and everybody was so kind."

Cary glanced up at his father, who gave his soft half-smile.

"You were a brave little girl not to be homesick."

"I did want to see Miss Arabella, and the pony. I had such a darling pony."

"Why, you can have a pony next summer," said Uncle Win. "I am very fond of riding."

Doris' face was filled with speechless delight.

After supper they sat round the fire and Cary asked her about the Old Boston. She had very good descriptive powers. Her life had been so circumscribed there that it had deepened impressions, and the young fellow listened quite surprised. Like his father he had known very little about girls in their childhood. She was so quaintly pretty, too, with the bow of dark ribbon high up on her head, amid the waving light hair.

Some time after Uncle Winthrop said:

"Doris, I have a letter from Miss Arabella. Would you not like to come in the study and read it?"

"Oh, yes," and she sprang up with the lightness of a bird.

He had cut around the great black seal. Sometime Doris might be glad to have the letter intact. There were no envelopes then besides those used for state purposes.

"Dear and Respected Sir," it began in the formal, old-fashioned manner. She had been rejoiced to hear of Doris' safe arrival and continued good health, and every day she saw the wisdom of the change, though she had missed the child sorely. Her sister had passed peacefully away soon after the departure of Doris, a loss to be accepted with resignation, since her life on earth had long ceased to have any satisfaction to herself. Her own health was very much broken, and she knew it would not be long before she should join those who had preceded her in a better land. When this occurred there would be some articles forwarded to him for Doris, and again she commended the little girl to his affectionate interest and care, and hoped she would grow into a sweet and useful womanhood and be all her parents could wish if they had lived.

"Dear Miss Arabella!" Doris wiped the tears from her eyes. How strange the little room must look without Miss Henrietta sitting at the window babbling of childish things! "And she is all alone with Barby. How sad it must be. I should not like to live alone."

Unconsciously she drew nearer Uncle Winthrop. He put his arm over her shoulder in a caressing manner, and his heart was moved with sympathy for the solitary lady across the ocean.

Doris thought of Aunt Priscilla and wondered whether she ever was lonesome.

Sunday was still bright, and somehow felt warm when contrasted with the biting weather of the last ten days. The three went to old Trinity Church, that stood then on a corner of Summer Street—a plain wooden building with a gambrel roof, quite as old-fashioned inside as out, and even now three-quarters of a century old. Up to the Revolution the king and the queen, when there was one, had been prayed for most fervently. The Church conceded this point reluctantly, since there were many who doubted the success of the struggle. But the clergy had resigned from King's Chapel and Christ Church. For a long while afterward Dr. Mather Byles had kept himself before the people by his wit and readiness for controversy, and the two old ladies, his sisters, were well known for their adherence to Royalist costumes and the unction with which they prayed for the king in their own house—with open windows, in summer.

In fact, even now Episcopalianism was considered rather foreign than of a home growth. But there had been such a divergence from the old-time faiths that people's prejudices were much softened.

It seemed quite natural again to Doris, and she had no difficulty in finding her places, though Cary offered her his prayer book every time. And it sounded so hearty to say "Amen" to the prayers, to respond to the commandments, and sing some of the old chants.

There was a short service in the afternoon, and in the evening she and Cary sang hymns. They were getting to be very good friends. Then on Christmas morning they all went again. There was a little "box and fir," and a branch of hemlock in the corner, but the people of that day would have been horrified at the greenery and the flowers met to hail the birth of Christ to-day.

They paused in the vestibule to give each other a cordial greeting, for the congregation was not very large.

A fine-looking elderly lady shook hands with Mr. Adams and his son.

"This is my little niece from abroad," announced the elder, "another of the Adams family. Her father was own nephew to Cousin Charles. Doris, this is Madam Royall."

"Poor Charles. Yes, I remember him well. Our children spied out the little girl in the sleigh with you on Saturday, and made no end of guesses. Is it the child who attends Mrs. Webb's school? Dorcas Payne goes there this winter, and she has been teasing to have her name changed to Doris, which she admires beyond measure."

"Yes," answered Doris timidly, as Madam Royall seemed addressing her. "I know Dorcas Payne."

"Oh, Mr. Adams, I have just thought—our children are going to have a little time to-night—not anything as pretentious as a party, a sort of Christmas frolic. Will you not come around and bring Cary and the little girl? You shall have some Christmas cake and wine with us, Cary can take tea with Isabel and Alice, and the little girl can have a good romp. Please do not refuse."

Cary flushed. Mr. Adams looked undecided.

"No, you shall not hunt about for an excuse. Dorcas has talked so much about the little girl that we are all curious to see her. Shouldn't you like a frolic with other little girls, my dear?"

Doris smiled with assenting eagerness.

"We shall surely look for you. I shall tell them all that you are coming, and that I have captured little Doris Adams."

"Very well," returned Mr. Adams.

"At four, exactly. The children's supper is at five."

Doris had tight hold of Uncle Winthrop's hand, and if she had not just come out of church she must have skipped for very gladness. For Dorcas Payne had talked about her cousins, the Royalls, and their charming grandmother, and the good times they had in their fine large house.

Uncle Win looked her all over as she sat at the dinner table. She was a pretty child, with her hair gathered up high and falling in a golden shower. Her frock was some gray woolen stuff, and he wondered vaguely if blue or red would have been better. He had seen little girls in red frocks; they looked so warm and comfortable in winter. Elizabeth Leverett would be shocked at the color, he knew. What made so many women afraid of it, and why did they cling to dismal grays and browns? He wished he knew a little more about girls.

They had a splendid young goose for the Christmas dinner, vegetables and pickles and jellies. Cider was used largely then; no hearty dinner would have been the thing without it. Even the Leveretts used that, while they frowned on all other beverages. And then the thick mince pie with a crust that fairly melted before you could chew it! One needed something to sustain him through the long cold winter, and the large rooms where you shivered if you went out of the chimney corner.

Doris stole a little while for her enchanting Primrose people, though Cary kept teasing by saying: "Has Moses gone to the Fair? Just wait until you see the sort of bargains he makes!"

Uncle Winthrop went out to Miss Recompense.

"She looks very plain for a little—well, I suppose it *is* a party, and I dare say there is another frock at the Leveretts'. I think the first time I saw her she had on something very pretty—silk, I believe it was. But there is no time to get it. Recompense, if you could find a ribbon or any suitable adornment to brighten her up. In that big bureau upstairs—I wish you would look."

Years ago the pretty things had been laid away. Recompense went over them every spring during house-cleaning time, to see that moths had not disturbed them. Thieves were never thought of. She always touched them with a delicate regard for the young wife she had never known.

She put a shawl about her now and went upstairs, unlocked the drawer of "trinkets," and peered into some of the boxes. Oh, here was a pretty bit of lace, simple enough for a child. White ribbons turned to cream, pale-blue grown paler with age, stiff brocaded ones, and down at the very bottom a rose color with just a simple silvery band crossing it at intervals. There was enough for a sash and a bow for the hair, and with the lace tucker it would be all right.

"Doris," she called over the baluster.

"Yes, ma'am," and Doris came tripping up, book in hand.

"Your uncle wants you fixed up a bit," she said, "and as you have nothing here I have looked up a few things. Let me fasten the tucker in your frock. There, that does look better. Madam Royall is quite dressy, like all fashionable people who go out and have company. I'm not much of a hand to fix up children, seeing that for years I have had none of it to do. But I guess I can manage to tie the sash. There, I think that will do."

"Oh, how lovely! How good of you, Miss Recompense."

Recompense Gardiner hated to take the credit for anything she had not done, but she had to let it go now.

"How to get this ribbon in your hair! I think it is too wide."

"Oh, can I have that too? Well, you see, you take up the curls this way and put the ribbon under. Can it be folded? Then you tie it on the top."

Miss Recompense did not make a very artistic bow, but Doris looked in the glass of the dressing table, and pulled and patted it a little, and said it was right and that she was a thousand times grateful.

The sober-minded woman admitted within herself that the child was greatly improved. Perhaps gay attire *did* foster vanity, yet it was pleasant for others to look upon.

"Run down and ask your uncle if you will do," exclaimed Miss Recompense, feeling that by his approval she would discharge her conscience from the sin, if sin it were.

She looked so dainty as she came and stood by him, and asked her question with such a bewitching flush, that he kissed her on the forehead for approval. But she put her soft young arms about his neck and kissed him back, and he held her there with a strange new warmth stirring his heart.

The old Royall house in Summer Street went its way three-quarters of a century ago. No one dreams now of the beautiful garden that surrounded it, and the blossoming shrubbery and beds of flowers from which nosegays were sent to friends, and the fruit distributed later on. It was an old house then, a great square, two-story building with a cupola railed around a flat place at the point of the roof, or what would have been the point if carried up. There were some rooms built out at the back, and an arbor—a covered sort of *allée* where the ladies sat and sewed at times and the children played. Thirty years before there had been many a meeting of friends to discuss the state of affairs. There had been disagreements, ruptures, quarrels made and healed. George Royall had gone back to England. Dwight Royall had fought on the side of the "Rebels." One daughter had married an English officer who had surrendered with Cornwallis and then returned to his native land. A younger son had married and died, and left two daughters to his mother's care, their own mother being dead. A widowed daughter had come home to live with her four children, the two youngest being girls. Dorcas Payne was a cousin to them on their father's side.

There were often guests staying with them, and the old house was still the scene of good times, as they were then: friends dropping in and finding ready hospitality. For though Madam Royall had passed the three score and ten, she was still intelligent and had been in her earlier years accomplished. She could play on her old-fashioned spinet for the children to dance, and sometimes she sang the songs of her youth, though her voice had grown a trifle unsteady in singing.

The sun was setting the west in a glow of magnificence as they walked up to the Royall house. Madam Royall and her daughter Mrs. Chapman were waiting to welcome them.

In this hall was the tall stove that was beginning to do duty for the cheerful hearthfire, and it diffused a delightful atmosphere of warmth. But you could see the blaze in the parlor and the dining room, where some friends were already assembled and having a game of cards. The sideboard, as was the custom then, was set out with a decanter of Madeira and one of sherry and the glasses, besides a great silver basin filled with nuts and dried fruit and another dish of crullers.

On the opposite side of the hall there was a hubbub of children's voices. Madam Royall ushered Mr. Adams into the dining room, left Cary to the attention of the two girls and their aunt, and took possession of Doris herself, removing her wraps and handing them to the maid. Then taking her hand she drew her into the room, kept mostly for dancing and party purposes.

CHAPTER XII

A CHILDREN'S PARTY

"This is Doris Adams, a little girl who came from England not long ago. You must make her welcome and show her what delightful children there are in Boston. These two girls are Helen and Eudora Chapman, my grandchildren, and the others are grandnieces and friends. Helen, you must do the honors."

Dorcas Payne came forward. "She goes to the same school that I do." She had been entertaining the girls with nearly all she knew about Doris. That Mr. Winthrop Adams was her uncle and guardian raised her a good deal in the estimation of Dorcas, for even then a man was thought unusually well off to be able to live without doing any real business.

"Would you like to play graces?" asked Eudora.

"I don't know," admitted Doris.

"We were playing. Grace and Molly, you go down that end of the room. Now, this is the way. When Betty tosses it you catch it on the sticks, so."

It seemed very easy when Eudora caught it and tossed it back, and Betty threw it again.

"Now you try," and she put the sticks in Doris' hands. "Oh, what tiny little hands you have, and as white as snow!"

Doris blushed. She threw the hoop and it "wabbled," but Betty, a bright, black-eyed girl, made a lunge or two, and caught it on the tip of one stick, and back it came. Doris was looking at her and never moved her hand.

"Pick it up and try again," said Eudora. "That isn't the right way, but we will excuse you this time."

Alas! this time Doris ran and brandished her stick in the air to no purpose.

"I would rather see you play," she said. "You are all doing it so beautifully."

"Then you stand here and watch."

It was very fascinating. There were three sets playing. Doris found that when a girl missed she gave up to some other companion. Her eyes could hardly move quickly enough to watch all the hoops. Now and then a girl was crowned,—that meant the hoops encircled her head,—and they all shouted.

Then Helen said they had played that long enough, and now they would try

"Hunt the slipper." The slipper was a pretty one, made of pink plush with a dainty heel and a shining buckle set in a small pink bow. Doris said "it looked like a Cinderella slipper."

"Oh, do you know about Cinderella? Do you know many stories?"

"Not a great many. Little Red Riding Hood and Beauty and the Beast, and a few in verses."

"I wish you knew something quite new. Oh!"

Eudora had forgotten to keep the slipper going. The girls were sitting in a ring, so she jumped up cheerfully and began to hunt. There were a great many little giggles and exclamations, and then someone said: "Oh, let's stop playing and tell riddles!"

That was a never-failing amusement. There were some very bright ones, some very puzzling ones. One girl asked how many baskets of dirt there were in Copp's Hill.

"Why, there can't anybody tell," said Helen. "You couldn't measure it that way."

Everybody looked at everybody else, and the glances finally grew indignant.

"There isn't any answer."

"Give it up?"

"Yes," cried the voices in unison.

"Why, one—if the basket is big enough."

"There couldn't be a basket made as large as that. You might as well ask how many drops of water there are in the sea, and then say only one because they all run together."

The girls applauded that, and, before anyone had thought of another, Miranda, —tall, black, imposing, with a gay turban wound round her head,— announced:

"De little misses were all disquested to walk out to de Christmas supper."

Grandmamma did not know how to leave her guests, and she was in the middle of a game of loo, but she had promised to sit at the head of the table, so Mrs. Chapman took her place. No one felt troubled because there were no boys at the party: the only boy of the house had gone out skating with some other boys.

It was quite a royal feast. There were thin bread and butter, dainty biscuits not much larger than the penny of that day, cold turkey and cold ham, and cake of every kind, it would seem, ranged around the iced Christmas cake that was surmounted by a wreath of some odd golden flowers that people dried and kept all winter for ornamental purposes.

They puzzled grandmamma with the two riddles, but she thought that about the sea the better one. And she said no one would ever have an opportunity to measure Copp's Hill, but for all that they did, if they had cared to.

The grown-up people had some tea and chocolate in the dining room, and seemed to be having as merry a time as the children. There was something infectious in the air or the house. Doris thought it very delightful. Her cheeks began to bloom in a wild-rose tint, and her eyes had a luminous look, as if happiness was shining through them.

Afterward grandmamma played on the spinet and they danced several pretty simple figures, ending with the minuet. When the clock struck seven someone came in a sleigh for four of the girls who lived quite near together. Pompey, the Royalls' servant, was to escort the others, and Betty March lived just across in Winter Street. When children went out the hours were kept pretty strictly. Seven o'clock meant seven truly, and not eight or nine.

Each child had a pretty paper box of candy, tied with a bright ribbon. Bonbons we should call them now. And they all expressed their thanks and made a courtesy as they reached the hall door.

"Have you had a good time?" asked Madam Royall, taking Doris by the hand.

"It's been just delightful, every moment," the child answered.

"And she's only looked on, grandmamma," exclaimed Eudora. "Now, let's us get real acquainted. We will go in the parlor and have a good talk."

"Very well," returned grandmamma. "I'll go and see what the *old* people are about."

"I am glad you don't have to go home so soon," began Helen. "Why don't you live with your Uncle Adams instead of in Sudbury Street? Are there any girls there?"

"One real big one who is sixteen. She has gone to Hartford now. That's Betty Leverett. And I went there first, because—well, Uncle Leverett came for me when the vessel reached Boston."

"Oh, he is your uncle, too! Did you come from another Boston, truly now?"

"Yes, it was Boston."

"And like this?"

"Oh, no."

"Did you know ever so many girls?"

"No. We lived quite out of the town."

"And, oh, were you not afraid to cross the ocean? Suppose there had been a pirate or something?"

"I didn't know anything about pirates," said Doris. "But I was afraid at first, when you could not see any land for days and days. There were two little girls and they had a doll. We played together and grew used to the water. But it was worse when it stormed."

"I should have been frightened out of my life. Grandmamma has been to England. We have some cousins there, but they are grown-up people and married. Which place do you like best?"

"I had no real relatives there after papa died. Oh, I like this Boston best."

Then they branched off into school matters. Eudora and her sister went to a Miss Parker, and to a writing school an hour in the afternoon. Eudora wished she was grown-up like Isabel and Alice, and could go out to real parties and have a silk frock. Grandmamma was going to give her one when she was fifteen.

A feeling of delicacy kept Doris from confessing that she owned the coveted article. Some of the girls had worn very pretty frocks. Eudora's was a beautiful soft blue, and had bands of black velvet and short sleeves with lace around them. But Doris had forgotten about her own attire, though she recalled the fact that there was only one little girl in a gray frock, and it didn't seem very pretty.

So they chattered on, and Eudora said they would have splendid times if she came in the summer. They had a big swing, and they went over on the Common and had no end of fun playing tag. The warm weather was the nicest, though there was great fun sledding and snowballing when the boys were not too rough. Oh, had she seen the forts and the great light out at Fort Hill? Wasn't it just grand?

"But, you know, Walter said if the redoubts had been stone instead of snow, the Rebels never could have taken them. You know, they called *us* Rebels then. And now we are a nation."

Doris wondered what a redoubt was, but she saved it to ask Uncle Win. She gave a sigh to think what an ignorant little girl she was.

"I think it is a great deal finer to be a country all by yourself and govern your own people. The King of England is half crazy, you know. You don't mind, do you, when we talk about the English? We don't really mean every person, and

137

our friends and—and all"—getting rather confused with distinctions.

"We mean the government," interposed Helen. "It stands to reason people thousands of miles away wouldn't know what is best for us. Wouldn't it be ridiculous if someone in Virginia should pretend to instruct grandmamma what to do? Grandmamma knows so much. And she is one of the handsomest old ladies in Boston. Oh, listen!"

A mysterious sound came from the kitchen. A fiddle was surely tuning up somewhere.

"The big folks are going to dance, and that is black Joe, Mr. Winslow's man."

Mr. Winslow and a young lady had arrived also. They tendered many apologies about their lateness.

The people in the dining room left the table and came out in the hall. Cary Adams had been having a very nice time, for a young fellow. Isabel poured the chocolate, and on her right sat a Harvard senior. Alice poured the tea, and beside her sat Cary, who made himself useful handing it about. He liked Alice very much. A young married couple were over on the other side, and now this addition and the fiddle looked suspicious.

"My dear Doris," exclaimed her uncle. He had been discussing Greek poets with the Harvard professor, and had really forgotten about her. "Are you tired? It's about time a young person like you, and an old person like me, went home."

He didn't look a bit old. There was a tint of pink in his cheeks—he had been so roused and warmed with his argument and his tea.

"Oh, do let Doris stay and see them dance, just one dance," pleaded Eudora. "We have been sitting here talking, and haven't tired ourselves out a bit."

The fiddler and the dancers went to the room where the children had their frolic. That was Jane Morse's cousin Winslow. How odd she should see him and hear black Joe, who fiddled like the blind piper. The children kept time with their feet.

The minuet was elegant. Then they had a cotillion in which there was a great deal of bowing. After that Mr. Adams said they must go home, and Madam Royall came and talked to Doris in a charming fashion, and then told Susan, the slim colored maid, to wrap her up head and ears, and in spite of Mr. Adams' protest Pompey came round with the sleigh.

"I hope you had a nice time," said Madam Royall, as she put a Christmas box in the little girl's hand.

"I'm just full of joy," she answered with shining eyes. "I couldn't hold any more unless I grew," laughingly.

They made her promise to come again, and the children kissed her good-by. Then they were whisked off and set down at their own door in no time.

"Now you must run to bed. Aunt Elizabeth would be horrified at your staying up so late."

Miss Recompense was—almost. She had been nodding over the fire.

They went upstairs together. She took a look at Doris, and suddenly the child clasped her round the waist.

"Oh, dear Miss Recompense, I was so glad about the beautiful sash. Most of the frocks were prettier than mine. Some had tiny ruffles round the bottom and the sleeves. But the party was so nice I forgot all about that. Oh, Miss Recompense, were you ever brimful of happiness, and you wanted to sing for pure gladness? I think that is the way the birds must feel."

No, Miss Recompense had never been that happy. A great joy, the delight of childhood, had been lost out of her life. She had been trained to believe that for every miserable day you spent bewailing your sins, a day in heaven would be intensified, and that happiness on earth was a snare of the Evil One to lead astray. She had gone out in the fields and bemoaned herself, and wondered how the birds *could* sing when they had to die so soon, and how anyone could laugh when he had to answer for everything at the Day of Judgment.

"Everybody was so delightful, though at first I felt strange. And I did not make out at all playing graces. That's just beautiful, and I'd like to know how. And now if you will untie the sash and put it away, and I am a hundred times obliged to you."

Some of the children she had known would have begged for the sash. Doris' frank return touched her. Mr. Adams no doubt meant her to keep it—she would ask him.

And then the happy little girl went to bed, while even in the dark the room seemed full of exquisite visions and voices that charmed her.

Cary had to go away the next morning. Uncle Win said he couldn't spare her, and sent Cato over to tell Mrs. Leverett. A young man came in for some instruction, and Doris followed the fate of the Vicar's household a while, until she felt she ought to study, since there were so many things she did not know.

Uncle Win found her in the chimney corner with a pile of books.

"What is it now?" he asked.

"I think I know *all* my spelling. But I can't get some of the addition tables right when I ask myself questions. I wish there had not been any nine."

"The world couldn't get along without the nine. It is very necessary."

"Most of the good things *are* hard," she said with a philosophic sigh.

He laughed.

"Eudora does not like tables either."

"I will tell you a famous thing about nine that you can't do with any other figure. How much is ten and ten?"

"Why, twenty, and ten more are thirty, and so on. It is easy as turning over

140

your hand."

"Ten and nine."

Doris looked nonplused and began to draw her brow in perplexed lines.

"Nine is only one less than ten. Now, if you can remember that——"

"Nineteen! Why, that is splendid."

"Now sixteen and nine?"

"Twenty-five," rather hesitatingly.

He nodded. "And nine more."

"Thirty-four. Oh, we made a rhyme. Uncle Winthrop, is it very hard to write verses? They are so beautiful."

"I think it is—rather," with his half-smile.

People had not had the leisure to be very poetical as yet. But through these years some children were being born into the world whose verses were to find a place by every fireside before the little girl said her last good-night to it. So far there had been some bright witticisms and sarcasms in rhyme, and the clergy had penned verses for wedding and funeral occasions. The Rev. John Cotton had indulged in flowing versification, and even Governor Bradford had interspersed his severer cares with visions of softer strains. Anne Dudley, the wife of Governor Bradstreet, with her eight children, had found time for study and writing, and about 1650 had a volume of verse published in London entitled "The Tenth Muse. Several poems compiled with a great variety of wit and learning. By an American Gentlewoman." And she makes this protest even then:

I am obnoxious to each carping tongue,
　　Who says my hand a needle better fits;
A poet's pen all scorn I thus should wrong,
　　For such despite they cast on female wits:
If what I do prove well it won't advance,
They'll say it's stolen, or else it was by chance.

There was also a Mrs. Murray and a Mercy Otis Warren, who evinced very fine intellectual ability; and Mrs. Adams had written letters that the world a hundred years later was to admire and esteem.

On the parlor table in some houses you found a thin volume of poems with a romantic history. A Mrs. Wheatley bought a little girl at the slave market one day, mostly out of pity. She learned to read very rapidly, and was so modest and thoughtful that as a young woman she was held in high esteem by Dr.

Sewall's flock at the Old South Church. She went abroad with her master's son before the breaking out of the war, and interested Londoners so much that her poems were published and she was the recipient of a good many attentions. Afterward they were reissued in Boston and met with warm commendations for the nobility of sentiment and smooth versification. So to Phillis Wheately belongs the honor of having been one of the first female poets in Boston.

And young men even now celebrated their sweethearts' charms in rhyme. Gay gallants wrote their own valentines. Young collegians struggled with Latin verse, and sometimes scaled the heights of Thessaly from whence inspiration sprang. But, for the most part, the temperaments that inclined to the worship of the Muses sought solace in Chaucer, Shakspere, and Milton while the later ones were winning their way.

Doris sighed over the doubtfulness in her uncle's tone. But it was music rather than poetry that floated through her brain.

"You might come and read a little Latin, and then we will have a talk in French. We will leave the prosaic part. What you will do in square root and cube root——"

"I am afraid I shall not grow at all. I'll just wither up. Isn't there some round root?"

"Yes, among vegetables."

They both laughed at that.

She did quite well in the Latin. Then she spelled some rather difficult words, and being in the high tide of French when dinner was announced, they kept on talking, to the great amusement of Miss Recompense, who could hardly convince herself that it really did mean anything reasonable.

Uncle Winthrop said then they certainly deserved some indulgence, and if she was not afraid of blowing away they would go out riding again. They took the small sleigh and he drove, and they turned down toward the stem end of the pear, and if Boston had not held on good and strong in those early years it might in some high wind have been twisted off and left an island.

It does not look, to-day, much as it did when Doris first saw it. Charles River has shrunken, Back Bay has been filled up. It has stretched out everywhere and made itself a marvelous city. The Common has changed as well, and is more beautiful than one could have imagined then, but a thousand old recollections cling to it.

They left the streets behind. Sleigh riding was the great winter amusement then, but you had to take it in cold weather, for the salt air all about softened the snow the first mild day. There was no factory smoke or dust to mar it, and it lay in great unbroken sheets. There were people skating on Back Bay, and chairs on runners with ladies well wrapped up in furs, and sleds of every description.

They came up around the other side and saw the wharves and the idle shipping and the white-capped islands in the harbor. Now the wind *did* nearly blow you away.

The next day was very lowering and chilly. Uncle Winthrop had to go to a dinner among some notables. Miss Recompense always brushed his hair and tied the queue. Young men did not wear them, but some of the older people thought leaving them off was aping youthfulness. He put on his black velvet smallclothes, his silk stockings and low shoes with silver buckles, his flowered waistcoat, his high stock and fine French broadcloth coat. His shirt front had two full ruffles beautifully crimped. Miss Recompense did it with a penknife.

"You look just like a picture, Uncle Winthrop," Doris exclaimed admiringly. "Party clothes *do* make one handsomer. I suppose it isn't good for one to be handsome all the time."

"We should grow too vain," he answered smilingly, yet he did enjoy the honest praise.

"Perhaps if we were used to it all the time it would not seem so beautiful. It would get to be everyday-like, and you would not think about it."

True enough. He had a fancy Madam Royall did not think half so much about her apparel as some of the more strenuous people who referred continually to conscience.

"Good-by. Maybe you will be in bed when I come back."

"Oh, will you be gone that late?" She stood upon a stool and reached over to give him a parting kiss, if she could not see him until to-morrow, and she did not even touch his immaculate ruffles.

It was growing dusky, and Miss Recompense was in and out, and was in no hurry for candlelight herself. Doris sat in a kind of chaotic thinking. Someone came up the steps, stamped his feet quite too noisily for Cato,—even if he had returned so soon,—knocked at the door, and then opened it.

"Oh, Uncle Leverett!" and she sprang up.

"Well, well, little runaway! I was quite struck when mother told me you were going to stay all the week. I wanted to see my little girl. It's lonesome without you and Betty, I can tell you—lonesome as the woods in winter; and as I couldn't get to see her, I thought I would run around this way and see you. The longest way round is the surest way home, I have heard"—with a twinkle in his eye. "Where's Uncle Win? What are you doing in the dark alone?"

"Uncle Win has gone to a grand dinner at the Exchange something. And he dressed all up. He looked splendid."

"I dare say. He isn't bad-looking in his everyday gear. And you are having a good time?"

"A most beautiful time, Uncle Leverett. I went to church Christmas morning. And a lady asked us both to a party—yes, it was a party. The grown people were by themselves, and the children—there were ten little girls—they had a grand supper and played games and told riddles, and we talked—"

"Where was this fine affair?"

"At Madam Royall's. And she was so kind and sweet and handsome."

"Well, I declare! Right in amongst the quality! I don't know what mother would say to a party. What a pity you didn't have that pretty frock!"

"I did wish for it at first, but we had such a nice time it made no difference. And then some more people came and Mr. Winslow and Black Joe, who was at Betty's party, and they danced. Cary went, too. He stayed after Uncle Win and I came home."

"Great doings. I am glad you are happy. But I shall be doubly glad to get you back. And now I must run off home."

Miss Recompense came in and lighted the candles. They were going to have supper in five minutes and he must take off his coat and stay.

"I've sort of run away, and no one would know where I am. Wife would keep supper waiting. No, I must hustle back, thanking you for the asking. I wanted to see Doris. Somehow we have grown so used to her already that the house seems kind of lost without her, Betty being away. We haven't had any letter from Hartford, but I dare say she is there all safe."

"Post teams do get delayed. Doris is well and satisfied. She and her uncle have great times studying."

"That is good. Wife worried a little about school. Now I must go. Good-night. You will surely be home on Saturday."

"Good-night," returned the soft voice.

Somehow the supper was very quiet. Doris had begun to read aloud to Miss Recompense "The Story of Rasselas, Prince of Abyssinia." She did not like it as well as her dear Vicar, but Uncle Win said it was good. He was not quite sure of the Vicar for such a child. So she read along very well for a while, and then she yawned.

"You were up late last night and you must go to bed," said the elder lady.

Doris was ready. She *was* sleepy, but somehow she did not drop asleep all in a minute. There was a grave subject to consider. All day she was thinking how splendid it would be if Uncle Win should ask her to come here and live. She liked him. She liked the books and the curiosities and the talks and the teaching. Uncle Win was so much more interesting than Mrs. Webb, who flung questions at you in a way that made you jump if you were not paying strict attention. There were other delights that she could not explain to herself. And the books, the leisure to sit and think. For careful Aunt Elizabeth said —"Have you hung up your cloak, Doris? Are you sure you know your spelling? I do wonder if you will ever get those tables perfect! The idea of such a big girl not knowing how to knit a stocking! Don't sit there looking into the fire and dreaming, Doris; attend to your book. Jimmie boy is away ahead of you in some things."

And here she could sit and dream. Of course she was not going to school. Miss Recompense did not think of something all the time. She had learned a sort of graciousness since she had lived with Mr. Winthrop Adams. True, she had nothing to worry about—no children to advance in life, no husband whose business she must be anxiously considering. She had a snug little sum of money, and was adding to it all the time, and she was still a long way from old age. Doris could not have understood the difference in both position and demands, but she enjoyed the atmosphere of ease. And there was a certain aspect of luxury, a freedom from the grinding exactions of conscience that had been trained to keep continually on the alert lest one "fall into temptation."

"He had wanted to see his little girl. He was lonesome without her."

She could see the longing in Uncle Leverett's face and hear his wistful voice there in the dark. He had come to the ship and given her the first greeting and brought her home. Yes, she supposed she *was* his little girl. Guardians were to take care of one's money; you did not have to live with them, of course. Uncle Leverett was something in a business way, too; and he loved her. She knew that without any explanation. She was quite sure Uncle Win loved her also, but her real place was in Sudbury Street.

Friday afternoon she was curled up by the fire reading, looking like a big kitten, if you had seen only her gray frock. Uncle Win had glanced at her every now and then. He did not mind having her around—not as much, in fact, as Cary, who tumbled books about and moved chairs noisily and kept one's nerves astir all the time, as a big healthy fellow whose body has grown so fast that he hardly knows what to do with his long arms and legs is apt to do.

Doris was like a little mouse. She never rattled the leaves when she turned them over, she never put books in the cases upside down, she did not finger papers or anything that lay on the table when she stood by it. He had a fancy that all children were meddlesome and curious and given to asking queer questions: these were the things he remembered about Cary in those first years of sorrow when he could hardly bear him out of his sight.

Instead, Doris was restful with her quaint ways. She did not run against chairs nor move a stool so that the legs emitted a "screak" of agony, and she could sit still for an hour at a time if she had a book. Of course, being a girl she ought to sew instead.

It was getting quite dusky. Uncle Winthrop came and stirred the fire and put on a pine log, then drew up his chair.

"Put away your book, Doris. You will try your eyes."

She shut it up and came and stood by him. He passed his arm around her.

"Uncle Win, there was a time when people had to read and sew by the blaze of logs and torches. There were no candles."

"They did it not so many years ago here. I dare say they are still doing it out in country places. They go to bed early."

"What seems queer to me is that people are continually finding out things. They must at one time have been very ignorant. No, they could not have been either," reflectively. "For just think how Adam named the animals. And Miss Arabella said that Job knew all about the stars and called them by their names. But perhaps it was the little things like candles and such. Yet they had lamps ever and ever so long ago."

"People seem to advance and then fall back. They emigrate and cannot take all their appliances with them, and they make simpler things to use until they have leisure and begin to accumulate wealth. You see, they could not bring a great deal from England or Holland in the vessels they had in early sixteen hundred. So they had to begin at the foundation in many things."

"It is all so wonderful when you really come to learn about it," she said with a gentle sigh.

The blaze was shining on her now, and bringing out the puzzles on the fair child's face. She was very intelligent, if she was slow at figures.

"Doris,"—after a long pause,—"how would you like to live here?"

"Oh, Uncle Win, it would be the most splendid thing——"

"I fancied you might like to change. And there are some matters connected with your education—why, what is it, Doris?"

She raised her eyes an instant, then they drooped and he saw the dark fringe beaded with tears. She took a long quivering inspiration.

"Uncle Win—I don't believe I can." The words came very slowly. "You see Betty is away, and Uncle Leverett missed me very much. He said the other night I was his little girl, and he was lonesome——"

"I shall be lonesome when you are gone."

"But you have so many books and things, and people coming, and—I should like to stay. Oh, I do like you so." She put her slim arm around his neck and laid her cheek against his. "Sometimes it seems as if you were like what I remember of papa. I only saw such a little of him, you know, after I went to England. But Aunt Elizabeth says it is the hard things that are right always. She would have Jimmie boy, you know, if I stayed, but Uncle Leverett wants me. I can just feel how it is, but I don't know how to explain it. He has always been so good to me. And that day on the ship he said, 'Is this my little girl?' and I was so glad to really belong to someone again——"

She was crying softly. He felt the tears on his cheek. Her simple heroism touched him.

"Yes, dear," he said with a comforting sound in his voice. "Perhaps it would be best to wait a little, until Betty returns, or in the summer. You can come over Friday night and spend Sunday, and brush up on Latin, and brush me up on French, and we will have a nice visit."

"Oh, thank you, thank you. Uncle Win—if I could be two little girls——"

"I want you all, complete. We will keep it to think about."

Then Miss Recompense said supper was ready, and Doris wiped the tears out of her eyes and smiled. But the pressure of her hand as they walked out confessed that she belonged to him.

CHAPTER XIII

VARIOUS OPINIONS OF LITTLE GIRLS

"You have kept up wonderfully for being absent a whole week. You haven't fallen back a bit," said Mrs. Webb.

Doris flushed with delight. The little training Uncle Winthrop had given her had borne fruit.

But she was shocked that Jimmie boy was so bad he had to be punished with the ruler. He had been punished twice in the week before.

"Don't you darst to tell grandmother," he said as they were turning into Sudbury Street. "If you do I'll—I'll"—she was a girl, and he couldn't punch her—"I won't take you on my sled."

"No. I won't tell."

"Honest and true? Hope to die?"

"I'll say honest and true."

"A little thing like that aint much, just two or three slaps. You ought to see the teacher at Salem? My brother Foster gets licked sometimes, and he makes us promise not to tell father."

James had stood a little in awe of Doris on the point of good behavior. But Sam had been up, and James had gone down to Aunt Martha's, and he felt a great deal bigger now.

Uncle Leverett was very glad to get his little girl back. They had heard from Betty, who had spent two delightful days with Mrs. Eastman, and then they had gone to Hartford together. Electa and the children were well, and she had a beautiful house with a Brussels carpet in the parlor and velvet furniture and vases and a table with a marble top. Betty sent love to everybody, and they were to tell Aunt Priscilla that the beaver bonnet was just the thing, and she was going to have the silk frock made over right away. Electa thought the India silk lovely, and she was so glad she had brought the extra piece along, for she was going to have the little cape with long tabs to tie behind, and she should use up every scrap putting a frill on it.

Aunt Priscilla had not waited until March, but taken another cold and was confined to the house, so Aunt Elizabeth went over quite often. Martha Grant proved very efficient, and she was industry itself. She, too, was amazed that Doris wasn't "put to something useful."

Doris had brought home a Latin book, but Aunt Elizabeth could not cordially indorse such a boyish study. Women were never meant to go to colleges. But she did not feel free to thwart Cousin Adams' plans for her.

He came over on Saturday and took her out, and they had a nice laughing French talk, though he admitted he and Miss Recompense had missed her very much. She told him about Betty, and what Mrs. Webb had said, and seemed quite happy.

Just at the last of the month they were all very much interested in a grand affair to which Uncle Winthrop was an invited guest. It was at the great Exchange Coffee House, and really in honor of the gallant struggle Spain had been making against the man who bid fair then to be the dictator of all Europe. On one throne after another he had placed the different members of his family. Joseph Bonaparte, who had been King of Naples, was summarily transferred to the throne of Spain, with small regard for the desires of her people. He found himself quite unable to cope with the insurgents rising on every hand. And America sent Spain her warmest sympathy.

Uncle Leverett read the account aloud from his weekly paper. Now and then there appeared a daily paper for a brief while, and a tolerably successful semi-weekly, but the real substantial paper was the weekly. How they would have found time then to read a morning and an evening paper—two or three, perhaps—is beyond comprehension. And to have heard news from every quarter of the globe before it was more than a few hours old would have seemed witchcraft.

Napoleon was now at the zenith of his fame. But the feeling of the country at his divorcing Josephine, who loved him deeply, was a thrill of indignation, for the tie of marriage was now considered irrevocable save for the gravest cause. That he should marry an Austrian princess for the sake of allying himself to a royal house and having an heir to the throne, which was nearly half of Europe now, was causing people even then to draw a parallel between him and our own hero, Washington. Both had started with an endeavor to free their respective countries from an intolerable yoke, and when this was achieved Washington had grandly and calmly laid down the burdens of state and retired to private life, while Napoleon was still bent upon conquest. The sympathies of America went out to all struggling nations.

There had been an ode read, and toasts and songs; indeed, it had called together the notable men of the city, who had partaken of a grand feast. It was much talked of for weeks; and Doris questioned Uncle Winthrop and began to be interested in matters pertaining to her new country.

She was learning a good deal about the city. Warren took her to Aunt

Priscilla's one noon, and came for her when they had "shut up shop." Aunt Priscilla did not mend rapidly. She called it being "pudgicky," as if there was no name of a real disease to give it. A little fresh cold, a good deal of weakness—and she had always been so strong; some fever that would persist in coming back even when she had succeeded in breaking it up for a few days. The time hung heavily on her hands. She did miss Betty's freshness and bright, argumentative ways. So she was glad to see Doris, for Polly sat out in the kitchen half asleep most of the time.

Solomon as well always seemed very glad to see Doris. He came and sat in her lap, and Aunt Priscilla told about the days when she was a little girl, more than fifty years ago. Doris thought life must have been very hard, and she was glad not to have lived then.

She did like Miss Recompense the best, but she felt very sorry for Aunt Priscilla's loneliness.

"She and Polly have grown old together, and they need some younger person to take care of them both," said Uncle Leverett. "She ought to take her comfort; she has money enough."

"It is so difficult to find anyone to suit," and Aunt Elizabeth sighed.

"I shall crawl out in the spring," declared Mrs. Perkins; but her tone was rather despondent.

Doris wondered when the spring would come. The snow and ice had never been entirely off the ground.

Besides going to Uncle Winthrop's,—and she went every other Saturday,—she had been asked to Madam Royall's to tea with the children. The elder lady had not forgotten her. Indeed, this was one of the houses that Mr. Adams thoroughly enjoyed, though he was not much of a hand to visit. But people felt then that they really owed their neighbors some social duty. There were not so many public amusements.

The Chapman children had real dolls, not simply rag babies; and the clothes were made so you could take them off. Doris was quite charmed with them. Helen's had blue eyes and Eudora's brown, but both were red-cheeked and had black hair, which was not really hair at all, but shaped of the composition and curled and painted over.

They had a grand long slide in their garden at the back. The servant would flood it over now and then and make it smooth as glass. Doris found it quite an art to stand up. Helen could go the whole length beautifully, and balance herself better than Eudora. But if you fell you generally tumbled over in the bank of snow and did not get hurt.

Playing graces was a great delight to her and after several trials she became quite expert. Then on one occasion Madam Royall found that she had a very sweet voice.

"You are old enough to learn some pretty songs, my child," she said. "I must speak to your uncle. When the weather gets pleasanter he must place you in a singing class."

Singing was quite a great accomplishment then. Very few people had pianos. But young ladies and young men would sometimes spend a whole evening in singing beautiful old songs.

In March there was a new President, Mr. Madison. Everybody was hoping for a new policy and better times, yet now and then there were quite sharp talks of war.

One day Mrs. Manning and the baby came in and made quite a visit. The baby was very sweet and good, with pretty dark eyes, and Mrs. Manning looked very much like Aunt Elizabeth. Mrs. Hollis Leverett came and spent the day, and young married women who had been Mary Leverett's friends came to tea. Warren went over in the old chaise and brought Aunt Priscilla. Everybody seemed personally aggrieved that Betty should stay away so long.

But Betty was having a grand time. Her letters to her mother were very staid and respectful, but there were accounts of dinners and evening parties and two or three weddings. Her brother King had given her a pretty pink silk, and that was made pompadour waist and had a full double plait at the back that hung down to the floor in a train. He had taken her and Electa to a grand affair where there were crowds of beautifully attired ladies. Betty did not call it a ball, for she knew they would all be shocked. And though her mother had written for her to come home, Mrs. King had begged for a little longer visit, as there seemed to be something special all the time.

"What extravagance for a young girl!" exclaimed Mrs. Manning. "Pink silk indeed, and a train! Betty will be so flighty when she comes back there will be no getting along with her. 'Lecty has grown very worldly, I think. I have never found any occasion for a pink silk."

Mrs. Leverett sighed. And Betty was not yet seventeen!

Mrs. Manning took James home with her, for she said grandmother was spoiling him. She kept the children with a pretty strict hand at home, and they soon jumped over the traces when you gave them a little liberty. She was very glad to have him go to school all winter and hoped he had made some improvement.

She was very brisk and energetic and was surprised to think they were letting

151

Doris grow up into such a helpless, know-nothing sort of girl. And her daughter of nine was like a steady little woman.

"Still it isn't wise to put too much on her," said Mrs. Leverett in mild protest. "Where one cannot help it, why, you must; but I think life is getting a little easier, and children ought to have their share of it."

"I'm not asking anything of her that I did not do," returned Mrs. Manning. "And I am proud of my training and my housekeeping."

"But it was so different then. Your father and I began life with only a few hundred dollars. Then there was his three years in the war, and people were doing everything for themselves—spinning and weaving and dyeing, and making clothes of every kind. To be sure I make soap and candles," laughing a little; "but we have only one cow now and give half the milk for her care. I really felt as if I ought not have Martha, but father insisted."

"I don't see why Doris couldn't have done a good deal instead of poring over books so much."

"Well—you see she isn't really our own. Cousin Winthrop has some ideas about her education. She will have a little money, too, if everything turns out right."

"It's just the way to spoil girls. And you will find, mother, that Betty will be none the better for her visit to 'Lecty. Dear me! I don't see how 'Lecty can answer to her conscience, spending money that way. We couldn't. It's wrong and sinful. And it's wrong to bring up any child in a helpless, do-little fashion."

They were sitting by the south window sewing, and Doris was at the other side of the chimney studying. Now and then she could not help catching a sentence. She wondered what little Elizabeth Manning was like, who could cook a meal, work butter, tend babies, and sew and knit stockings. She only went to school in the winter; there was too much work to do in the summer. She was not left alone now; one of the Manning aunts had been staying some time. This aunt was a tailoress and had been fitting out Mr. Manning, and now James must go home to have some clothes made.

Jimmie boy privately admitted to Doris that he would rather stay at grandmother's. She was a good deal easier on him than his mother, and he didn't mind Mrs. Webb a bit. "But you just ought to see Mr. Green. He does lick the boys like fury! And there's such lots of errands to do home. Mother never gives you a chunk of cake either. I don't see why they couldn't all have been grandmothers instead of mothers."

James was not the first boy who had wished such a thing. But he knew he had to go home, and that was all there was about it.

Martha wanted to go also. She had bought a good stout English cambric—lively colored, as she called it—and a nice woolen or stuff frock, as goods of that kind was often called. She was going to do up her last summer's white frock to be married in. They would have a wedding supper at her father's and then go home, and begin housekeeping the next morning. Mrs. Leverett added a tablecloth to her store.

Betty must be sent for imperatively. Her mother was afraid she would be quite spoiled. And she could not help wishing that Mrs. King would be a little more careful and not branch out so, and Mary take life a little easier, for Mr. Manning was putting by money and had his large farm clear.

Then Aunt Priscilla was suddenly at sea. Jonas Field had bought a place of his own where he could live over the store. In spite of a changed name, King Street had dropped down and down, and was now largely given to taverns. The better class had kept moving out and a poorer class coming in, with colored people among them. No one had applied for the store, but a man who wanted to keep a tavern combined with a kind of sailor lodging house had made her a very good offer to buy the property.

"I'm going to live my time out in this very house," declared Aunt Priscilla with some of her olden energy. "I came here when I was married and I'll stay to be buried. By the looks of things, it won't be a great many years. And I haven't made a sign of a will yet! Not that the Perkinses would get anything if I died in this state—that aint the word, but it means the same thing, not having your will made, and I aint quite sure after all that would be right. I worked and saved, and I had some when we were married, but husband had farsight, and knew how to turn it over. Some of his money ought to go back to his folks."

This had been one of the decisions haunting Aunt Priscilla's conscience. Down at the bottom she had a strict sense of justice.

"It is hardly nice to go there any more," said Aunt Elizabeth. "And I shall not enjoy a young girl like Betty running over there, if Aunt Priscilla shouldn't be very well, and she is breaking. Polly gets worse and really is not to be trusted."

It was Polly after all who settled the matter, or the summons that came to Polly one night. For in the morning, quite late, after a good deal of calling and scolding, Aunt Priscilla found she had taken the last journey. It was a great shock. Jonas Field's errand boy was dispatched to the Leveretts'.

The woman who came soon gave notice that she "couldn't stay in no such neighborhood for steady company."

Mr. Leverett and Cousin Adams urged her to sell. If there should be war she might not have a chance in a long while again.

"But I don't know the first thing in the world to do," she moaned. "I haven't a chick nor a child to care about me."

"Come over and stop with us a bit until you can make some plans. There's two rooms upstairs in which you could housekeep if you wanted to. Our family gets smaller all the time. But if you liked to live with us a spell——" said Mr. Leverett.

"I don't know how 'Lizabeth could stand an old woman and a young one"— hesitatingly.

"If you mean Doris, she is going over to Winthrop's," he replied.

"Ready to jump at the chance, I'll warrant. You can't count on children."

"No, Aunt Priscilla, she didn't jump. She's a wise, fond little thing. Win asked her about Christmas, and she wouldn't consent until Betty came back, for fear we would be lonesome. It quite touched me when I heard of it. Win has some ideas about her education, and I guess he's nearer right. So that needn't trouble you. It would be so much better for you to sell."

"I'll think it over," she said almost gruffly, for she was moved herself. "I never could get along with this Rachel Day. She doesn't allow that anyone in the world knows anything but herself, and I kept house before she was born. I don't like quite such smart people."

Miss Hetty Perkins came in to offer her services as housekeeper. Every now and then she had "edged round," as Aunt Priscilla expressed it. Everybody said Hetty was closer than the skin, but then she had no one except herself to depend upon. And Amos Perkins called to see if Aunt Priscilla had anyone she could trust to do her business. He heard she was going to sell.

"I haven't made up my mind," she answered tartly. She was not fond of Amos either.

Then the would-be purchaser found he could have a place two doors below. He did not like it as well, but it would answer.

"It seems as if I was bound to have a rum shop and a sailor's boarding-house under my nose. There'll be a crowd of men hanging round and fiddling and carousing half the night. I don't see what's getting into Boston! Places that were good enough twenty year ago are only fit for tramps, and decent people have to get out of the way, whether they will or no."

Betty came home the last of March. She looked taller—perhaps it was because she wore her dresses so long and her hair so high. She had a pretty new frock—a rich warm brown ground, with little flowers in green and yellow and a kind of dull red sprinkled all over it. It had come from New York, and was called delaine. She had discarded her homespun woolen. And, oh, how stylishly pretty she was, quite like the young ladies at Madam Royall's!

She held Doris to her heart and almost smothered her, kissing her fondly.

"You have grown lovely by the minute!" she cried. "I was so afraid someone would cut your hair. 'Lecty said at first that I had only one idea, and that was Doris Adams, I talked about you so much. And she's wild to see you. She's quite grand and full of fun, altogether different from Mary. Mary holds onto every penny until I should think she'd pinch it thin. And I've had the most magnificent time, though Hartford is nothing compared to Boston. It is like a country place where you know everybody that is at all worth knowing. I have such lots of things to tell you."

It came rather hard to take up the old routine of work, and get up early in the morning. She was dismayed by the news that Aunt Priscilla was coming and Doris going.

"Though I don't know," she declared after reflecting a day or two on the subject. "I'll have such a good excuse to go to Uncle Win's, and we can have delightful talks. But Aunt Priscilla is certainly a dispensation of Providence equal to St. Paul's thorn in the flesh."

"I've made her some visits this winter, and she has been real nice," said Doris. "I shouldn't mind her at all now. And I told Uncle Win that I would like to be two little girls, so one *could* stay here. I love Uncle Win very much. I love your father too."

"Is there anybody in the whole wide world you do not love?"

Doris flushed. She had not been able to feel very tenderly toward Mrs. Manning, and Mrs. Hollis Leverett talked about her being so backward, and such a "meachin" little thing.

"I dare say if the truth was known, her mother died of consumption. And that great mop of hair is enough to take the strength out of any child. I wouldn't have it on Bessy's head for an hour," declared Mrs. Hollis.

But Bessy told her in a confidential whisper that she thought her curls the sweetest thing in the world, and when she was a grown-up young lady she meant to curl her hair all over her head.

Doris was glad Uncle Winthrop did not find any fault with them.

Of course she should be sorry to go. It was curious how one could be glad and sorry in a breath.

Mrs. Leverett went over to Aunt Priscilla's to help pack. Oh, the boxes and bundles and bags! They were tied up and labeled; some of them had not been opened for years. Gowns that she had outgrown, stockings she had knit, petticoats she had quilted—quite a fashion then.

"It's lucky we have a big garret," said Mrs. Leverett. "And whatever will you do with them?"

"There's that flax wheel—it was grandmother's. She was like Benjamin Franklin, who gave his sister Jane a spinning wheel on her wedding day: she gave me that. And Jane's gone, though I did hear someone bought the wheel for a sort of keepsake. Oh, Elizabeth, I don't know what *you* will do with all this old trumpery!"

Elizabeth hardly knew either. It was good to have children and grandchildren to take some of these things just to keep one from hoarding up. Elizabeth, sweet soul, remembered the poor at her gates as well. But most people were fond of holding onto everything until their latest breath. There was some virtue in it, for the later generations had many priceless heirlooms.

One of the south rooms was emptied, and after a great deal of argument Aunt Priscilla was prevailed upon to use her best chamber furniture for the rest of her life. She had not cared much for the housekeeping project, and decided she would rather board a while until she could get back some of her strength.

"What are you going to do with Solomon?" asked Doris.

"Well—I don't know. Aunt Elizabeth doesn't like cats very much. He's such a nice fellow, I should hate to leave him behind and have him neglected. But it's bad luck to move cats."

"I should like to have him."

"Would you, now? He's almost like a human. I've said that many a time; and he went round asking after Polly just as plain as anyone could. I declare, it made my heart ache. Polly had been a capable woman, and Mr. Perkins bought her, so I didn't feel free to turn her away when he was gone. And I'd grown used to a servant, too. I don't know what I should have done without her the two years he was ailing. Though when she came to be forgetful and lose her judgment it did use to try me. But I'm glad now I kept her to the end. I'd borrowed a sight of trouble thinking what I'd do if she fell sick, and I might just as well have trusted the Lord right straight along. When I come to have this other creetur ordering everything, and making tea her way,—she will boil it and you might as well give me senna,—then I knew Polly had some sense and memory, after all. You can't think how I miss her! I'm sorry for every bit of fault I've found these last two years."

Aunt Priscilla stopped to take breath and wipe her eyes. Polly's death had opened her mind to many things.

Doris sat and stroked Solomon and rubbed him under the throat. Now and then he looked up with an intent, asking gaze, and a solemn flick of one ear, as if he said, "Can't you tell me where Polly is gone?"

"You'd have to ask Uncle Winthrop. And I don't know what Miss Recompense would say."

"She likes cats."

"Oh. Well, I'm afraid Uncle Winthrop doesn't."

"If he *should*," tentatively.

"I think I'd miss Solomon a good deal. But he'd be a bother to keep at the Leveretts'. I would like him to have a good home. And he is very fond of you."

Uncle Win was over the very next day, and Doris laid the case before him.

"I like the picture of comfort a nice cat makes before the fire. I haven't any objection to cats in themselves. But I dislike cat hairs."

"Uncle Win, I could brush you off. And Solomon has been so well trained. He has a box with a cushion, so he never jumps up in chairs. And he has a piece of blanket on the rug where he lies. He loves me so, and Aunt Elizabeth can't bear cats. Oh, I wish I might have him."

"I'll talk to Miss Recompense. She's having a little room fixed up for you just off of hers. It opens on the hall, and it has a window where you can see the sun rise. I think through the summer you need not go to school, but study at home as you did Christmas week."

"That will be delightful! And I shall be so glad when it is truly spring."

It had been a long cold winter, but now there were signs everywhere of a curious awakening among the maples. Some were already out in red bloom. The grass had begun to spring up in its soft green, though there were patches of ice in shady places and a broad skim along the edge of the Charles River marsh. But the bay and the harbor were clear and beautiful.

Betty and Doris had confidential chats after they were in bed—in very low tones, lest they should be heard.

"Everybody would be shocked to see how really gay Electa is. There are very religious people in Hartford, too, who begin on Saturday night. But the men insist upon parties and dinners, and they bring their fashions up from New York. Boston is just as gay in some places, and Jane Morse has had a splendid time this winter going to dances. The gentlemen who come to Mr. King's are so polite, some of them elegant. I envy 'Lecty. It's just the kind of world to live in."

"And I want to hear about your pink silk."

"I left it at 'Lecty's. It was too gay to bring home. It would have frightened everybody. And 'Lecty thinks of going to New York next winter, and if she does she will send for me. I should have had to rumple it all up bringing it home, and I don't believe I'd had a chance to wear it. I have the other two, and Mat thought the blue and white one very pretty. Mat laughs at what he calls Puritanism, and says the world is growing broader and more generous. He is a splendid man too, and though he is making a good deal of money he doesn't think all the time of saving, as Mary and her husband do. He is good to the poor, and generous and kind, and wants everyone to be happy. Of course they go to church, but there is a curious difference. I sometimes wonder who is right and if it *is* a sin to be happy."

Doris' mind had no especial theological bent, and her conscience had not been trained to keep on the alert.

"It was very nice in him to give it to you. And you must have looked lovely in it."

"Oh, the frock," Betty laughed. "Yes, I did. And when you know you look nice you stop feeling anxious about it. It was just so at Jane's party. But I should have been mortified in my gray woolen gown. Well—the mortification may be good, but it isn't pleasant. I wore the pink silk to the weddings and to some dinners. Dinners are quite grand things there, but they last so long I should call them suppers. And sometimes there is a grand march afterward, which is a kind of stately dancing. It has been just delightful. I don't know how I will settle down and wash and iron and scrub. But I would a great deal rather be in 'Lecty's place than in Mary's, and saving up money to buy farms isn't everything to life. I think the Mannings worship their farms and stock a good deal more than 'Lecty and Mat do their fine house and their money and all."

Her admirers and her conquests she confided to Janie Morse. There was one very charming young man that she liked a great deal, but her sister said she was too young to keep company, and there might be next winter in New York.

It spoke volumes for the wholesome, sensible nature of Betty Leverett that she could take her olden place in the household, assist her mother, and entertain her father with the many interesting events of her gay and happy winter.

CHAPTER XIV

IN THE SPRING

The matter had settled itself so easily that Doris could not find much opportunity for sorrow, nor misgivings for her joy. She could not see the struggle there had been in Uncle Leverett's mind, and the sturdy common sense that had come to his assistance. He could recall habits of second-cousin Charles that were like a woman's for daintiness, and Winthrop Adams had the same touch of refinement and delicacy. It was in the Adams blood, doubtless. Aunt Priscilla had not a large share, but he had noted some of it in Elizabeth. It pervaded every atom of Doris' slender body and every cell of her brain. She never would take to the rougher, coarser things of life; indeed, why should she when there was no need? He had wandered so far from the orthodox faith that he began to question useless discipline.

Winthrop could understand and care for her better. She would grow up in his house to the kind of girl nature had meant her to be. Here the useful, that might never come in use, would be mingled and confused with what was necessary. He had watched her trying to achieve the stocking that all little girls could knit at her age. It was as bad as Penelope's web. Aunt Elizabeth pulled it out after she had gone to bed, and knit two or three "rounds," so as not to utterly discourage her inapt pupil. But Doris had set up some lace on a "cushion," after Madam Sheafe's direction, and it grew a web of beauty under her dainty fingers.

It was not as if Doris would be quite lost to them. They would see her every day or two. And when it was decided that Aunt Priscilla would come he was really glad. Aunt Priscilla's captious talk did not always proceed from an unkindly heart.

Betty made a violent protest at first.

"After all, it will not be quite so bad as I thought," she admitted presently. "I shall go to Uncle Win's twice as often, and I have always been so fond of him. And things *are* prettier there, somehow. There is a great difference in the way people live, and I mean to change some things. It isn't because one is ashamed to be old-fashioned; some of the old ways are lovely. It is only when you tack hardness and commonness on them and think ugliness has a real virtue in it. We will have both sides to talk about. But if you were going back to England, it would break my heart, Doris."

Doris winked some tears out of her eyes.

She thought her room at Uncle Win's was like a picture. The wall was whitewashed: people thought then it was much healthier for sleeping chambers. The floor was painted a rather palish yellow. There was only one window, but the door was opposite, and a door that opened into the room of Miss Recompense. The window had white curtains with ruffled edges, made of rather coarse muslin, but it was clear, and looked very tidy. Miss Recompense had found a small bedstead among the stored-away articles. It had high posts and curtains and valance of pale-blue flowered chintz. There was a big bureau, a dressing table covered with white, and a looking glass prettily draped. At the top of this, surmounted by a gilt eagle, was a marvelous picture of a man with a blue coat and yellow smallclothes handing into a boat a lady who wore a skirt of purple and an overdress of scarlet, very much betrimmed, holding a green parasol over her head with one hand and placing a slippered foot on the edge of the boat. After a long while Doris thought she should be much relieved to have them sail off somewhere.

There were two quaint rush-bottomed chairs and a yellow stool, such as we tie with ribbons and call a milking stool. A nice warm rug lay at the side of the bed, and a smaller one at the washing stand. These were woven like rag carpet, but made of woolen rags with plenty of ends standing up all over, like the surface of a Moquette carpet. They were considered quite handsome then, as they were more trouble than braided rugs, and so soft to the foot. Some strenuous housekeepers declared them terrible dust catchers.

Doris' delight in the room amply repaid Miss Recompense. She had learned her way about, and could come down alone, now that the weather had grown pleasanter, and she was full of joy over everything. Occasionally Uncle Winthrop would be out, then she and Miss Recompense would have what they called a "nice talk."

Miss Recompense Gardiner was quite sure she had never seen just such a child. Indeed at five-and-forty she was rather set in her ways, disliked noise and bustle, and could not bear to have a house "torn up," as she phrased it. Twelve years before she had come here to "housekeep," as the old phrase went. She had not lacked admirers, but she had been very particular. Her sisters said she was a born old maid. There was in her soul a great love of refinement and order.

Mr. Winthrop Adams just suited her. He was quiet, neat, made no trouble, and did not smoke. That was a wretched habit in her estimation. Cousin Charles used to come over, and different branches of the family were invited in now and then to tea. Cary was a rather proper, well-ordered boy, trained by his mother's sister, who had married and gone away just before the advent of Miss Gardiner. There had been some talk that Mr. Winthrop might espouse

Miss Harriet Cary in the course of time, but as there were no signs, and Miss Cary had an excellent offer of marriage, she accepted it.

Cary went to the Latin School and then to Harvard. He was a fair average boy, a good student, and ready for his share of fun at any time. His father had marked out his course, which was to be law, and Cary was indifferent as to what he took up.

So they had gone on year after year. It promised a pleasant break to have the little girl.

The greatest trouble, Miss Recompense thought, would be making Solomon feel at home. Doris brought his cushion, and the box he slept in at night was sent. Warren brought him over in a bag and they put him in the closet for the night. He uttered some pathetic wails, and Doris talked to him until he quieted down. He was a good deal frightened the next morning, but he clung to Doris, who carried him about in her arms and introduced him to every place. He was afraid of Mr. Adams and Cato, his acquaintance with men having been rather limited. After several days he began to feel quite at home, and took cordially to his cushion in the corner.

"He doesn't offer to run away," announced Doris to Aunt Priscilla. "He likes Miss Recompense. Uncle Winthrop thinks him the handsomest cat he has ever seen."

"Poor old Polly! She set a great deal of store by Solomon. I never did care much for a cat, but I do think Solomon was most as wise as folks. I don't know what I should have done last winter when I was so miserable if it had not been for him. He seemed to take such comfort that it was almost as good as a sermon. And sometimes when he purred it was like the sound of a hymn with the up and down and the long notes. I don't believe he would have stayed with anyone else though. Child, what is there about you that just goes to the heart of even a dumb beast?"

Doris looked amazed, then thoughtful. "I suppose it is because I love them," she said simply.

There was a great stir everywhere, it seemed. The slow spring had really come at last. The streets were being cleared up, the gardens put in order, some of the houses had a fresh coat of paint; the stores put out their best array, the trees were misty-looking with tiny green shoots, and the maples Doris thought wonderful. There were four in the row on Common Street; one was full of soft dull-red blooms, one had little pale-green hoods on the end of every twig, another looked as if it held a tiny scarlet parasol over each baby bud, and the fourth dropped clusters of brownish-green fringe.

"Oh, how beautiful they are!" cried Doris, her eyes alight with enthusiasm.

And then all the great Common began to put on spring attire. The marsh grass over beyond sent up stiff green spikes and tussocks that looked like little islands, and there were water plants with large leaves that seemed continually nodding to their neighbors. The frog concerts at the pond were simply bewildering with the variety of voices, each one proclaiming that the reign of ice and snow was at an end and they were giving thanks.

"They are so glad," declared Doris. "I shouldn't like to be frozen up all winter in a little hole."

Miss Recompense smiled. Perhaps they *were* grateful. She had never thought of it before.

Doris did not go back to Mrs. Webb's school, though that lady said she was sorry to give her up. Uncle Win gave her some lessons, and she went to writing school for an hour every day. Miss Recompense instructed her how to keep her room tidy, but Uncle Win said there would be time enough for her to learn housekeeping.

Then there were hunts for flowers. Betty came over; she knew some nooks where the trailing arbutus grew and bloomed. The swamp pinks and the violets of every shade and almost every size—from the wee little fellow who sheltered his head under his mother's leaf-green umbrella to the tall, sentinel-like fellow who seemed to fling out defiance. Doris used to come home with her hands full of blooms.

The rides too were delightful. They went over the bridges to West Boston and South Boston and to Cambridge, going through the college buildings—small, indeed, compared with the magnificent pile of to-day. But Boston did seem almost like a collection of islands. The bays and rivers, the winding creeks that crept through the green marsh grass, the long low shores held no presentiment of the great city that was to be.

Although people groaned over hard times and talked of war, still the town kept a thriving aspect. Men were at work leveling Beacon Hill. Boylston Street was being made something better than a lane, and Common Street was improved. Uncle Winthrop said next thing he supposed they would begin to improve him and order him to take up his house and walk. For houses were moved even then, when they stood in the way of a street.

The earth from the hill, or rather hills, went to fill in the Mill Pond. Lord Lyndhurst had once owned a large part, but he had gone to England to live. Charles Street was partly laid out—as far as the flats were filled in. It was quite entertaining to watch the great patient oxen, which, when they were standing still, chewed their cud in solemn content and gazed around as though they could predict unutterable things.

From the house down to Common Street was a kind of garden where Cato raised vegetables and Miss Recompense had her beds of sweet and medicinal herbs. For then the housekeeper concocted various household remedies, and made extracts by the use of a little still for flavoring and perfumery. She gathered all the rose leaves and lavender blossoms and sewed them up in thin muslin bags and laid them in the drawers and closets.

And, oh, what roses she had then! Great sweet damask roses, pink and the loveliest deep red, twice as large as the Jack roses of to-day. And trailing pink and white roses climbing over everything. Aunt Elizabeth said Miss Recompense could make a dry stick grow and bloom.

Uncle Winthrop found a new and charming interest in the little girl. She was so fond of taking walks and hearing the legends about the old places. She could see where the old beacon had stood when the place was called Sentry Hill, and she knew it had been blown down in a gale, and that on the spot had been erected a beautiful Doric column surmounted by an eagle, to commemorate "the train of events that led to the American Revolution and finally secured liberty and Independence."

But the State House had made one great excavation, and the Mill Pond Corporation was making others, and they were planning to remove the monument.

"We ought to have more regard for these old places," Uncle Win used to say with a sigh.

Cary had not been a companionable child. He was a regular boy, and the great point of interest in Sentry Hill for him was batting a ball up the hill. It was a proud day for him when he carried it farther than any other boy. He was fond of games of all kinds, and was one of the fleetest runners and a fine oarsman, and could sail a boat equal to any old salt, he thought. He was a boy, of course, and Uncle Win did not want him to be a "Molly coddle," so he gave in, for he did not quite know what to do with a lad who could tumble more books around in five minutes than he could put in order in half an hour, and knew more about every corner in Old Boston than anyone else, and was much more confident of his knowledge.

But this little girl, who soon learned the peculiarity of every tree, the song of the different birds, and the season of bloom for wild flowers, and could listen for hours to the incidents of the past, that seem of more vital importance to middle-aged people than the matters of every day, was a veritable treasure to Mr. Winthrop Adams. He did not mind if she could not knit a stocking, and he sometimes excused her deficiencies in arithmetic because she was so fond of hearing him read poetry. For Doris thought, of all the things in the world, being able to write verses was the most delightful, and that was her aim when she was a grown-up young lady. She did pick up a good deal of general knowledge that she would not have acquired at school, but Uncle Win wasn't quite sure how much a girl ought to be educated.

She began to see considerable of the Chapman girls, and Madam Royall grew very fond of her. But she did not forget her dear friends in Sudbury Street. Sometimes when Uncle Win was going out to a supper or to stay away all the evening she would go up and spend the night with Betty, and sit in the old corner, for it was Uncle Leverett's favorite place whether there was fire or not. He was as fond as ever of listening to her chatter.

She always brought a message to Aunt Priscilla about Solomon. Uncle Winthrop thought him the handsomest cat he had ever seen, and now Solomon was not even afraid of Cato, but would walk about the garden with him, and Miss Recompense said he was so much company when she, Doris, was out of the house.

Indeed, he would look at her with inquiring eyes and a soft, questioning sound in his voice that was not quite a mew.

"Yes," Miss Recompense would say, "Doris has gone up to Sudbury Street. We miss her, don't we, Solomon? It's a different house without her."

Solomon would assent in a wise fashion.

"I never did think to take comfort in talking to a cat," Miss Recompense would say to herself with a touch of sarcasm.

About the middle of June, when roses and spice pinks and ten-weeks' stocks, and sweet-williams were at their best, Mr. Adams always gave a family gathering at which cousins to the third and fourth generation were invited. Everything was at its loveliest, and the Mall just across the street was resplendent in beauty. Even then it had magnificent trees and great stretches of grass, green and velvety. Already it was a favorite strolling place.

Miss Recompense had sent a special request for Betty on that particular afternoon and evening. There was to be a high tea at five o'clock.

"I shall have my new white frock all done," said Betty delightedly. "There is just a little needlework around the neck and the skirt to sew on."

"But I wouldn't wear it," rejoined her mother. "You may get a fruit stain on it, or meet with some accident. Miss Recompense will expect you to work a little."

"Have you anything new, Doris?"

"Oh, yes," replied Doris. "A white India muslin, and a cambric with a tiny rosebud in it. Madam Royall chose them and ordered them made. And Betty, I have almost outgrown the silk already. Madam Royall is going to see about getting it altered. And in the autumn Helen Chapman will have a birthday company, and I am invited already, or my frock is," and Doris laughed. "She has made me promise to wear it then."

"You go to the Royalls' a good deal," exclaimed Aunt Priscilla jealously. She was sitting in a high-backed chair, very straight and prim. She was not quite at home yet, and kept wondering if she wouldn't rather have her own house if she could get a reasonable sort of servant. Still, she did enjoy the sociable side of life, and it was pleasant here at Cousin Leverett's. They all tried to make her feel at home, and though Betty tormented her sometimes by a certain argumentativeness, she was very ready to wait on her. Aunt Priscilla did like to hear of the delightful entertainments her silk gown had gone to after being hidden away so many years. As for the hat, a young Englishman had said "She looked like a princess in it."

"You are just eaten up with vanity, Betty Leverett," Aunt Priscilla tried to rejoin in her severest tone.

Doris glanced over to her now.

"Yes," she answered. "Uncle Winthrop thinks I ought to know something about little girls. Eudora is six months older than I am. They have such a magnificent swing, four girls can sit in it. Helen is studying French and the young ladies can talk a little. They do not see how I can talk so fast."

Doris laughed gleefully. Aunt Priscilla sniffed. Winthrop Adams would make a flighty, useless girl out of her. And companying so much with rich people would fill her mind with vanity. Yes, the child would be ruined!

"And we tell each other stories about *our* Boston. This Boston," making a pretty gesture with her hand, "has the most splendid ones about the war and all, and the ships coming over here almost two hundred years ago. It is a long while to live one hundred years, even. But I knew about Mr. Cotton and the lady Arabella Johnston. They had not heard about the saint and how his body was carried around to make it rain."

"To make it rain! Whose body was it, pray?" asked Aunt Priscilla sharply, scenting heresy. She was not quite sure but so much French would shut one out from final salvation. "Did you have saints in Old Boston?"

"Oh, it was the old Saint of the Church—St. Botolph." Doris hesitated and glanced up at Uncle Leverett, who nodded. "He was a very, very good man," she resumed seriously. "And one summer there was a very long drought. The grass all dried up, the fruit began to fall off, and they were afraid there would be nothing for the cattle to feed upon. So they took up St. Botolph in his coffin and carried him all around the town, praying as they went. And it began to rain."

"Stuff and nonsense! The idea of reasonable human beings believing that!"

"But you know the prophet prayed for rain in the Bible."

"But to take up his body! Are they doing it now in a dry time?" Aunt Priscilla asked sarcastically.

"They don't now, but it was said they did it several times, and it always rained."

"They wan't good orthodox Christians. No one ever heard of such a thing."

"But our orthodox Christians believed in witches—even the descendants of this very John Cotton who came over to escape the Lords Bishops," said Warren.

"And, unlike Mr. Blacksone, stayed and had a hard time with the Lords Brethren," said Mr. Leverett. "I hardly know which was the worst"—smiling with a glint of humor. "And you more than half believe in witches yourself, Aunt Priscilla."

"I am sure I have reason to. Grandmother Parker was a good woman if ever there was one, and she *was* bewitched. And would it have said in the Bible —'Thou shalt not suffer a witch to live,' if there had not been any?"

"They were telling stories at Madam Royall's one day. And sometime Uncle Winthrop is going to take us all to Marblehead, where Mammy Redd lived. Eudora said this:

"'Old Mammy Redd
Of Marblehead
Sweet milk could turn
To mold in churn.'

And Uncle Winthrop has a big book about them."

"He had better take you to Salem. That was the very hot-bed of it all," said Warren.

Doris came around to Aunt Priscilla. "Did your grandmother really see a witch?" she asked in a serious tone.

"Well, perhaps she didn't exactly *see* it. But she was living at Salem and had a queer neighbor. One day they had some words, and when grandmother went to churn her milk turned all moldy and spoiled the butter. Grandmother didn't even dare feed it to the pigs. So it went on several times. Then another neighbor said to her, 'The next time it happens you just throw a dipper-full over the back log.' And so grandmother did. It made an awful smell and smoke. Then she washed out her churn and put it away. She was barely through when someone came running in, and said, 'Have you any sweet oil, Mrs. Parker? Hetty Lane set herself afire cleaning the cinders out of her oven, and she's dreadfully burned. Come right over.' Grandmother was a little afraid, but she went, and, sure enough, it had happened just the moment she threw the milk in the fire. One side of her was burned, and one hand. And although the neighbors suspected her, they were all very kind to her while she was ill. But grandmother had no more trouble after that, and it was said Hetty Lane never bewitched anybody again."

"It's something like the kelpies and brownies Barby used to tell about that were in England long time ago," said Doris, big-eyed. "They hid tools and ate up the food and spoiled the milk and the bread, turning it to stone. They went away—perhaps someone burned them up."

Aunt Priscilla gave her sniff. To be compared with such childish stuff!

"It was very curious," said Mrs. Leverett. "I have always been glad I was not alive at that time. Sometimes unaccountable things happen."

"Did you ever see a truly witch yourself, Aunt Priscilla?" asked the child.

"No, I never did," she answered honestly.

"Then I guess they did go with the fairies and kelpies. Could I tell your story over sometime?" she inquired eagerly.

Telling ghost stories and witch stories was quite an amusement at that period.

"Why, yes—if you want to." She was rather pleased to have it go to the Royalls'.

"The last stitch," and Betty folded up her work. "Come, Doris, say good-night, and let us go to bed."

Doris put a little kiss on Aunt Priscilla's wrinkled hand.

CHAPTER XV

A FREEDOM SUIT

Aunt Priscilla had a dozen changes of mind as to whether to go to Cousin Adams' or not. But Betty insisted. She trimmed her cap and altered the sleeves of her best black silk gown. The elderly people were wearing "leg-o'-mutton" sleeves now, while the young people had great puffs. Long straight Puritan sleeves were hardly considered stylish. And then Cousin Win sent the chaise up for her.

Mrs. March, Cary's aunt, had come up to Boston to make a little visit. Mr. March was a ship builder at Plymouth. She was quite anxious to see this cousin that Cary had talked about so much, and she was almost jealous lest he should be crowded out of his rightful place. She had no children of her own, but her husband had four when they were married. So a kind of motherly sympathy still went out to Cary.

Betty came over in the morning. She and Miss Recompense were always very friendly. They talked of jells and jams and preserves; it was too early for any fresh fruit except strawberries, and Cato always took a good deal of pains to have these of the very nicest.

The wide fireplace was filled in with green boughs and the shining leaves of "bread and butter." The rugs were taken up and the floor had a coat of polish. The parlor was wide open, arrayed in the stately furnishings of a century ago. There were two Louis XIV. chairs that had really come from France. There were some square, heavy pieces of furniture that we should call Eastlake now. And the extravagant thing was a Brussels carpet with a scroll centerpiece and a border in arabesque.

The guests began to come at two. Miss Recompense and Betty had been arranging the long table with its thick basket-work cloth that was fragrant with sweet scents. Betty wore her blue and white silk, as that had met with some mishaps at Hartford. Miss Recompense had on a brown silk with a choice bit of thread lace, and a thread lace cap. Many of the elderly society ladies wore immense headgears like turbans, with sometimes one or two marabou feathers, which were considered extremely elegant. But Miss Recompense kept to her small rather plain cap, and looked very ladylike, quite fit to do the honors of the house.

Some of the cousins had driven in from Cambridge and South Boston. Miss Cragie, who admired her second-cousin Adams very much, and it was said would not have been averse to a marriage with him, came over from the old house that had once been Washington's headquarters and was to be more famous still as the home of one of America's finest poets. She took a great interest in Cary and made him a welcome guest.

We should call it a kind of lawn party now. The guests flitted around the garden and lawn, inspected the promising fruit trees, and were enthusiastic over the roses. Then they wandered over to the Mall and discussed the impending changes in Boston, and said, as people nearly always do, that it would be ruined by improvements. It was sacrilegious to take away Beacon Hill. It was absurd to think of filling in the flats! Who would want to live on made ground? And where were all the people to come from to build houses on these wonderful streets? Why, it was simply ridiculous!

There were some young men who felt rather awkward and kept in a little knot with Cary. There were a few young girls who envied Betty Leverett her at-homeness, and the fact that she had spent a winter in Hartford. Croquet would have been a boon then, to make a breach in the walls of deadly reserve.

Elderly men smoked, walked about, and talked of the prospect of war. Most of them had high hopes of President Madison just now.

Doris was a point of interest for everybody. Her charming simplicity went to all hearts. Betty had dressed her hair a dozen different ways, but found none so pretty as tying part of the curls on top with a ribbon. She had grown quite a little taller, but was still slim and fair.

Miss Cragie took a great fancy to her and said she must come and spend the day with her and visit the notable points of Cambridge. And next year Cary would graduate, and she supposed they would have a grand time.

The supper was quite imposing. Cato's nephew, a tidy young colored lad, came from one of the inns, and acquitted himself with superior elegance. It was indeed a feast, enlivened with bright conversation. People expected to talk then, not look bored and indifferent. Each one brought something besides appetite to the feast.

Afterward they went out on the porch and sang, the ice being broken between the younger part of the company. There were some amusing patriotic songs with choruses that inspired even the older people. "Hail, Columbia!" was greeted with applause.

There were sentimental songs as well, Scotch and old English ballads. Two of Cary's friends sang "Queen Mary's Escape" with a great deal of spirit. Then Uncle Win asked Doris if she could not sing a little French song that she sang for him quite often, and that was set to a very touching melody.

She hung back and colored up, but she did want to please Uncle Win. She was standing beside him, so she straightened up and took a step out, and holding his hand sang with a grace that went to each heart. But she hid herself behind Uncle Win's shoulder when the compliments began. Cary came around, and said "She need not be afraid; it was just beautiful!"

After that the company began to disperse. Everybody said "It always was delightful to come over here," and the women wondered how it happened that such an attractive man as Mr. Winthrop Adams had not married again and had someone to entertain regularly.

There was a magnificent full moon, and the air was delicious with fragrance. One after another drove away, or taking the arm of a companion uttered a cordial good-night. Mr. Adams had sent some elderly friends home in a carriage, and begged the Leveretts to wait until it came back.

Warren had not been very intimate with the young collegian; their walks in life lay quite far apart. But Cary came and joined them as they were all out on the porch.

"I hope you had a pleasant time," he began. "If it had not been a family party I should have asked the club to come over and sing some of the college songs. Arthur Sprague has a fine voice. And you sing very well, Warren."

"I have been in a singing class this winter, I like music so much."

"You ought to hear half a dozen of our fellows together! But this little bird warbled melodiously," and he put his arm over the shoulder of Doris. "I did not know she could move an audience so deeply."

"I was so frightened at first," began Doris with a long breath. "I don't mind singing for Uncle Win, and one day when there were some guests Madam Royall asked me to sing a little French song she had known in her youth. Isn't it queer a song should last so long?"

"The fine songs ought to last forever. I hope we will have some national songs presently besides the ridiculous 'Yankee Doodle.' It doesn't seem quite so bad when it is played by the band and men are marching to it."

Cary straightened himself up. Being slender he often allowed his shoulders to droop.

"Now you look like a soldier," exclaimed Warren.

"I'd like to be one, first-rate. I'd leave college now and go in the Navy if there was another boy to follow out father's plans. But I can't bear to disappoint him. It's hard to go against your father when you are all he has. So I suppose I will go on and study law, and some day you will hear of my being judge. But we are going to have a big war, and I would like to take a hand in it. I wish I was twenty-one."

"I shall be next month. I am going to have a little company. I'd like you to come, Cary."

"I just will, thank you. What are you going to do?"

"I shall stay with father, of course. I have been learning the business. I think I shouldn't like to go to war unless the enemy really came to us. I should fight for my home."

"There are larger questions even than homes," replied Cary.

Betty came around the corner of the porch with Uncle Win, to whom she was talking in her bright, energetic fashion. Aunt Elizabeth said it was very pleasant to see so many of the relatives again.

"The older generation is dropping out, and we shall soon be among the old people ourselves," Mr. Leverett said. "I was thinking to-night how many youngish people were here who have grown up in the last ten years."

"We each have a young staff to lean upon," rejoined Mr. Adams proudly, glancing at the two boys.

The carriage came round. Aunt Priscilla shook hands with Cousin Winthrop, and said, much moved:

"I've had a pleasant time, and I had a good mind not to come. I'm getting old and queer and not fit for anything but to sit in the corner and grumble, instead of frolicking round."

"Oh, don't grumble. Why, I believe I am going backward. I feel ten years younger, and you are not old enough to die of old age. Betty, you must keep prodding her up."

He handed her in the carriage himself, and when they were all in Doris said:

"It seems as if I ought to go, too."

Uncle Win caught her hand, as if she might run away.

"I do think Cousin Winthrop has improved of late," said Mrs. Leverett. "He has gained a little flesh and looks so bright and interested, and he talked to all the folks in such a cordial way, as if he was really glad to see them. And those strawberries did beat all for size. Betty, the table looked like a feast for a king, if they deserve anything better than common folks."

"Any other child would be clear out of bonds and past redemption," declared Aunt Priscilla. "Everybody made so much of her, as if it was her party. And how the little creetur does sing! I'd like to hear her praising the Lord with that voice instead of wasting it on French things that may be so bad you couldn't say them in good English."

"That isn't," replied Betty. "It is a little good-night that her mother used to sing to her and taught her."

Aunt Priscilla winked hard and subsided. A little orphan girl—well, Cousin Winthrop would be a good father to her. Perhaps no one would ever be quite tender enough for her mother.

Everybody went home pleased. Yet nowadays such a family party would have been dull and formal, with no new books and theaters and plays and tennis and golf to talk about, and the last ball game, perhaps. There had been a kind of gracious courtesy in inquiries about each other's families—a true sympathy for the deaths and misfortunes, a kindly pleasure in the successes, a congratulation for the younger members of the family growing up, a little circling about religion and the recent rather broad doctrines the clergy were entertaining. For it was a time of ferment when the five strong points of Calvinism were being severely shaken, and the doctrine of election assaulted by the doctrine that, since Christ died for all, all might in some mysterious manner share the benefit without being ruled out by their neighbors.

Winthrop Adams would hardly have dreamed that the presence of a little girl in the house was stirring every pulse in an unwonted fashion. He had brooded over books so long; now he took to nature and saw many things through the child's fresh, joyous sight. He brushed up his stories of half-forgotten knowledge for her; he recalled his boyhood's lore of birds and squirrels, bees and butterflies, and began to feast anew on the beauty of the world and all things in their season.

It is true, in those days knowledge and literature were not widely diffused. A book or two of sermons, the "Pilgrim's Progress," perhaps "Fox's Book of Martyrs," and the Farmer's Almanac were the extent of literature in most families. Women had too much to do to spend their time reading except on Saturday evening and after second service on the Sabbath—then it must be religious reading.

But Boston was beginning to stir in the education of its women. Mrs. Abigail Adams had said, "If we mean to have heroes, statesmen, and philosophers, we should have learned women." They started a circle of sociality that was to be above the newest pattern for a gown and the latest recipe for cake or preserves. A Mrs. Grant had written a volume called "Letters from the Mountains," which they interested themselves in having republished. Hannah Adams had written some valuable works, and was now braiding straw for a living; and Mrs. Josiah Quincy exerted herself to have so talented a woman placed above indigence. She also endeavored to have Miss Edgeworth's "Moral Tales" republished for young people. Scott was beginning to infuse new life with his wonderful tales, which could safely be put in the hands of younger readers. The first decade of the century was laying a foundation for the grand work to be done later on. And with nearly every vessel, or with the travelers from abroad, would come some new books from England. Though they were dear, yet there were a few "foolish" people who liked a book better than several dollars added to their savings.

Warren's freedom suit and his freedom party interested Doris a great deal. Since Betty's return there had been several evening companies, with the parlor opened and the cake and lemonade set out on the table instead of being passed around. Betty and Jane Morse were fast friends. They went "uptown" of an afternoon and had a promenade, with now and then a nod from some of the quality. Betty was very much elated when Cary Adams walked home with her one afternoon and planned about the party. He would ask three of the young fellows, and with himself they would give some college songs. He knew Miss Morse's cousin, Morris Winslow, very well—he met him quite frequently at the Royalls'. Indeed, Cary knew he was a warm admirer of Isabel Royall.

After all, the much-talked-of suit was only a best Sunday suit of black broadcloth. Doris looked disappointed.

"Did you expect I would have red and white stripes down the sides and blue stars all over the coat?" Warren asked teasingly. "And an eagle on the buttons? I am afraid then I should be impressed and taken out to sea."

"Betty," she said afterward, "will you have a freedom suit when you are twenty-one. And must it be a black gown?"

"I think they never give girls that," answered Betty laughingly. "Theirs is a wedding gown. Though after you are twenty-one, if you go anywhere and earn money, you can keep it for yourself. Your parents cannot claim it."

Warren had a holiday. His father said he did not want to see him near the store all day long. He went over to Uncle Win's, who was just having some late cherries picked to grace the feast, and he was asked into the library, where Uncle Win made him a very pleasant little birthday speech and gave him a silver watch to remember the occasion by. Warren was so surprised he hardly knew how to thank him.

Betty was sorry there could be no dancing at the party, especially as Mr. Winslow had offered black Joe. But mother would be so opposed they did not even suggest it.

The young people began to gather about seven. They congratulated the hero of the occasion, and one young fellow recited some amusing verses. They played games and forfeits and had a merry time. The Cambridge boys sang several beautiful songs, and others of the gay, rollicking order. The supper table looked very inviting, Betty thought. Altogether it was a great pleasure to the young people, who kept it up quite late, but then it was such a delightful summer night! Doris thought the singing the most beautiful part of all.

Warren's great surprise occurred the next morning. There was a new sign up over the door in the place of the old weather-beaten one that his father had admitted was disgraceful. And on it in nice fresh lettering was:

F. LEVERETT & SON.

"Oh, father!" was all he could say for a moment.

"Hollis was a good, steady boy—I've been blest in my boys, and I thank God for it, so when Hollis was through with his trade, and had that good opportunity to go in business, I advanced him some money. He has been prospered and would have paid it back, but I told him to keep it for his part. This will be your offset to it. Cousin Winthrop is coming down presently, and Giles Thatcher, and we will have all the papers signed, so that if anything happens to me there will be no trouble. You've been a good son, Warren, and I hope you will make a good, honorable man."

The tears sprang to Warren's eyes. He was very glad he had yielded some points to his father and accepted obedience as his due to be rendered cheerfully. For Mr. Leverett had never been an unreasonable man.

Uncle Win congratulated him again. Betty and her mother went down in the afternoon to see the new sign. Aunt Priscilla thought it rather risky business, for being twenty-one didn't always bring good sense with it, and too much liberty was apt to spoil anyone with no more experience than Warren.

Betty said Aunt Priscilla must have something to worry about, which was true enough. She had come to the Leveretts' to see how she could stand "being without a home," as she phrased it. But she found herself quite feeble, and with a cough, and she admitted she never had quite gotten over the winter's cold which she took going to church that bitter Sunday. As just the right person to keep her house had not come to hand, and as it really was cheaper to live this way, and gave one a secure feeling in case of illness, she thought it best to go on. Elizabeth Leverett made her feel very much at home. She could go down in the kitchen and do a bit of work when she wanted to, she could weed a little out in the garden, she could mend and knit and pass away the time, and it was a pleasure to have someone to converse with, to argue with.

She had been in great trouble at first about black Polly. That she had really entertained the thought of getting rid of her in a helpless old age seemed a great sin now.

"And the poor old thing had been so faithful until she began to lose her memory. How could I have resolved to do such a thing!" she would exclaim.

"You never did resolve to do it, Aunt Priscilla," Mr. Leverett said one day. "I am quite sure you could not have done it when it came to the pinch. It was one of the temptations only."

"But I never struggled against it. That is what troubles me."

"God knew just how it would end. He did not mean the poor creature to become a trouble to anyone. If he had wanted to try you further, no doubt he would have done it. Now, why can't you accept the release as he sent it? It seems almost as if you couldn't resign yourself to his wisdom."

"You make religion so comfortable, Foster Leverett, that I hardly know whether to take it that way. It isn't the old-fashioned way in which I was brought up."

"There was just one Doubting Thomas among the Twelve," he replied smilingly.

There was little need of people going away for a summering then, though they did try to visit their relatives in the country places about. People came up from the more southern States for the cool breezes and the pleasant excursions everywhere. There were delightful parties going out almost every day, to the islands lying off the city, to the little towns farther away, to some places where it was necessary to remain all night. Madam Royall insisted upon taking Doris with the girls for a week's excursion, and she had a happy time. Cary went to Plymouth to his aunt's, and was fascinated with sea-going matters and the naval wars in progress. Josiah March was a stanch patriot, and said the thing would never be settled until we had taught England to let our men and our vessels alone.

Only a few years before our commerce had extended over the world. Boston —with her eighty wharves and quays, her merchants of shrewd and sound judgment, ability of a high order and comprehensive as well as authentic information—at that time stood at the head of the maritime world. The West Indies, China,—though Canton was the only port to which foreigners were admitted,—and all the ports of Europe had been open to her. The coastwise trade was also enormous. From seventy to eighty sail of vessels had cleared in one day. Long Wharf, at the foot of State Street, was one of the most interesting and busy places.

The treaty between France and America had agreed that "free bottoms made free ships," but during the wars of Napoleon this had been so abridged that trade was now practically destroyed. Then England had insisted upon the right of search, which left every ship at her mercy, and hundreds of our sailors were being taken prisoners. There was a great deal of war talk already. Trade was seriously disturbed.

There was a very strong party opposed to war. What could so young a country, unprepared in every way, do? The government temporized—tried various methods in the hope of averting the storm.

People began to economize; still there was a good deal of money in Boston. Pleasures took on a rather more economical aspect and grew simpler. But business was at a standstill. The Leveretts were among the first to suffer, but Mr. Leverett's equable temperament and serene philosophy kept his family from undue anxiety.

"It's rather a hard beginning for you, my boy," he said, "but you will have years enough to recover. Only I sometimes wish it could come to a crisis and be over, so that we could begin again. It can never be quite as bad as the old war."

Doris commenced school with the Chapman girls at Miss Parker's. Uncle Win had a great fancy for sending her to Mrs. Rowson.

"Wait a year or so," counseled Madam Royall. "Children grow up fast enough without pushing them ahead. Little girlhood is the sweetest time of life for the elderly people, whatever it may be for the girls. I should like Helen and Eudora to stand still for a few years, and Doris is too perfect a little bud to be lured into blossoming. There is something unusual about the child."

When anyone praised Doris, Uncle Win experienced a thrill of delight.

Miss Parker's school was much more aristocratic than Mrs. Webb's. There were no boys and no very small children. Some of the accomplishments were taught. French, drawing and painting, and what was called the "use of the globe," which meant a large globe with all the countries of the world upon it, arranged to turn around on an axis. This was a new thing. Doris was quite fascinated by it, and when she found the North Sea and the Devonshire coast and the "Wash" the girls looked on eagerly and straightway she became a heroine.

But one unlucky recess when she had won in the game of graces a girl said:

"I don't care! That isn't anything! We beat your old English in the Revolutionary War, and if there's another war we'll beat you again. My father says so. I wouldn't be English for all the gold on the Guinea coast!"

"I am not English," Doris protested. "My father was born in this very Boston. And I was born in France."

"Well, the French are just as bad. They are not to be depended upon. You are a mean little foreign girl, and I shall not speak to you again, there now!"

Doris looked very sober. Helen Chapman comforted her and said Faith Dunscomb was not worth minding.

She told it over to Uncle Win that evening.

"I suppose I can never be a real Boston girl," she said sorrowfully.

"I think you are a pretty good one now, and of good old Boston stock," he replied smilingly. "Sometime you will be proud that you came from the other Boston. Oddly enough most of us came from England in the beginning. And the Faneuils came from France, and they are proud enough of their old Huguenot blood."

She had been to Faneuil Hall and the Market with Uncle Winthrop. They raised all their vegetables and fruit, unless it was something quite rare, and Cato did the family marketing.

Only a few years before the Market had been enlarged and improved. Fifty years earlier the building had burned down and been replaced, but even the old building had been identified with liberty of thought, and had a well-known portrait painter of that day, John Smibert, for its architect. In the later improvements it had been much enlarged, and the beautiful open arches of the ground floor were closed by doors and windows, which rendered it less picturesque. It was the marketplace *par excellence* then, as Quincy Market came in with the enterprise of the real city. But even then it rejoiced in the appellation of "The Cradle of Liberty," and the hall over the market-space was used for political gatherings.

Huckster and market wagons from the country farms congregated in Dock Square. The mornings were the most interesting time for a visit. The "quality" came in their carriages with their servant man to run to and fro; or some young lady on horseback rode up through the busy throng to leave an order, and then the women whose servant carried a basket, or those having no servant carried their own baskets, and who went about cheapening everything.

So Doris was quite comforted to know that Peter Faneuil, who was held in such esteem, had not even been born in Boston, and was of French extraction.

But girls soon get over their tiffs and disputes. Play is the great leveler. Then Doris was so obliging about the French exercises that the girls could not stay away very long at a time.

Miss Parker's typified the conventional idea of a girl's education prevalent at that time: that it should be largely accomplishment. So Doris was allowed considerable latitude in the commoner branches. Mrs. Webb had been exacting in the few things she taught, especially arithmetic. And Uncle Win admitted to himself that Doris had a poor head for figures. When she came to fractions it was heartrending. Common multiples and least and greatest common divisors had such a way of getting mixed up in her brain, that he felt very sorry for her.

She brought over Betty's book in which all her sums in the more difficult rules had been worked out and copied beautifully. There were banking and equation of payments and all the "roots" and progression and alligation and mensuration.

"I don't know what good they will really be to Betty," said Uncle Win gravely. Then, as his face relaxed into a half-smile, he added: "Perhaps Mary Manning's fifty pairs of stockings she had when she was married may be more useful. Betty has a good head and "twinkling feet." Did you know a poet said that? And another one wrote:

"'Her feet beneath her petticoat,
Like little mice stole in and out
    As if they feared the light;
But, oh, she dances such a way!
No sun upon an Easter day
    Is half so fair a sight.'"

"Oh, Uncle Win, that's just delightful! Did your poet write any more such dainty things, and can I read them? Betty would just go wild over that."

"Yes, I will find it for you. And we won't worry now about the hard knots over in the back of the arithmetic."

"Nor about the stockings. Miss Isabel is knitting some beautiful silk ones, blossom color."

Ladies and girls danced in slippers then and wore them for evening company, and stockings were quite a feature in attire.

Uncle Win was too indulgent, of course. Miss Recompense said she had never known a girl to be brought up just that way, and shook her head doubtfully.

Early in the new year an event happened, or rather the tidings came to them that seemed to have a bearing on both of these points. An old sea captain one day brought a curious oaken chest, brass bound, and with three brass initials on the top. The key, which was tied up in a small leathern bag, and a letter stowed away in an enormous well-worn wallet, he delivered to "Mr. Winthrop

Adams, Esq."

It contained an unfinished letter from Miss Arabella, beginning "Dear and Honored Sir," and another from the borough justice. Miss Arabella was dead. The care of her sister had worn her so much that she had dropped into a gentle decline, and knowing herself near the end had packed the chest with some table linen that belonged to the mother of Doris, some clothing, two dresses of her own, several petticoats, two pairs of satin slippers she had worn in her youth and outgrown, and six pairs of silk stockings. Doris would grow into them all presently.

Then inclosed was a bank note for one hundred pounds sterling, and much love and fond remembrances.

The other note announced the death of Miss Arabella Sophia Roulstone, aged eighty-one years and three months, and the time of her burial. Her will had been read and the bequests were being paid. Mr. Millington requested a release before a notary, and an acknowledgment of the safe arrival of the goods and the legacy, to be returned by the captain.

Mr. Adams went out with the captain and attended to the business.

Doris had a little cry over Miss Arabella. It did not seem as if she could be eighty years old. She could recall the sweet, placid face under the snowy cap, and almost hear the soft voice.

"That is quite a legacy," said Uncle Win. "Doris, can you compute it in dollars?"

We had come to have a currency of our own—"decimal" it was called, because computed by tens.

We still reckoned a good deal in pounds, shillings, and pence, but ours were not pounds sterling.

Doris considered and knit her delicate brows. Then a soft light illumined her face.

"Why, Uncle Win, it is five hundred dollars! Isn't that a great deal of money for a little girl like me? And must it not be saved up some way?"

"Yes, I think for your wedding day."

"And then suppose I should not get married?"

CHAPTER XVI

A SUMMER IN BOSTON

The Leveretts rejoiced heartily over Doris' good fortune. Aunt Priscilla began to trouble herself again about her will. She had taken the usual autumnal cold, but recovered from it with good nursing. Certainly Elizabeth Leverett was very kind. Aunt Priscilla had eased up Betty while her mother spent a fortnight at Salem, helping with the fall sewing and making comfortables. And this time she brought home little Ruth, who was thin and peevish, and who had not gotten well over the measles, that had affected her eyes badly. Ruth was past four.

"I wish Mary did not take life so hard," said Mrs. Leverett with a sigh. "They have been buying a new twenty-acre pasture lot and two new cows, and it is just drive all the time. That poor little Elizabeth will be all worn out before she is grown up. And Ruth wouldn't have lived the winter through there."

Ruth was extremely troublesome at first. But grandmothers have a soothing art, and after a few weeks she began to improve. The visits of Doris fairly transported her, and she amused grandpa by asking every morning "if Doris would come to-day," having implicit faith in his knowledge of everything.

Aunt Priscilla counted on the visits as well. She kept her room a good deal. Ruth's chatter disturbed her. Pattern children brought up on the strictest rules did not seem quite so agreeable to her as the little flower growing up in its own sweetness.

Betty used to walk a short distance home with her, as she declared it was the only chance she had for a bit of Doris. She was very fond of hearing about the Royalls, and now Miss Isabel's engagement to Mr. Morris Winslow was announced.

Warren declared Jane was quite "top-loftical" about it. She had been introduced to Miss Isabel at an evening company, and then they had met at Thayer's dry goods store, where she and Mrs. Chapman had been shopping, and had quite a little chat. They bowed in the street, and Jane was much pleased at the prospect of being indirectly related.

But Betty had taken tea at Uncle Winthrop's with Miss Alice Royall, who had come over with the two little girls to return some of the visits Doris had made. The girls fell in love with bright, versatile Betty, and Alice was much interested in her visit to Hartford, and thought her quite charming.

Then it was quite fascinating to compare notes about Mr. Adams with one of his own kin. Alice made no secret of her admiration for him; the whole family joined in, for that matter. Young girls could be a little free and friendly with elderly gentlemen without exciting comment or having to be so precise.

When Jane said "Cousin Morris told me such or such a thing," Betty was delighted to reply, "Yes, Doris was speaking of it." The girls were the best of friends, but this half-unconscious rivalry was natural.

Mrs. Leverett had no objections to the intimacy now. Betty was older and more sensible, and now she was really a young lady receiving invitations, and going out to walk or to shop with the girls. For hard as the times were, a little finery had to be bought, or a gown now and then.

Mrs. King had not gone to New York, though her husband had been there on business. She would have been very glad of Betty's company; but with little Ruth and Aunt Priscilla, Betty felt she ought not leave her mother. And, then, she was having a young girl's good time at home.

Mrs. Leverett half wished Jane might "fancy Warren." She was a smart, attractive, and withal sensible girl. But Warren was not thinking of girls just now, or of marrying. The debating society was a source of great interest and nearly every "talk" turned on some aspect of the possible war. His singing class occupied him one evening, and one evening was devoted to dancing. He liked Jane very much in a friendly fashion, and they went on calling each other by their first names, but if he happened to drop in there was almost sure to be other company.

The "Son" on the business sign over the doorway gave him a great sense of responsibility, especially now when everything was so dull, and money, as people said, "came like drawing teeth," a painful enough process in those days.

Finally Miss Isabel Royall's wedding day was set for early in June. The shopping was quite an undertaking. There were Thayer's dry-goods store and Daniel Simpson's and Mr. Bromfield's, the greater and the lesser shops on Washington and School streets. It was quite a risk now ordering things from abroad, vessels were interfered with so much. But there were China silks and Canton crape,—a beautiful material,—and French and English goods that escaped the enemy; so if you had the money you could find enough for an extensive wedding outfit. At home we had also begun to make some very nice woolen goods.

May came out full of bloom and beauty. Such a shower of blossoms from cherry, peach, pear, and apple would be difficult now to imagine. For almost every house had a yard or a garden. Colonnade Row was among the earliest places to be built up compactly of brick and was considered very handsome for the time.

But people strolled around then to see the beautiful unfolding of nature. There was the old Hancock House on Beacon Street. The old hero had gone his way, and his wife was now Madam Scott, and lived in the same house, and though the garden and nursery had been shorn of much of their glory, there were numerous foreign trees that were curiously beautiful, and people used to make at least one pilgrimage to see these immense mulberry trees in bloom.

The old Bowdoin garden was another remarkable place, and the air around was sweet for weeks with the bloom of fruit trees and later on the grapes that were raised in great profusion. You sometimes saw elegant old Madam Bowdoin walking up and down the garden paths and the grandchildren skipping rope or playing tag.

But Summer Street, with its crown of beauty, held its head as high as any of its neighbors.

"I don't see why May should be considered unlucky for weddings," Isabel protested. "I should like to be married in a bower of apple blossoms."

"But isn't a bower of roses as beautiful?"

"And the snow of the cherries and pears! Think of it—fragrant snow!"

But Isabel gave parties to her friends, and they took tea out under the great apple tree and were snowed on with every soft wave of wind.

It was not necessary then to go into seclusion. The bride-elect took pleasure in showing her gowns and her finery to her dearest friends. She was to be married in grandmother's brocade. Her own mother had it lent to her for the occasion. It was very handsome and could almost "stand alone." There were great flowers that looked as if they were embroidered on it, and now it had assumed an ivory tint. Two breadths had been taken out of the skirt, people were so slim at present. But the court train was left. The bertha, as we should call it now, was as a cobweb, and the lace from the puff sleeve falling over the arm of the same elegant material.

It was good luck to borrow something to be married in, and good luck to have something old as well as the something new.

Morris Winslow had been quite a beau about town. He was thirty now, ten years older than Isabel. He had a big house over in Dorchester and almost a farm. He owned another in Boston, where a tavern of the higher sort was kept and rooms rented to bachelors. He had an apartment here and kept his servant Joe and his handsome team, besides his saddle horse. He was rather gay, but of good moral character. No one else would have been accepted as a lover at the Royalls'.

Jane was invited to one of the teas. People had not come to calling them "Dove" parties yet, nor had breakfasts or luncheon parties come in vogue for such occasions. There were about a dozen girls. They inspected the wedding outfit, they played graces, they sang songs, and had tea in Madam Royall's old china that had come to America almost a hundred years before.

Afterward several young gentlemen called, and they walked up and down in the moonlight. A young lady could invite her own escort, especially if she was "keeping company." Sometimes the mothers sent a servant to fetch home their daughters.

Of course Jane had an invitation to the wedding. Alice and a friend were to be bridesmaids, and the children were to be gowned in simple white muslin, with bows and streamers of pink satin ribbon and strew roses in the bride's path. They were flower maidens. Dorcas Payne was asked, and Madam Royall begged Mr. Adams to allow his niece to join them. They would all take it as a great favor.

"The idea!" cried Aunt Priscilla; "and she no relation! If the queen was to come to Boston I dare say Doris Adams would be asked to turn out to meet her! Well, I hope her pretty face won't ever get her into trouble."

It was a beautiful wedding, everybody said. The great rooms and the halls were full of guests, but they kept a way open for the bride, who came downstairs on her lover's arm, and he looked very proud and manly. The bridesmaids and groomsmen stood one couple at each side. The little girls strewed their flowers and then stood in a circle, and the bride swept gracefully to the open space and turned to face the guests. The maid was a little excited when she pulled off the bride's glove, but all went well, and Isabel Royall was at her very best.

While the kissing and congratulations were going on, four violins struck up melodious strains. It was just six o'clock then. The bride and groom stood for a while in the center of the room, then marched around and smiled and talked, and finally went out to the dining room, where the feast was spread, and where the bride had to cut the cake.

Cary Adams was among the young people. He was a great favorite with Alice, and a welcome guest, if he did not come quite as often as his father.

One of the prettiest things afterward was the minuet danced by the four little girls, and after that two or three cotillions were formed. The bride danced with both of the groomsmen, and the new husband with both of the bridesmaids. Then their duty was done.

They were to drive over to Dorchester that night, so presently they started. Two or three old slippers were thrown for good luck. Several of the younger men were quite nonplused at this arrangement, for they had planned some rather rough fun in a serenade, thinking the bridal couple would stay in town.

There were some amusements, jesting and laughter, some card-playing and health-drinking among the elders. The guests congratulated Madam Royall nearly as much as they had the bride. Then one after another came and bade her good-night, and took away their parcel of wedding cake to dream on.

"Oh," cried Doris on the way home,—the night was so pleasant they were walking,—"oh, wasn't it splendid! I wish Betty could have been there. Cary, how old must you be before you can get married?"

"Well—I should have to look up a girl."

"Oh, take Miss Alice. She likes you ever so much—I heard her say so. But you haven't any house like Mr. Winslow. Uncle Win, couldn't he bring her home to live with us?"

Cary's cheeks were in a red flame. Uncle Win laughed.

"My dear," he began, "a young man must have some business or some money to take care of his wife. She wouldn't like to be dependent on his relatives. Cary is going to study law, which will take some years, then he must get established, and so we will have to wait a long while. He is too young. Mr. Winslow is thirty; Cary isn't twenty yet."

"Oh, dear! Well, perhaps Betty will get married. The girl doesn't have to be so old?"

"No," said Uncle Win.

Betty came over the next morning to spend the day and help Miss Recompense to distill. She wanted to hear the first account from Doris and Uncle Win, to take off the edge of Jane's triumphant news.

They made rose water and a concoction from the spice pinks. Then they preserved cherries. Uncle Win took them driving toward night and said some day they would go over to Dorchester. He had several friends there.

The next excitement for Doris was the college commencement. Mr. Adams was disappointed that his son should not stand at the head of almost everything. He had taken one prize and made some excellent examinations, but there were many ranking as high and some higher.

There were no ball games, no college regattas to share honors then. Not that these things were tabooed. There were some splendid rowing matches and games, but then young men had a desire to stand high intellectually.

A long while before Judge Sewall had expressed his disapproval of the excesses at dinners, the wine-drinking and conviviality, and had set Friday for commencement so that there would be less time for frolicking. The war, with its long train of economies, and the greater seriousness of life in general, had tempered all things, but there was gayety enough now, with dinners given to the prize winners and a very general jollification.

Doris went with Uncle Winthrop. Commencement was one of the great occasions of the year. All the orations were in Latin, and the young men might have been haranguing a Roman army, so vigorous were they. Many of the graduates were very young; boys really studied at that time.

The remainder of the day and the one following were given over to festivities. Booths were everywhere on the ground; colors flying, flowers wreathed in every fashion, and so much merriment that they quite needed Judge Sewall back again to restrain the excesses.

Mr. Adams and Doris went to dine at the Cragie House, and Doris would have felt quite lost among judges and professors but for Miss Cragie, who took her in charge. When they went home in the early evening the shouts and songs and boisterousness seemed like a perfect orgy.

Someone has said, with a kind of dry wit, "Wherever an Englishman goes courts and litigation are sure to prevail." Certainly our New England forefathers, who set out with the highest aims, soon found it necessary to establish law courts. In the early days every man pleaded his own cause, and was especially versed in the "quirks of the law." Jeremy Gridley, a graduate of Harvard, interested himself in forming a law club in the early part of the previous century to pursue the study enough "to keep out of the briars." And to Justice Dana is ascribed the credit of administering to Mr. Secretary Oliver, standing under the Liberty Tree in a great assemblage of angry townspeople, an oath that he would take no measures to enforce the odius Stamp Act of the British Parliament or distribute it among the people.

And now the bar had a rank of its own, and Winthrop Adams had a strong desire to see his son one of the shining lights in the profession. Cary had a fine voice and was a good speaker. More than once he had distinguished himself in an argument at some of the debates. To be admitted to the office of Governor Gore was considered a high honor then, and this Mr. Adams gained for his son. Cary had another vague dream, but parental authority in well-bred families was not to be disputed at that period, and Cary acquiesced in his father's decision, since he knew his own must bring about much discussion and probably a refusal.

Mrs. King came to visit her mother this summer. She left all her children at home, as she wanted to visit round, and was afraid they might be an annoyance to Aunt Priscilla. Little Ruth had gone home very much improved, her eyes quite restored.

Uncle Winthrop enjoyed Mrs. King's society very much. She was intelligent and had cultivated her natural abilities, she also had a certain society suavity that made her an agreeable companion. Doris thought her a good deal like Betty, she was so pleasant and ready for all kinds of enjoyment. Aunt Priscilla considered her very frivolous, and there was so much going and coming that she wondered Elizabeth did not get crazy over it.

They were to remove to New York in the fall, Mr. King having perfected his business arrangements. So Betty would have her winter in the gay city after all.

There were many delightful excursions with pleasure parties up and down the bay. The Embargo had been repealed, and the sails of merchant ships were again whitening the harbor, and business people breathed more freely.

There were Castle Island, with its fortifications and its waving flag, and queer old dreary-looking Noddle's Island, also little towns and settlements where one could spend a day delightfully. Every place, it seemed to Doris, had some queer, interesting story, and she possessed an insatiable appetite for them. There was the great beautiful sweep of Boston Bay, with its inlets running around the towns and its green islands everywhere—places that had been famous and had suffered in the war, and were soon to suffer again.

Mrs. King had a friend at Hingham, and one day they went there in a sort of family party. Uncle Winthrop obtained a carriage and drove them around. It was still famous for its wooden-ware factories, and Uncle Win said in the time of Governor Andros, when money was scarce among the early settlers, Hingham had paid its taxes in milk pails, but they decided the taxes could not have been very high, or the fame of the milk pails must have been very great.

Mrs. Gerry said in the early season forget-me-nots grew wild all about, and the ground was blue with them.

"Oh, Uncle Win, let us come and see them next year," cried Doris.

Then they hunted up the old church that had been nearly rent asunder by the bringing in of a bass viol to assist the singers. Party spirit had run very high. The musical people had quoted the harps and sacbuts of King David's time, the trumpets and cymbals. At last the big bass viol won the victory and was there. And the hymn was:

"Oh, may my heart in tune be found,
Like David's harp of solemn sound."

But the old minister was not to be outdone. The hymn was lined off in this fashion:

"Oh, may my heart go diddle, diddle,
Like Uncle David's sacred fiddle."

There were still a great many people opposed to instrumental music and who could see no reverence in the organ's solemn sound.

Uncle Winthrop smiled over the story, and Betty said it would do to tell to Aunt Priscilla.

Betty begged that they might take Doris to Salem with them. Doris thought she should like to see the smart little Elizabeth, who was like a woman already, and her old playfellow James, as well as Ruth, who seemed to her hardly beyond babyhood. And there were all the weird old stories—she had read some of them in Cotton Mather's "Magnalia," and begged others from Miss Recompense, who did not quite know whether she believed them or not, but she said emphatically that people had been mistaken and there was no such thing as witches.

"A whole week!" said Uncle Winthrop. "Whatever shall I do without a little girl that length of time?"

"But you have Cary now," she returned archly.

Cary was a good deal occupied with young friends and college associates. Now and then he went over to Charlestown and stayed all night with one of his chums.

"I suppose I ought to learn how it will be without you when you want to go away in real earnest."

"I am never going away."

"Suppose Mrs. King should invite you to New York? She has some little girls."

"You might like to go," she returned with a touch of hesitation.

"To see the little girls?" smilingly.

"To see a great city. Do you suppose they are very queer—and Dutch?"

He laughed at that.

"But the Dutch people went there and settled, just as the Puritans came here.

And I think I like the Dutch because they have such a merry time at Christmas. We read about them in history at school."

"And then the English came, you know. I think now there is not much that would suggest Holland. I have been there."

Then Doris was eager to know what it was like, and Uncle Winthrop was interested in telling her. They forgot all about Salem—at least, Doris did until she was going to bed.

"If you *do* go you must be very careful a witch does not catch you, for I couldn't spare my little girl altogether."

"Uncle Winthrop, I am going to stay with you always. When Miss Recompense gets real old and cannot look after things I shall be your housekeeper."

"When Miss Recompense reaches old age I am afraid I shall be quaking for very fear."

"But it takes a long while for people to get very old," she returned decisively.

Betty came over the next day to tell her they would start on Thursday morning, and were going in a sloop to Marblehead with a friend of her father's, Captain Morton.

It was almost like going to sea, Doris thought. They had to thread their way through the islands and round Winthrop Head. There was Grover's Cliff, and then they went out past Nahant into the broad, beautiful bay, where you could see the ocean. It seemed ages ago since she had crossed it. They kept quite in to the green shores and could see Lynn and Swampscott, then they rounded one more point and came to Marblehead, where Captain Morton stopped to unload his cargo, while they went on to Salem.

At the old dock they were met by a big boy and a country wagon. This was Foster Manning, the eldest grandson of the family.

"Oh," cried Betty in amazement, "how you have grown! It *is* Foster?"

He smiled and blushed under the sunburn—a thin, angular boy, tall for his age, with rather large features and light-brown hair with tawny streaks in it. But his gray-blue eyes were bright and honest-looking.

"Yes, 'm," staring at the others, for he had at the moment forgotten his aunt's looks.

Betty introduced them.

"I should not have known you," said Aunt Electa. "But boys change a good deal in two years or so."

They were helped in the wagon, more by Betty than Foster, who was evidently very bashful. They drove up past the old Court House, through the main part of the town, which even then presented a thriving appearance with its home industries. But the seaport trade had been sadly interfered with by the rumors and apprehensions of war. At that time it was quaint and country-looking, with few pretensions to architectural beauty. There was old Gallows Hill at one end, with its haunting stories of witchcraft days.

The irregular road wandered out to the farming districts. Many small towns had been set off from the original Salem in the century before, and the boundaries were marked mostly by the farms.

Betty inquired after everybody, but most of the answers were "Yes, 'm" and "No, 'm." When they came in sight of the house Mrs. Manning and little Ruth ran out to welcome the guests, followed by Elizabeth, who was almost as good as a woman.

The house itself was a plain two-story with the hall door in the middle and a window on each side. The roof had a rather steep pitch in front with overhanging eaves. From this pitch it wandered off in a slow curve at the back and seemed stretched out to cover the kitchen and the sheds.

A grassy plot in front was divided by a trodden path. On one side of the small stoop was a great patch of hollyhocks that were tolerated because they needed no special care. Mrs. Manning had no time to waste upon flowers. The aspect was neat enough, but rather dreary, as Doris contrasted it with the bloom at home.

But the greetings were cordial, only Mrs. Manning asked Betty "If she had been waiting for someone to come and show her the way?" Ruth ran to Doris at once and caught her round the waist, nestling her head fondly on the bosom of the guest. Elizabeth stood awkwardly distant, and only stared when Betty presented her to Doris.

They were ushered into the first room, which was the guest chamber. The floor was painted, and in summer the rugs were put away. A large bedstead with faded chintz hangings, a bureau, a table, and two chairs completed the furniture. The ornaments were two brass candlesticks and a snuffers tray on the high mantel.

Here they took off their hats and laid down their budgets, and then went through to mother's room, where there were a bed and a cradle, a bureau, a big chest, a table piled up with work, a smaller candlestand, and a curious old desk. Next to this was the living-room, where the main work of life went on. Beyond this were a kitchen and some sheds.

Baby Hester sat on the floor and looked amazed at the irruption, then began to whimper. Her mother hushed her up sharply, and she crept out to the living-room.

"We may as well all go out," said Mrs. Manning. "I must see about supper, for that creature we have doesn't know when the kettle boils," and she led the way.

Elizabeth began to spread the tea table. A youngish woman was working in the kitchen. The Mannings had taken one of the town's poor, who at this period were farmed out. Sarah Lewis was not mentally bright, and required close watching, which she certainly received at the Mannings'. Doris stood by the window with Ruth, until the baby cried, when her mother told her to take Hester out in the kitchen and give her some supper and put her to bed. And then Doris could do nothing but watch Elizabeth while the elders discussed family affairs, the conversation a good deal interrupted by rather sharp orders to Sarah in the kitchen, and some not quite so sharp to Elizabeth.

Supper was all on the table when the men came in. There were Mr. Manning, Foster and James, and two hired men.

"You must wait, James," said his mother—"you and Elizabeth."

The guests were ranged at one end of the table, the hired men and Foster at the other. Elizabeth took some knitting and sat down by the window. The two younger children remained in the kitchen.

Doris was curiously interested, though she felt a little strange. Her eyes wandered to Elizabeth, and met the other eyes, as curious as hers. Elizabeth had straight light hair, cut square across the neck, and across her forehead in what we should call a bang. "It was time to let it grow long," her mother admitted, "but it was such a bother, falling in her eyes." Her frock, whatever color it had been, was now faded to a hopeless, depressing gray, and her brown gingham apron tied at the waist betrayed the result of many washings. She was thin and pale, too, and tired-looking. Times had not been good, and some of the crops were not turning out well, so every nerve had to be strained to pay for the new lot, in order that the interest on the amount should not eat up everything.

Afterward the men went to look to the cattle, and Mrs. Manning, when she had given orders a while in the kitchen, took her guests out on the front porch. She sat and knit as she talked to them, as the moon was shining and gave her light enough to see.

When the old clock struck nine, Mr. Manning came through the hall and stood in the doorway.

"Be you goin' to sit up all night, mother?" he inquired.

"Dear, no. And I expect you're all tired. We're up so early in the morning here that we go to bed early. And I was thinking—Ruth needn't have gone upstairs, and Doris could have slept with Elizabeth——"

"I'll go upstairs with Doris, and 'Lecty may have the room to herself," exclaimed Betty.

Grandmother Manning had a room downstairs, back of the parlor, and one of the large rooms upstairs, that the family had the privilege of using, though it was stored nearly full with a motley collection of articles and furniture. This was her right in the house left by her husband. But she spent most of her time between her daughter at Danvers and another in the heart of the town, where there were neighbors to look at, if nothing else.

Doris peered in the corners of the room by the dim candlelight.

"It's very queer," she said with a half-smile at Betty, glancing around. For there were lines across on which hung clothes and bags of dried herbs that gave the room an aromatic fragrance, and parcels in one corner piled almost up to the wall. But the space to the bed was clear, and there were a stand for the candle and two chairs.

"The children are in the next room, and the boys and men sleep at the back. The other rooms have sloping roofs. And then there's a queer little garret. Grandmother Manning is real old, and some time Mary will have all the house to herself. Josiah bought out his sisters' share, and Mrs. Manning's runs only as long as she lives."

"I shouldn't want to sleep with Elizabeth. I love you, Betty."

Betty laughed wholesomely. "You will get acquainted with her to-morrow," she said.

Doris laid awake some time, wondering if she really liked visiting, and recalling the delightful Christmas visit at Uncle Winthrop's. The indefinable something that she came to understand was not only leisure and refinement, but the certain harmonious satisfactions that make up the keynote of life from whence melody diffuses itself, were wanting here.

They had their breakfast by themselves the next morning. Friday was a busy day, but all the household except the baby were astir at five, and often earlier. There were churning and the working of butter and packing it down for customers. Of course, June butter had the royal mark, but there were plenty of people glad to get any "grass" butter.

Betty took Doris out for a walk and to show her what a farm was like. There was the herd of cows, and in a field by themselves the young ones from three months to a year. There were two pretty colts Mr. Manning was raising. And there was a flock of sheep on a stony pasture lot, with some long-legged, awkward-looking lambs who had outgrown their babyhood. Then they espied James weeding out the garden beds.

Betty sat down on a stone at the edge of the fence and took out some needlework she carried around in her pocket. Doris stood patting down the soft earth with her foot.

"Do you like to do that?" she asked presently.

"No, I don't," in a short tone.

"I think I should not either."

"'Taint the things you like, it's what has to be done," the boy flung out impatiently. "I'm not going to be a farmer. I just hate it. When I'm big enough I'm coming to Boston."

"When will you be big enough?"

"Well—when I'm twenty-one. You're of age then, you see, and your own master. But I might run away before that. Don't tell anyone that, Doris. Gewhilliker! didn't I have a splendid time at grandmother's that winter! I wish I could live there always. And grandpop is just the nicest man I know! I just hate a farm."

Doris felt very sorry for him. She thought she would not like to work that way with her bare hands. Miss Recompense always wore gloves when she gardened.

"I'd like to be you, with nothing to do."

That was a great admission. The winter at Uncle Leverett's he had rather despised girls. Cousin Sam was the one to be envied then. And it seemed to her that she kept quite busy at home, but it was a pleasant kind of business.

She did not see Elizabeth until dinner time. James took the men's dinner out to the field. They could not spend the time to come in. And after dinner Betty harnessed the old mare Jinny, and took Electa, Doris, and little Ruth out driving. The sun had gone under a cloud and the breeze was blowing over from the ocean. Electa chose to see the old town, even if there were but few changes and trade had fallen off. Several slender-masted merchantmen were lying idly at the quays, half afraid to venture with a cargo lest they might fall into the hands of privateers. The stores too had a depressed aspect. Men sat outside gossiping in a languid sort of way, and here and there a woman was tending her baby on the porch or doing a bit of sewing.

"What a sleepy old place!" said Mrs. King. "It would drive me to distraction."

CHAPTER XVII

ANOTHER GIRL

Saturday afternoon the work was finished up and the children washed. The supper was eaten early, and at sundown the Sabbath had begun. The parlor was opened, but the children were allowed out on the porch. Ruth sprang up a time or two rather impatiently.

"Sit still," said Elizabeth, "or you will have to go to bed at once."

"Couldn't I take her a little walk?" asked Doris.

"A walk! Why it is part of Sunday!"

"But I walk on Sunday with Uncle Winthrop."

"It's very wicked. We *do* walk to church, but that isn't anything for pleasure."

"But uncle thinks one ought to be happy and joyous on Sunday. It is the day the Lord rose from the dead."

"It's the Sabbath. And you are to remember the Sabbath to keep it holy."

"What is the difference between Sabbath and Sunday?"

"There aint any," said James. "There's six days to work, and I wish there was two Sundays—one in the middle of the week. The best time of all is Sunday night. You don't have to keep so very still, and you don't have to work neither."

Elizabeth sighed. Then she said severely, "Do you know your catechism, James?"

"Well—I always have to study it Sunday morning," was the rather sullen reply.

"Maybe you had better go in and look it over."

"You never do want a fellow to take any comfort. Yes, I know it."

"Ruth, if you are getting sleepy go to bed."

Ruth had leaned her head down on Doris' shoulder.

"She's wide awake," and Doris gave her a little squeeze that made her smile. She would have laughed outright but for fear.

Elizabeth leaned her head against the door jamb.

"You look so tired," said Doris pityingly.

"I am tired through and through. I am always glad to have Saturday night come and no knitting or anything. Don't you knit when you are home?"

"I haven't knit—much." Doris flushed up to the roots of her fair hair, remembering her unfortunate attempts at achieving a stocking.

"What do you do?"

"Study, and read to Uncle Winthrop, and go to school and to writing school, and walk and take little journeys and drives and do drawing. Next year I shall learn to paint flowers."

"But you do some kind of work?"

"I keep my room in order and Uncle Win trusts me to dust his books. And I sew a little and make lace. But, you see, there is Miss Recompense and Dinah and Cato."

"Oh, what a lot of help! What does Miss Recompense do?"

"She is the housekeeper."

"Is Uncle Winthrop very rich?"

"I—I don't know."

"But there are no children and boys to wear out their clothes and stockings. There's so much knitting to be done. I go to school in winter, but there is too much work in summer. Doris Adams, you are a lucky girl if your fortune doesn't spoil you."

"Fortune!" exclaimed Doris in surprise.

"Yes. I heard father talk about it. And all that from England! Then someone died in Boston and left you ever so much. I suppose you will be a grand lady!"

"I'd like to be a lovely old lady like Madam Royall."

"And who is she?"

Doris was in the full tide of narration when Mrs. Manning came to the hall door. She caught some description of a party.

"Elizabeth, put Ruth to bed at once and go yourself. Doris, talking of parties isn't a very good preparation for the Sabbath. Elizabeth, when you say your prayers think of your sins and shortcomings for the week, and repent of them earnestly."

Ruth had fallen asleep and gave a little whine. Her mother slapped her.

"Hush, not a word. You deserve the same and more, Elizabeth! James, go in and study your catechism over three times, then go to bed."

Doris sat alone on the doorstep, confused and amazed. She was quite sure now she did not like Mrs. Manning, and she felt very sorry for Elizabeth. Then Betty came out and told her some odd Salem stories.

They all went to church Sabbath morning, in the old Puritan parlance. Doris found it hard to comprehend the sermon. Many of the people from the farms brought their luncheons, and wandered about the graveyard or sat under the shady trees. At two the children were catechised, at three service began again.

Mrs. King took Doris and Betty to dine with a friend of her youth, and then went back to the service out of respect to her sister and brother-in-law. Little Ruth fell asleep and was punished for it when she reached home. The children were all fractious and their mother scolded. When the sun went down there was a general sense of relief. The younger ones began to wander around. The two mothers sauntered off together, talking of matters they preferred not to have fall on the ears of small listeners.

Betty attracted the boys. Foster could talk to her, though he was much afraid of girls in general.

Doris and Elizabeth sat on the steps. Ruth was running small races with herself.

"Would you rather go and walk?" inquired Elizabeth timidly.

"Oh, no. Not if you like to sit still," cheerfully.

"I just do. I'm always tired. You are so pretty, I was afraid of you at first. And you have such beautiful clothes. That blue ribbon on your hat is like a bit of the sky. And God made the sky."

The voice died away in admiration.

"That isn't my best hat," returned Doris simply. "Cousin Betty thought the damp of the ocean and running out in the dust would ruin it. It has some beautiful pink roses and ever so much gauzy stuff and a great bow of pink satin. Then I have a pink muslin frock with tiny green and brown sprigs all over it, and a great sash of the muslin that comes down to the hem. The Chapman girls have satin ribbon sashes, but Miss Recompense said she liked the muslin better."

"Do you have to wear just what she says?"

"Oh, no. Madam Royall chooses some things, and Betty. And Cousin King brought me an elegant sash, white, with flowers all over it. I have ever so many pretty things."

"Oh, how proud you must feel!" said the Puritan maid half enviously.

"I don't know"—hesitatingly. "I think I feel just nice, and that is all there is about it. Uncle Win likes what they get for me—men can't buy clothes, you know, and if he is pleased and thinks I look well, that is the end of it."

"Oh, how good it must feel to be happy just like that. But are you quite sure," lowering her voice to a touch of awe, "that you will not be punished in the next world?"

"What for? Doesn't God mean us to be happy?"

"Well—not in this world, perhaps," answered the young theologian. "But you don't have anything in heaven except a white robe, and if you haven't had any pretty things in this world——"

"I wish I could give you some of mine." Doris slipped her soft warm hand over the other, beginning to grow bony and strained already.

"They wouldn't do me any good," was the almost apathetical reply. "I only go to church, and mother wouldn't let me wear them."

"Do you like to go to church?"

"I hate the long sermons and the prayers. Oh, that is dreadful wicked, isn't it? But I like to see the people and hear the talk, and they do have some new clothes; and the sitting still. When you've run and run all the week and are tired all over, it's just good to sit still. And it's different. I get so tired of the same things all the time and the hurry. Do you know what I am going to do when I am a woman?"

"No," replied Doris with a look of interested inquiry.

"I'm going to have one room like grandmother Manning, and live by myself. I shan't have any husband or children. I don't want to be sewing and knitting and patching continually, and babies are an awful sight of trouble, and husbands are just thinking of work, work all the time. Then I shall go visiting when I like, and though I shall read the Bible I won't mind about remembering the sermons. I'll just have a good time by myself."

Doris felt strangely puzzled. She always wanted a good time with someone. The great pleasure to her was having another share a joy. And to live alone was almost like being imprisoned in some dreary cell. Neither could she think of Helen or Eudora living alone—indeed, any of the girls she knew.

"Now you can go on about the wedding party," said Elizabeth after a pause. "And you really danced! And you were not afraid the ground would open and swallow you?"

"Why, no," returned Doris. "There are earthquakes that swallow up whole towns, but, you see, the good and the bad go together. And I never heard of anyone being swallowed up——"

"Why, yes—in the Bible—Korah, Dathan, and Abiram."

"But they were not dancing. I think,"—hesitatingly,—"they were finding fault with Moses and Aaron, and wanting to be leaders in some manner."

"Well—I am glad it wasn't dancing. And now go on quick before they come back."

Elizabeth had never read a fairy story or any vivid description. She had no time and there were no books of that kind about the house. She fairly reveled in Doris' brilliant narrative. She had seen one middle-aged couple stand up to be married after the Sunday afternoon service, and she had heard of two or three younger people being married with a kind of wedding supper. But that Doris should have witnessed all this herself! That she should have worn a wedding gown and scattered flowers before the bride!

Ruth was tired of running. "I'm sleepy," she said. "Unfasten my dress, I want to go to bed."

Betty and the boys were coming up the path, with the shadowy forms of the grown people behind them. Mr. Manning had been taking a nap on the rude kitchen settee, his Sunday evening indulgence. Now he came through the hall.

"Boys, children, it's time to go to bed. You are all sleepy enough in the mornin', but you would sit up half the night if someone did not drive you off."

"Oh, I wish you lived here, Aunt Betty," said Foster for a good-night.

Betty and Doris were almost ready for bed when there was a little sound at the door, pushed open by Elizabeth, who stood there in her plain, scant nightgown with a distraught expression, as if she had seen a ghost.

"Oh, Aunt Betty or Doris, *can* you remember the text and what the sermon was about? We always say it to mother after tea Sabbath evening, and she'll be sure to ask me to-morrow morning. And I can't think! I never scarcely do forget. Oh, what shall I do!"

Her distress was so genuine that Betty folded her in her arms. Elizabeth began to cry at the tender touch.

"There, little Bessy, don't cry. Let me see—I remember I was preaching another sermon to myself. It was—'Do this and ye shall live.' And instead of all the hard things he put in, I thought of the kindly things father was always doing, and Uncle Win, and mother, and the pleasant things instead of the severe laws. And when he reached his lastly he said no one could keep all the laws, and because they could not the Saviour came and died, but he seemed to preach as if the old laws were still in force, and that the Saviour's death really had not changed anything. That was in the morning. And the afternoon was the miracle of the loaves and fishes."

"Yes—I could recall that. But I was sure mother would ask me the one I had forgotten. It always happens that way. Oh, I am so glad. Dear Aunt Betty! And if I was sometimes called Bessy, as you called me just now, or Betty, or anything besides the everlasting 'Lisbeth. Oh, Doris, how happy you must be ——"

"There, dear," said Betty soothingly, "don't cry so. I will write out what I can recall on a slip of paper and you can look it over in the morning. I just wish you could come and make me a visit, and go over to Uncle Win's. Yes, Doris *is* a happy little girl."

"But I have everything in the world," said Doris with a long breath. "I am afraid I could not be so happy here. Oh, can't we take Elizabeth home with us? Betty, coax her mother."

"It wouldn't do a bit of good. You can't coax mother. And there is always so much work in the summer. I am afraid she wouldn't like it—even if you asked her."

"But James came, and little Ruth——"

"They were too young to work. Oh, it would be like going to heaven!"

"It may be sometime, little Bessy. You can dream over it."

"Good-night. Would you kiss me, Doris?"

The happy girl kissed her a dozen times instead of once. But her deep eyes were full of tears as she turned to Betty when the small figure had slipped away.

"Yes, it is a hard life," said Betty. "It seems as if children's lives ought to be happier. I don't know what makes Mary so hard. I'm sure she does not get it from father or mother. She appears to think all the virtue of the world lies in work. I wonder what such people will do in heaven!"

"Oh, Betty, do try to have her come to Boston. I know Uncle Win will feel sorry for her."

Those years in the early part of the century were not happy ones for childhood in general. Too much happiness was considered demoralizing in this world and a poor preparation for the next. Work was the great panacea for all sorts of evils. It was seldom work for one's neighbors, though people were ready to go in sickness and trouble. It was adding field to field and interest to interest, to strive and save and wear one's self out and die.

Elizabeth was up betimes the next morning, and there lay the paper with chapter and verse and some "remarks." Her heart swelled with gratitude as she ran downstairs. Sarah had made the "shed" fire and the big wash kettle had been put over it. She was rubbing out the first clothes, the nicest pieces.

"Now fly round, 'Lisbeth," said her mother. "You've dawdled enough these few days back, and there'll be an account to settle presently. I suppose your head was so full of that bunch of vanity you never remembered a word of the sermon yesterday. What was the text in the morning?"

Elizabeth's pale face turned scarlet and her lip quivered; her slight frame seemed to shrink a moment, then in a gasping sort of way she gave chapter and verse and repeated the words.

"I don't think that was it," said her mother sharply. "Ruth was in a fidget just as the text was given out. Wasn't that last Sunday's text?"

"Some of the others may remember," the child said in her usual apathetical voice.

"Well, you needn't act as if you were going to have a hysteric! Hand me that dish of beans. Your father likes them warmed over. Quick, there he comes now. You stir them."

A trivet stood on the glowing coals, and the pan soon warmed through. Father and the men took their places. Foster came in sleepily.

"Where's James?" inquired his mother.

"I don't want him in the field to-day. He can weed in the garden. You send him with the dinners."

"Where was yesterday morning's text, Foster?" Mrs. Manning asked sharply.

The boy looked up blankly. As there was no Sunday evening examination it had slipped out of his mind.

"It was something about—keeping the law—doing——"

James entered at that moment and had heard the question and hesitating reply.

"I can't remember chapter and verse, but it was short, and I just rammed the words down in my memory box. 'Do this and ye shall live.'"

"James, no such irreverence," exclaimed his father.

Elizabeth in the kitchen drew a long breath of relief. She wondered whether his mother would have taken Aunt Betty's word.

Monday morning was always a hard time. Sarah required looking after, for her memory lapses were frequent. Mr. Manning said a good birch switch was the best remedy he knew. But though a hundred years before people had thought nothing of whipping their servants, public opinion was against it now. Mrs. Manning did sometimes box her ears when she was over-much tired. But she was a very faithful worker.

Elizabeth gave Ruth and baby Hester their breakfast. Then Betty came down, and insisted upon getting the next breakfast while Mrs. Manning hung up her first clothes. She had been scolding to Betty about people having no thought or care as to how they put back the work with their late breakfast. But when Betty cooked and served it, and insisted upon washing up the dishes; and Doris amused the baby, who was not well, and helped Ruth shell the pease for dinner; when the washing and churning were out of the way long before noon, and Elizabeth was folding down the clothes for ironing while Sarah and her mother prepared the dinner and sent it out to the men—the child couldn't see that things were at all behindhand.

Sarah and Elizabeth ironed in the afternoon. Mrs. Manning brought out her sewing and Betty helped on some frocks for the children. Two old neighbors came in to supper, bringing two little girls who were wonderfully attracted by Doris and delighted to be amused in quite a new fashion. But Elizabeth was too busy to be spared.

After supper was cleared away and the visitors had gone Elizabeth brought her knitting and sat on the stoop step in the moonlight.

"Oh, don't knit!" cried Doris. "You look so tired."

"I'd like to go to bed this minute," said the child. "But last week I fell behind. You see, there are so many to wear stockings, and the boys do rattle them out so fast. We try to get most of the new knitting done in the summer, for autumn brings so much work. And if you will talk to me—I like so to hear about Boston and Madam Royall's beautiful house and your Uncle Win. It must be like reading some interesting book. Oh, I wish I could come and stay a whole week with you!"

"A week!" Doris laughed. "Why, you couldn't see it all in a month, or a year. Every day I am finding something new about Boston, and Miss Recompense remembers so many queer stories. I'm going to tell her all about you. I know she'll be real nice about your coming. Everything is as Uncle Win says, but he always asks her."

Doris could make her little descriptions very vivid and attractive. At first Elizabeth replied by exclamations, then there was quite a silence. Doris looked at her. She was leaning against the post of the porch and her needles no longer clicked, though she held the stocking in its place. The poor child had fallen fast asleep. The moonlight made her look so ghostly pale that at first Doris was startled.

The three ladies came out, but Elizabeth never stirred. When her mother spied her she shook her sharply by the shoulder.

"Poor child!" exclaimed Mrs. King. "Elizabeth, put up your work and go to bed."

"If you are too sleepy to knit, put up your work and go out and knead on the bread a spell. Sarah always gets it lumpy if you don't watch her," said Mrs. Manning.

Elizabeth gathered up her ball and went without a word.

"I'll knit for you," said Betty, intercepting her, and taking the work.

"Mary, you will kill that child presently, and when you have buried her I hope you will be satisfied to give Ruth a chance for her life," exclaimed Mrs. King indignantly.

"I can't afford to bring my children up in idleness, and if I could, I hope I have too great a sense of responsibility and my duty toward them. I was trained to work, and I've been thankful many a time that *I* didn't have to waste grown-up years in learning."

"We didn't work like that. Then father had given some years to his country and we *were* poor. You have no need, and it is cruel to make such a slave of a child. She does a woman's work."

"I am quite capable of governing my own family, Electa, and I think I know what is best and right for them. We can't afford to bring up fine ladies and teach them French and other trumpery. If Elizabeth is fitted for a plain farmer's wife, that is all I ask. She won't be likely to marry a President or a foreign lord, and if we have a few hundred dollars to start her in life, maybe she won't object."

"You had better give her a little comfort now instead of adding farm to farm, and saving up so much for the woman who will come in here when you are dead and gone. Think of the men who have second and third wives and whose children are often turned adrift to look out for themselves. Hundreds of poor women are living hard and joyless lives just to save up money. And it is a shame to grind their children to the lowest ebb."

Mrs. Manning was very angry. She had no argument at hand, so she turned in an arrogant manner and said austerely:

"I had better go and look after my daughter, to see that she doesn't work herself quite to death. But I don't know what we should do without bread."

"Now you have done it!" cried Betty. "I only hope she won't vent her anger on the poor child."

"It is a curious thing," said Mrs. King reflectively, "that women—well, men too—make such a point of church-going on Sunday, and hardly allow the poor children to draw a comfortable breath, and on Monday act like fiends. Women especially seem to think they have a right to indulge in dreadful tempers on washing day, and drive all before them. Think of the work that has been done in this house to-day, and the picture of Elizabeth, worn out, falling asleep over her knitting. I should have sent her to bed with the chickens. I'd like to take her home with me, but it would spoil her for the farm."

Betty knit away on the stocking. "I can't see what makes Mary so hard and grasping," she said. "It troubles mother a good deal."

When they went in the house was quiet and the kitchen dark. Mrs. Manning sat sewing. Their candles were on the table. Betty and Mrs. King said a cordial good-night.

The sisters-in-law were to come the next day, and grandmother Manning, with an addition of four children. The Salem sister, Mrs. Gates, was stout and pleasant; the farmer sister thin and with a troublesome cough, and she had a young baby besides her little girl of six. She was to make a visit in Salem, and doctor somewhat, to see if she could not get over her cough before cold weather.

The children were turned out of doors on the grassy roadside, where they couldn't hurt anything. Mrs. Gates and Betty helped in the kitchen, and after the dinner was cleared away Elizabeth was allowed to put on her second-best gingham and go out with the children. They ran and played and screamed and laughed.

"I'd a hundred times rather sit still and hear you talk," she said to Doris. "And I'm awful sorry to have you go to-morrow. Even when I am busy it is so nice just to look at you, with your beautiful hair and your dark eyes, and your skin that is like velvet and doesn't seem to tan or freckle. Foster hates freckles so."

Doris flushed at the compliment.

"I wonder how it would seem to be as pretty as you are? And you're not a bit set up about your fine clothes and all. I s'pose when you're born that way you're so used to it, and there aint anything to wish for. I'm so glad you could come. And I do hope you will come again."

They parted very good friends. Mrs. King had been quite generous to the small people, and Mrs. Manning really loved her sister, although she considered her very lax and extravagant. No one could tell what was before him, and thrift and prudence were the great virtues of those days. True, they often degenerated into penuriousness and labor that was early and late—so severe, indeed, it cost many a life; and the people who came after reaped the benefit.

CHAPTER XVIII

WINTER AND SORROW

"Oh, Uncle Win," exclaimed Doris, "I can't be sorry that I went to Salem, and I've had a queer, delightful time seeing so many strange things and hearing stories about them! But I am very, very glad to get back to Boston, and gladdest of all to be your little girl. There isn't anybody in the whole wide world I'd change you for!"

Her arms were about him. He was so tall that she could not quite reach up to his neck when he stood straight, but he had a way of bending over, and she was growing, and the clasp gave him a thrill of exquisite pleasure.

"I've missed my little girl a great deal," he said. "I am afraid I shall never want you to go away again."

"The next time you must go with me. Though Betty was delightful and Mrs. King is just splendid."

They had famous talks about Salem afterward, and the little towns around. Miss Recompense said now she shouldn't know how to live without a child in the house. Mrs. King went home to her husband and little ones, and Doris imagined the joy in greeting such a fond mother. Uncle Win half promised he would visit New York sometime. Even Aunt Priscilla was pleased when Doris came up to Sudbury Street, and wanted her full share of every visit. And they were all amazed when she went over to Uncle Win's to spend a day and was very cordial with Miss Recompense. They had a nice chat about the old times and the Salem witches and the dead and gone Governors—even Governor and Lady Gage, who had been very gay in her day; and both women had seen her riding about in her elegant carriage, often with a handsome young girl at her side.

She had some business, too, with Uncle Win. They were in the study a long while together.

"Living with the Leveretts has certainly changed Aunt Priscilla very much," he said later in the evening to Miss Recompense. "I begin to think it is not good for people to live so much alone when they are going down the shady side of life. Or perhaps it would not be so shady if they would allow a little sun to shine in it."

Solomon was full of purring content and growing lazier every day. Latterly he had courted Uncle Win's society. There was a wide ledge in one of the southern windows, and Doris made a cushion to fit one end. He loved to lie here and bask in the sunshine. When there was a fire on the hearth he had another cushion in the corner. Sometimes he sauntered around and interviewed the books quite as if he was aware of their contents. He considered that he had a supreme right to Doris' lap, and he sometimes had half a mind to spring up on Uncle Win's knee, but the invitation did not seem sufficiently pressing.

Cary was at home regularly now, except that he spent one night every week with a friend at Charlestown, and went frequently to the Cragies' to meet some of his old chums. He had not appeared to care much for Doris at first, and she was rather shy. Latterly they had become quite friends.

But it seemed to Doris that he was so much gayer and brighter at Madam Royall's, where he certainly was a great favorite. Miss Alice was very brilliant and charming. They were always having hosts of company. Mr. and Mrs. Winslow were at the head of one circle in society. And this autumn Miss Jane Morse was married and went to live in Sheaffe Street in handsome style. She had done very well indeed. Betty was one of the bridesmaids and wore a white India silk in which she looked quite a beauty.

Miss Helen Chapman was transferred to Mrs. Rowson's school to be finished. Doris and Eudora still attended Miss Parker's. But Madam Royall had treated the girls to the new instrument coming into vogue, the pianoforte. It's tone was so much richer and deeper than the old spinet. She liked it very much herself. Doris was quite wild over it. Madam Royal begged that she might be allowed to take lessons on it with the girls. Uncle Winthrop said in a year or two she might have one if she liked it and could learn to play.

She and Betty used to talk about Elizabeth Manning. There was a new baby now, another little boy. Mrs. Leverett made a visit and brought home Hester, to ease up things for the winter. Elizabeth couldn't go to school any more, there was so much to do. She wrote Doris quite a long letter and sent it by grandmother. Postage was high then, and people did not write much for pure pleasure.

And just before the new year, when Betty was planning to go to New York for her visit to Mrs. King, a great sorrow came to all of them. Uncle Leverett had not seemed well all the fall, though he was for the most part his usual happy self, but business anxieties pressed deeply upon him and Warren. He used to drop in now and then and take tea with Cousin Winthrop, and as they sat round the cheerful fire Doris would bring her stool to his side and slip her hand in his as she had that first winter. She was growing tall quite rapidly now, and pretty by the minute, Uncle Leverett said.

There was no end of disquieting rumors. American shipping was greatly interfered with and American seamen impressed aboard British ships by the hundreds, often to desert at the first opportunity. Merchantmen were deprived of the best of their crews for the British navy, as that country was carrying on several wars; and now Wellington had gone to the assistance of the Spanish, and all Europe was trying to break the power of Napoleon, who had set out since the birth of his son, now crowned King of Rome, to subdue all the nations.

The *Leopard-Chesapeake* affair had nearly plunged us into war, but it was promptly disavowed by the British Government and some indemnity paid. There was a powerful sentiment opposed to war in New York and New England, but the people were becoming much inflamed under repeated outrages. Young men were training in companies and studying up naval matters. The country had so few ships then that to rush into a struggle was considered madness.

Mr. Winthrop Adams was among those bitterly opposed to war. Cary was strongly imbued with a young man's patriotic enthusiasm. There was a good deal of talk at Madam Royall's, and a young lieutenant had been quite a frequent visitor and was an admirer also of the fair Miss Alice. Then Alfred Barron, his friend at Charlestown, had entered the naval service. Studying law seemed dry and tiresome to the young fellow when such stirring events were happening on every side.

Uncle Leverett took a hard cold early in the new year. He was indoors several days, then some business difficulties seemed to demand his attention and he went out again. A fever set in, and though at first it did not appear serious, after a week the doctor began to look very grave. Betty stopped her preparations and wrote a rather apprehensive letter to Mrs. King.

One day Uncle Win was sent for, and remained all the afternoon and evening. The next morning he went down to the store.

"I'm afraid father's worse," said Warren. "His fever was very high through the night, and he was flighty, and now he seems to be in a sort of stupor, with a very feeble pulse. Oh, Uncle Win, I haven't once thought of his dying, and now I am awfully afraid. Business is in such a dreadful way. That has worried him."

Mr. Adams went up to Sudbury Street at once. The doctor was there.

"There has been a great change since yesterday," he said gravely. "We must prepare for the worst. It has taken me by surprise, for he bid fair to pull through."

Alas, the fears were only too true! By night they had all given up hope and watched tearfully for the next twenty-four hours, when the kindly, upright life that had blessed so many went to its own reward.

To Doris is seemed incredible. That poor Miss Henrietta Maria should slip out of life was only a release, and that Miss Arabella in the ripeness of age should follow had awakened in her heart no real sorrow, but a gentle sense of their having gained something in another world. But Uncle Leverett had so much here, so many to love him and to need him.

Death, the mystery to all of us, is doubly so to the young. When Doris looked on Uncle Leverett's placid face she was very sure he could not be really gone, but mysteriously asleep.

Yes, little Doris—the active, loving, thinking man had "fallen on sleep," and the soul had gone to its reward.

Foster Leverett had been very much respected, and there were many friends to follow him to his grave in the old Granary burying ground, where the Fosters and Leveretts rested from their labors. There on the walk stood the noble row of elms that Captain Adino Paddock had imported from England a dozen years before the Revolutionary War broke out, in their very pride of strength and grandeur now, even if they were leafless.

It seemed very hard and cruel to leave him here in the bleakness of midwinter, Doris thought. And he was not really dead to her until the bearers turned away with empty hands, and the friends with sorrowful greeting passed out of the inclosure and left him alone to the coming evening and the requiem of the wind soughing through the trees.

Doris sat by Miss Recompense that evening with Solomon on her lap. She could not study, she did not want to read or sew or make lace. Uncle Winthrop had gone up to Sudbury Street. All the family were to be there. The Kings had come from New York and the Mannings from Salem.

"Oh," said Doris, after a long silence, "how can Aunt Elizabeth live, and Betty and Warren, when they cannot see uncle Leverett any more! And there are so many things to talk about, only they can never ask him any questions, and he was so—so comforting. He was the first one that came to me on the vessel, you know, and he said to Captain Grier, 'Have you a little girl who has come from Old Boston to New Boston?' Then he put his arm around me, and I liked him right away. And the great fire in the hall was so lovely. I liked everybody but Aunt Priscilla, and now I feel sorry for her and like her a good deal. Sometimes she gets queer and what she calls 'pudgicky.' But she is real good to Betty."

"She's a sensible, clear-headed woman, and she has good solid principles. I do suppose we all get a little queer. I can see it in myself."

"Oh, dear Miss Recompense, you are not queer," protested Doris, seizing her hand. "When I first came I was a little afraid—you were so very nice. And then I remembered that Miss Arabella had all these nice ways, and could not bear a cloth askew nor towels wrinkled instead of being laid straight, nor anything spilled at the table, nor an untidy room, and she was very sweet and nice. And then I tried to be as neat as I could."

"I knew you had been well brought up." Miss Recompense was pleased always to be compared to her "dear Miss Arabella." There was something grateful to her woman's heart, that had long ago held a longing for a child of her own, in the ardent tone Doris always uttered this endearment.

"Miss Recompense, don't you think there is something in people loving you? You want to love them in return. You want to do the things they like. And when they smile and are glad, your whole heart is light with a kind of inward sunshine. And I think if Mrs. Manning would smile on Elizabeth once in a while, and tell her what she did was nice, and that she was smart,—for she is very, very smart,—I know it would comfort her."

"You see, people haven't thought it was best to praise children. They rarely did in my day."

"But Uncle Leverett praised Warren and Betty, and always said what Aunt Elizabeth cooked and did was delightful."

"Foster Leverett was one man out of a thousand. They will all miss him dreadfully."

Aunt Priscilla would have been amazed to know that Mr. Leverett had been in the estimation of Miss Recompense an ideal husband. Years ago she had compared other men with him and found them wanting.

Uncle Win was much surprised to find them sitting there talking when he came home, for it was ten o'clock. Cary returned shortly after, and the two men retired to the study. But there was a curious half-dread of some intangible influence that kept Doris awake a long while. The wind moaned outside and now and then raised to a somber gust sweeping across the wide Common. Oh, how lonely it must be in the old burying ground!

Mr. Leverett's will had been read that evening. The business was left to Warren, as Hollis had most of his share years before. To the married daughters a small remembrance, to Betty and her mother the house in Sudbury Street, to be kept or sold as they should elect; if sold, they were to share equally.

Mrs. King was very well satisfied. In the present state of affairs Warren's part was very uncertain, and his married sisters were to be paid out of that. The building was old, and though the lot was in a good business location, the value at that time was not great.

"It seems to me the estate ought to be worth more," said Mrs. Manning. "I did suppose father was quite well off, and had considerable ready money."

"So he did two years ago," answered Warren. "But it has been spent in the effort to keep afloat. If the times should ever get better——"

"You'll pull through," said Hollis encouragingly.

He had not suffered so much from the hard times, and was prospering.

The will had been remade six months before, after a good deal of consideration.

When Mrs. King went home, a few days after, she said privately to Warren: "Do not trouble about my legacy, and if you come to hard places I am sure Matt will help you out if he possibly can."

Warren thanked her in a broken voice.

Mr. King said nearly the same thing as he grasped the young fellow's hand.

They were a very lonely household. Of course, Betty could not think of going away. And now that they knew what a struggle it had been for some time to keep matters going comfortably, they cast about to see what retrenchment could be made. Even if they wanted to, this would be no time to sell. The house seemed much too large for them, yet it was not planned so that any could be rented out.

"If you're set upon that," said Aunt Priscilla, "I'll take the spare rooms, whether I need them or not. And we will just go on together. Strange though that Foster, who was so much needed, should be taken, and I, without a chick or a child, and so much older, be left behind."

There was a new trustee to be looked up for Doris. A much younger man was needed. If Cary were five or six years older! Foster Leverett's death was a great shock to Winthrop Adams. Sometimes it seemed as if a shadowy form hovered over his shoulder, warning him that middle life was passing. He had a keen disappointment, too, in his son. He had hoped to find in him an intellectual companion as the years went on, but he could plainly see that his heart was not in his profession. The young fellow's ardor had been aroused on other lines that brought him in direct opposition to the elder's views. He had gone so far as to ask his father's permission to enlist in the navy, which had been refused, not only with prompt decision, but with a feeling of amazement that a son of his should have proposed such a step.

Cary had the larger love of country and the enthusiasm of youth. His father was deeply interested in the welfare and standing of the city, and he desired it to keep at the head. He had hoped to see his son one of the rising men of the coming generation. War horrified him: it called forth the cruel and brutal side of most men, and was to be undertaken only for extremely urgent reasons as the last hope and salvation of one's country. We had gained a right to stand among the nations of the world; it was time now that we should take upon ourselves something higher—the cultivation of literature and the fine arts. To plunge the country into war again would be setting it back decades.

He had taken a great deal of pleasure in the meetings, of the Anthology Club and the effort they had made to keep afloat a *Magazine of Polite Literature.* The little supper, which was very plain; the literary chat; the discussions of English poets and essayists, several of which were reprinted at this era; and the encouragement of native writers, of whom there were but few except in the line of sermons and orations. By 1793 there had been two American novels published, and though we should smile over them now we can find their compeers in several of the old English novels that crop out now and then, exhumed from what was meant to be a kindly oblivion.

The magazine had been given up, and the life somehow had gone out of the club. There was a plan to form a reading room and library to take its place. Men like Mr. Adams were anxious to advance the intellectual reputation of the town, though few people found sufficient leisure to devote to the idea of a national literature. Others said: "What need, when we have the world of brilliant English thinkers that we can never excel, the poets, and novelists! Let us study those and be content."

The incidents of the winter had been quite depressing to Mr. Adams. Cary was around to the Royalls' nearly every evening, sometimes to other places, and at discussions that would have alarmed his father still more if he had known it. The young fellow's conscience gave him many twinges. "Children, obey your parents" had been instilled into every generation and until a boy was of age he had no lawful right to think for himself.

So it happened that Doris became more of a companion to Uncle Win. They rambled about as the spring opened and noted the improvements. Old Frog Lane was being changed into Boylston Street. Every year the historic Common took on some new charm. There was the Old Elm, that dated back to tradition, for no one could remember its youth. She was interested in the conflicts that had ushered in the freedom of the American Colonies. Here the British waited behind their earthworks for Washington to attack them, just as every winter boys congregated behind their snowy walls and fought mimic battles. Indeed, during General Gage's administration the soldiers had driven the boys off their coasting place on the Common, and in a body they had gone to the Governor and demanded their rights, which were restored to them. Many a famous celebration had occurred here, and here the militia met on training days and had their banquets in tents. At the first training all the colored population was allowed to throng the Common; but at the second, when the Ancient and Honorable Artillery chose its new officers, they were strictly prohibited.

Many of the ropewalks up at the northern end were silent now. Indeed, everybody seemed waiting with bated breath for something to happen, but all nature went on its usual way and made the town a little world of beauty with wild flowers and shrubs and the gardens coming into bloom, and the myriads of fruit trees with their crowns of snowy white and pink in all gradations.

"I think the world never was so beautiful," said Doris to Uncle Winthrop.

It was so delightful to have such an appreciative companion, even if she was only a little girl.

Cary's birthday was the last of May, and it was decided to have the family party at the same time. Cary's young friends would be invited in the evening, but for the elders there would be the regular supper.

"You will have your freedom suit, and afterward you can do just as you like," said Doris laughingly. She and Cary had been quite friendly of late, young-mannish reserve having given place to a brotherly regard.

"Do you suppose I *can* do just as I like?" He studied the eager face.

"Of course you wouldn't want to do anything Uncle Win would not like."

Cary flushed. "I wonder if fathers always know what is best? And when you are a man——" he began.

"Don't you want to study law?"

"Under some circumstances I should like it."

"Would you like keeping a store or having a factory, or building beautiful houses—architecture, I believe, the fine part is called. Or painting portraits like Copley and Stuart and the young Mr. Allston up in Court Street."

"No, I can't aspire to that kind of genius, and I am sure I shouldn't like shop-keeping. I am just an ordinary young fellow and I am afraid I shall always be a disappointment to the kindest of fathers. I wish there were three or four other children."

"How strange it would seem," returned Doris musingly.

214

"I am glad he has you, little Doris."

"Are you really glad?" Her face was alight with joy. "Sometimes I have almost wondered——"

"Don't wonder any more. You are like a dear little sister. During the last six months it has been a great pleasure to me to see father so fond of you. I hope you will never go away."

"I don't mean to. I love Uncle Win dearly. It used to trouble me sometimes when Uncle Leverett was alive, lest I couldn't love quite even, you know," and a tiny line came in her smooth brow.

"What an idea!" with a soft smile that suggested his father.

"It's curious how you can love so many people," she said reflectively.

At first the Leveretts thought they could not come to the party, but Uncle Winthrop insisted strongly. Some of the other relatives had lost members from their households. All the gayety would be reserved for the evening. But Cary said they would miss Betty very much.

They had a pleasant afternoon, and Betty was finally prevailed upon to stay a little while in the evening. Cary was congratulated by the elder relatives, who said many pleasant things and gave him good wishes as to his future success. One of the cousins proposed his health, and Cary replied in a very entertaining manner. There was a birthday cake that he had to cut and pass around.

"I think Cary has been real delightful," said Betty. "I've never felt intimately acquainted with him, because he has always seemed rather distant, and went with the quality and all that, and we are rather plain people. Oh, how proud of him Uncle Win must be!"

He certainly was proud of his gracious attentions to the elders and his pleasant way of taking the rather tiresome compliments of a few of the old ladies who had known his Grandfather Cary as well as his Grandfather Adams.

Aunt Elizabeth and Aunt Priscilla sat up in the room of Miss Recompense with a few of the guests who wanted to see the young people gather. There were four colored musicians, and they began to tune their instruments out on the rustic settee at the side of the front garden, where the beautiful drooping honey locusts hid them from sight and made even the tuning seem enchanting. Girls in white gowns trooped up the path, young men in the height of fashion carried fans and nosegays for them; there was laughing and chattering and floating back and forth to the dressing rooms.

Madam Royall came with Miss Alice and Helen, who was allowed to go out occasionally under her wing. Eudora had been permitted just to look on a while and to return with grandmamma.

The large parlor was cleared of the small and dainty tables and articles likely to be in the way of the dancers. The first was to be a new march to a patriotic air, and the guests stood on the stairs to watch them come out of the lower door of the long room, march through the hall, and enter the parlor at the other door. Oh, what a pretty crowd they were! The old Continental styles had not all gone out, but were toned down a little. There were pretty embroidered satin petticoats and sheer gowns falling away at the sides, with a train one had to tuck up under the belt when one really danced. Hair of all shades done high on the head with a comb of silver or brilliants, or tortoise shell so clear that you could see the limpid variations. Pompadour rolls, short curls, dainty puffs, many of the dark heads powdered, laces and frills and ribbons, and dainty feet in satin slippers and silken hose.

After that they formed quadrilles in the parlor. There was space for three and one in the hall. Eudora and Doris patted their feet on the stairs in unison, and clasping each other's hands smiled and moved their heads in perfect time.

Aunt Priscilla admitted that it was a beautiful sight, but she had her doubts about it. Betty was sorry there was such a sad cause for her not being among them. Even Cary had expressed regrets about it.

Then the Leveretts and Madam Royall went home. A few of the elders had a game of loo, and Mr. Adams played chess with Morris Winslow, whose pretty wife still enjoyed dancing, though he was growing stout and begged to be excused on a warm night.

They played forfeits afterward and had a merry time. Then there was supper, and they drank toasts and made bright speeches, and there was a great deal of jesting and gay laughter, and much wishing of success, a judgeship in the future, a mission abroad perhaps, a pretty and loving wife, a happy and honorable old age.

They drank the health of Mr. Winthrop as well, and congratulated him on his promising son. He was very proud and happy that night, and planned within his heart what he would do for his boy.

Doris kept begging to stay up a little longer. The music was so fascinating, for the band was playing soft strains out on the front porch while the guests were at supper. She sat on the stairs quite enchanted with the gay scene.

The guests wandered about the hall and parlor and chatted joyously. Then there was a movement toward breaking up.

Miss Alice espied her.

"Oh, you midget, are you up here at midnight?" she cried. "Have we done Cary ample honor on his arrival at man's estate?"

"You were all so beautiful!" said Doris breathlessly. "And the dancing and the music: It was splendid!"

Helen kissed her good-night with girlish effusion. Some of the other ladies spoke to her, and Mrs. Winslow said: "No doubt you will have a party in this old house. But you will have a girl's advantage. You need not wait until you are twenty-one."

When the last good-nights were said, and the lights put out, Cary Adams wondered whether he would have the determination to avow his plans.

CHAPTER XIX

THE HIGH RESOLVE OF YOUTH

War was declared. The President, James Madison, proclaimed it June 18, 1812. Hostilities opened promptly. True, England's navy was largely engaged with France in the tremendous effort to keep Napoleon confined within the boundaries that he had at one time assented to by treaty, but at that period she had over a thousand vessels afloat, while America had only seventeen warships in her navy to brave them.

There was a call for men and money. The Indian troubles had been fomented largely by England. There had been fighting on the borders, but the battle of Tippecanoe had broken the power of Tecumseh—for the time, at least. But now the hopes of the Indian chieftain revived, and the country was beset by both land and naval warfare.

The town had been all along opposed to war. It had been said of Boston a few years before that she was like Tyre of old, and that her ships whitened every sea. Still, now that the fiat had gone forth, the latent enthusiasm came to the surface, and men were eager to enlist. A company had been studying naval tactics at Charlestown, and most of them offered their services, filled with the enthusiasm of youth and brimming with indignation at the treatment our sailors were continually receiving.

Still, the little navy had proudly distinguished itself in the Mediterranean, and the *Constitution* had gained for herself the sobriquet of "Old Ironsides"—a Boston-built vessel, though the live oak, the red cedar, and the pitch pine had come from South Carolina. But Paul Revere had furnished the copper bolts and spikes, and when the ship was recoppered, later on, that came from the same place. Ephraim Thayer, at the South End, had made her gun carriages, and her sails were manufactured in the Old Granary building.

"A bunch of pine boards with a bit of striped bunting" had been the enemy's disdainful description of our youthful navy. And now they were to try their prowess with the Mistress of the Seas, who had defeated the combined navies of Europe. No wonder the country stood astounded over its own daring.

Everything afloat was hurriedly equipped as a war vessel. The solid, far-sighted men of New York and New England shook their heads over the great mistake Congress and the President had made.

Warren Leverett began to talk about enlisting. Business had been running behind. True, he could appeal to his brother-in-law King. He had sounded Hollis, who declared he had all he could do to keep afloat himself.

Mrs. Leverett besought him to take no hasty step. What could they do without him? They might break up the home. Electa would be glad to have Betty—there were some things she could do, but Aunt Priscilla—whose health was really poor——

Aunt Priscilla understood the drift presently, and the perplexity. Warren admitted that if he had some money to tide him over he would fight through. The war couldn't last forever.

"And you never thought of me!" declared Aunt Priscilla, pretending to be quite indignant. "See here, Warren Leverett, when I made my will I looked out for you and Betty. Mary Manning shan't hoard up any of my money, and 'Lecty King, thank the Lord, doesn't want it. So if you're to have it in the end you may as well take some of it now, fursisee. I shall have enough to last my time out. And I'm settled and comfortable here and don't want to be routed out and set down elsewhere."

Warren and his mother were surprised and overcome by the offer. He would take it only on condition that he should pay Aunt Priscilla the interest.

But his business stirred up wonderfully. Still, they all felt it was very generous in Aunt Priscilla, whose money had really been her idol.

Doris had gone over from her music lesson one afternoon. They were always so glad to see her. Aunt Priscilla thought a piano in such times as these was almost defying Providence. But even the promise of that did not spoil Doris, and they were always glad to see her drop in and hear her dainty bits of news.

They wanted very much to keep her to supper.

"Why, they"—which meant the family at home—"will be sure you have stayed here or at the Royalls'. Mr. Winslow has given ever so much money toward the fitting out of a vessel. They are all very patriotic. And Cary's uncle, Mr. March, has gone in heart and hand. I don't know which is right," said Betty with a sigh, "but now that we are in it I hope we will win."

But Doris was afraid Miss Recompense would feel anxious, and she promised to come in a few days and stay to supper.

It was very odd that just as she reached the corner Cousin Cary should cross the street and join her.

"I have been down having a talk with Warren," he said as if in explanation. "I wish I had a good, plodding business head like that, and Warren isn't lacking in the higher qualities, either. If there was money enough to keep the house going, he would enlist. He had almost resolved to when this stir in business came."

"Oh, I don't know what his mother would have done! If Uncle Leverett was alive——"

"He would have consented in a minute. Someone's sons must go," Cary said decisively. "No, don't go straight home—come over to the Common. Doris, you are only a little girl, but I want to talk to you. There is no one else——"

Doris glanced at him in amazement. He was quite generally grave, though he sometimes teased her, and occasionally read with her and explained any difficult point. But she always felt so like a very little girl with him.

They went on in silence, however, until they crossed Common Street and passed on under the magnificent elms. Clumps of shrubbery were blooming. Vines ran riotously over supports, and roses and honeysuckle made the air sweet.

"Doris,"—his voice had a little huskiness in it,—"you are very fond of father, and he loves you quite as if you were his own child. Oh, I wish you were! I wish he had half a dozen sons and daughters. If mother had lived——"

"Yes," Doris said at length, in the long silence broken only by the song and whistle of myriad birds.

"I don't know how to tell you. I can't soften things, incidents, or explanations. I am so apt to go straight to the point, and though it may be honorable, it is not always wisest or best. But I can't help it now. I have enlisted in the navy. We start for Annapolis this evening."

"Oh, Cary! And Uncle Win——"

"That is it. That gives me a heartache, I must confess. For, you see, I can't go and tell him in a manly way, as I would like. We have had some talks over it. I asked him before I was of age, and he refused in the most decisive manner to consider it. He said if I went I would have to choose between the country and him, which meant—a separation for years, maybe. It is strange, too, for he is noble and just and patriotic on certain lines. I do think he would spend any money on me, give me everything I could possibly want, but he feels in some way that I am his and it is my duty to do with my life what he desires, not what I like. I am talking over your head, you are such a little girl, and so simple-hearted. And I have really come to love you a great deal, Doris."

She looked up with a soft smile, but there were tears in her eyes.

"You see, a big boy who has no sisters doesn't get used to little girls. And when he really begins to admire them they are generally older. Then, I have always been with boys and young men. I was glad when you came, because father was so interested in you. And I thought he had begun to love you so much that he wouldn't really mind if I went away. But, you see, his heart would be big enough for a houseful of children."

"Oh, why do you go? He will be—broken-hearted."

"Little Doris, I shall be broken-hearted if I stay. I shall begin to hate law— maybe I shall take to drink—young fellows do at times. I know I shall be just good for nothing. I should like best to talk it over dispassionately with him, but that can't be done. We should both say things that would hurt each other and that we should regret all our lives. I have written him a long letter, but I wanted to tell someone. I thought of Betty first, and Madam Royall, but no one can comfort him like you. Then I wanted you to feel, Doris, that I was not an ungrateful, disobedient son. I wish we could think alike about the war, but it seems that we cannot. And because you are here,—and, Doris, you are a very sweet little girl, and you will love him always, I know,—I give him in your charge. I hope to come back, but the chances of war are of a fearful sort, and if I should not, will you keep to him always, Doris? Will you be son and daughter to him as you grow up—oh, Doris, don't cry! People die every day, you know, staying at home. I have often thought how sad it was that my mother and both your parents should die so young———"

His voice broke then. They came to a rustic seat and sat down. He took her hand and pressed it to his lips.

"If I shouldn't ever come back"—tremulously—"I should like to feel at the last moment there was someone who would tell him that my very latest thought was of him and his tender love all my twenty-one years. I want you to make him feel that it was no disrespect to him, but love for my country, that impelled me to the step. You will understand it better when you grow older, and I can trust you to do me full justice and to be tender to him. And at first, Doris, when I can, I shall write to you. If he doesn't forbid you, I want you to answer if I can get letters. This is a sad, sad talk for a little girl———"

Doris tried very hard not to sob. She seemed to understand intuitively how it was, and that to make any appeal could only pain him without persuading. If she were as wise and bright as Betty!

"That is all—or if I said any more it would be a repetition, and it is awfully hard on you. But you will love him and comfort him."

"I shall love him and stay with him all my life," said Doris with tender solemnity.

They were both too young to understand all that such a promise implied.

"My dear little sister!" He rose and stooping over kissed her on the fair forehead. "I will walk back to the house with you," he added as she rose.

Neither of them said a word until they reached the corner. Then he took both hands and, kissing her again, turned away, feeling that he could not even utter a good-by.

Doris stood quite still, as if she was stunned. She was not crying in any positive fashion, but the tears dropped silently. She could not go indoors, so she went down to the big apple tree that had a seat all around the trunk. Was Uncle Win at home? Then she heard voices. Miss Recompense had a visitor, and she was very glad.

The lady, an old friend, stayed to supper. Uncle Win did not make his appearance. Doris took a book afterward and sat out on the stoop, but reading was only a pretense. She was frightened now at having a secret, and it seemed such a solemn thing as she recalled what she had promised. She would like to spend all her life with Uncle Win; but could she care for him and make him happy, when the one great love of his life was gone?

Miss Recompense walked out to the gate with her visitor, and they had a great many last bits to say, and then she watched her going down the street.

"Child, you can't see to read," she said to Doris. "I think it is damp. You had better come in. Mr. Adams will not be home before ten."

Doris entered the lighted hall and stood a moment uncertain.

"How pale and heavy-eyed you look!" exclaimed Miss Recompense. "Does your head ache? Have they some new trouble in Sudbury Street?"

"Oh, no. But I am tired. I think I will go to bed. Good-night, dear Miss Recompense," and she gave her a gentle hug.

She cried a little softly to her pillow. Had Cary gone? When Uncle Win came home he would find the letter. She dreaded to-morrow.

Cary had one more errand before he started. He had said good-by to them at Madam Royall's and announced his enlistment, but he had asked Alice to meet him at the foot of the garden. They were not lovers, though he was perhaps quite in love. And he knew that he had only to speak to gain his father's consent and have his way to matrimony made easy, since it was Alice Royall. But he had never been quite sure that she cared for him with her whole soul, as Isabel had cared for Morris Winslow. And if he won her— would he, could he go away?

He used to wonder later on how much was pure patriotism and how much a desire to stand well with Alice Royall. She was proudly patriotic and had stirred his blood many a time with her wishes and desires for the country. Grandmamma Royall had laughed a little at her vehemence, and said it was fortunate she was not a boy.

"I should enlist at once. Or what would be better yet, I would beg brother Morris to fit out a war ship, and look up the men to command it, and go in *any* capacity. I should not wait for a high-up appointment."

When Cary confessed his step first to her, she caught his hands in hers so soft and delicate.

"I knew you were the stuff out of which heroes were made!" she cried exultantly. "Oh, Cary, I shall pray for you day and night, and you will come back crowned with honors."

"If I come back——"

"You will. Take my word for your guerdon. I can't tell you *how* I know it, but I am sure you will return. I can see you and the future——"

She paused, flushed with excitement, her eyes intense, her rosy lips tremulous, and looked, indeed, as if she might be inspired.

So she met him again at the garden gate for a last good-by. Young people who had been well brought up did not play at love-making in those days, though they might be warm friends. A girl seldom gave or received caresses until the elders had signified assent. An engagement was quite a solemn thing, not lightly to be entered into. And even to himself Cary seemed very young. All his instincts were those of a gentleman, and in his father he had had an example of the most punctilious honor.

They walked up and down a few moments. He pressed tender kisses on her fair hand, about which there always seemed to cling the odor of roses. And then he tore himself away with a passionate sorrow that his father, the nearest in human ties of love, could not bid him Godspeed.

The next morning Doris wondered what had happened. There was a loneliness in the very air, as there had been when Uncle Leverett died. The sky was overcast, not exactly promising a storm, but soft and penetrative, as if presaging sorrow.

Oh, yes, she remembered now. She dressed herself and went quietly downstairs.

"You may as well come and have your breakfast," exclaimed Miss Recompense. "Your uncle sent down word that he had a headache and begged not to be disturbed. He was up a long while after he came home last night; it must have been past midnight when he went to bed. I wish he did not get so deeply interested in improvements and everything. And if we are to be bombarded and destroyed I don't see any sense in laying out new streets and filling up ponds and wasting the money of the town."

It seemed to Doris as if she could not swallow a mouthful. She tried heroically. Then she went out and gathered a bunch of roses for Uncle Win's study. She generally read French and Latin a while with him in the morning. Then she made her bed, dusted her room, put her books in her satchel and went to school in an unwilling sort of fashion. How long the morning seemed! Then there was a half-hour in deportment—we should call it physical culture at present. All the girls were gay and chatty. Eudora told her about a new lace stitch. Grandmamma had been out yesterday where there was such an elegant Spanish woman with coal-black eyes and hair. Her family had fled to this country to escape the horrors of war. They had been rich, but were now quite poor, and she was thinking of having a needlework class.

Did Eudora know Cary had gone away?

Uncle Win came out to dinner. She was a little late. He glanced up and gave a faint half-smile, but, oh, how deadly pale he was!

"Dear Uncle Winthrop—is your headache better?" she asked with gentle solicitude.

"A little," he said gravely.

It was a very quiet meal. Although Mr. Winthrop Adams had a delicate appearance, he was rarely ill. Now there were deep rings under his eyes, and the utter depression was sad indeed to behold.

Doris nearly always ran in the study and gossiped girlishly about the morning's employments. Now she sauntered out on the porch. There was neither music nor writing class. She wondered if she had better sew. She was learning to do that quite nicely, but the stocking still remained a puzzle.

"Doris," said a gentle voice through the open window; and the sadness pierced her heart.

She rose and went in. Solomon lay on his cushion in the corner, and even he, she thought, had a troubled look in his eyes. Uncle Win sat by the table, and there lay Cary's letter.

She put her arms about his neck and pressed her soft warm cheek against his, so cool that it startled her.

"My clear little Doris," he began. "I am childless. I have no son. Cary has gone away, against my wishes, in the face of my prohibition. I do not suppose he will ever return alive. And so I have given him up, Doris"—his voice failed him. He had meant to say, "You are all I have."

"Uncle Win—may I tell you—I saw him yesterday in the afternoon. And he told me he had enlisted——"

"Oh, then, you know!" The tone somehow grew harder.

"Dear Uncle Win, I think he could not help going. He was very brave. And he was sorry, too. His eyes were full of tears while he was talking. And he asked me——"

"To intercede for him?"

"No—to stay here with you always. He said I was like a little sister. And I promised. Uncle Win, if you will keep me I will be your little girl all my life long. I will never leave you. I love you very dearly. For since Uncle Leverett went away I have given you both loves."

She stood there in silence many minutes. Oh, how comforting was the clasp of the soft arms about his neck, how consoling the dear, assuring voice!

"Will you tell me about it?" he said at length.

She was a wise little thing, though I think her chief wisdom lay in her desire not to give anyone pain. Some few sentences she left out, others she softened.

"Oh," she said beseechingly, "you will not be angry with him, Uncle Winthrop? I think it is very brave and heroic in him. It is like some of the old soldiers in the Latin stories. I shall study hard now, so I can read about them all. And I shall pray all the time that the war will come to an end. We shall be so proud and glad when he returns. And then you will have two children again."

"Yes—we will hope for the war to end speedily. It ought never to have begun. What can we do against an enemy that has a hundred arms ready to destroy us? Little Doris, I am glad to have you."

Winthrop Adams was not a man to talk over his sorrows. He had been wounded to the quick. He had not dreamed that his son would disregard his wishes. His fatherly pride was up in arms. But he did not turn his wounded side to the world. He quietly admitted that his son had gone to Annapolis, and received the congratulations of friends who sincerely believed it was time to strike.

Salem was busy at her wharves, where peaceable merchantmen were being transformed into war vessels. Charlestown was all astir, and sailors donned the uniform proudly. New York and Baltimore joined in the general activity. The *Constellation* was fitting out at Norfolk. The *Chesapeake*, the *United States*, and the *President* were to be made famous on history's page.

Privateers without number were hurried to the fore.

The *Constitution* had quite a reception in New York, and she started out with high endeavors. She had not gone far, however, before she found herself followed by three British frigates, and among them the *Guerriere*, whose captain Commodore Hull had met in New York. To be captured in this manner—for fighting against such odds would be of no avail—was not to be thought of, so there was nothing but a race before him. If he could reach Boston he would save his ship and his men, and somewhere perhaps gain a victory.

Ah, what a race it was! The men put forth all their strength, all their ingenuity. At times it seemed as if capture was imminent. By night and by day, trying every experiment, working until they dropped from sheer fatigue, and after an hour or two of rest going at it again—Captain Hull kept her well to the windward, and with various maneuverings puzzled the pursuers. Then Providence favored them with a fine, driving rain, and she flew along in the darkness of the night, hardly daring to hope, but at dawn, after a three days' race, Boston was in sight, and her enemies were left behind.

But that was not in any sense a complete victory, and she started out again to face her enemy and conquer if she could, for her captain knew the British ship *Guerriere* was lying somewhere in wait for her. Everybody prayed and hoped. Firing was heard, but at such a distance from the harbor nothing could be decided.

The frontier losses had been depressing in the extreme. Boston had hung her flags at half-mast for the brave dead. But suddenly a report came that the *Constitution* had been victorious, and that the *Guerriere* after having been disabled beyond any power of restoration, had been sent to a watery grave.

In a moment it seemed as if the whole town was in a transport of joy. Flags were waving everywhere, and a gayly decorated flotilla went out in the harbor to greet the brave battle-scarred veteran. And when the tale of the great victory ran from lip to lip the rejoicing was unbounded. A national salute was fired, which was returned from the ship. The streets were in festive array and crowded with people who could not restrain their wild rejoicing. The *Guerriere*, which was to drive the insolent striped bunting from the face of the seas, had been swept away in a brief hour and a half, and the bunting waved above her grave. That night the story was told over in many a home. The loss of the *Constitution* had been very small compared to that of the *Guerriere*, which had twenty-three dead and fifty-six wounded; and Captain Dacres headed the list of prisoners.

There was a grand banquet at the Exchange Coffee House. The freedom of the city was presented to Captain Hull, and New York sent him a handsome sword. Congress voted him a gold medal, and Philadelphia a service of plate.

At one blow the prestige of invincibility claimed for the British navy was shattered. And now the *Constitution's* earlier escape from the hot chase of the three British frigates was understood to be a great race for the nation's honor and welfare, as well as for their own lives, and at last the baffled pursuers, out-sailed, out-maneuvered, dropped behind with no story of success to tell, and were to gnaw their hearts in bitterness when they heard of this glorious achievement.

Uncle Winthrop took Doris and Betty out in the carriage that they might see the great rejoicing from all points. Everywhere one heard bits of the splendid action and the intrepidity of Captain Hull and his men.

"I only wish Cary had been in it," said Betty with sparkling eyes.

Warren told them that when Lieutenant Read came on deck with Captain Hull's "compliments, and wished to know if they had struck their flag," Captain Dacres replied:

"Well—I don't know. Our mizzenmast is gone, our mainmast is gone, and I think you may say on the whole that we have struck our flag."

One of the points that pleased Mr. Adams very much was the official report of Captain Dacres, who "wished to acknowledge, as a matter of courtesy, that the conduct of Captain Hull and his officers to our men had been that of a brave enemy; the greatest care being taken to prevent our losing the smallest trifle, and the kindest attention being paid to the wounded."

More than one officer was to admit the same fact before the war ended, even if we did not receive the like consideration from our enemies.

"I only wish Cary had been on the *Constitution*," said Betty eagerly. "I should be proud of the fact to my dying day, and tell it over to my grandchildren."

A tint of color wavered over Uncle Winthrop's pale face. No one mentioned Cary, out of a sincere regard for his father, except people outside who did not know the truth of his sudden departure; though many of his young personal friends were aware of his interest and his study on the subject.

Old Boston had a gala time surely. The flags floated for days, and everyone wore a kind of triumphant aspect. That her own ship, built with so much native work and equipments, should be the first to which a British frigate should strike her colors was indeed a triumph. Though there were not wanting voices across the sea to say the *Guerriere* should have gone down with flying colors, but even that would have been impossible.

Miss Recompense and Uncle Winthrop began to discuss Revolutionary times, and Doris listened with a great deal of interest. She delighted to identify herself strongly with her adopted country, and in her secret heart she was proud of Cary, though she could not be quite sure he was right in the step he had taken. They missed him so much. She tried in many ways to make up the loss, and her devotion went to her uncle's heart.

If they could only hear! Not to know where he was seemed so hard to bear.

CHAPTER XX

A VISITOR FOR DORIS

Doris was in the little still-room, as it was called—a large sort of pantry shelved on one side, and with numerous drawers and a kind of dresser with glass doors on another. By the window there were a table and the dainty little still where Miss Recompense made perfumes and extracts. There were boxes of sweet herbs, useful ones, bottles of medicinal cordials and salves. Miss Recompense was a "master hand" at such things, and the neighbors around thought her as good as a doctor.

It was so fragrant in this little room that Doris always had a vague impression of a beautiful country. She had a kind of poetical temperament, and she hoped some day to be able to write verses. Helen Chapman had written a pretty song for a friend's birthday and had it set to music. The quartette sang it so well that the leading paper had praised it. There was no one she could confess her secret ambition to, but if she ever *did* achieve anything she would confide in Uncle Winthrop. So she sat here with all manner of vague, delightful ideas floating through her brain, steeped with the fragrance of balms and odors.

"Please, 'm," and Dinah stood in the door in all the glory of her gay afternoon turban, which seemed to make her face more black and shining—"Please, 'm, dere's a young sojer man jus' come. He got a bundle an' he say he got strict d'rections to gib it to missy. An' here's de ticket."

"Oh, for me!" Doris took it eagerly and read aloud, "Lieutenant E. D. Hawthorne." "Oh, Miss Recompense, it's from Cary, I know," and for a moment she looked undecided.

Miss Recompense had on her morning gown, rather faded, though she had changed it for dinner. Her sleeves were pushed above the elbow, her hands were a little stained, and just now she could not leave her concoction without great injury to it, though it was evidently improper for a child like Doris, or indeed a young lady, to see a strange gentleman alone. And Mr. Adams was out.

Doris cut the Gordian knot by flashing through the kitchen and entering the lower end of the hall. The young man stood viewing "The Destruction of the Spanish Armada." But he turned at the sort of bird-like flutter and glanced at the vision that all his life long he thought the prettiest sight he had ever beheld.

She had on a simple white frock, though it was one of her best, with a narrow embroidered ruffle around the bottom that Madam Royall had given her. When it was a little crumpled she put it on for afternoon wear. The neck was cut a small square with a bit of edging around it, gathered with a pink ribbon tied in a bow in front. She still wore her hair in ringlets; it did not seem to grow very fast, but she had been promoted to a pompadour, the front hair being brushed up over a cushion. That left innumerable short ends to curl in tiny tendrils about her forehead. Oddly enough, too, she had on a pink apron Betty had made out of the best breadth of a pink India lawn frock she had worn out. It had pretty pockets with a bow of the same.

"Miss Doris Adams," exclaimed the young lieutenant. "I should have known you in a minute, although you are——" He paused and flushed, for Cary had said, "She isn't exactly handsome, but very sweet-looking with pretty, eager eyes and fair hair." He checked himself suddenly, understanding the impropriety of paying her the compliment on the end of his tongue, but he thought her an enchanting picture. "You are larger than I supposed. Adams always said 'My little cousin.'"

"I was little when I first came. And I have grown ever so much this summer —since Cary went away. Oh, have you seen him? How is he? Where is he?"

Doris had a soft and curiously musical voice, the sound that lingered with a sort of cadence. Her eyes shone in eager expectation, her curved red lips were dewy sweet.

"He is well. He has sailed on the *United States* as midshipman. I saw him at Annapolis—indeed, we came quite near being on the same vessel. He is a fine young fellow, but he doesn't look a day over eighteen. And there *is* a family resemblance," but he thought Doris would make a much handsomer young woman than Cary would a young man. "And I have a small packet for you that I was to deliver to no one else."

He held it out to her with a smile. It was sealed, and was also secured with a bit of cord, which, of course, should have been a thread of silk, but we saved our refinements of chivalry for other purposes.

"He is going to make a fine, earnest, patriotic sailor. You will never hear anything about him that you need be ashamed of. He told me his father wasn't quite reconciled to the step, but after this splendid victory in Boston harbor— to strain a little point," laughingly, "the town may well be proud of the courageous navy. And I hope you will hear good news of him. One thing you may be sure of—he will never show the white feather."

Oh, how her eyes glistened! There were tears in them as well.

"He described the house to me, and the town. I have never been in Boston before, and have come from Washington on important business. I return this evening. I don't know when I shall see him again, and letters to vessels are so uncertain. That seems the hardest part of it all. But he may happen in this very port before a great while. One never knows. Believe that I am very glad to have the opportunity of coming myself, and if in the future I should run across him on the high seas or the shore even,"—smiling again,—"I shall feel better acquainted and more than ever interested in him. There is one great favor I should like to ask—could you show me the study? Adams talked so much about that and his father."

"It is here." Doris made a pretty gesture with her hand, and he walked to the door, glancing around. There was the high backed chair by the table with its covering of Cordovan leather, and he could imagine the father sitting there.

"One would want a year to journey around these four walls," he said with a soft sigh. "A library like this is an uncommon sight. And you study here? Adams said you had been such a comfort and pleasure to his father. Oh, what a magnificent cat!"

"Kitty is mine," said Doris. She crossed over to the window, and Solomon rose to his fullest extent, gave a comfortable stretch, and rubbed the cheek of his young mistress, then arched his back, studied the visitor out of sleepy green eyes and began to turn around him three times in cat fashion.

They both laughed at that. Did Doris know what a pretty picture she made of herself in her girlish grace?

"Thank you. What a splendid old hall! I should like to spend a day looking round. But I had only the briefest while, and I was afraid I should not get here. So I must be satisfied with my glimpse. I shall hope that fate will send me this way again when I have more leisure. May I pay a visit here?"

"Oh, yes," returned Doris impulsively. "And I can never tell you how glad I am for this," touching the little packet caressingly to her cheek. "There isn't any word with enough thanks and gratitude in it."

"I am glad to have earned your gratitude. And now I must say farewell, for I know you are impatient to read your letter."

He stepped out on the porch and bowed with a kind of courtly grace. Doris realized then that he was a very handsome young man.

"Miss Doris,"—he paused halfway down the steps,—"I wonder if I might be so bold as to ask for yonder rose—the last on its parent stem?"

Thomas Moore had not yet immortalized "The Last Rose of Summer" and given it such pathetic possibilities.

"Oh, yes," she said. "That is a late-blooming rose—indeed, it blooms twice in the season." Only this morning she had gathered a bowl of rose leaves for Miss Recompense, and this one had opened since. She broke the stem and handed it to him. "It is a very little gift for all you have brought me," she added in a soft, heart-felt tone.

"Thank you. I shall cherish it sacredly."

Miss Recompense had hurried and donned a gingham gown and a fresh cap. She had come just in time to see the gift, and the manner in which the young man received it alarmed her. And when he had walked down to the street he turned and bowed and made a farewell gesture with his hand.

Doris had nothing to cut the cord around the packet, so she bit it with her pretty teeth and tore off the wrapper, coming up the steps. Then raising her eyes she sprang forward.

"Oh, dear Miss Recompense, letters, see! A letter from Cary all to myself, and one for Uncle Win! I'll just put that on his table to be a joyful surprise. And may I come and read mine to you? He was in such a hurry, though really I did not ask him to stay. Was that impolite?"

"No—under the circumstances." She cleared her throat a little, but the lecture on propriety would not materialize.

"'Dear little Doris.' Think of that—wouldn't Cary be surprised to see how much I have grown! May I sit here?"

Miss Recompense was about to decant some of her preparations. Doris took the high stool and read eagerly, though now and then a little break came in her voice. The journey to Annapolis with half a dozen college chums bent on the same errand, the being mustered into the country's service and assigned to positions, meeting famous people and hearing some thrilling news, and at last the order for sailing, were vivid as a picture. She was to let Madam Royall and the household read all this, and he sent respectful regard to them all, and real love to all the Leveretts. There had been moments when he was wild to see them again, but after all he was prouder than ever to be of service to his country, who needed her bravest sons as much now as in her seven years' struggle.

There was a loose page beginning "For your eyes alone, Doris," and she laid it by, for she felt even now that she wanted to cry over her brave cousin. Then he spoke of Lieutenant Hawthorne, who had been instrumental in getting him his appointment, and who had undertaken to see that this would reach her safely. And so many farewells, as if he could hardly say the very last one.

Miss Recompense wiped her eyes and stepped about softly, as if her whole body was pervaded with a new tenderness. She made little comments to restore the equilibrium, so that neither would give way to undue emotion.

"Miss Recompense, do you think I might run up to Aunt Elizabeth's with my letter? They will all want to hear."

"Why—I see no objections, child. And then if you wanted to go to Madam Royall's—but I think they will keep you to tea at Sudbury Street. Let Betty or Warren walk home with you. Take off your apron."

Doris read half a dozen lines of her own personal letter and laid it in the bottom of her workbox, that had come from India, and had a subtle fragrance. She did not want to cry in real earnest, as she felt she should, with all these references to Uncle Win. She tied on her hat and said "Good-afternoon," and really did run part of the way.

They were just overflowing with joy to hear, only Betty said, "What a shame Cary had to go before the glorious news of the *Constitution*! There was a chance of two days after he had written his letter, so he might have heard." Postage was high at that time and mails uncertain, so letters and important matters were often trusted to private hands. Then Lieutenant Hawthorne had not gone to Boston as soon as he expected.

Betty had some news too. Mr. and Mrs. King were going to Washington, perhaps for the greater part of the winter.

As they walked home Betty rehearsed her perplexities to Doris. It was odd how many matters were confided to this girl of thirteen, but she seemed so wise and sensible and sympathetic.

"If it wasn't quite such hard times, and if Warren could marry and bring Mercy home! She's an excellent housekeeper, just the wife for a struggling young man, mother admits. But whether *she* would like it, and whether Aunt Priscilla would feel comfortable, are the great questions. She's been so good to Warren. Mary badgered him dreadfully about her part. If Mary was a little more like Electa!"

Warren had been keeping company with Mercy Gilman for the last year. She was a bright, cheerful, industrious girl, well brought up, and the engagement was acceptable to both families. Young people paid more deference to their elders then. Warren felt that he could not go away from home, and surely there was room enough if they could all agree.

"It's odd how many splendid things come to Electa, though it may be because she is always willing to take advantage of them. They have rented their house in New York and are to take some rooms in Washington. Bessy and Leverett are to be put in school, and she takes the two little ones. Their meals are to be sent in from a cook shop. Of course she can't be very gay, being in mourning. Everybody says Mrs. Madison is so charming."

"Oh, I wish you could go," sighed Doris.

"And Mary is always wondering why I do not come and stay with her, and sew and help along. Oh, Doris, what if I should be the old maid aunt and go visiting round! For there hasn't a soul asked me to keep company yet," and Betty laughed. But she was not very anxious on the subject.

They reached the corner and kissed each other good-night. Miss Recompense sat on the stoop with a little shawl about her shoulders. She drew Doris down beside her and inquired about her visit.

While there was much that was stern and hard and reticent in the Puritan character, there was also an innate delicacy concerning the inward life. They made few appeals to each other's sympathies. Perhaps this very reserve gave them strength to endure trials heroically and not burden others.

Miss Recompense had judged wisely that Mr. Adams would prefer to receive his missive alone. His first remark had been the usual question:

"Where is Doris?"

"Oh, we have had quite an adventure—a call from a young naval officer. Here is his card. He brought letters to you and Doris, and she was eager to take hers over to Betty. She will stay to supper."

He scrutinized the card while his breath came in strangling gasps, but he preserved his composure outwardly.

"Did you—did he——" pausing confusedly.

"I did not see him," returned Miss Recompense quietly. "I was not in company trim, and he asked for Doris. I dare say he thought her a young lady."

"Is he staying in Boston?" fingering the card irresolutely.

"He was to return to Washington at once. He had come on some urgent business."

Mr. Adams went through to his study. He looked at the address some moments before he broke the seal, but he found the first lines reassuring.

"Will you have supper now?" asked Miss Recompense from the doorway.

"If convenient, yes." He laid down his letter and came out in the hall. "Doris told you all her news, I suppose?"

"She read me her letter. Cary seems to be in good spirits and position. He spoke very highly of Lieutenant Hawthorne."

"The accounts seem very satisfactory."

Then they went out to the quiet supper. A meal was not the same without Doris.

All the evening he had remained in his room, reading his son's letter more than once and lapsing into deep thought over it. He heard the greetings now, and came out, inquiring after the folks in Sudbury Street, sitting down on the step and listening with evident pleasure to Doris' eager chat. It was bedtime when they dispersed.

"Uncle Win," Doris said the next morning, "there is a page in my letter I would like you to read. And do you think I might go home with Eudora and take dinner at Madam Royall's? Cary sent them some messages."

"Yes, child," he made answer.

They were indeed very glad, but like Betty they could not help wishing he had been on the famous *Constitution*. Alice was particularly interested, and said she should watch the career of the *United States*.

After that the ice seemed broken and no one hesitated to mention Cary. But Mr. Winthrop said to Doris:

"My dear child, will you give me this leaf of your letter. I know Cary did not mean it for my eyes, but it is very precious to me. Doris, how comes it that you find the way to everybody's heart?"

"And you will forgive him, Uncle Win? He was so brave——" Her voice trembled.

"I have forgiven him, Doris. If I should never see him again,—you are young and most likely will,—assure him there never was a moment that I ceased to love him. Perhaps I have not taken as much pains to understand him as I might have. I suppose different influences act upon the new generation. If we should both live to welcome him back——"

"Oh, we must, Uncle Win."

"If he has you——" Oh, what was he saying?

"You will both have me. I shall stay here always."

He stooped and kissed her.

The other alternative, that Cary might not return, they banished resolutely. But it drew them nearer together in unspoken sympathy.

Everybody noted how thin and frail-looking Mr. Adams had grown. Doris became his constant companion. She had a well-trained horse now, and they rode a good deal. Or they walked down Washington street, where there were some pretty shops, and met promenaders. They sauntered about Cornhill, where Uncle Win picked up now and then an odd book, and they discovered strange things that had belonged to the Old Boston of a hundred years agone. There was quite an art gallery in Cornhill kept by Dogget & Williams—the nucleus of great things to come. It was quite the fashion for young ladies to drop in and exercise their powers of budding criticism or love of art. Now and then someone lent a portrait of Smibert's or Copley's, or you found some fine German or English engravings. An elder person generally accompanied the younger people. The law students, released from their labors, or the young society men, would walk home beside the chaperone, but talk to the maidens.

Then Uncle Winthrop committed a piece of great extravagance, everybody said—especially in such times as these, when the British might take and destroy Boston. This was buying a pianoforte. Madam Royall approved, for Doris was learning to play very nicely. An old German musician, Gottlieb Graupner, who was quite a visitor at the Royall house, had imported it for a friend who had been nearly ruined by war troubles and was compelled to part with it. Mr. Graupner and a knot of musical friends used to meet Saturday evenings in old Pond Street, and with a few instruments made a sort of orchestra. As a very great favor, friends were occasionally invited in.

There was a new organist at Trinity Church, a Mr. Jackson, who was trying to bring in the higher class cathedral music. The choir of Park Street Church, some fifty in number, was considered one of the great successes of the day, and people flocked to hear it. Puritan music had been rather doleful and depressing.

There was quite a discussion as to where the piano should stand. They had very little call to use the parlor in winter. Uncle Winthrop's friends generally visited him in the study. The spacious hall was the ordinary living-room, and Doris begged that it might be kept here—for the winter, at least.

Oh, what a cheerful sound the music made in the old house! Uncle Win would bring out a book of poems, often Milton's "L'Allegro" and half read, half listen, to the entrancing combination. Dinah declared "It was like de w'ice ob de Angel Gabriel hisself." Miss Recompense enjoyed the grand old hymns that brought back her childhood.

Solomon at first made a vigorous protest. He seemed jealous of the pretty fingers gliding over the keys, and would spring up to cover them or rest on her arms. But when he found he was banished to the kitchen every evening, he began to consider and presently gave in. He would sit beside Uncle Win in dignified protest, looking very "dour," as a Scotchman would say.

And then the country was electrified with the news of another great victory. Off the Canary Islands, Captain Decatur, with the frigate *United States*, met the *Macedonian*, one of the finest of the British fleet. The fight had been at close quarters with terrific broadsides. After an hour and a half, with her fighting force disabled, the *Macedonian* struck her colors. Her loss in men killed and wounded was over one hundred, and the *United States* lost five killed and seven wounded.

The American vessel brought her prize and prisoners into port amid general acclaim. The *Macedonian* was repaired and added to the fast-increasing navy, that was rapidly winning a world-wide reputation. And when she came up to New York early in January with "The compliments of the season," there was great rejoicing. Samuel Woodworth, printer and poet, wrote the song of the occasion, and Calvert, another poet, celebrated the event in an ode.

Captain Carden was severely censured by his own government, as Captain Dacres had been, for not going down with flying colors instead of allowing his flag to be captured and his ship turned to the enemy's advantage. Instead of jeering at the navy of "pine boards and striped bunting," it was claimed the American vessels were of superior size and armament and met the British at unfair advantage, and that they were largely manned by English sailors.

There was an enthusiastic note from Cary. He was well, and it had been a glorious action. Captain Carden had been a brave gentleman, and he said regretfully, "Oh, why do we have to fight these heroic men!"

But Betty had the letter of triumph this time. Mrs. King was a delightful correspondent, though she was always imploring Betty to join her.

There had been a ball and reception given to several naval officers who were soon to go away. The President, engaged with some weighty affairs, had not come in yet, but the Secretary of the Navy, Mr. Hamilton, and no end of military and naval men, in gold lace and epaulettes and gleaming swords, were present, and beautiful, enthusiastic women in shimmering silks and laces. One did not have to get a new gown for every occasion in those days.

There was a little lull in the dancing. Mrs. Madison, who was charmingly affable, was seated with a group of men about her, when there was a stir in the hall, and a sudden thrill of expectancy quivered through the apartment. Ensign Hamilton, son of the Secretary, and several midshipmen entered, and the young man went straight to his father with the captured flag of the *Macedonian*. Such a cheer as rent the air! Ladies wiped their eyes and then waved their handkerchiefs in the wild burst of joy. They held the flag over the heads of the chief officer while the band played "Hail, Columbia!" Then it was laid at the feet of Mrs. Madison, who accepted it in the name of the country with a charming and graceful speech. Afterward it was festooned on the wall with the flag of the *Guerriere*.

"So, you see, Cary has been the hero of a great victory," said Betty enthusiastically; "but we all wish it had been 'off Boston Light' instead of on the distant ocean. And it is a shame not to be in Washington. Electa seems to be going everywhere and seeing everything, 'in spite of her being the mother of four children,' as Aunt Priscilla says. And the ladies dress so beautifully. We shall come to be known as 'plain Boston' presently."

There was no Worth or Pingat to charge enormous prices. Patterns were passed around. Ladies went visiting and took their sleeves along to make, or their ruffles to plait, and altered over their brocades and paduasoys and crapes, and some darned Brussels "footing" until it was transformed into really handsome lace. They could clean their feathers and ribbons, and one wonders how they found time for so many things. They were very good letter writers too. Dolly Madison and Mrs. Adams are fresh and interesting to-day.

But Boston could rejoice, nevertheless. To the little girl Cary was invested with the attributes of a hero. He even looked different to her enchanted eyes.

Uncle Win used to smile with grave softness when she chattered about him. At first it had given him a heartache to hear Cary's name mentioned, but now it was like a strain of comforting music. Only he wondered how he ever would have lived without the little girl from Old Boston.

She used to play and sing "Hail, Columbia!"—for people were patriotic then. But the sweetest of all were the old-fashioned ones that his wife had sung as a young girl, daintily tender love songs. Sometimes he tried them with her, but his voice sounded to himself like a pale ghost out of the past, yet it still had a mournful sweetness.

But with the rejoicing we had many sorrows. Our northern frontier warfare had been full of defeats; 1813 opened with various misfortunes. Ports were blockaded, business dropped lower and lower. Still social life went on, and in a tentative way intellectual life was making some progress.

The drama was not neglected either. The old Boston Theater gave several stirring representations that to-day would be called quite realistic. One was the capture of the *Guerriere* with officers, sailors and marines, and songs that aroused drooping patriotism. Perhaps the young people of that time enjoyed it as much as their grandchildren did "H. M. S. Pinafore."

Doris liked the rare musical entertainments. People grew quite used to seeing Mr. Winthrop Adams with the pretty, bright, growing girl, who might have been his daughter. It was a delight to her when anyone made the mistake. Occasionally an old gentleman remembered her grandfather, and the little boy Charles who went to England.

Then in the early summer Mrs. King came on for a visit, and brought her eldest child Bessy, a bright, well-trained little girl.

There had been a good deal of trouble at the Mannings', and grandmother had gone back and forth, making it very confining for Betty. Crops had proved poor in the autumn; the children had the measles and Mrs. Manning a run of fever. Elizabeth had taken a cold in the early fall and had a troublesome cough all winter. Mrs. Leverett wanted to bring her home for a rest, but Mrs. Manning could not spare her, with all the summer work, and the warm weather would set her up, she was quite sure.

The country was drawing a brief breath of relief. There had been the magnificent victories on the Lakes and some on the land, and now and then came cheering news of naval successes. Everybody was in better spirits. Mrs. King seemed to bring a waft of hope from the Capital itself, and the Leverett house was quite enlivened with callers. Invitations came in for dinners and suppers and evening parties. Madam Royall quite claimed her on the strength of the Adams relation, and also Doris, who was such a favorite. Doris and little Bessy fraternized at once, and practiced a duet for the entertainment of Uncle Winthrop, who praised them warmly.

She planned to take Betty back to New York with her.

"But I can't go," declared Betty. "Warren must not be taxed any more heavily, so there would be no hope of having help, and mother cannot be left alone."

"Is there any objection to Mercy coming? Why doesn't Warren marry? That would relieve you all. I suppose it *is* best for young people to have a home by themselves, but if it isn't possible—and I'd like to know how we are going to get along in heaven if we can't agree with each other here on earth!" Mrs. King inquired.

"That sounds like father," said Betty laughingly, yet the tears came to her eyes. "Poor father! He did not suppose we would have such hard times. If the war would only end. You see,"—after a pause,—"we are not quite sure of Aunt Priscilla. She's changed and softened wonderfully, and she and mother get along so well. She insisted upon paying a generous board, and she was good to Warren."

"I must talk it over with mother. There is no need of having your life spoiled, Betty."

For Betty was a very well-looking girl, arch and vivacious, and her harvest time of youth must not be wasted. Mrs. King was really glad she had no entanglement.

Mrs. Leverett had no objections to a speedy marriage If Mercy could be content. Warren had thought if he could be prosperous he would like to buy out Betty's share if she married. "And my share will be mine as long as I live," added the mother. "But Warren is fond of the old house, and Hollis has a home of his own. You girls will never want it."

Warren was delighted with what he called "Lecty's spunk." For Aunt Priscilla agreed quite readily. It was dull for Betty with two old people. Mercy would have her husband.

So the wedding day was appointed. Mercy had been a year getting ready. Girls began soon after they were engaged. Mrs. Gilman was rather afraid the thing wouldn't work, but she was sure Mercy was good tempered, and she had been a good daughter.

They made quite a "turning round." Mrs. Leverett went upstairs to Betty's room, which adjoined Aunt Priscilla's, and she gave some of her furniture for the adornment of the bridal chamber.

It was a very quiet wedding with a few friends and a supper. At nine o'clock the new wife went to Sudbury Street. Mrs. Gilman had some rather strict ideas, and declared it was no time for frolicking when war was at our very door, and no one knew what might happen, and hundreds of families were in pinching want.

Mercy was up the next morning betimes and assisted her new mother with the breakfast. Warren went down to his shop. But they had quite an elaborate tea drinking at the Leveretts', and some songs and games in the evening. Mercy *did* enjoy the wider life.

Mrs. Manning had come in for the wedding and a few days' stay, though she didn't see how she could be spared just now, and things would get dreadfully behindhand. Mrs. King was to go home with her and make a little visit. Bessy thought she would rather stay with Doris, and she was captivated with the Royall House and Eudora. The children never seemed in the way of the grown people there, and if elderly men talked politics and city improvements, —quite visionary, some thought them,—the young people with Alice and Helen had the garden walks and the wide porch, and discussed the enjoyments of the time with the zest of enthusiastic inexperience but keen delight.

CHAPTER XXI

ELIZABETH AND—PEACE

Mrs. King brought back Elizabeth Manning, a pale, slim ghost of a girl, tall for her age—indeed, really grown up, her mother said. Of the three girls Bessy King had the most indications of the traditional country girl. A fine clear skin, pink cheeks and a plump figure, and an inexhausible flow of spirits, ready for any fun or frolic.

Doris was always well, but she had the Adams complexion, which was rather pale, with color when she was warm, or enthusiastic or indignant. The pink came and went like a swift summer cloud.

"I do declare," exclaimed Aunt Priscilla, "if 'Lecty King doesn't beat all about getting what she wants, and making other people believe they want it, too! Warren might as well have been married in the winter, and Mercy would have been company for Betty. She never liked to run out and leave me alone. Mercy seems a nice, promising body, and Warren might as well be happy and settled as not. And 'Lecty's been to Washington and dined with the President and Mrs. Madison, and I'll venture to say there was something the President's wife consulted her about. And all the big captains and generals, and what not! And here's the quality of Boston running after her and asking her out just as if we had nothing to feed her on at home. She don't do anything, fursisee, but just look smiling and talk. But my opinion is that Elizabeth Manning hasn't a very long journey to the graveyard. I don't see what Mary's been thinking about."

Mrs. King took her niece to Dr. Jackson, one of the best medical authorities of that day, and he looked the young girl over with his keen eyes.

"If you want the real truth," said the doctor, "she has had too much east wind and too much hard work. The children of this generation are not going to stand what their mothers did. A bad cold or two next winter will finish her, but with care and no undue exposure she may live several years. But she will never reach the three score and ten that every human being has a right to."

Uncle Winthrop sent the carriage around every day to the Leveretts'. They had given up theirs before Mr. Leverett's death. He and Doris took their morning horseback rides and scoured the beautiful country places for miles around, until Doris knew every magnificent tree or unusual shrub or queer old house and its history. These hours were a great delight to him.

Elizabeth had often gone down to Salem town, but her time was so brief and there was so much to do that she "couldn't bother." And she wondered how Doris knew about the shops in Essex Street and Federal Street and Miss Rust's pretty millinery show, and Mr. John Innes' delicate French rolls and braided bread, and Molly Saunders' gingerbread that the school children devoured, and the old Forrester House with its legends and fine old pictures and the lovely gardens, the wharves with their idle fleets that dared not put out to sea for fear of being swallowed up by the enemy.

Uncle Winthrop had taken her several times when some business had called him thither. But, truth to tell, she had never cared to repeat her visit to Mrs. Manning's.

The piano was like a bit of heaven, Elizabeth thought, the first time she came over to visit Doris.

"Oh," she said, with a long sigh, pressing her hand on her heart, for the deep breaths always hurt her, "if I was only prepared to go to heaven I shouldn't want to stay here a day longer. When they sing about 'eternal rest' it seems such a lovely thing, and to 'lay your burdens down.' But then there's 'the terrors of the law,' and the 'judgments to come,' and the great searching of the hearts and reins—do you know just what the reins are?"

No, Doris didn't. Heaven had always seemed a lovely place to her and God like a father, only grander and tenderer than any human father could be.

Then they talked about praying, and it came out that Doris said her mother's prayers still in French and her father's in English.

"Oh," exclaimed Elizabeth, horrified, "I shouldn't dare to pray to God in French—it would seem like a mockery. And 'Now I lay me down to sleep' is just a baby prayer, and really isn't pouring out your own soul to God."

Doris asked Uncle Winthrop about it.

"My child," he said with grave sweetness, "you can never say any better prayers of your own. The Saviour himself gave us the comprehensive Lord's Prayer. And are all the nations of the earth who cannot pray in English offering God vain petitions? You will find as you grow older that no earnest soul ever worships God in vain, and that religion is a life-long work. I am learning something new about it every day. And I think God means us to be happy here on earth. He doesn't save all the joys for heaven. He has given me one," and he stooped and kissed Doris on the forehead. "Poor Elizabeth," he added—"make her as happy as you can!"

When Mrs. King proposed to take Betty to New York for the whole of the coming winter there was consternation, but no one could find a valid objection. It was a somewhat expensive journey, and winter was a very enjoyable season in the city. Then another year something new might happen to prevent—there was no time like the present.

No one had the courage to object, though they did not know how to spare her. Aunt Priscilla sighed and brought out some beautiful long-laid-away articles that Electa declared would make over admirably.

"Where do you suppose Aunt Priscilla picked up all these elegant things?" asked Electa. "I never remember seeing her wear them, though she always dressed well, but severely plain. And Uncle Perkins was quite strict about the pomps and vanities of the world."

And so Aunt Priscilla put away the last of her idols and the life she had coveted and never had. But perhaps the best of all was her consideration for others, the certainty that it was quite as well to begin some of the virtues of the heavenly world here on earth that they might not seem strange to one.

Mrs. Manning sent in for Elizabeth.

"Well—you do seem like a different girl," her father declared, looking her over from head to foot. "You've had a good rest now, and you'll have to turn in strong and hearty, for Sarah's gone, and Ruth isn't big enough to take hold of everything. So hunt up your things while I'm doing some trading."

Elizabeth only had time for the very briefest farewells. Mrs. King sent a little note containing the doctor's verdict, but Mrs. Manning was indignant rather than alarmed.

It was lonesome when they were all gone. Eudora Chapman went to a "finishing school" this autumn, and Doris accompanied her—poor Doris, who had not mastered fractions, and whose written arithmetic could not compare with Betty's. She had achieved a pair of stockings after infinite labor and trouble. They *did* look rowy, being knit tighter and looser. But Aunt Priscilla gave her a pair of fine merino that she had kept from the ravages of the moths. Miss Recompense declared that she had no one else to knit for.

There were expert knitters who made beautiful silk stockings, and Uncle Winthrop said buying helped along trade, so why should Doris worry when there were so many more important matters?

The little girl and her uncle kept track of what was going on in the great world. Napoleon the invincible had been driven back from Russia by cold and famine, forced to yield by the great coalition and losing step by step until he was compelled to accept banishment. Then England redoubled her efforts, prepared to carry on the war with us vigorously. Towns on the Chesapeake were plundered and burned, and General Ross entered Washington, from which Congress and the President's family had fled for their lives. America was again horror stricken, but gathering all her energies she made such a vigorous defense as to convince her antagonist that though cast down she could never be wholly defeated.

But this attack gave us the inspiration of one of our finest deathless songs. A Mr. Francis S. Key, a resident of Georgetown, had gone down from Baltimore with a flag of truce to procure the release of a friend held as prisoner of war, when the bombardment of Fort McHenry began. All day long he watched the flag as it floated above the ramparts. Night came on and it was still there. And at midnight he could see it only by "the rockets' red glare," while he and his friends tremulously inquired if the "flag still waved o'er the Land of the Free." Oh, what joy must have been his when it "caught the gleam of the morning's first beam." He had put the night watch and the dawn in a song that is still an inspiration.

And now convinced, the enemy withdrew. There were talks of peace, though we did not abate our energies. And the indications of a settlement brought about another wedding at the Royall house.

Miss Alice had been a great favorite with the young men, and her ardent patriotism had inspired more than one, as it had Cary Adams, with a desire to rush to his country's defense. There were admirers too, but most of them had been kept at an intangible distance. At last she had yielded to the eloquence of young Oliver Sargent, who was in every way acceptable. Grandmother Royall expected to give her an elegant wedding along in the winter.

The Government was to send out another commissioner to consult with those already at Ghent, and Mr. Sargent had been offered the post of private secretary. He was to sail from New York, but he obtained leave to spend a few days in Boston to attend to some affairs. He went at once to Madam Royall and laid his plans before her. He wanted to marry Alice and take her with him, as he might be gone a long while. Alice was nothing loath, for the journey abroad was extremely tempting.

But what could one do in such a few days? And wedding clothes——

"Save the wedding gear until we come back," said the impatient young lover. "Alice can get clothes enough abroad."

It was quite a new departure in a wedding. Invitations were always sent out by hand, even for small evening parties, and often verbally given. A private marriage would not have suited old Madam Royall. So the house was crowded at eleven in the morning, and the bride came through the wide hall in a mulberry-colored satin gown and pelisse that had been made two weeks before for ordinary autumn wear. But her bonnet was white with long streamers, and her gloves were white, and she made a very attractive bride, while young Sargent was manly and looked proud enough for a king. At twelve they went away with no end of good wishes, and an old slipper was thrown after the carriage.

Mrs. Morris Winslow had two babies, and was already growing stout. But the departure of Alice made a great break.

"But it is the way of the world and the way of God that young people should marry," said Madam Royall. "I was very happy myself."

"Oh," exclaimed Doris eagerly that evening, her eyes aglow and her cheeks pink with excitement—"oh, Uncle Win, do you think there will be peace?"

"My little girl, it is my prayer day and night."

"And then Cary will come home."

It had been a long while since they had heard. Cary had been transferred from the *United States*, that had lain blockaded in a harbor many weary weeks. But where he was now no one could tell.

People began to take heart though the fighting had not ceased. And it was odd that a dozen years before everybody had looked askance at dancing, and now no one hesitated to give a dancing party. The contra-dance and cotillions were all the rage. Sometimes there was great amusement when it was a draw dance, for then you had to accept your partner whether or no.

Whole families went, grandmothers and grandchildren. There were cards and conversation circles for those who did not care to join the mazy whirls. And the suppers were quite elegant, with brilliant lamps and flowers, plate and glass that had come through generations. Fruits and melons were preserved as long as possible, and a Turkish band in fine Oriental costume was often a feature of the entertainment.

Doris had charming letters from Betty, a little stilted we should call them now, but very interesting. Mr. King was confident of peace. Doris used to read them to Aunt Priscilla, who said Betty was very frivolous, but that she always had a good time, and perhaps good times were not as wicked as people used to think.

Mrs. Leverett went to Salem in November. Her namesake had taken a cold and had some fever, and she asked for grandmother continually. Mercy did finely at housekeeping, and so the weeks ran along, the invalid being better, then worse, and just before Christmas the frail little life floated out to the Land of Rest.

"Oh, poor little Elizabeth!" cried Doris. "If she could have been real happy!

But there never seemed any time. Uncle Win, they are not so poor that they have to work so hard, are they?"

"No, dear. Mr. Manning has money out at interest, besides his handsome farm. But a great many people think there is solid virtue in working and saving. I suppose it makes them happy."

Doris was puzzled. She said the same thing to Aunt Priscilla, who took off her glasses, rubbed them with a bit of old silk and wiped the tears out of her eyes.

"I think we haven't had quite the right end of it," she began after a pause. "I was brought up that way. But then people had to spin and weave for themselves, and help the men with the out-of-doors work. The children dropped corn, and potatoes, and there was always weeding. There was so much spring work and fall work, and folks couldn't be comfortable if they saw a child playing 'cat's cradle.' They did think Satan was going about continually to catch up idle hands. Well maybe if I'd had children I'd 'a' done the same way."

"Oh, you wouldn't, Aunt Priscilla, I know," said Doris with the sweetest faith shining in her eyes. "Elizabeth thought you such a comfortable old lady. She said you never worried at anyone."

"That is because I have come to believe the worrying wrong. The Lord didn't worry at people. He told them what to do and then he let them alone. And Foster Leverett was about the best man I ever knew. He didn't even worry when times were so bad. Everybody said his children would be spoiled. They were out sledding and sliding and skating, and playing tag in summer. They've made nice men and women."

"Oh, I remember how friendly he looked that day he came on the vessel. And how he said to Captain Grier, 'Is there a little girl for me that has come from Old Boston?' He might have said something else, you know. 'A little girl for me' was such a sweet welcome, I have never forgotten it."

"Yes—I was here the night you came. We had been waiting. And the red cloak and big bonnet with the great bow under your chin, and a silk frock ———"

"Did I look very queer?" Doris laughed softly.

"You looked like a picture, though that wan't my idea of what children should be."

"Miss Recompense has them put away to keep. I outgrew them, you know. What would you have done with me?"

Aunt Priscilla's pale face wrinkled up and then smoothed out.

"I've come to the conclusion the Lord knows his business best and is capable of attending to it. When we meddle we make a rather poor fist of it. Betty has a lot of morning-glories out there," nodding her head, "and I said to her 'They're poor frail things: why not put out a hop vine or red beans? They can't stand a bit of sun, like Jonah's gourd.' But she only laughed—her father had that way when he didn't want to argue. When they came to bloom they were sights to behold, like the early morning when the sun is rising, and you see such beautiful colors. They used to nod to each other and swing back and forth, like people coming to call, then they said good-by and were off. The Lord meant 'em just to look pretty and they did."

"Uncle Win likes them so much. Miss Recompense had a whole lattice full of them. Oh, did you mean I was like a morning glory? Haven't I some other uses?"

"You're always fresh and blossoming every day. That's a use. You come in with a little greeting that warms one's heart. You were a great delight to Uncle Leverett, and I don't know what Uncle Winthrop would have done without you, Cary being away. And how Solomon took to you, when he was awful shy of strangers! He must have liked you uncommon to be willing to stay in a strange place, for cats cannot bear to be moved about. Maybe 'twould been the same if you had not been so pretty to look at, but the Lord made you the way he wanted you, and you haven't spoiled yourself a bit."

Doris blushed. Compliments were quite a new thing with Aunt Priscilla.

"What would you have done with me?" Doris asked again, after a long pause.

"You won't like to hear it. I ought to confess it because it was a sin, a sort of meddling with the Lord's plans. You see, I'd taken it in my head that someone would have to give you a home. It didn't seem as if that old ma'shland would be good for anything, and I knew your father wasn't rich. Winthrop Adams was one of the finicky kind and quite put about to know what to do with you. So I thought if there didn't any place open, for Elizabeth Leverett was quite wrapped up in her grandchildren, that"—hesitatingly—"when things were straightened out a bit, I'd offer——"

"That would have been good of you——"

"No, it wasn't goodness," interrupted Aunt Priscilla. "I thought I should want someone, with Polly getting old. I'd have expected you to work, though I'd have done the fair thing by you, and left you some money in the end. I was a little jealous when everybody took to you so. I was sure you'd be spoiled. And, though you've got that music thing and go among the quality, and are pretty as a pink, and Winthrop Adams thinks you a nonesuch, you come in here in plain everyday fashion and talk and read and make it sunshiny for everybody. So, you see, the Lord knew, and it is just as if he said, 'Priscilla

Perkins, your way doesn't suit at all. There's something in the world besides work and saving money. There's room enough in the world for a hill of potatoes and a morning-glory made of silk and dew if it doesn't bloom but just one morning. It's a smile, and there are others to follow, and it is a thousand times better than frowns.'"

"And if there had been no money, and I had wanted a home, would you have given me one?" she asked in a soft, tremulous tone.

"Yes, child. And I couldn't have worked you quite like poor little Elizabeth was worked. I didn't think there *was* so much money, or that that lady in England would have left you a legacy or that Winthrop Adams would come to believing that he couldn't live without you."

"Then you were kind to have a plan about it, and I am glad to know it."

She had been sitting on Aunt Priscilla's footstool, but she rose and twined her arms about the shrunken neck, and kissed the wrinkled forehead. She saw a homeless little girl going to sheltering care, with a kindly remembrance at the last. Someone else might have thought of the exactions.

"You make the thing look better than it was," Aunt Priscilla cried with true humility. "But the Lord put you in the right place."

She saw the mean and selfish desire, the wish to get rid of a faithful old woman who might prove a burden. It was a sin like the finery she had longed for and bought and laid away. She had not worn the finery, she had not sent away the poor black soul, she had not been a hard taskmistress to the child, but early training had added the weight of possible sins to the actual ones.

Christmas morning Doris was surprised by a lovely gift. In a small box by her plate, with best wishes from Uncle Winthrop, lay a watch and chain, a dainty thing with just "Doris" on the plain space in the center that overlay another name that had once been there. It had undergone some renovation at the jeweler's hands, after lying untouched more than twenty years. Winthrop Adams had kept it for a possible granddaughter, but he knew now no one could cherish it more tenderly than Doris.

January, 1815, came in. People counted the days. But it was not until the middle of February that Boston town was one morning electrified by the ringing of bells and the shouts of men and boys, who ran along the streets crying "Peace! Peace! Peace!" Windows were raised; people ran out, so eager were they. Of all glorious words ever uttered none fell with such music on the air. Could it be true?

Uncle Winthrop put on his surtout with the great fur collar. Then he looked at Doris.

"Wrap yourself up and come along," he said huskily.

Already people were hanging flags out of the windows and stringing them across the streets. Every sled and sleigh had some sort of banner, if nothing more than white or brown paper with the five welcome letters, and everybody was shouting. Some men were carrying high banners with the words in blue or red on a white ground. When they came to State Street it was impassable. Cornhill was jammed. The *Evening Gazette* office had the announcement, thirty-two hours from New York (there was no telegraph or railroad train then):

"Sir: I hasten to acquaint you for the information of the public of the arrival here this afternoon of H. Br. M. sloop of war *Favorite*, in which has come passenger Mr. Carroll, American Messenger, having in his possession A Treaty of Peace."

They passed that word from the nearest, standing by the bulletin, to the farther circles, and in five minutes the crowd knew it by heart. On the Commons the drums were beating, the cannons firing, and people shouting themselves hoarse.

Mr. Adams went around to the Royall house, and that looked like a hotel on a gala day, and was nearly as full of people. The treaty had been signed on Christmas Eve. The President had now to issue a decree suspending hostilities. But one of the most brilliant battles had been fought on the 8th of January at New Orleans, under General Jackson—a farewell shot.

For a week no one could think or talk of anything else. Then the official accounts having been received from Washington, there were plans for a grand procession. An oratorio was given at the Stone Chapel in the morning. Madam Royall had managed to obtain seats for Mr. Winthrop and Doris with her party. The church was crowded. American and British officers in full uniform were side by side,—as happy to be at peace as the rulers themselves, —chatting cordially with each other.

The State House was decorated with transparencies, and there were to be fireworks in the evening. The procession marched around the Common, with the different trades drawn on sleds. Printers struck off hand-bills with the word "Peace!" printed on them and distributed them among the crowd. The carpenters were erecting a Temple of Peace. The papermakers had long strips of red, white, and blue: every trade had hit upon some signification of the general joy.

Uncle Win sent Cato round for Mercy and Warren Leverett to come to tea, and then they went out to see the illumination and the fireworks. Old Boston had suffered a great deal from the war, and her rejoicing was as broad as her sorrow had been deep.

As if that was not enough, there was to be a grand Peace Ball. The gentry did not so often patronize public balls, but this was an exception. Uncle Winthrop procured a ticket for Warren and his wife. Mrs. Gilman was shocked, and Mercy like a modern woman declared she had nothing to wear. But Aunt Priscilla brought out her last remnant of gorgeousness, a gray satin that looked very youthful draped with sheer white.

"I feel just as if I was going to be married over again," Mercy declared laughingly; and Warren said she had never looked so beautiful.

Uncle Winthrop left Doris' adornments to Madam Royall and Mrs. Chapman. She and Eudora had the same kind of gowns—sheer, dotted muslin trimmed with rows of white satin ribbon, and the bodice with frills of lace and bows of ribbon.

The hairdresser did her hair in a multitude of puffs and curls that made her look quite like a young lady. She was still very slim, but growing tall rapidly. In fact, as Uncle Winthrop looked at her he realized that she could not always remain a little girl.

Concert Hall was brilliantly illuminated and decorated with flags and flowers. A platform surrounded the floor, and many people preferred to be spectators or just join in the march. There were some naval as well as military officers, and Doris kept a sharp watch, for it almost seemed as if she might come upon Cary. Oh, where would he hear the declaration of peace!

The dancing was quite delightful to most of the young people. Even those who just walked about, looked happy, and little knots chatted and smiled, adding a certain interest to the scene. The supper was very fine, and after that many of the quality retired, leaving the floor to those who had come to dance.

Doris looked bright the next morning as she came to breakfast in her blue flannel frock and lace tucker, and her hair tied up high with a red ribbon, which with her white skin "made the American colors," Helen Chapman said.

"I am glad to get back my little girl," Uncle Winthrop exclaimed, as he placed his hands lightly on her shoulders. "You looked strange to me last night. Doris, how tall you are growing!" in half-surprise.

"That is an Adams trait, Aunt Priscilla would say. And do you remember that I am fifteen?"

"Isn't there some way that girls can be set back?" he asked with feigned anxiety.

"I've heard of their being set back after they reached thirty or forty," said Miss Recompense.

"I don't want to wait so long," returned Uncle Winthrop with a smile.

250

"There were some beautiful old ladies there last night," said Doris. "The one with black velvet and diamonds—Madam Bowdoin. Is that Aunt Priscilla's friend?"

"I suppose so. Mr. Perkins was held in high esteem, and Aunt Priscilla used to go about in her carriage then."

"And Madam Scott! Uncle Win, to think she was John Hancock's wife, and he signed the Declaration of Independence!"

"And after that I wouldn't have married anybody," declared Miss Recompense with haughty stiffness.

The enthusiasm did not die out at once. When men or women met they had to talk over the good news. Warren Leverett declared that business was reviving. Mercy told Uncle Winthrop that she had never expected to see so many famous people under such grand conditions as a Peace Ball, and that it would be something to talk about when she was an old lady. Aunt Priscilla listened to the accounts with deep interest.

"And I looked like a real young lady," said Doris. "I was frightened when I came to think about it. I would like to stay a little girl for years and years. But I would not have missed the ball for anything. I do not believe there will ever be such a grand occasion again."

CHAPTER XXII

CARY ADAMS

It took a good while in those days for the news of peace to go around the world. But there was a general reign of peace. The European countries had mostly settled their difficulties; there was royalty proper again on the throne of France. Napoleon swept through his hundred brilliant days, and was banished for life to the rocky isle of St. Helena; the young King of Rome was a virtual prisoner to Austria, and Russia and Prussia began to breathe freely once more.

The United States had won a standing among the nations. Her indomitable courage, her successes against tremendous odds, had impressed Europe with her vitality and determination.

One by one the ships came back to home ports. Mr. Adams and Doris watched and listened to every bit of news eagerly.

The old apothecary's shop on Washington Street, to begin a famous history a decade later as "The Old Corner Bookstore," was even then a rendezvous for the news of the day. People paused going up and down, and each one added his bit to the general fund, or took with him the knowledge he was eagerly seeking.

And when someone said, "Heard from your son yet, Mr. Adams?" he could only make a negative gesture.

"If there isn't some word of Cary Adams soon, his father will never live to welcome him home," said Madam Royall to her daughter. "He grows thinner every day. What a perfect Godsend Doris has been!"

Madam Royall was hale and hearty though she had lived through many sorrows.

The coveted news came first from Betty. She had written a letter to send by a private messenger, and opened it to add this postscript:

"Mr. Bowen is waiting for this letter. Mr. King has just come in with the news that two ships have arrived at Portsmouth. Among the officers is 'Lieutenant Cary Adams.' That is all we know."

"Oh, Uncle Win!" Doris' eyes swam in tears of joy. "Read Betty's postscript." Then she ran out of the room and had a good cry by herself, though why anyone should want to cry over such joyful news she could not quite understand.

Afterward she tied on her hat and ran over to Madam Royall's and then up to Sudbury Street. For in those days people were wont to say to their neighbors, "Come, rejoice with me!"

When she returned home the house was very quiet. Solomon came and rubbed against her in mute inquiry. No one was in the study. She went out to the kitchen.

"Don't disturb your uncle, Doris," said Miss Recompense. "The news quite overcame him. He has gone to lie down."

After dinner she went out again for some lessons. Oh, how bright the world looked, though it was a day in later March, but the wind had a Southern softness. Soon the wild flowers would be out. There was a very interesting new study, botany, that the previous autumn had taken groups of girls out in the lanes and fields, and some had ventured to visit the Botanic Gardens at Harvard University. Doris was much interested in it.

Uncle Winthrop came to supper, and Doris played and sang for him during the evening. For though Cary was the uppermost thought in both hearts, they could not talk about him.

It was a tedious post journey from Washington to Boston. One had to possess one's soul in patience. But the letter came at length.

Cary had to go to Washington, as there was some prize money and claims to be inquired into. He had handed in his resignation, and should hereafter be a private citizen of dear old Boston. There was much more that gladdened his father's heart and betrayed a manly spirit.

Betty returned home, though Mrs. King declared she only lent her for a visit. She was very stylish now, and was studying French, for it might be possible that Mr. King would go abroad and take his wife and Betty.

"I do wonder if you will ever settle down?" exclaimed Mrs. Leverett anxiously. That meant marriage and housekeeping.

Betty laughed. "You know I have settled to be the old maid aunt," she returned. "But I am going to have a good young time first. And, mother, you can hardly realize what a fine, generous, broad-minded man Mat King has made."

There were lovely odds and ends of attire, dainty slippers, long gloves that came to your very shoulders, vandyke capes of beautiful lace, buckles that looked like diamonds, ribbons and belts and sashes. Mercy said Betty could go down to Washington Street and open a fancy-goods store. And, oh, the delightful things she had seen and done, the skating parties in the winter, the sleigh rides when one stopped at a cozy, well-kept tavern and had a dainty supper and a dance. The drives down around the Battery and Bowling Green, and the promenades. There were still a good many military men in New York, but it had not suffered as much from the war as Boston.

But Boston was growing beautiful by the hour, with her pretty private gardens and hundreds of fruit trees blooming everywhere, and the great Common where people went for walks on sunny afternoons.

Miss Recompense had a gorgeous tulip bed and some lilies of the valley, which were quite a new thing. Cato trimmed and trained the roses and vines, and the old Adams house was quite a bower of beauty.

One April afternoon Doris sat by the study window doing some lace work, while Solomon lay curled up on the sill. She kept glancing out. People were quite given to going around this corner to get into Common Street. She liked to see them. Now and then a friend nodded. Uncle Win had been reading aloud from "Jerusalem Delivered," but Doris thought it rather prosy, and strayed off into her own thoughts.

A tall, soldierly fellow came up the street, looked, hesitated, opened the gate softly, and glanced down at the tulips. He was quite imposing as to figure, and his complexion was bronzed, the ends of his brown hair rather long and curling. He was in citizen clothes, and Doris wondered why she should think of Lieutenant Hawthorne. She had expected Cary in all the glory of a naval uniform—a slim, fair, boyish person with a light springy walk. It never could be Cary!

"Oh, Uncle Win, quick!" as the step sounded on the porch. "It is—someone ——" She was so little certain she could not utter a name.

Uncle Winthrop went out, opened the door, and his son put his arms about the father's neck. If there had been need of words neither could have uttered them for many minutes.

When Miss Recompense cleaned house a week or two before the piano had been moved into the parlor. The door stood open so that it could have the warmth of the hall fire. The two entered it when they had found their voices.

"It *is* Cary," thought Doris with a sense of disappointment, though why she could not have told.

Half an hour afterward they came out to the study.

"Oh, Doris!" Cary cried, "how you have changed and grown. I shouldn't have known you! I've been carrying about with me the remembrance of a little girl.

In my mind you have been no taller, no older, and yet I might have known—why, we shall have to get acquainted all over again."

Doris blushed. "I am sure I have not changed as much as you. I did not think it could be you."

"Someone at Annapolis before we went out designated me as 'That consumptive-looking young fellow.' But I have grown strong and hearty, and no doubt I shall come to fourscore. I do not mean that it shall be all labor and sorrow, either."

Then Cary made the rounds of the house. Miss Recompense was as much amazed as Doris had been. Cato and Dinah were overjoyed. He had hardly dared dream that nothing would be changed, that more than the old love would be given back. He had gone away a boy, nurtured in the restraints of wise Puritanism that made a lasting mark on New England character; he had come home a man of experience, of deeper thought, of higher understanding and stronger affection. He was proud that he had done his duty as a citizen of the republic, but he knew now that neither naval or military life was to his taste. Henceforth he was to be a son in the old home.

Doris left them talking when she went to bed, a little hurt and jealous that she was no longer first, that she could not be all to Uncle Win. It gave her a kind of solitary feeling.

The old house took on an aspect of intense interest. There was a continual going and coming and enough congratulations for a wedding feast. All Cary's friends vied with each other in warm welcomes, and Madam Royall claimed him with the old time cordiality.

Was there any disappointment about Alice?

He had a boy's thought the first few months about winning glory for her, of coming back to her, and perhaps laying his triumphs at her feet. But the real work, the anxieties, the solemn fact of taking one's life in one's hands and realizing how near death might be, had changed him month by month, until he had only one prayer left—that he might see his father again. If she was happy —she surely had her heart's choice—he was satisfied. They had never really been lovers.

When the first excitement of welcome was over there were many things to think about. His interrupted career was one. Governor Gore had been chosen United States Senator the year before, but he still kept his office, and very kindly greeted the return of his student, offering him still greater advantages. Here the young Daniel Webster, a lad fresh from the country, had won the friendship of his master, and after a brief trial in New Hampshire had returned to Boston.

Boston town began to experience the beneficent power of peace. Languishing industries revived. Commerce had been crippled by the war, but the inhabitants of New England had learned the value of their own ingenuity and industry to supply needs, and now they were roused to the fact there was an outside world to supply as well.

Improvements started up on every side. There was even talk of transforming the town into a city. Indeed, it had never been a formally incorporated town. The Court of Assistants one hundred and seventy years before had changed the name from Tri-Mountain to Boston, and it had taken the privileges of a town. But there were many grave questions coming to the front.

The family party at the Adams house this year seemed to include half of Boston. One by one the old relatives had dropped out. Some of the younger ones had gone to other cities.

Madam Royall came over to be mistress of ceremonies. For besides the ovation to the returned lieutenant, Miss Doris Adams was to be presented as a full-fledged young lady, and she wore her pretty gown made for the Peace Ball, and pink roses. Miss Betty Leverett was quite a star as well. Miss Helen Chapman was engaged, and Eudora was a favorite with the young gentlemen.

"I shall be so sorry when they are all gone," declared Madam Royall. "I do love young people, but I am afraid my fourth generation will not grow up in time for me to enjoy them. You must keep good watch over Doris lest some wolf enters the fold and carries off the sweet child."

Uncle Win smiled and then looked grave. Doris carried off—oh, no, he could never spare her!

Cary Adams had not forgotten how to dance, and every girl he asked was delighted with the opportunity. It seemed rather queer to Doris to accept or decline on her own responsibility.

A week or two later, when they had settled to quite regular living, Cary came out and sat on the step one evening.

"Doris," he began, "do you remember the letter I sent you by a Lieutenant Hawthorne—that first letter——" What a flood of remembrances it brought!

"Oh, yes." She had begun to feel very much at home with Cary—his little sister, as he called her. "And I must tell you a queer thing—the day you came home—when I looked down the path—I thought of him. You had changed so. I don't know what sent him to my mind."

"That was odd. He is in town. He called on me to-day. For the last year he has been Captain Hawthorne, and he is a splendid fellow. He has been sent to the Charlestown Navy Yard, and may be here the next three months, for now the Government is considering a navy. Well—we did some splendid fighting with the old ships. But oh, Doris, you can't imagine how homesick I was. I had half a mind to show the white feather and come home."

"Oh, you couldn't have done it, Cary!"

"No, I couldn't when it came to the pinch. But if I had gone with father's consent! I understood then what it would be never to see him again. I think I shall be a better son all my life for the lesson."

"Yes," in her gentle approving fashion.

"Hawthorne wants to come over here," Cary said presently. "I think my father would like him, though I notice he has an aversion to military or naval men. But I shall never go away again unless the country is in great danger."

"I should like to see him. I wonder if he has changed as much as you?"

"I think not," and Cary laughed. "He was twenty-four then, and sort of settled into manhood, while I was a rather green stripling."

"You are losing some of the 'sea tan,' as Madam Royall calls it. I am glad of it. I like you best fair."

"Captain Hawthorne is a very handsome man. I ought to feel flattered to be mistaken for him."

"Is he?" returned Doris simply.

"Don't you remember him?"

"I remember that he asked me for a rose and I gave it to him. It was the last one on the bush. I was so glad to get the letter I couldn't think of anything else."

So Cary brought him over to tea one afternoon. Doris noted then that he was extremely good-looking and very entertaining. Besides, he had a fine tenor voice and they sang songs together.

Uncle Winthrop was troubled at first. Captain Hawthorne's enthusiasm for his profession was so ardent that Mr. Adams was alarmed lest it might turn Cary's thoughts seaward again. But he found presently that Cary's enlisting had been that of a patriotic, high-spirited boy, and that he had no real desire for the life.

What a summer it was! Betty was over often, Eudora was enchanted with the Adams house, and there was a bevy of girls who brought their sewing and spent the afternoon on the stoop. Sometimes Uncle Win came out and read to them. There were several new English poets. A Lord Byron was writing the cantos of a beautiful and stirring poem entitled "Childe Harold" that abounded in fine descriptions. There were "The Lady ol the Lake" and "Marmion," and there was a queer Scotchy poet by the name of Burns, who had a dry wit—and few could master the tongue. A whole harvest of delight was coming over from England.

There were so many curious and lovely places within a few hours sail or drive. Captain Hawthorne had spent most of his life in Maryland, and this scenery was new. They made up parties for the day, or Betty, Doris, and Uncle Winthrop and the captain went in a quartette.

"I don't know," Uncle Win said one day with a grave shake of the head. "Do you not think I am rather an old fellow to go careering round with you young people?"

"But, you see, someone would have to go," explained Doris. "Young ladies can't go out with a young man alone. It would have to be Aunt Elizabeth, or Mrs. Chapman, and I would so much rather have you. It's nice to be just by ourselves."

"The captain seems to like Betty very much."

"Indeed he does," answered Doris warmly.

Occasionally Cary would get off and join them. But he was trying hard to catch up. He had gotten out of study habits, and some days he found it quite irksome, for he was fond of pleasure, and it seemed to him that Betty was extremely charming, and Doris quaint, and Eudora vivacious to the point of wit.

One warm August afternoon he sat alone, having resolved to master a knotty point. What were the others doing? he wondered.

There was a step, and he glanced up.

"Oh," nodding to Captain Hawthorne, "I was just envying you and all the others, and wondering where you were on pleasure bound."

"It was not pleasure, but hard work over at the yard to-day. However, I have the evening, and feel like inviting myself to partake of a cup of the comforting tea Miss Recompense brews."

"Come along then. I have put in a good day and am conscience-clear."

Cary began to pile up his books.

"I have only about a fortnight more," Captain Hawthorne said slowly.

Cary changed his coat and locked his desk. "Well?" as the caller was watching him earnestly.

"Adams, do you mean—do you expect to marry your cousin?" Hawthorne asked abruptly.

"My cousin? Betty or Doris?"

"Doris."

"Why—no, I never thought of it. And I have a sight of work to do before I marry."

"Then—I suppose you never suspected such a thing—but I am in love with her."

"In love with Doris! Why, she's just a child."

"I dare say I shall have to serve seven years before I can get your father's consent. She will be older then. I was listening to a romantic story about an old house where a handsome girl leaned out of a window and her beauty attracted an English officer passing by, who said to himself that was the one woman for him, and long afterward he went back, found her, and married her."

"A handsome Miss Sheafe. Yes." Cary smiled.

"See here, Cary Adams." Hawthorne took a small leather case out of his pocket. Between two cards was a pressed rose. "When I took your packet to Miss Doris Adams almost four years ago, I gave it into the hands of the sweetest little girl I ever saw. If I had been less of a gentleman I must have kissed her. I espied one rose in the garden and asked her for it. This is the rose she gave me. I meant to come North and find her, and when I asked for leave of absence to visit Boston this business was put in my charge. Then I said, 'I will look up the little girl, who must be a large girl now, and woo her with the sincerest regard.' It shall go hard indeed with me if I cannot win her. But I have fancied of late that you——"

"She is very dear to me and to my father. But I had not thought——"

"Then I take my chances. As I said, I will wait for her. She is still very young, and I should feel conscience-smitten to rob your father. Sometime you may want to bring the woman you love to the old home, and then it will not be so hard. I could keep true to her the whole world over; and if she promises, she will keep true to me."

Cary Adams was deeply moved. Such devotion ought to win a reward. How blind he and his father had been, thinking of Betty Leverett.

Oh, how could they let Doris go! Yet a lover like this was not to be curtly refused.

"I shall not stand in your way," quietly.

"Thank you a thousand times. But if she had been for you, as I feared, I should have proved man enough to keep silent and go my way. It has been a happy summer, and in two weeks more it will end. Still, I may be able to get an appointment here. I shall try for it and return."

"Come," said Cary Adams, and he went out feeling there had been a great change in the world, and he was wrapped about with some mysterious influence.

Doris had thought of Captain Hawthorne on the day of his, Cary's, return. How many times besides had she thought of him? And she had recalled giving him the rose.

CHAPTER XXIII

THE COST OF WOMANHOOD

A happy fortnight. It was worth all the after-pain to have it to remember. When Boston was a great city half a century later, and there had been another war, and Captain Hawthorne had risen in the ranks and been put on the retired list, he came a grizzled old man to find the place that had always lived in his remembrance. But the old house had been swept away by the march of improvement, the rounding corner straightened and given over to business, and the Common was magnificent in beauty. The tall, thin, scholarly man had gone to the wife of his youth. Doris, little Doris, was very happy. So what did it matter?

There was a succession of lovely days. One morning, early, Captain Hawthorne joined Doris and her uncle in a long ride over on Boston Neck. They found an odd old tavern kept by a sailor who had been round the world and taken a hand in the "scrimmage," as he called it, and with his small prize money bought out the place. There was some delightful bread and cold chicken, wine and bottled cider equal to champagne. There was another long lovely day when with Betty they went up to Salem and drove around the quaint streets and watched the signs of awakening business. There was Fort Pickering, the lighthouse out on the island, the pretty Common, the East India Marine Society's hall with its curiosities (quite wonderful even then), and the clean streets with their tidy shops, the children coming from school, the housewives going about on errands. Foster Manning drove his grandmother down to join them; and he was almost a young man now. He told Doris they all missed Elizabeth so much, but he was glad she had had that nice visit to Boston.

So the days drifted on; Doris unconsciously sweet in her simplicity, yet so innocent that the lover began to fear while he hoped.

Uncle Winthrop had gone to a meeting of the Historical Society. Miss Recompense had a neighbor in great trouble that she was trying to console out in the supper room, where they could talk unreservedly. Cary was in the study, and the two were sauntering around the fragrant walks where the grassy beds had recently been cut. There was no moon, and the whole world seemed soft and still, as if it was listening to the story Captain Hawthorne had to tell, as if it was in love with itself.

"Oh," interrupted Doris with a sharp, pained cry, "do not, please do not! I never dreamed—I—shall never go away from Uncle Winthrop. I do not want any other love. I thought it was—Betty. Oh, forgive me for the pain and disappointment. I seem even to myself such a little girl——"

"But I can wait years. I wanted you to know. Oh, Doris, as the years go on can you not learn to love me? I will be patient and live in the sweet, grand hope that some day——"

"No, no; do not hope. I cannot promise. Oh, you are so noble and upright, can you not accept this truth from me? For it would only be pain and disappointment in the end."

No, she did not love him. Her sweet soul was still asleep within her fair body. He was too really honorable to persist.

"Doris," he said,—what a sweet girl's name it was!—"five years from this time I shall come back. You will be a woman then, you are still a child. And if no other lover has won you, I shall ask again."

He pressed her hand to his lips. Then he led her around to the porch, and bade her a tender good-night. He would not embarrass her by any longer stay.

She ran up the steps. Cary intercepted her in the hall.

"Has he gone? Doris——"

"Oh, *did* you know? How could you let him!" she cried in anguish. "How could you!"

"Doris—my dear little sister, he loved you so. But I wish it had been Betty. Oh, don't cry. You have done nothing. I am sorry, but he would not have been satisfied if he had not spoken. He wanted to ask father first, but I hated to have *him* pained if it was not necessary——"

"Thank you for that, Cary. Do not tell him. You will not?" she pleaded, thinking of the other first.

"No, dear. We must shield him all we can."

Yes, they would try always. There was a little rift in the cloud of pain.

The next evening Captain Hawthorne came over to bid them a formal good-by. Helen Chapman and her lover and Eudora were there, so it was an unembarrassing affair with many good wishes on both sides.

Doris thought she would like to run away and hide. It seemed as if the whole story was written in her face. Betty suspected, but she loved her too well to tease. And almost immediately Helen announced her arrangements. She was to be married in October. Doris and Cary must stand with her, and one of the Chapman cousins with Eudora. Another warm girl friend and her lover would complete the party. Grandmamma had stipulated that Mr. Harrison Gray should cast in his lot with them for a year. Mr. Sargent had been attached to the embassy at London and they would remain two years longer at least. Madam Royall could not bear to have the family shrink so rapidly.

Betty was to go away again. Mr. and Mrs. Matthias King came together this time to see old friends and Boston, that Mr. King found wonderfully changed. He was to go to France on business for the firm of which he was a member, and be absent a year at least. It would be such a splendid chance for Betty. They were to take their own little Bessy and leave the three younger children with a friend who had a school for small people and who would give them a mother's care.

There was a little grandson in Sudbury Street, and Mercy had proved a very agreeable daughter-in-law. Warren had begun to prosper again, and was full of hope. The children at Hollis Leverett's were growing rapidly. They no longer said "little Sam." He was almost a young man. He had taken the Franklin prize at the Latin School and was now apprenticed to an architect and builder, and would set up for himself when he came of age, as Boston had begun to build up rapidly. But he couldn't help envying Cousin Cary Adams his prize money and wondering what he meant to do with it.

An invitation to go to Paris was not to be lightly declined then, any more than it would be now. Mrs. Manning did not see "how Betty could leave mother for so long," but Mrs. Leverett was in good health, and though she hated to have her go so far away, there really could be no objection, when Matthias King was so generous.

"I am going to have some of my good times while we are together and able to enjoy them," he said to Mrs. Leverett. "I shall have to leave Electa alone every now and then while I am about business, and it will be such a comfort to her to have Betty. No doubt, we shall marry her to a French count."

"Oh, no, bring her back to me," said Betty's mother.

There was quite a stir among Betty's compeers. She was congratulated and envied, and they begged her to write everything she could about French fashions. How lucky that she had been studying French!

Aunt Priscilla had a hard struggle with conscience about a matter that she felt to be quite a duty. Giving away finery that you would never wear was one thing, but your money was quite another.

"Betty," she said, "I'm going to make you a little gift. If you shouldn't want to use it maybe Mat will see some way to invest it for you. When the trouble came to Warren, I said he might as well have his part as to wait until I was dead and gone. I have been paid over and over again in comfort. He grows so much like your father, Betty. And he's weathered through the storm and stress. So I'll do the same by you, and if you never get any more you must be content."

It was an order for five hundred dollars. Winthrop Adams would see it paid.

Betty was quite overwhelmed. "I ought to give half of it to mother!" she cried.

"No, no. Your mother will have all she needs. The Mannings would borrow it of her to buy more ground with. I've no patience with all their scrimping, and sometimes I give thanks that poor Elizabeth is out of it all. Don't have an anxious thought about money where you mother is concerned."

"What a comfort you are, Aunt Priscilla."

"Well, it took years enough to teach me that anybody needed comforting."

As for Doris, she was so busy that she could hardly think about herself or Captain Hawthorne. She did wish he had not loved her. If she had known about the rose her heart would have been still more sore and pitiful.

Betty went before the wedding. They took a sloop to New York and were to leave there for Havre.

Madam Royall had this wedding just to her fancy, and it was quite a fine affair. Cary looked very nice, Doris thought, for the sea tan had nearly all bleached out. His figure was compact, and he had a rather soldierly bearing. He was quite a hero, too, to his old college mates, some of whom had not considered him possessed of really strong characteristics.

But the young ladies were proud of his notice and attention, and there was no end of invitations from their mothers when they were going to have evening companies.

The cold weather came on apace. Mr. Adams seemed to feel it more and gave up his horseback rides. He interested himself very much in the library plans, but he grew fonder of staying at home, and Doris was such a pleasant companion. Cary had never been fond of poetry, and now he threw himself into his profession with a resolve to stand high. Manhood's ambition was so different from the lukewarm endeavors of the boy.

His father did enjoy his earnestness very much. Sometimes he roused himself to argue a point when two or three young men dropped in, and the old fire flashed up, though he liked best his ease and his poets, or Doris reading or singing some old song. But he did not lose his interest in the world's progress or that of his beloved city.

Doris was very happy in a young girl's way. One did not expect to fill every moment with pleasure, or go to parties or the theater every evening. There were other duties and purposes to life. As Aunt Priscilla did not go out after the cold weather set in, she ran up there nearly every day with some cheerful bit of gossip. Madam Royall had grown very fond of her as well. There was the dancing class; and the sewing class, when they made garments for poor people; and shopping—even if one did not buy much, for now such pretty French and English goods were shown again. Then one stopped in the confectioner's on Newberry Street and had a cup of hot coffee or tea if it was a cold day; or strolled down Cornhill to see what new books had come over from London, for the Waverley novels had just begun, and everybody was wondering about the author. Or you went to Faneuil Hall to see Trumbull's Declaration of Independence, which was considered a very remarkable work. There were the sleigh-rides, when you went out in style and had a supper and a dance; and the sledding parties, that were really the most fun of all, when you almost forgot you were grown-up.

Cary was always ready to attend his cousin, though she quite as often went out with Mr. and Mrs. Gray and Eudora. When he thought of it, it did seem a little curious that Doris had no special company.

But a girl was not allowed to keep special company until the family had consented and she was regularly engaged. Young men and girls came to sing, for a piano was a rarity; there were parties going here and there, but Doris never evinced any particular preference.

So spring came again and gardening engrossed Doris. She had been learning housekeeping in all its branches under the experienced tuition of Miss Recompense and Dinah. A girl who did not know everything from the roasting of a turkey to the making of sack-posset, and through all the gradations of pickling and preserving, was not considered "finished."

Doris was very fond of the wide out-of-doors. She often took her work, and Uncle Winthrop his book, and sat out on a rustic seat at the edge of the Common, which was beginning to be beautiful, though it was twenty years later that the Botanic Garden was started. But now that our ships were going everywhere, curious bulbs and plants were brought from Holland and from the East Indies by sea captains. And they found wonderful wild flowers that developed under cultivation. Brookline was a great resort on pleasant days, with its meadows and wooded hillsides and beautiful gardens. Colonel Perkins had all manner of foreign fruits and flowers that he had brought home from abroad, and had a greenhouse where you could often find the grandmother of the family, who was most generous in her gifts. There were people who thought you "flew in the face of Providence" when you made flowers bloom in winter, but Providence seemed to smile on them.

Over on the Foster estate at Cambridge there was a genuine hawthorn. People made pilgrimages to see it when it was white with bloom and diffusing its peculiar odor all about. There were the sweet blossoms of the mulberry and the honey locust, and the air everywhere was fragrant, for there were so few factories, and people had not learned to turn waste materials into every sort of product and make vile smells.

Cary sometimes left his books early in the afternoon and went driving with them. If he did not appreciate poetry so much, he was on the lookout for every fine tree and curious flower, and twenty years later he was deep in the Horticultural Society.

Uncle Winthrop bought a new low carriage this summer. For anyone else but a grave gentleman it would have looked rather pronounced, but it was so much easier to get in and out. And Doris in her sweet unconsciousness never made any bid for attention, but people would turn and look at them as one looks at a picture.

Thirty years or so afterward old ladies would sometimes say to the daughters of Doris:

"My dear, I knew your mother when she was a sweet, fresh young girl and used to go out driving with her uncle. Mr. Winthrop Adams was one of the high-bred, delicate-looking men that would have graced a court. There wasn't a prettier sight in Boston—and, dear me! that was way back in '16 or '17. How time flies!"

They heard from Betty occasionally. The letters were long and "writ fine," though happily not crossed. They should have been saved for a book, they were so chatty. In August one came to Doris that stirred up a mighty excitement. Betty had a way of being quite dramatic and leading up to a climax.

A month before they had met a delightful Frenchman, a M. Henri de la Maur, twenty-five or thereabouts, and found him an excellent cicerone to some remarkable things they had not seen. He was much interested in America and its chief cities, especially Boston, when he found that was Betty's native town.

And one day he told them of a search he had been making for a little girl. The De la Maurs had suffered considerably under the Napoleonic *régime*, and had now been restored to some of their rights. There was one estate that could not be settled until they found a missing member. They had traced the mother, who had died and left a husband and a little girl—Jacqueline. "That is such a common name in France," explained Betty. She had been placed in a convent, and that was such a common occurrence, too. Then she had been taken to the North of England. He had gone to the old town, but the child's father had died and some elderly relatives had passed away, and the child herself had been sent to the United States. Everybody who had known her was dead or had forgotten.

"And I never thought until one day he said Old Boston," confessed Betty, "when I remembered suddenly that your mother's name was Jacqueline Marie de la Maur in the old marriage certificate. We had been talking of it a week or more, but one hears so many family stories here in Paris, and lost and found inheritances. But I almost screamed with surprise, and added the sequel; and he was just overjoyed, and brought the family papers. He and your mother are second- and third-cousins. It is queer you should have so many far-off relations, and so few near-by ones, and be mixed up in so many romances.

"The fortune sounds quite grand in francs, but if we enumerated our money by quarters of dollars, we might all be rich. It is a snug little sum, however, and they are anxious to get it settled before the next turn in the dynasty, lest it might be confiscated again. So M. Henri is coming home with us, and we shall start the first day of September, as Mr. King has finished his business and Electa is wild to see her children. I think I shall give 'talks' all winter and invite you over to Sudbury Street, with your sewing, for I never shall be talked out."

It was wonderful. Doris had to read the letter over and over. It had listeners at the Royall house who said it was a perfect romance, and at the Leveretts' they rejoiced greatly.

"I declare!" exclaimed Aunt Priscilla, "if you should live to be fifty or sixty, and everybody go on leaving you fortunes, you won't know what to do with your money. They're filling up the Mill Pond and the big ma'sh and going to lay out streets. I wouldn't have believed it! Foster Leverett held on to his legacy because he couldn't sell it, and now Warren has been offered a good sum. Mary Manning will pinch herself blue to think she sold out when she did. I'm just glad for Warren. And Cary'll know so much law that he will look out for you."

It was a beautiful autumn, for a wonder. Summer seemed loath to depart or allow the flame-colored finger of Fall to place her seal on the glowing foliage. But it was the last of October when Betty reached Boston, convoyed by a very old-time New England woman going on to Newburyport.

"For you know," said Betty, "the French are very particular about a young woman traveling alone, but we did have a hunt to find someone coming to

Boston. Otherwise M'sieur Henri—you see how apt I am in French—could not have accompanied me."

M. de la Maur was a very nice-looking young man, not as tall as Cary, but with a graceful and manly figure, soft dark eyes, and hair that just missed being black, a clear complexion and fine color, and a small line of mustache. As to manners he was really charming, and so well-read that Mr. Winthrop Adams took to him at once. He was conversant with Voltaire and Rousseau, the plays of Racine and Molière, and the causes that had led to the French Revolution, and had been in Paris through the famous "Hundred Days." Of course he was bitter against Napoleon.

The inheritance part was soon settled. Doris would have about three thousand dollars. But De la Maur took a great fancy to Boston, and the Royall family approved of him. Mr. and Mrs. Sargent had returned this fall and the old house was a center of attractive gayeties.

"Do you know, I think Cousin Henri is in love with Betty," said Doris, with a feminine habit of guessing at love matters. "But she insists she will never live abroad, and Cousin Henri thinks Paris is the center of the world."

"How will they manage?"

Doris laughed. She did not just see herself.

But Betty's romance came to light presently. It had begun during her winter in New York, but it had not run smoothly. Betty had a rather quick wit and was fond of teasing, and there had been "differences" not easily settled. Mr. Harman Gaynor had risen to the distinction of a partnership in the King firm, and on meeting Betty again, with the young Frenchman at her elbow, had presented his claim in such a way that Betty yielded. When Mr. Gaynor came to Boston to have a conference with Mrs. Leverett—for fathers and mothers still had authority in such matters—Betty's engagement was announced and the marriage set for spring.

Somehow it was a delightful winter. But after a little one person began to feel strangely apprehensive, and this was Cary Adams.

"I suppose Doris and her third- or fourth-cousin will make a match?" Madam Royall said one evening when they had been playing morris and she had won the rubber. "How can you let her go away?"

"She will never leave father," exclaimed Cary confidently.

There was a sudden stricture all over his body. It seemed as if some cold hand had clutched both heart and brain.

He walked home in the bright, fresh air. It was barely ten. He passed De la

Maur on the way and they greeted each other. The parlor windows were darkened, his father was alone in the study, and everyone else had gone to bed.

"I wish you had been home," said his father glancing up. "De la Maur has been reciting Racine, and I have never heard anything finer! I wish he could read Shakspere. He certainly is a delightful person, so cultured and appreciative. It makes me feel that we really are a new people."

Could no one see the danger? How happened it his father was so blind? Did Doris really care? She had not loved Captain Hawthorne, a man worthy of any woman's love. Cary had a confident feeling that in five years they would see him again. But he would be too old for Doris—thirteen years between them. Yet his father had been fifteen years older than his mother. Doris was so guileless, so simply honest, and if she loved—how curiously she had kept from friendships or intimacies with young men! Eudora had a train of admirers. So had Helen and Alice in their day.

When he had met Mrs. Sargent he knew it had only been a boyish fancy for Alice Royall, and it had merely shaped and strengthened the ardent desire of youth to go to his country's defense. He was a man now, and capable of loving with supreme tenderness and strength. Yet he had seen no woman to whom he cared to pour out the first sweet draught of a man's regard.

But Doris must not go away, she could not.

Morning, noon, and night he watched her. She prepared his father's toast, she chatted with him and often coaxed him to taste this or that, for his appetite was slender. On sunny mornings they went to drive, or if not she brought her sewing and sat in the study, listened and discussed the subjects he loved, and was enthusiastic about the Boston that was to be, that they both saw with the eye of faith. While he took his siesta she ran up to Sudbury Street, or did an errand. Later in the afternoon there would be calls. There was a sideboard at the end of the hall where a bottle or two of wine were kept, as was the custom then, and a plate of cake.

Doris brought in a fashion of offering tea or sometimes mulled cider on a cold day. But Miss Recompense made delicious tea, and some of the gentlemen took it just to see Doris drop in the lump of sugar so daintily.

If they were at home there was always company in the evening, unless the night was very stormy. De la Maur generally made one of the guests. If they were alone they had a charming evening in the study.

The young Frenchman was most punctilious. He might take a few cousinly freedoms, but he never offered any that were lover-like. So it was the more easy for Doris to persuade herself that it was merely relationship. Occasionally the eloquence of his eyes quite unnerved her. She cunningly sheltered herself beside Eudora when it was possible.

But De la Maur's regard grew apace. It would not be honorable to come without declaring his intentions. And the American fashion of being engaged was extremely fascinating to him. He wanted the more than cousinly privileges.

So it happened one night Betty and Warren came over with a piece of music Mrs. King had sent, a song by Moore, the Irish poet. Doris went to the parlor to try it. That was De la Maur's golden opportunity, and he could not allow it to slip. In a most deferential manner he laid his case before her relative and guardian and begged permission to address Miss Doris.

Winthrop Adams was utterly amazed at the first moment. Then he recovered himself. Doris *was* a young lady. One friend and another was being given in marriage, and Doris naturally would have lovers. There was one that he had hoped—but he had never seen any real indication.

"It is true that I like my own Paris best, but if Miss Doris longed to stay here a few years, I would make myself content. But you will understand—I could not come any longer without explaining; and this time you allow young people—betrothment—looks so attractive. May I ask and learn her sentiments, since young ladies choose for themselves?"

What could he do but consent? If Doris should not love him——

"Good-night Uncle Win," cried Betty from the hall. "Good-night, M. De la Maur."

Doris was replacing some music in the portfolio. Cousin Henri crossed the room and she saw a mysterious sweetness in his face as he took her hand.

"*Ma chère amie* Cousin Doris, I have just explained to your uncle my sentiments concerning you, and have his permission to ask for your regard. I love you very dearly. Will you be my wife?"

Doris drew her hand away and was pale and red by turns, while her throat constricted and her breath came in great bounds.

"I am so sorry. I tried not to be—I did not want anything like this to happen—but sometimes I felt afraid," she stammered in her embarrassment. "I like you very much. But I do not want to marry or to be engaged. I shall stay with my uncle. I shall never go away from the country of my adoption."

"But if I were willing to remain a while—so long as your uncle lived? I do not wonder you love him very much. He is a charming gentleman. I have no parents to bid me stay at home, I need consult only you and myself."

"Oh, no, no! Do not compel me to pain you by continued refusals. I cannot consent. I will always be friend and cousin—I do not love anyone——"

"Then if you do not love anyone this friendship might ripen into a sweet regard. Oh, Doris, I had hardly thought so deep a love possible."

His imploring tone touched her. But she drew back farther and said in a more decisive tone: "Oh, no, no! I cannot promise."

He was too gentlemanly to persist in his pleading. But he was confident he had Mr. Adams on his side. And at home the desires of parents and guardians counted for a great deal.

"My dear cousin, will you talk this matter over with your uncle? You may look at it in a different light. And I shall remain your ardent admirer until I am convinced. Since you have no lover——"

Doris Adams suddenly straightened her pliant young figure. Some dignity was born in her face and in the clear eyes she raised, too pure to doubt anything or to fear anything, sure for a moment that she possessed every pulse and thought and knowledge of her own soul, then beset by a strange shadowy misgiving that she had reached a curious crisis in her life that she did not know of an instant ago.

But she said bravely, though there was a quiver in her breath that she tried to keep from her voice:

"Let us remain cousins merely. My duty is here. My love is here also—to the best of fathers, the tenderest of friends. I cannot share it with anyone."

De la Maur bowed and went slowly out of the apartment.

CHAPTER XXIV

THE BLOOM OF LIFE—LOVE

Doris flew to the study. Uncle Winthrop's eyes were bent on his book and his face partly turned aside. He had been making a brave fight. A man of a less fine strain of honor would not have answered the brave young lover as he had done. He could not have answered him thus if he had not liked Henri de la Maur so well, and loved Doris with such singleness of heart.

He heard her step and put out his hand without moving. His tone was very low.

"Is it—France?"

"France! Oh, Uncle Win! When I belong to you and Boston?"

Her arms were around his neck. His heart, his whole body, seemed to give one great throb of joy as he drew her down to his knee. There had been only one other experience in life as sweet.

"And you would have sent me away!" with a soft, broken upbraiding in which love was uppermost.

"No, child, no. God forbid, Doris, now that you are *not* going, I will confess —I think I should have died before the parting came. But, my little girl, I must say this in memory of two sweet years of wedded life—there is no happiness comparable to it. And to accept your youth, your golden period that never dawns but once on any human being, to gladden my declining years would be a selfish sin. I once had a dream—but it came to naught"—he drew a long breath as if the remembrance pained him. "You must be quite free, dear, to love and to marry. All these years with you have been so precious, but sometime I shall go my way, and I could not bear the thought of your being left alone!"

"I shall stay with you. I—there can never be any home like this—any love like yours——"

The hall door opened and shut slowly. That was Cary's step. She could not meet him here. She kissed Uncle Win vehemently and flashed past the young man standing there almost in the doorway with a white, strained face. The great armchair was in her way and she half stumbled over it. Then some other arms caught her and she had no strength to struggle. Did she want to?

"Doris! Doris! Was it true what you said just now—that no home could be like this, and your love for him, which has been that of a tender daughter—his love for you—is there room for another regard still? for, Doris, I love you! I want you. I have been wild and jealous since I have suspected, since I have really known or guessed your cousin's intentions. I did not suspect at first—there were Betty and Eudora—and an old regard waiting for you, but now I can think of only one thing, that has been in my mind day and night for the last fortnight, that I love you as well as the others; only it seems a small and ignoble matter to appeal to your affection for my father and the old home. But I want your love, your sweetness, your precious faith, the trust of your coming womanhood, your own sweet self. I'm not a handsome fellow like Captain Hawthorne, nor accomplished like De la Maur, but I shall love you to my life's end, Doris!"

They sat down on the step of the old staircase and he could feel the tremble in every pulse of her slim young figure. Was it the strange mystery that had come to her half an hour ago in the parlor opposite, a something that was not knowledge, but a vague consciousness that there was a person in the world who could say the words that would thrill her with delight instead of bringing sorrow and regret!

"All that is a very illogical and incoherent presentation. I must do better when I come to argue my first case," and he gave a joyous little laugh. For he knew if Doris meant to say him "Nay," she would not let her head droop on his shoulder, or yield to the clasp of his arm. And suddenly his soul was filled with infinite pity for Hawthorne, and—yes—he felt sorry for De la Maur.

"Doris—is it a little for my own sake?"

A breath of happy content swept over her like a summer wind coming from some mysterious world.

"You have been an angel of comfort to both of us. I don't know what I should have done in that unhappy time if it had not been for you. But Hawthorne's regard made it a point of honor with me. Could you have loved him, Doris? He is such a fine fellow."

He noted the little shrinking, he was holding her so close.

"Not in that way," and her reply was a soft whisper.

"Thank Heaven! But I want to hear you say—oh, my darling, I want the assurance that I shall be dear to you, that it is not all because——"

"I should stay for Uncle Win's sake. I think Miss Recompense finds a great many sources of happiness in a single life. But if I promised you, it would be because—because—I loved you."

"Then promise me," he cried enraptured. "I love you dearly, if I haven't been much of a lover. I have said to myself that I was waiting for Hawthorne's five years to end, or to do something worthy of you. And now, Doris, I know what fighting means, and I would fight to the death for you. I am afraid I shall be selfish and exigent to the last degree."

He felt the delicate revelation in the warmth of her cheek, the tremble of the soft hands, the relaxation of her whole body. And a kind of solemn exultation filled his soul. Except the youthful episode with Alice Royall, he had never sincerely cared for any woman, and he was very glad he could give Doris the first offering of a man's love as he understood it now.

And then for a long while neither spoke, except in kisses—love's own language. Every moment the mystery seemed to grow upon Doris, to unfold as well, to pass the line of girlhood, to accept the crown of a woman's life. It had been very simply sweet. Some other woman might have made a rather tragic episode of her two lovers. Doris pitied them sincerely, but they both had the deepest sympathy from Cary Adams.

"Let us go to him," Cary exclaimed presently, rising, with his arm still about her.

There were two wax candles burning in their sconces that had been made over forty years ago in Paul Revere's foundry. By the softened light Cary glanced at the flushed face, downcast eyes and dewy, tremulous lips. Half the sweet story was still untold, but there would be years and years. Oh, Heaven grant they might have them together! And at this instant he was filled with a profound sympathy for his father's loss and lonely life.

They walked slowly through the hall and paused a moment in the doorway. Winthrop Adams was leaning his head on his hand, and the lamp a little at the side threw up his thin, finely cut features, as if they had been done in marble, and he was almost as pale. The exultation went out of the soul of the young lover, and a rush of tenderness such as he had never experienced before swept through him.

"Father," he said softly, touching him on the shoulder, "father—will you give me Doris, for your claim is first? Will you accept me as her lover, sometime to be her husband, always to be your son, and your daughter?"

Winthrop Adams rose half-bewildered. Had the secret hope of his soul unfolded in blessed fruition? He looked from one to the other, then his glance rested on his son—their eyes met, and in that instant they came to know each other as they never had before, to understand, to comprehend all that was in the tie of nature. He laid one hand on his son's shoulder, the other clasped the slim virginal figure, no longer a little girl, but whose girlhood and affectionate

274

devotion would always fill both hearts.

"Doris, my child—you are quite sure——" He could not have his son defrauded of any sweetness.

Doris raised her downcast eyes and smiled, while the pink flush was like a rosy gleam of sunrise. Then she laid her hand over both of the others' in a tender, caressing fashion. But she was too deeply moved for words.

Winthrop Adams kissed her fair brow, but her lover kissed her on the sweet, rosy lips.

They announced the engagement almost at once. It was done partly for De la Maur's sake, though after the first he took it quite philosophically. There were three people supremely happy over it. Miss Recompense, Madam Royall,— who declared she would have been disappointed in Providence if it had been any other way,—and Cousin Betty, who was happy as a queen in her own life, though why we should make royalty a synonym for happiness I do not know.

"You never could have left Uncle Win," wrote Betty, "and Cary could not have gone away, neither could he have brought home a strange woman. This was the only satisfactory ending. But I hope you will be awfully in love with each other and sweet—and silly and all that. I am sorry for Captain Hawthorne, for, Doris, he loved you sincerely, but your French cousin can console himself with an English rhyme:

"'If she be not fair for me,
What care I how fair she be?'"

And oddly enough a few months later he did console himself with Eudora Chapman.

Just a few years afterward there was a great time in Boston. For she had adopted a charter and become a real city, after long and earnest discussion. There was a grand celebration and no end of dinners, and young Cary Adams made one of the addresses. Mr. Winthrop Adams insisted that his life work was done, but he lived to be interested in many more improvements, and some charming grandchildren.

"But after all," Doris would declare, "splendid as it is going to be, I am glad to belong to Old Boston with her lanes and byways and rough hills and marsh lands, with their billowy grasses and wild flowers, and great gardens full of fruit trees, and the little old shops and people sitting on front stoops sewing or reading or chatting cozily. And what a pleasure it will be by and by to tell the children that I was a little girl in Old Boston."

THE END.